CENTER
STREET

LARGE
PRINT

Date: 11/7/12

LP FIC DEKKER
Dekker, Ted,
The sanctuary

THE SANCTUARY

1

MY NAME IS RENEE Gilmore, but really, this is Danny's story.

Danny, the one who saved me. The one who helped me believe in love again. My precious Danny—my priest who was no longer a priest, because he never really had much love for religion. My mentor, my rock, my lover, who was locked away in prison because of me.

For three years he was behind bars. During this time, and with his patient help, I put all my guilt behind me. My mind was sound, my world was whole, my bank account was full, my debt was paid, and my enemies were long gone.

Or so I thought.

The truth is, my greatest enemy was always myself. I was always a calculating person, carefully managing my life to keep everything in order. I have an inordinate capacity to rise up with strength and deal with the fires of crises when I have to, but my first reaction to the most severe crises looks more like a meltdown than an uprising. Like an engine woefully cranking and grinding before it fires and comes to life with an earsplitting roar.

On the morning that my world melted down in earnest, I was standing in my kitchen, trying to decide what I should eat for breakfast. Normally this was an easy task, because I was a person of habit. If I didn't perceive my world as ordered, anxiousness could creep into my mind like an obsessive ghost. It's often small things that bother fractured people, because we're convinced that small things always add up to big things, and those big things turn into goblins that gobble us up if we're not careful.

An unmade bed, for example, soon becomes sheets on the floor. Then pillows on the carpet, joined by dirty socks and shoes and books and belts and newspapers and empty cartons and dirt, all adding up to heaps of garbage attracting rats and roaches. A dirty plate in the sink soon becomes a pile of moldy dishes surrounded by half-eaten pans of lasagna and crusted silverware and leaking bottles of liquid soap and oily pots and pans, providing lots of places for all those rats and roaches to nest and feed as they plot your demise. The bathroom—mercy, don't get me started on the horrors of where a wet toothbrush might ultimately lead.

A little disorder gives way to complete chaos and before you know it, you're holed up in the last corner, armed with an old .38 Special and only two bullets to fend off the army of rats daring you to take a shot while they scurry over the piles of moldy rubbish. The way to avoid chaos is to maintain perfect order in all things, including what you put in your mouth.

I know that people who don't deal with obsessive compulsions find this a tad annoying, but the truth is, we're all fractured in some respect. We just demonstrate our brokenness in unique ways. Some with a steely resolve that covers up the wounding but keeps even the

3

closest friend out. Some with food or other sensory addictions. Some by keeping so busy they don't have time to really know themselves at all. Others simply live in denial.

Danny, the man I loved more than my own life, believed our thoughts and emotions aren't really us at all. We are consciousness separate from thoughts, beliefs, and emotions, temporarily cohabitating with them until the day we die. In reality, we are love and can best find God's love when we are still and aware in the present, beyond thought and emotion. But then, Danny was a priest.

Breathe, Renee, he often said. *Let it all go. Live in the present, not in fear of the future, which is only an illusion.*

Easier said than done.

I tried, trust me, but for the most part I was bound to maintain a semblance of peace by keeping my world straight. For me that had somehow translated into starting every day with a breakfast of one hard-boiled egg, half of a grapefruit with a light sprinkling of sugar, and a single glass of orange juice.

Dressed in yellow-checkered short flannel pajama bottoms and a matching top, I stood in the middle of my two-bedroom condo kitchen on Long Beach's north side, staring at the refrigerator, thinking that I really should get a life and eat something other than my habitual breakfast.

The refrigerator was white, as were the toaster, the GE electric can opener, the wooden paper-towel holder, the Black & Decker coffee machine, the dish washer, and the stove-top—all as spotless, gleaming, and shiny as the polished chrome faucet.

I stepped up and pulled open the refrigerator. Eggs: two dozen, stacked in two clear plastic trays on the right, flush with the forward edge of the glass shelf. Orange juice: one half-empty, clear plastic container beside the eggs. Grapefruits: three, in a wooden bowl below. There was more in there: Zico coconut water, cheese, butter, tomatoes—the usual stuff any vegetarian might keep, each item neatly in its place. But all I could really see were the eggs, the grapefruit, and the OJ.

These observations were more subconscious than conscious, I suppose. Most people have similar kinds of thoughts; they just don't identify and order them the way some of us tend to.

It took me seven minutes to boil the egg, cut the grapefruit, and pour the orange juice into a tall, narrow glass. Then another three minutes to wash and dry the boiling pot, clean the serrated knife, wipe down and shine the counter, the sink, and the faucet. I called it my ten-minute breakfast prep.

Satisfied, I slid onto the high-backed bar stool at the white-tiled breakfast bar, crossed one leg over the other, and ate my breakfast as I always did, beginning with a sip of orange juice followed by a bite of egg.

My therapist, Laura Ashburn, claimed that I had at least borderline obsessive-compulsive disorder characterized by persisting thoughts and impulses that caused severe anxiety, despite the realization that those thoughts were irrational. Evidently these thoughts translate into worries about cleanliness and order, among other things. I followed her advice and tried Zoloft, then Prozac, but neither helped much and both gave me a case of nightly sweats. They say the average mattress is home to entire colonies of microscopic, squirming mites that if not routinely eradicated quickly multiply to half the weight of the mattress. Give them a nightly diet of sweat and you'll soon be sleeping on a swarm of mites who might prefer you to the mattress.

Worse, the Prozac leaking out of your pores as you sleep doesn't calm down mites the way it soothes humans; it turns them into vicious little mutants that grow into rat-sized fiends with a taste for flesh. This theory grown from my overactive imagination wasn't based on any actual research, naturally, and I didn't really believe it, but it kept me seeking alternative solutions. Danny would say those fears weren't the real me, no more than the anxiety was.

Truthfully, I'm quite normal.

My mother and father divorced when I was a teenager, at which time my father vanished from my life. I left Atlanta at age twenty after my mother was killed in a car crash, and I made my way to California with fifteen thousand dollars of a life insurance payout in my pocket, determined to begin a new life in the world of cosmetology.

That didn't quite work out as planned. For a couple of years I seemed to have it all: classes at Beautiful Styles Cosmetology in Burbank, a livable apartment, cash for what I needed when I needed it. But my money ran out before I could properly monetize my new skills, and I'd somehow (for the life of me I still can't figure out why) hooked up with the wrong crowd. What had started out as just another way to make ends meet led me to experiment with various substances and landed me at the mercy of some very nasty people.

I may have fallen flat on my face, but what counted was that since then I'd become a whole person again, ready to take on the world.

Well, sort of.

I lifted my glass and washed down the last of my boiled egg, then got up and washed the plate, the spoon, and the glass. They all fit nicely into their respective cupboards and drawers.

I walked into my bedroom and glanced at the green-and-yellow-checkered comforter pulled smooth under twin matching pillow shams. Atop this was a fluffy white tiger. There were two nightstands holding crystal lamps, the oak rocking chair in the corner, the small walk-in closet filled with every article of clothing I could possibly want, which wasn't all that much. The golden corduroy-covered sofa set in the living room, the desk and computer in my office—none of them was really mine. Danny had bought them for me.

Danny Hansen, the priest who was no longer a priest, incarcerated in my place, serving a fifty-year sentence. My husband who had never legally been my husband, though that made no difference to me. I didn't need a piece of paper to prove my love for him.

The phone out on the breakfast bar rang and I swiveled my head. It wasn't often I received a call at nine o'clock in the morning. My first thought was that it would be a sales call of some kind. Either that or the prison, calling to inform me that something terrible had happened to Danny.

Ring...

I hurried back to the kitchen and snatched up the receiver on the fourth ring, saw that the caller ID read *Private*, and pressed the handset to my cheek. "Hello?"

For a moment I thought I could hear gentle breathing. I was tempted to feel some alarm, but I let it go, reasoning that it was only the hiss of distant static. I was too paranoid.

My imagination knew no bounds. It was no

one. Or maybe it really was someone breathing.

No, only static.

I hung up and turned back toward the bedroom, dismissing unreasonable thoughts as they strung through my mind. Danny was calling me from a guard's cell phone, bloodied and lying on the side of the road where the transport van had tipped over, killing everyone but him. He was hurt and couldn't speak. He needed my help.

But I knew it wasn't anything like that. It had to be a wrong number.

A knot tightened in my gut as I headed into the bathroom. It's hard for me to express just how much I loved Danny. Maybe if you knew him the way I did, you'd understand.

He'd grown up during the war in Bosnia and at fifteen watched Orthodox Christians rape and murder his mother and sisters. Danny had done what any devastated young man might do in such a violent setting: he found a gun, hid behind the stove in his house, and then shot the men who killed his family.

Over the next four years he threw himself into the war and became one of the best-known assassins in that gut-wrenching conflict. When the fighting ended he came to the United States and became a priest in honor of his mother, a devout Catholic. He wanted to do his part in righting what was wrong in the world from the vantage of someone who'd seen horrible injustice.

But Danny's desire to help brutalized victims like his mother and sisters was his undoing. It began several years after he'd become a priest, while he was aiding a boy who'd been victimized by a pedophile. The pedophile managed to get out of prison, thanks to his father, who was a judge. Then he killed the boy whose testimony had helped convict him.

Outraged, Danny had forced the pedophile into a warehouse and cut off his penis. He didn't mean to kill, but the man had bled out. Rather than turn himself in, Danny justified and covered up the murder, something he came to regret years after meeting me.

That was Danny's first victim in this country. Over the next decade there were more, many more, all as deserving of harsh judgment, all untouched by the law. He always gave his subjects one chance to change, and if they refused, he changed them permanently, as he put it. He wasn't a serial killer with a pathological compulsion to kill, but a vigilante of sorts, all the while also serving the oppressed as a priest, however unorthodox his methods.

He was an outlaw, in the same way those who assisted Jews in Nazi Germany had been outlaws. In the same way Martin Luther, Gandhi, and Jesus had all stepped beyond the law to serve truth and justice in their day.

In that way, Danny and I were similar. I was one of those abused victims he'd come to save. I too took the life of a man who would have otherwise destroyed his wife and children, knowing the law would never save them. I'm not trying to justify what either of us did. It was terribly wrong. I had accepted responsibility for my crimes and fully intended on paying the price, really, I had.

But Danny and I fell in love, and at the last minute he stepped in and took the fall for what I had done, demanding that I remain free. He knew war; he knew prisons. He insisted that the prison system would chew me up and destroy me, and he couldn't live with that. No amount of objection on my part could change his mind.

After receiving the breathy phone call, I stepped up to the bathroom mirror, withdrew my week-old toothbrush from its holder, applied a thin line of toothpaste to the brush, turned on the faucet, wet the bristles, and started on my lower left molars. Teeth are far more delicate than most people realize. Even a small speck of food can quickly cause a rotting mess if left alone.

Danny was in prison and I was alone. Desperately alone and all too aware that it was my fault.

The phone rang again and I hurried to rinse my brush and mouth. An image of Danny struggling to push the buttons on a cell phone as he lay in a pool of blood next to a transport van returned to my mind. Or maybe he'd crawled into the tall grass by now and was hiding from the guards until I could come to his rescue.

Crazy, I know, but that's what went through my mind.

I rushed back through my bedroom, rounded the door frame, and snatched the phone from its cradle.

Private.

This time there could be no mistaking the sound on the line. It wasn't static. It was breathing.

I listened for a long moment, undeniably unnerved. The difference between static and heavy breathing is actually quite distinct, and when the certainty that I was listening to the latter settled into my mind, my own breathing became shallow.

It could be some morning drunk who'd called the wrong number twice in a row. It could be Danny hidden in the grass unable to speak because his throat was cut, or afraid that he'd be heard if he tried. It could be a maniac breathing down my neck.

I had to know which.

"Danny?"

More breathing, heavy. A man filled with perverted fantasies. One of my neighbors peeking at me through a hole in the wall. A grocery store clerk who moonlighted with a knife and a rope.

I started to hang up the phone but only got as far as the first twitch of my bicep when the breathing became a low, thick voice that short-circuited the nerves in my arm.

"I know about you, Renee." Another breath. And then, "The priest is going to die."

Click. The phone in my fist went dead. The room began to spin.

My full meltdown began then, when I first learned that Danny was going to die.

2

AT THE PRECISE moment that Renee Gilmore heard those fateful words, Danny Hansen sat in a waiting room outside the warden's office in the Basal Institute of Corrections and Rehabilitation, southeast of Wrightwood, just west of Interstate 15. The transfer from Ironwood State Prison had started at 2:00 a.m. and taken seven hours, fewer than three of which were spent in the transport van, or "the chain" as some called it.

He'd followed instructions without misstep as he always did. He was polite, spoke only when spoken to, stayed to himself, and arrived a few hours earlier in relatively good spirits.

Three years of incarceration in the overcrowded California prison had convinced him
that he truly was an outlaw, on the inside as
much as on the outside. He would do his time
as required by the law, but in his heart he still
lived beyond any law that conflicted with the
greater truth.

The system liked to say that an inmate had
the choice of doing either hard time or smooth
time. Danny had done neither. He was doing
his time. Nothing more, nothing less.

They said that in prison it's better to fight and
gain respect than to run and lose your dignity.
They said that steering clear of trouble has a
price. That the fight picks you—you don't pick
the fight.

All true, of course, but Danny didn't care
about the injustice inflicted upon him and
didn't try to change the convict code that administered it. He took his abuse in stride, like a
concrete wall, without retaliating and without
suffering more than one shallow wound from a
shank in his side. Compared to the physical and
mental wounds he'd suffered in the Bosnian
War, the abuse at Ironwood had been wholly
tolerable.

The suffering of *other* inmates preyed upon by the hustlers and gangbangers who ran the prison, however, had been much more difficult to stomach.

And even more, his separation from the one person he loved more than his own freedom tore through his heart like a strand of barbed wire. In so many ways, Renee was his life. Concrete walls stood between them, but they lived together as one in his mind. Her voice whispered in his ears without end.

If something bothered Renee, it bothered Danny. If bedbugs were overtaking her world, they were consuming his. If she preferred grapefruit over oranges, he wanted two of them, no matter how bitter they tasted. If she wondered why the world was upside down, so did he, always with a gentle reply and a nudge toward a less fretful analysis, but he could never simply dismiss her concerns. They were her truth.

She could not know how desperately he missed her, how her safety and happiness consumed him, how deep the sorrow of their separation ran through him. If she knew the full extent of his concern for her, she would only suffer more than she already did, because Renee loved him more than she knew how to love herself.

She paced through his heart every waking moment, occupied with inconsequential concerns that meant nothing to him except that they were hers. The rest of him was doing time in a society called prison, hidden away from the rest of the world. A totally self-contained culture, as alien as Mars to those who lived on the outside; a universe unto itself with a whole different set of rules and values. As members of this subculture, inmates became a new kind of creature. But what kind?

Ninety percent of all those incarcerated would reenter society, as they should. If all those incarcerated were kept behind bars, a full half of America's population would be in prison. The real question was, in what condition would a person released from prison emerge? Would he be a properly punished and reformed person ready to tackle life's challenges while following the rules, or an embittered, hardened person armed with new, more violent survival skills?

The puppies, as Danny sometimes thought

of those called newbies, worried him the most. You could slap a puppy for jumping up on your leg and peeing on your foot in their exuberance to experience life, much like you could slap an eighteen-year-old for possession of pot. But put the puppy in a cage with raging bulldogs for a few years and they would come out far less playful and far more apt to bite.

In the American prison system, the weak were often forced to become strong to survive the preying wolves, too often becoming wolves themselves. Nonviolent offenders often learned violence; young prisoners who had been caught on the wrong side of their pursuit of pleasure often learned that aggression and anger were required to survive. Some called the American prison system a monster factory, an environment that far too often fractured those who entered it.

At Ironwood, Danny had expected nothing because little was offered. He'd learned to live in a quiet place deep in his mind, compromised only by the intense suffering of others whom he was powerless to help. Unlike most prison puppies, Danny had embraced his new life and learned to be reasonably content with his situation.

But after only a few hours at Basal, he wondered if his determination to be content with nothing might be compromised here. If Ironwood was a prison that offered nothing, Basal appeared to be one that offered everything.

Awareness of this hit him the moment he stepped from the van beyond the sally port and breathed his first lungful of mountain air. Having survived three deadly summers in stifling one-hundred-degree weather at Ironwood, he'd lost sight of how pleasurable clean, cool air could feel.

The lawn wasn't brown or gray, but green. The building itself was constructed in the shape of a massive cross—four wings to accommodate the inner workings of the prison. The outer walls were formed of beautiful stone blocks, and steps that led up to an arched entry might have been mistaken for the welcoming gateway to a picturesque cathedral, if not for the words stamped above bolted black iron doors that identified it as a correctional facility. Ironic, he thought, a prison built like a cathedral.

A single motto embossed in the iron framework identified the prison's ideology: *An Eye for an Eye*.

"Let's go." The guard's voice brought him down to earth, and he'd followed the man through the main entrance into Basal. The processing room was carpeted, and the furnishings were made of expensive wood with bowls of candies on the counter. The guards were dressed in smart black slacks and could have been mistaken for hotel concierges rather than trained security personnel overseeing hardened criminals.

As the only transfer that morning, he'd met no other prisoners. After an hour of waiting in the comfortably furnished reception room, he began to wonder if Basal was actually a facility for the mentally ill. A new kind of sanitarium. Perhaps he'd been admitted to test his sanity. Other than the fact that it was a new experimental prison with better accommodations, he knew little about Basal.

No one spoke to him other than to give him simple directions, another oddity compared to the constant orders of Ironwood guards. When he finally approached the counter and politely asked the woman if Basal was a maximum-security prison, she'd simply informed him that the warden would explain everything when they met later that morning. Warden Marshall Pape personally saw to the welcoming and indoctrination of each new member, she said.

Member, not inmate or prisoner.

The entrance examination consisted of a thorough physical and a medical-history questionnaire administered by a white-coated physician in a small room that might be found in any doctor's office. Basal's version of a strip search.

Dressed in new blue slacks and a tan, short-sleeved button-front shirt they'd given him, Danny now sat in an upper level waiting area that would make a fine addition to any downtown Los Angeles attorney's firm. The six chairs were padded, the brown carpet was new. There were brass lamps on both end tables, a bookcase full of law books, three *Ficus* plants in off-white ceramic pots, and two recent copies of *National Geographic* magazine on the oak coffee table. A guard sat in a chair by the door, reading a copy of *Sports Illustrated*.

Danny could have easily rushed him and

taken him out before other guards responded, if he were predisposed to do so. They hadn't taken the typical precautions of placing him in chained ankle or wrist restraints.

Odd. Why?

There were at least half a dozen objects in the room that someone with Danny's training and skill could fashion into a weapon. The ceramic pots could be shattered and a shard used as a shank; the heavy wire harp used to support either lamp shade could be used as a lethal whip or a spike; the globe on two overhead dome lights as well as the glass from any of the incandescent bulbs would be as effective as razor blades in the right hands. His, for example.

From what he'd seen so far, the only clear indicators that Basal was a high-security facility were the series of locked doors that separated the administrative wing from the rest of the prison, the twin heavy-gauge doors at the entrance, and the three impassable perimeter fences around the entire compound.

The warden's door opened. A tall man with a balding head, dressed in dark brown slacks and a white shirt, filled the frame and stared at

Danny with drooping blue eyes. This was the warden. Marshall Pape.

Danny stood. The man's cheekbones were high, hardening his long face, but otherwise he looked like any middle-aged executive who might be seen entering or leaving a bank.

"Welcome to hell," Pape said.

His eyes held on Danny for a long beat before a smile brightened his face.

"So to speak. Please. Come in."

Danny dipped his head and walked into the room. The door closed quietly behind him and an electric latch fell into place, sealing him off from any attempt to get out using the warden as a hostage.

Three red camera lights winked at them from the corners of the ceiling. Whoever had constructed this new facility had surely covered all the bases using less conventional and far more sophisticated measures than in older prisons. For all Danny knew, there was a gun trained on his head at that very moment, waiting for him to grab a pen on the warden's cherrywood desk in an attempt to stab him.

The office was large and plush, with dark wood-paneled walls, bookcases, globes, several lamps, and two large family portraits. These showed a gray-haired woman, presumably the warden's wife, and two adolescent children, a boy and a girl. A sheer lace curtain covered the room's only window.

"Have a seat, Danny." The warden's voice was low and soothing. He indicated one of three high-backed leather chairs positioned opposite his desk. "Just so you know, this interview is being watched and recorded. Do you have a family?"

"No, sir."

"No?" He looked at one of the family portraits. "That's too bad. Everyone needs a family. There's nothing more important in this world than loving and being loved by your family. It's why I do what I do, you know. To keep families like mine safe. Society demands this from me, and I would give my life for it."

Danny said nothing.

The warden slowly opened a file folder, studied Danny for a moment, then settled into his chair.

"Let's start at the beginning, if you don't mind. Do you know how many people in the United States are incarcerated, Mr. Hansen?"

"No."

"According to the latest statistics, one out of every hundred adults in America is behind bars at any given time. Purely by the numbers, the average adult male in this country stands a fifteen percent chance of being imprisoned sometime during his life. Does that strike you as high?"

He'd heard it was ten percent. "It does."

"Yes, it does. And thank you for being so direct in your responses. I appreciate that."

Danny nodded.

"The sheer number of people imprisoned in this country becomes truly alarming when you consider that, although the Unites States makes up only five percent of the world's population, it has twenty-five percent of the world's prison population. On average, our incarceration rate is five times the rest of the world. Per capita, we have six times the incarceration rate of Canada, twenty times that of Japan. That's a seven hundred percent increase since 1970. Few realize it, but the United States is fast becoming a penal colony. Does this alarm you?"

"It does."

"Bear with me, because I need you to understand where I'm headed with all of this. One out of every thirty-one men in the United States today is either in jail today or under the supervision of corrections. The recidivism rate in California is seventy percent. As you know, the gyms at Ironwood are no longer used for recreation but to house hundreds of bunk beds, an attempt to handle more than twice the number of prisoners the facility was designed to hold. And through it all you have to ask yourself one question: why? Why are so many people going to prison, Danny? And why are seventy percent of those released being dragged back into prison?"

It sounded like a rhetorical question, so Danny said nothing.

"Go ahead, take a stab at an answer."

"Because they exit the system more hardened than when they entered it," Danny said. "Survival in the system requires adaptation to the environment. It's only human."

"Only human, very good. It's America's biggest tragedy. We have these manufacturing plants called prisons that accept deviants, turn them into hardened criminals, and send them back out into the world to wreak havoc. It's like boot camp for storm troopers."

"Not everyone who comes out—"

"Shut up, Danny."

The man's tone surprised him. But then Pape smiled. "This is a nice prison, you'll see that, but we have rules. One of those rules is that you will speak to me only when I ask you to. It may seem harsh, but it's one of the ways we maintain order. Fair?"

"Fair."

The warden continued. "Now, not all those who enter the monster factory come out as hardened criminals. But you, being a man of the cloth, surely realize that we are all monsters in need of help, don't you?"

Danny remained silent, not sure if he was expected to respond.

"That was a question, Danny. You may respond."

"I would say everyone needs help."

"Because we are all monsters?"

"I wouldn't necessarily go that far."

Pape kept his eyes steady above a gentle smile. "Then maybe you'll learn that in here. To the earlier point, you're right. A third of those who leave prison never return to it. But that leaves two-thirds who yield to the machinery and come out ready to prey on the weak. It's not society's intention, naturally, but it's real, nonetheless. You have to wonder why society doesn't rise up in protest and insist the government close down these manufacturing plants for criminals, don't you?"

Danny wasn't sure how to respond to such a sweeping generalization of the system, but Pape compelled him to answer. "Perhaps."

"No matter how you look at it, the system in this country's a hopeless mess," Pape said. "And no one has the will to fix it. That, my friend, is where I come in. Basal is the first facility to look the problem square in the eyes and fix what's broken, from the ground up. It's why the department of corrections signed off on spending $150 million to build and operate Basal. It took too many years and far too much political maneuvering to line up everyone, but now we have it. It's my turn to help fix the world."

His voice was like a purr, comforting, engendering trust. The warden looked down at the file and picked up a sheet of photocopied snapshots that Danny recognized from his original processing.

"I see you've put on a few muscles since they first sent you away. You like working out?"

"It helps me focus, yes."

"Good. You're going to need that focus to become a better man in here, Danny. All of it."

The warden set the pictures down and folded his hands on the desk.

"I'm guessing that you're wondering why you were transferred to our facility? Am I correct?"

"The question has crossed my mind, yes."

"For starters you should know that I'm very particular about who I invite into the program. Each candidate is carefully vetted. No attitudes, no violent criminals, no gang members, no racists, no drug addicts. We operate near full capacity. You're the first transfer in four months. I accept only two kinds of members: those with very long or indeterminate life sentences who have proven they can follow rules, and the newly incarcerated who believe they are innocent. It's critical that all of our members get off on the right foot, which is why I personally indoctrinate them. Consider this your gateway into a new world. Within these walls you will find true life or you will find hell. Do you understand?"

"Yes." Danny watched him, intrigued.

"Do you know what the word *basal* means?"

"It means 'basic.'"

"That's right. I like to think of it as foundational. Everything at Basal is about getting back to the basics of the human condition. The foundation of our souls. Who we are and who we are meant to be. As a priest, I'm sure you can appreciate that?"

"I'm no longer a priest," Danny said. "But yes, I think I understand."

"At Ironwood you were seen as a number. FX49565, to be precise. But I look at you and I see a human being who stands about six feet tall with brown hair and blue eyes. You're thirty-six and weigh 217 pounds, most of it muscle. More important, you seem to have the intellect of a scholar and the resolve of a thoughtful, disciplined man."

Danny wasn't quite sure how to take the warden. He spoke sincerely with a calm and soothing voice, but there was something odd about his stare.

"Still, let's not mince words. You've slipped. Fallen. You are broken and it's my job to fix you. This is Basal, and in Basal we go back the basics. The very basics. Do you understand?"

"Most of it, yes."

"Not all of it?"

"Some things take time to understand."

"You don't think you're broken?"

"As you said, aren't we all?"

"Yes, but not all of us are priests who murder. And if I were to guess, there are more than two bodies out there killed by your hand."

So the warden knew about that as well. "I was in the Bosnian War."

"Did I ask you to explain yourself? You have a way with judges as well, I understand." The man drilled him with his blue eyes. "And district attorneys," Pape said. "You cut a deal. In exchange for your confession to the murders of Jonathan Bourque and Darby Gordon, the DA agreed to no press. No death penalty. Fifty years in prison. You waived appeal. Why? Probably because doing so typically limits the inquiry to a simple identification of the victim's bodies rather than a full investigation, which would produce evidence needed in the event of an appeal. Which leads me to believe you're hiding something. Are you hiding something, Danny?"

The man's assumptions were correct. How

he'd come to the conclusion so easily was dis-
concerting. A full investigation of the facts surrounding the victims might have produced
forensic evidence that incriminated someone
else. Someone Danny loved more than he loved
his own life.

"Perhaps you're hiding something about
Renee?" the warden said.

A chill rode Danny's spine. What had a moment ago been deep concern immediately grew
to alarm. How could the warden even guess
such a thing?

Pape picked up a sheet of paper from the file.
"A Renee Gilmore, if I'm right. Ring a bell?"

"She's a very good friend," Danny said. "We
go way back."

"Yes, I bet you do." He set the paper down
and closed the file. "You must understand what
I'm driving at."

But Danny didn't understand.

"The fact is, you're broken. A priest, no less,
who has failed in the worst of ways. As the book
says: 'Any man who falls from the grace of his
brothers is no brother at all.' Isn't that right?"

"I'm sorry, I don't recall that passage. Where's
it from?"

The warden wagged his head at the book-shelf to his left. "Take your pick."

The books on the middle shelf made up what appeared to be a nearly exhaustive library of holy books from all the world's major religions, and as many smaller ones. The Muslim Quran, the Christian Bible, the Jewish Talmud, the Hindu Bhagavad Gita, the *Analects of Confucius*, and more, all lined up in no particular order.

"My point is simple," Pape said. "Basal isn't here to destroy you, however deserving you are, or to keep you away from society, but to *fix* you while you can still be saved. To rehabilitate you in a way that no other facility can possibly hope to. You won't simply do time here, Danny. You will either find a new life and a reduced sentence, or you will find real trouble. Are you agreeable to that?"

Danny couldn't mistake the irony of the warden's words. As a priest, he'd been the defender of the abused, the weak, the outcasts trampled under the heavy feet of powerful men. He'd confronted such powerful men, given them one chance to change their oppressive ways, and if they failed he'd change their ways for them. Often with a bullet to the head.

And now he was being confronted with the same choice. Change or be changed. Forever.

"As you see fit," Danny said.

"And I see fit that every man must first recognize their true nature and come face-to-face with who they really are in full confession. This must happen before they can turn around and begin the true path of repentance and rehabilitation. As the good books say, only when you realize just how wretched you are can you climb to freedom. Will you allow me to take you on that journey, Danny?"

"As long as I'm in your facility, my life isn't my own," Danny replied. "It's yours."

The warden stared at him for a few seconds and then slowly offered a slight smile. "And so it is. In Basal, I am God. And if you're going to reenter that fallen world out there, you must first understand the true nature of reward for good behavior and punishment for deviant behavior."

He slid a piece of paper across the desk and set a pen on top of it. "You are required to sign this waiver to participate in our program. Basal is outside the rest of the system, and as such there are special restrictions and rules. Take a moment to read it before you sign it."

Danny scanned the one-page document, which consisted of a list of behavioral rules and the forfeiture of several basic rights associated with visitation, mail, phone calls, and due process.

Most lifers who'd spent time in another prison would see the waiver as a small price to pay for a more comfortable stay and an earlier release. Fish—new guys—who believed they were innocent might be less likely to sign, unless they had no case or representation. Clearly, the warden only wanted those who fit a particular profile in his prison.

The waiver's restrictions might make contact with Renee more difficult, but there was now another consideration boring through Danny's mind. The warden seemed to suspect more about Renee than was on the books. How, Danny didn't know, but the fact that Pape might represent a danger to Renee compelled Danny to learn more about the severity of the warden's threat. He couldn't do so locked down at Ironwood.

Danny signed the waiver.

"Thank you." The warden stood, slid his chair under his desk, and began to pace, hands now behind his back.

"My prison is unlike any other, hidden from prying eyes, and I intend to keep it that way. Consider yourself fully isolated from the influences that corrupted you. That includes phone calls, mail, and visitation, which are earned privileges. Not easily earned, as you will see. I have the full support of the director who oversees this prison, and he's given me full authority. Due process is in place, but it's quick, and my word stands without question."

He pulled the translucent lace drape aside with a long finger and peered outside.

"As you have likely noted, we don't favor typical prison slang. It's critical that members forget everything they think they know about prison. This isn't a prison, it's my sanctuary. It's a proper reflection of authentic life. I'm sure a man of the cloth can appreciate that."

He released the curtain and continued down the length of his desk.

"We have three populations in our sanctuary. The commons wing is occupied by what's called the general population at other institutions. A smaller privileged wing is for those who reject deviant behavior and demonstrate sincere progress. And then we have the meditation floor, what you might think of as administrative segregation, or the hole. It's a travesty that inmates aren't rewarded for good behavior in most prisons, wouldn't you agree?"

"I can see that."

"It's an equal travesty that they aren't punished for deviant behavior. In our sanctuary reward is both earned and coveted. Do good and you will be richly rewarded. But fail me and you will suffer. As the book says, 'An eye for an eye.' Isn't that how it works?"

Danny's mind was still on how Pape seemed to know so much about him. Typically a warden knew only what was in a prisoner's file, which rarely held all the details of his crime. In the warden's careful vetting process, he had obviously dug much deeper. Everything he'd mentioned was a matter of record somewhere.

"I asked a simple question, Danny. Please answer."

"You would like my true opinion?"

"Would I have asked for it if I didn't?"

"Then I would say an eye for an eye is best replaced by forgiveness, love, and mercy."

The warden nodded. "Yes, you would. We may have challenges, you and I. But in the end, you will see my wisdom. We don't have an orientation period. You will leave me and go straight to the commons, where you will either learn the way things work on your own or be helped along by my staff. A handbook in your cell will lay out all of our rules, but let me highlight a few I'm partial to."

He cleared his throat and brought the back of his hand across his lips as if to dry them, then placed his fingertips on the desktop.

"Foul language is not permitted under any circumstance. It only reinforces learned behavior. Violence of any nature is strictly prohibited unless approved by me. Any form of sexual conduct is strictly prohibited unless I deem it to be appropriate. This includes any form of homosexuality, masturbation, or inciting lewd discussion. Is that clear?"

"Yes, sir."

"Some of the rules may seem pointless. I would advise you to follow them all to the letter. They're in place to help you learn obedience, regardless of the nature of that obedience. Any infraction will be grounds for swift disciplinary action in a manner I see fitting. Is that clear?"

"Yes."

"Good." He pressed the button on an intercom to his right. "Shari, please send Bostich in to transfer our new member to the commons."

He returned his attention to Danny. "As I'm sure you know, priests on the inside are often misjudged by others. They will see you as scum, an understandable sentiment. One of our members, a lifer named Bruce Randell, has a particular dislike of your kind for good reason and will try to make your life complicated. He's not a kind man. I assume you will stay clear of him?"

"I will do my best."

"I doubt your best will be good enough. Randell is a violent man."

"And yet he's in your prison."

The warden smiled. "Yes, well, I do make exceptions to the rules when it suits our collective goal. A wolf or two in the sheep pen keeps everyone on their toes."

Danny had kept his former occupation to himself at Ironwood, because a priest in prison was too quickly suspected as a sex offender, the worst possible classification among prisoners. Even the most hardened criminals refused to tolerate rapists and pedophiles.

It was senseless that a murderer could so harshly judge a rapist, but the society called prison had its own code, as unflinching as any law.

It was ironic that Danny's first victim had been a sexual predator.

The latch on the door hummed and snapped open. Bostich stepped in and looked at Danny. The man was in his thirties and wore a buzz cut, black slacks, and a black short-sleeved shirt. His hair was bleached, if Danny was right. Yellowish brows hung over dark eyes, which were an oddity in his pale, blotchy face. The man was average height, but strong, with thick fingers.

His eyes skirted to the warden. "Sir."

"Take our priest to his quarters," Pape said.

"Yes, sir."

Danny stood and walked to the door. He knew nothing about Bostich other than that he was likely the primary enforcer at Basal. Already, he didn't like the man. But this was his old judgmental nature rising. He set his disfavor aside and offered Bostich a nod, which was returned by an unflinching stare.

"Oh, and Danny..."

He turned to face the warden.

"There's a rapist in our sanctuary who continues to insist on his innocence. A dense young man named Peter Manning. I want you to see to him, help him understand his true wretchedness, the first step toward rehabilitation. Can you do that?"

Danny hesitated. "I will do my best."

Pape tapped his fingertips on the desk and smiled. "Surely you know how to handle people who harbor dark secrets. How you handle Peter may very well determine how it goes for you in Basal. Hell is a miserable place, Danny. Take care not to join Peter there."

3

AS I SAID, my meltdown really began with that first breathy phone call.

The priest is going to die.

Danny. He was talking about Danny. I stood rigid for a count of three and then I was flying toward my bedroom. My first thought was of the nine-millimeter—the gun in the back of my closet, the one I hadn't touched in three years. But my determination never to touch it again was already halfway out the window, because the nine-millimeter was the only thing I had that could blow a hole through the head of the man who'd just spoken to me on the phone. I wouldn't hesitate if it meant protecting Danny.

I made it to the edge of the bed before my mind caught up. I didn't need a gun; I needed Danny. And Danny was in prison.

I spun around and hurried back to the phone, thinking that Danny was probably already in transit to Basal. The images of that overturned transport van winked on, then off. Too neurotic. Impossible.

The phone was harping its disconnect alert when I snatched it off the counter. I got a dial tone and with a shaking finger dialed the all-too-familiar phone number for Ironwood State Prison, whispering reason to myself.

The line began to ring. I scanned the walls of my condo for holes and a peeping eye. But I would have noticed; I was too observant in my own environment to miss something so obvious. Who would want to watch me? One of Danny's old enemies. Or mine. Ghosts from the past, that's who.

Calm down, Renee. Take a deep breath.

"Ironwood State Prison."

"Yes, can you connect me with the warden?"

A pause. I sounded like a frantic girlfriend or wife. The prison probably got them all the time.

"May I ask who's calling?"

I calmed my voice as best I could. "Renee Gilmore."

The phone clicked, then began to ring through to the warden's office. In prison, the warden might be God, but to get through to God you had to get through his secretary who, in this case, went by the name Susan Johnson.

"Warden's office."

"Thank God, thank God." Still way too hyper. "I'm sorry, this is Renee Gilmore and my...a friend of mine is incarcerated there. Danny Hansen. FX49565. He was scheduled to be transferred today."

"What can I do for you, Ms. Gilmore?" Her tone was flat, the kind you might expect from someone trying to cope in a prison stuffed with twice as many inmates as the two thousand or so it was built to hold.

"I need to find Danny."

"I'm sorry—"

"I know you can't just put me through, but I just received a threat on his life and if anything happens to him, I swear...You've got to get a message to him."

"I'm sorry, but—"

"At least put him into segregation."

"Calm down. If you'd let me get a word in edgewise I'd tell you that my records show that he was taken out at four this morning."

"Four? He's gone?"

"Try Basal, Mrs. Hansen."

"Gilmore," I said, barely hearing myself, and hung up.

I'd never been to Basal—no reason to. But I'd looked it up a few days earlier and printed out a map when Danny told me he was being transferred. There was no helpful information on the Internet, only a sentence saying that it was an experimental state facility geared toward rehabilitation for three hundred inmates. The prison system in California was stressed beyond capacity, in large part due to the fact that half of the prisoners who served their time came out of prison more jacked up than when they went in. The state had the highest recidivism rate in the country.

The state aimed to change that and was searching for answers. Basal had gone live three years ago as part of that effort. As far as I was concerned, that much was good news. A prison devoted to rehabilitation had to be better than the overcrowded gangland called Ironwood.

Then again, that was all I knew about Basal. All the other prisons in the California Department of Corrections and Rehabilitation had websites that provided at least a peek into their mysterious worlds.

Not Basal. It was sealed up and locked down like Area 51. Tucked away in the Angeles National Forest south of Wrightwood, off of Lone Pine Canyon Road.

Images of Nazi concentration camps that experimented on prisoners flashed through my mind. This was America, not Poland, but Basal was also a prison, and the prison system was a world unto itself, hidden from the rest of society. And I have an active imagination.

The drive from Ironwood to Basal would take only a few hours. Danny had arrived and was probably already processed by now. Why would someone call me if they wanted to hurt Danny? Maybe it was a prank call. Or a ghost from the past come back to haunt Danny on the outside. Danny and me.

I know about you, Renee.

That first part of the call ballooned in my head and for a moment I wondered if it was part of a dream. No, I was awake. I might have had something close to OCD, and sure, I was a bit neurotic, but I wasn't crazy and I wasn't hallucinating.

I thumbed in 4-1-1 and paced. When I asked for the number for the Basal Institute of Corrections and Rehabilitation, the operator put me through.

A warm female voice answered my call. "Basal."

"Yes, uh…hi. This is the prison?"

"The Basal Institute, that is correct. How may I direct your call?"

"I'm looking for a prisoner who was transferred this—"

"Hold on."

She shuffled me on to the appropriate party. It was a real place with a real voice that didn't sound like it belonged to a Nazi doctor. That was good, right?

"Basal."

This second voice didn't sound so warm.

"Yes, I'm trying to reach an inmate who was transferred to your institution from Ironwood this morning. A Danny Hansen. Can you tell me if—"

"Visitation is by approval only, every Tuesday."

"Well, fine, then I would like to schedule a visit."

"I'm sorry, it doesn't work like that here. Visitation is an earned privilege. Once the member in question has earned visitation rights, you may request a visit, assuming you are approved."

"I've already been approved."

"Not for Basal, you aren't."

The revelation set me back. It had taken me weeks to get approval to visit Danny at Ironwood.

"Why not?"

"The regulations at other institutions don't apply at Basal. I'm sorry, but you'll have to wait, like everyone else."

"Then I can schedule a call with him."

"No, ma'am. Phone calls are also an earned privilege. You have to understand, we're not like the other prisons."

"Then how do I get in touch with him?" I demanded.

"You don't get in touch with him. Not until he earns the privilege and you're approved."

"How long does that take?"

"I can't make any promises."

"How long?" I snapped, aware I was starting to boil over but unable to calm myself.

"A month or two." Her tone was now not only flat but unyielding.

"I'm supposed to wait two full months before I talk to him? That's ridiculous!"

"We're not a resort, ma'am."

"Can I get him a message?"

"Once he earns mail privilege—"

"I don't have time to wait for him to earn his privileges, or send a letter. I need to get him a message now! His life depends on it."

"Are you his attorney?"

"No, I'm—"

"Then you'll have to wait until he earns the right to receive messages. Now if you'll excuse me—"

"Wait!"

I'd been pacing back and forth in front of the breakfast bar like a caged cat, hair on end, and I knew that I wouldn't get anywhere with this Nazi unless I calmed down. So I stopped, took a deep breath, and placed my free hand on the counter.

"Fine. Okay, can you at least tell me if he arrived."

I heard the faint clatter of keys on a keyboard. "His name?"

"Danny," I said. "Danny Hansen. FX49565."

"We wouldn't use his corrections number. Danny Hansen, you said?"

"Yes, Danny Hansen."

The phone went silent. In an age when the Internet is faster than light, I always wondered why the prison computers are so slow.

"He's here," she finally said.

"He's safe?"

"He's here, that's all I can say."

My hand-on-the-counter trick failed me; my fingers coiled into a fist. "Someone called me a few minutes ago and threatened to kill him! Now don't just sit there and tell me I can't get that message to him. I want to speak to the warden!"

"I'm afraid that won't be possible."

"Why not?"

"The warden doesn't take unofficial calls."

"This *is* an official call!"

"I'm sorry, but I have to terminate this call."

"Wait! At least tell the warden what I told you."

She didn't respond. But neither did she hang up. So I surged ahead.

"Please, I'm begging you. Someone wants to kill Danny, you have to tell the warden that much. Aren't life threats part of your concern?"

"I'll tell him," she said.

"You do that," I snapped, and I disconnected.

I was a mess, and it took me ten minutes to calm down enough to start from the top and start thinking straight. The way I saw it I had three options.

One, I could sit around and wait for another breathy phone call, which in my condition was a clear impossibility.

Two, I could hire an attorney and get a message to Danny that way, but it would still take a day or two, at least.

Or, three, I could go to where Danny was and try to make something happen another way. What way, I had no idea. And that was a problem. Which brought me back to option two, which seemed as pointless to me.

I was pacing when the doorbell startled me. Other than UPS deliveries from Amazon or a visit from either Jane or Sarah, my bell rarely rang. Jane, who'd rescued me from a dead battery in the parking lot two years earlier, had become my closest friend, and although she lived in a unit at the end of the complex, she knew to call first if she wanted to swing by. Same with Sarah, who I'd met at the school for truckers—long story.

I crossed to the door and cautiously peered through the eyehole. On the landing stood a rather large woman, warped by the lens so that she looked like a bowling pin wearing a blue dress. I released both dead bolts, cracked the door a foot, and peered out.

"Renee Gilmore?" the woman asked.

"I'm sorry, who are you?"

In her hands she held what appeared to be a shoebox. She glanced around nervously. Her brown hair hung to her shoulders, crinkled by a bad do-it-at-home perm—surely she hadn't actually paid someone to do that to her. She towered over me, all 250 pounds of her.

"You're Renee Gilmore?"

"Yes."

"Can I come in?"

"Come in? Why?"

"I'd rather not say, not out here."

"Why not?"

She hesitated, fiddling with her thick fingers. Her pink polish was a good two weeks old, judging by the growth at the base of her nails. Chipped and scratched.

"Do you know a priest at Basal?" she asked in a husky voice.

Every alarm in my mind clanged to life. First a phone call, and now this? The woman went from being messy tramp to lifeline in less time than I could think it. I scanned the parking lot and sidewalks. "You're alone?"

"Yes."

"Who are you? How did you get here?"

"Constance. I got here on the bus. That's all I can say." She looked around again, like someone frightened she might be seen talking to me. If she was scared, I had even more reason to be.

I pulled the door open. "Hurry."

"Thank you."

As soon as she stepped in, I closed and locked the door. "Don't touch anything." That sounded rude. "I mean, I just cleaned. So what do you know about Danny? Have you seen him?"

"No. No, it's not like that. I—"

"But you've heard from him? Or about him?"

"I was told to deliver this." She held out the shoebox.

"What is it?"

"I don't know."

"Will it explode?"

"Hasn't yet. Please, just take it."

I took the box from her and examined the lid, which was sealed shut with masking tape. No name, no address, just an old Nike shoebox that held something other than a pair of shoes, judging by how light it was.

"I should open it?" I asked.

"Not now. I have no idea what it is. I was just told to give it to you, that's all."

"Where'd you get it?"

"You have to believe me, I have no idea what it's about." She hesitated. "But there's something else."

"What?"

She glanced around as if putting off saying what she really wanted to say.

"Do you mind if I have a drink of water?"

Not sure what else to do, I set the box on the counter, crossed to the cupboard, pulled out a glass, and filled it from the filtered-water spout at the sink. I handed her the glass. "Here."

"Can I sit down?"

My first thought was *No, we don't have time*

*for sitting, just say it! And why'd you bring me
a box?* But I immediately realized how absurd
that would sound.

So I rounded the counter and waved her into
the living room. "Sure, sit."

"I have to get back. If Bruce finds out I told
you this he'd flip his lid."

"Bruce who? Tell me what?" She'd crossed to
the couch but hadn't taken a seat. "Sit down."

Constance settled to the couch. Her glass was
still full. She was trying to work up the nerve
to tell me something. Already, my mind was
seeing Danny lying in the center of the prison
yard, bleeding on the ground with a shank
sticking out of his back.

"Please, just say it. What's happened to him?"

"Nothing that I know of. But he might be in
some trouble."

"What trouble?"

"I talked to Bruce two days ago. Bruce Randell. He's in Basal."

"Your husband?"

"No."

"Girlfriend? Sister?"

"Let's just say we know each other. He went
down on a distribution conviction eight years

ago and was transferred to Basal after it opened."

I sat down on the edge of the stuffed chair facing her. "And? What about the priest?"

"If this gets back to Bruce…He's got connections on the outside."

"Whatever you tell me, I swear, not a soul will know."

She nodded once. "Bruce once told me he was sexually molested by a priest when he was a boy. No one can know that or he'd hit the ceiling. For two years, when he was thirteen. He went back when he was eighteen and killed the priest who did it. I'll deny that if it ever comes back on me."

"It won't. I promise."

"I'm only telling you so that you know why I'm here."

"Which is what? He hates priests and Danny's a priest?"

"He talked about the priest transferring to Basal and said I'd be getting a box he wanted me to deliver to someone. He said I'd know who when I got the box."

"Me?"

She stared at me and nodded once.

My heart was pounding. The phone call suddenly made more sense to me. But why me? How could Bruce know about me? Or get my number? Two thoughts crammed into my mind. The first was that he knew more than a few things about me.

The second was that both Danny and I were dead.

I stood up and looked at the shoe box. "What's in the box?"

"I swear, I don't know what's in the box. Money, for all I know. I shouldn't be telling you this."

In that moment, confronted by what seemed like certainty, I felt my mind rewinding, becoming the mind of the woman I'd been three years earlier, before Danny had fixed me.

"Why didn't you go to the warden with this?" I asked.

"I can't. You don't understand, I should have just dropped the box off and left."

"Who gave it to you?"

"I don't know."

"What do you mean, you don't know? They gave it to you, right? They were wearing a mask?"

"It was left for me with a note with your name and address on it. I'm not going to sit here and tell you how or why I have to do this. Let's just say I have a conscience. But Bruce can hurt anyone he wants to, including me."

So then. There it was. We were dead. But I wasn't feeling fear; I was feeling rage. The kind I hadn't felt for three years. And that box was calling to me, daring me to open that lid.

I sat down and drilled her with a stare. "That's it?"

"I had to tell you."

"So what am I supposed to do?"

She shrugged. "Warn the priest."

"Warn him? I can't even get a phone call through to him! They've cut me off!"

The woman pushed herself up using the arm-rest. "Can he handle himself?"

I couldn't believe she was just going to dump this on me and leave. "He's in for murder, isn't he?" I said. "But he doesn't like to hurt people. You don't know anyone else on the inside I can get to? Someone in food services? A cop? A guard?"

"Not at Basal, no way. I'm sorry, honey, I don't know what to tell you. I did what I had to, you understand. With any luck he sees it coming and gets himself put in segregation."

She headed for the door, stepped outside without a backward glance, and left me alone in silence.

I locked the door behind her and stared at the old shoe box. I knew whatever it contained couldn't be good. Images of white anthrax powder and homemade bombs filled my head. But there was that breathy phone call, and there was Bruce, and there was Danny, and there was that box. I had to know what was in that box.

So I withdrew a knife from the drawer, sliced the masking tape, and lifted the lid.

Inside the box lay some tissue paper. On that tissue paper sat a small plastic bag. There was a bloody finger in the bag.

4

BEYOND THE ADMINISTRATIVE wing, Basal looked fairly typical for any newly constructed prison, Danny thought. But as Bostich ran down a short summary of the layout and basic expectations, it was clear that there was far more to the facility's inner workings than first met the eye.

The large cross-shaped structure was divided into four operational wings referred to by their compass location with a large, domed common area at its hub. The two-story north wing, where Danny was admitted, held all administrative functions, which centered on the warden. The south wing was used for services including the infirmary, food preparation and dining, laundry, maintenance, commissary, and programs. Members were housed in one of three wings. The longer west or "commons" wing consisted of ninety cells with a maximum capacity of 180 members. The shorter east or "privileged" wing consisted of fifty units called rooms rather than cells, many of which were single occupancy. And the basement or "meditation" floor was reserved for up to fifty less-responsive members.

There were two yards—one small patch off the hub, and a much larger park that surrounded the entire facility, a privileged area reserved only for the east wing members accessed through the back of their quarters.

Bostich led Danny through a secured door into the hub, where perhaps forty members loitered around fixed tables or on brown couches that faced a small television playing HGTV. The rest were either on the yard, in the rec room, or in their cells, Bostich said. Commoners weren't permitted to work.

Most prisons had work programs ranging from common maintenance to skilled labor—

employment that kept inmates occupied for six to eight hours a day, earning a maximum of ninety-five cents an hour, half of which went to pay fines. A man dressed in jeans and a blue button-front shirt paused his mopping of the gray floor and leaned on his mop to watch Danny. Jeans. An employee, yes, but an inmate? The privileged class.

Odd. Work, however menial the task, tended to keep prisoners occupied and out of trouble. Here, that privilege was reserved for those who'd graduated to the east wing. The employed would control the prison's entire underground commerce, which in most prisons consisted of extorting, hustling, and trading of both legal goods, such as potato chips or coffee, or contraband, such as tobacco, prison brew, or drugs. Goods smuggled in or purchased by the wealthy at the commissary were the currency in most prisons, and those prisoners who had the most to trade typically had the most power, just like in all societies.

Giving those in the privileged wing that balance of power by offering them an easy way to make extra money would create class envy. Violence or threats of violence would be used to extort or rob the upper class in many prison systems.

Evidently, Basal wasn't home to typical prisoners.

The walls and floor were concrete, painted a shiny gray. Guarded steel doors controlled passage into each of the four wings. Black-and-yellow-striped tape ran along the floor, marking walkways and restricted areas. No pictures or images on the walls, no plants or decorations of any kind.

The silence struck Danny as he followed Bostich across the hub toward a guarded door with a sign that said Commons above it. The hub was massive, hollowed like an echo chamber beneath a large glass dome, and yet an eerie quiet hovered about the several dozen members who quietly watched him. No one seemed to be speaking.

They were all dressed in the same blue slacks and tan short-sleeved shirts, staring with interest. A cross-section of ages was represented, but fewer younger prisoners than at Ironwood.

Respect was critical in prison, not of correctional officers as much as of other inmates. Cross into the personal space of a CO and you were likely to be ignored unless you were belligerent.

But disrespecting another inmate with anything from a harsh look to an angry word could earn you unending trouble.

Take a man's freedom and he will cling to those few needs that make him human: his need for respect and his need for dignity. Take those and he will become an animal.

Treat a man like you treat an animal, and to the extent he is able, he will treat you like one. Respect and dignity—these were the lifeblood of the convict code, a convention that had as much if not more bearing on how a prison ran than the official prison protocol.

What few on the outside seemed to realize was that humans were human, regardless of which society they lived in. Government, hierarchy of power, and expectation of social conformity were as real in the prison society as in any other. Rob the members of their dignity and they would only learn to rob others of theirs. Hence, the monster factory.

Bostich nodded at a brown-headed, lanky CO standing by the entrance to the commons wing. "Danny Hansen, 297, new arrival."

The guard checked a box on his clipboard. "Seventy-one."

"Let's go."

Bostich led him down a wide hall with two floors of barred cells on the left. Metal stairs rose to a second tiered row with a four-foot walkway for access to cells set back from the railing. Same gray floor, same painted cinderblock walls as in the hub. All of it scrubbed clean and shiny new. A guard station manned by a young officer who leaned back in his chair behind several monitors was centered on the opposite wall. Beyond him was a passage to what Danny guessed to be the showers. He'd seen no public phones yet.

The cell Bostich took him to was located on the second tier, three quarters of the way down the hall. The front wall of each cell consisted of vertical bars and a barred door, allowing unrestricted view of the interior.

"Here you go." Bostich opened the unlocked door to a cell with the number 71 stenciled above it. "Everything you've been issued is on the top bunk, including a handbook with the rules. I suggest you familiarize yourself with it."

"Thank you." Danny stepped inside and scanned the cell.

Eight feet wide if you wore large shoes, maybe twelve deep. Two long strides by four shorter strides. A bunk bed on the right, opposite two standing lockers. Beyond the bunk, a single metal sink attached to a single metal toilet, no seat.

On the top bunk, his kit. Two additional pair of blue slacks, two more tan shirts, two white T-shirts, two pair of white boxer shorts, two pair of black socks, one yellow towel, one yellow washcloth, one set of white sheets, one gray blanket with blue stripes at the top, one bar of soap half the size of his fist, a tube of Crest toothpaste, one yellow toothbrush, one red disposable razor with a worthless blade, and two roles of single-ply toilet paper. These and the clothes he wore were now his only earthly possessions. They'd taken the rest when he'd entered the facility.

His cellie was an organized, educated man, judging by the clean sink, the folded clothes on the end of his bed, and the philosophy books stacked neatly on the top of the first locker. No TV, no music player, no electronics of any kind in sight.

The cell door clanked shut but remained unlocked. Lockdown would come at night with lights out.

When Danny turned around, Bostich was gone. There was no further explanation of the prison protocol, no introduction to the facilities, no assembly-line pickup of issued items.

But clearly, that was part of the program. He was being watched carefully. What he did now would determine what happened to him.

And he would do what he always did. Time.

He would go through the motions, naturally. He would eat what they gave him to eat, try to sleep when they told him to sleep, walk around the yard when they allowed him to do so, avoid the hustlers, read anything and everything he could get his hands on, make polite conversation with whoever was predisposed to join him, and he would think.

But mostly he would simply do his time, decades of it, trying to figure out who he really was and then attempting to live a life behind bars that allowed him to be that self. Because truthfully, behind bars a man has only himself and time.

His memory of his past life hung in his mind like a distant fog, surreal now after three years.

It was hard to believe he'd been that fifteen-year-old boy in Bosnia whose mother and sisters were raped and killed...that child who became a man when he took a pistol and shot the men who destroyed them...that young soldier who became feared for his efficiency.

And that priest, who took the lives of far too many people when he became their judge, jury, and executioner. Through it all he'd learned two things about himself, the part of him that had been buried under years of suffering and rage in a brutal war: he would far rather be a lover than a fighter, and he made for a terrible priest. And yet he would always be known for that, wouldn't he?

The priest who killed.

Danny had finished making his bed and putting his few items in the second locker when the rap of knuckles on steel interrupted his thoughts. At the door stood an older, skinny man with gray hair and a matching goatee, grinning. One tooth missing. Eyes as bright as the blue sky.

"Hello, cellie." The man opened the door, stepped in, and extended his hand. "Simon Godfrey's my name. Welcome to your basal cell in-carcinoma, home of the diseased, deviants unfortunate enough to be caught. Basal, institute for the wayward."

Danny took the cool, thin hand. "Danny Hansen."

"Good name," the man said, still grinning. His eyes sparkled with life. "The word is you're a priest. Now, what on earth is a priest doing in this sanctuary for the wicked?"

The man was either daft or exceptionally witty, and Danny thought the latter. Translation: *What are you in for?* It was typically a guarded question on the inside, not the first question asked. Godfrey was either too new or too long in the system to care.

"How did you know I was a priest?"

"Everyone knows, that's why. The captain announced it two days ago. A priest is coming, he said."

"The captain?"

"Bostich."

"He said that?"

"He did. And you know what that means."

"He announced that?"

"He announced that."

"How?"

"A man with many questions." He slapped Danny on the shoulder and stepped past him. "I like that, Father. I like that a lot. He told Randell, who told his bunch of knuckleheads, who told the rest." Knuckleheads, prison slang for those bucking the system and doing hard time. Godfrey faced the metal toilet, unzipped his trousers, and let loose a stream into the toilet bowl. "Loudmouth works better than the loud-speaker inside. Problem with the loudspeaker is, no one listens. But put it out on loudmouth and in five minutes the whole club knows." He zipped up and turned around. "Wouldn't you agree?"

"Makes sense."

"How long?"

"Fifty years."

The man whistled. "Me, I got life. Do you want me to wash my hands?"

Danny found the man's unpretentious audacity disarming and oddly comforting.

"I want you to do whatever it is you need to do."

"Then I won't bother," Godfrey said. "Not to worry, I didn't touch myself. Have a seat and let me tell you how it is before you head out to meet the wolves, though to be fair, there's only one real wolf in this place and you already met him."

He sat on the lower bunk and patted the mattress. Danny felt obliged to humor the man.

"You've been around, so you know that a priest has it coming from both sides. There's those who assume you're a sexual predator, and you know how that goes. And then there's the rest, who think a man of the cloth breaking the law just ain't right. So you're screwed either way."

"Assuming I'm a priest. Which I'm not."

"I'm assuming you were at one time."

"I gave it up before I confessed."

"To what?"

Back to the start. He decided it wouldn't hurt to leak the right story.

"Let's just say I helped the wayward see the light using a little too much force."

"Hmmm. And these wayward, did they deserve it?"

Danny considered the question only a moment. "No more than I did."

The man grinned from ear to ear. "So now I really like you. Unfortunately, Bostich doesn't, that much I can assure you. I'm assuming you got the speech from the warden?"

"We spoke, yes."

"Two kinds of prisoners, right? Fish and indeterminate lifers. But there's a third group in here: the knuckleheads he brings in for one reason and one reason alone—to test the rest. In his twisted way of thinking, you see, he has to make this grand sanctuary of his as similar to his understanding of the world as possible. That means there's got to be a carrot and there's got to be a whip, and he's going to help you decide which one you want. But what fun is all that without temptation? So, yes, he brings in the knuckleheads to either entice you into wickedness or push you over the edge. If your edge was violence, he's going to push you there again. Trust me on that."

Perhaps. But Danny had lost his stomach for violence three years ago. The only edge Danny had now was Renee. As long as she was safe, he would not bend.

"I'm no longer a violent man," he said.

"All I'm saying," Godfrey continued, "is that Bostich, who's a devil, has his orders, and unless I'm a fool those orders are to break you down before he breaks you in."

None of this concerned Danny for the simple

reason that he was powerless to change any of it. There was only so much the authorities could do to a person in an American prison, and none of it compared to the suffering he'd experienced in Bosnia as a younger man. His vow of nonviolence could not be compromised.

"They can try," Danny said. "I suppose I deserve whatever comes my way."

"You do realize what the carrot is, don't you?" Godfrey asked, then answered himself. "The privileged wing. You follow the rules, all the rules, rules, rules, and you live life large until you get out on early release, assuming you still want it. All things become new, my man, that's the carrot." He formed an imaginary ball with his thin, blue-veined hands. "A paradise overflowing with milk and honey, that's the ticket. The Pape's kingdom, right here on earth. They live in apartments over there, man! With their own bathrooms and flatscreen TVs. They wear what they want, they get all the jobs. Better food, a cinema room, a full weight room, a gym with nets. Heck, if you believe the rumors, they get booty calls over there."

"And yet you're still here," Danny said.

Godfrey lowered his hands and flashed his

missing-toothed smile. "Because I can't seem to keep my mouth shut. The warden doesn't like my little slipups. He's got all the privileged guys in tow, see?" He stabbed his forehead with a bony finger. "But I got too much up here for him. The only thing that keeps me out of trouble is that no one has the brains to listen."

His confession made Danny wonder why he'd been placed with Godfrey. Clearly, the warden wanted him to hear all of this.

"How long have you been here?" he asked.

"Two years. Give me another two and I just might see it like the rest. It gets to you, you know. Don't think it doesn't. Once you buy into it all, you're stuck. The strange thing is, the Pape's philosophy actually seems to work. Basal is probably the smoothest-running correctional facility in the country."

"Why wouldn't it be? The warden handpicks his prisoners."

"True. He's even got the knuckleheads by the gonads. It's not just the carrot, my friend. There's more down in that basement than a cold hole. You buck the system and you pay a price."

Godfrey glanced at the bars and lowered his voice. "In my time I've seen three men commit suicide, all of them knuckleheads, and I swear not one of them did it to themselves. That's just the way it is. He's got a little heaven and a little hell laid out like a smorgasbord, and he makes the choice pretty easy. Just like on the outside."

"Hustlers?"

"Sure, we got all kinds, everybody has their thing, but it's all pretty much either aboveboard or immediately exposed and punished. Nothing happens the warden doesn't know about, trust me. If there's a hustle going on, it's only because he allows it. There's no freedom here. Pape controls every syllable uttered in this prison. Sometimes I think half the staff doesn't even know what's really happening."

"So it's not all aboveboard."

"I'm not talking about the hustles and tattoos or what not. I'm talking about what's *really* going on. And visitation? Forget it."

It was the first thing Godfrey said that struck a raw nerve.

"Unless you're in the east wing, and then only if he can trust you. 'Come out from among them and be separate,' as the book says. Keeps you safe from what destroyed you, he says."

"I'm surprised his policy isn't challenged."

"By who? You have an attorney?"

"No need for one."

"Exactly. Like you said, he handpicks his prisoners. The ones who don't have a case or the resources to bring a case. You have anyone on the outside who would help you?"

His mind filled with an image of Renee marching up to the gate upon learning that she was barred from visiting him. She would go ballistic if she learned that contact with him was being cut off indefinitely.

Danny stood and ran his fingers through his hair. On the other hand, if he could manage his way into the east wing and earn both visitation rights and an early release, he would be able to tend to her needs.

Dear God, he missed her. It was difficult to reveal the true nature of his longing to be with her without causing her more anxiousness. If she knew the extent of the suffering their separation caused him, she would never consider moving on to build a new life without him. And yet, considering her nature, he was sure she needed constant companionship. His own need for her loyalty and love was superseded by his need to see her at peace and comfortable, even if the transition proved to be difficult.

But now…what if there was a way to get out early? A legal way.

"How long does it take to get into the east wing? Assuming you play by the warden's rules."

Godfrey shrugged. "I've seen it done in six months. But he cycles them out as fast as they go in. Any deviant behavior, and I mean crossing-the-road-on-the-wrong-day kind of deviant behavior, and you're back where you started from. Welcome to the sanctuary, Priest."

"Please, don't call me that."

"No? Might as well get used to it, they're already calling you that." The older man stood. "If I was you—and this is just me, understand—I would learn the rules, follow his laws to the letter, and take your abuse. Let them think they're breaking you. It's in their blood. In the Pape's universe, everyone is guilty and deserves punishment. Heck, he'd put the whole world in here if he could. Follow the Godfrey and you won't go wrong."

"I'll keep that in mind."

"And so that you know, the only people who will talk to you during your so-called indoctrination are those the warden's determined fit to speak to you. You'll feel like a leper out there, but it's by design. The good news is, you get me. If you let me, I'll talk your ear off."

"Speak all you like. Although I'd prefer it if you didn't snore too loudly."

"Then we're good. I'll sleep with my blanket over my head."

Danny chuckled. "No need, my friend."

Godfrey gave him a whimsical look. "You may insist, my priest."

"What do you know about an inmate named Peter Manning?"

"Members, not inmates. Remember that. And the guards are facilitators. They're just here to help us see the light. The warden's very particular about words. And whatever you do, don't swear. It took me three months to learn how to speak right." He walked to the bars and peered down the tier. "Why do you ask about Peter?"

"The warden asked me to help him out."

Godfrey looked away, frowning. "Pete's in for statutory rape. He's twenty years old and his story's going to break your heart and get you in trouble, mark my words. He moves like clock-work—he'll be in the dining room in half an hour. You can hear the story from him if you can get him to talk. But I'm warning you, tread carefully. You can't save him."

"I'm not here to save anyone."

The man didn't respond, but his eyes betrayed his thoughts clearly enough. *We'll just see about that.* You never knew what kind of cell mate you would find in prison. Danny couldn't imagine a better one than this old character who spoke what was on his mind.

"Just curious," Danny said, "since you asked me, what's your story?"

"Me? I was once a philosophy professor at UCLA. That was sixteen years ago. I've been serving Father Time ever since for a crime I didn't commit."

"And what crime was that?"

"I was framed for the tsunami that killed all those people in Indonesia. Unfortunately, I no longer have the resources to appeal the verdict."

He said it without the slightest hint of humor. "But don't you worry about that, Priest. You have bigger worries."

"Is that right? And what would they be?"

"Bruce Randell," Godfrey said. "You're not careful and he'll kill you."

5

SEEING THE MANGLED, bloodied finger in a shoe box, I reacted as any normal person sent a piece of her husband's body might. I rushed to the sink and threw up.

My illness came at the thought of that finger belonging to Danny, but whether it actually *was* Danny's finger, I couldn't know. It was way too mangled to tell. Either way, my world was caving in on itself. Danny's life was in danger. So was mine.

I stood over the sink, shaking, mind racing. I couldn't go to the police, that much I knew. Whoever was behind this knew too much about our past. Questions would be asked.

People would talk. Both Danny and I would go down.

I didn't have time to figure out who Bruce Randell was by researching the particulars of his incarceration and looking for details about his case. That was a long shot at best. I had to get to Danny, and there was only one way I knew to get to him. I had to go to Basal.

Impulsively, without even taking the time to look again, I wiped the vomit off my lips, grabbed the shoe box, and dumped the contents, tissue and all, into the garbage disposal. I flipped the switch. Three seconds of chunking and scraping later, the thing was gone, and only then did I wonder if I'd sent valuable evidence into the sewer system.

Danny had once cut things off of people. Maybe someone was returning the favor.

I had to get to Danny. He had to be alive. I knew that from my call to Basal earlier. If he was alive, I would find a way to get to him.

Basal was located in the high country, north of Rancho Cucamonga, far beyond my regular stomping grounds, which pretty much consisted of my condo, north Long Beach, and Ironwood State Prison. I wasn't one for exploring just for the thrill of it. For starters, I hated the traffic in Southern California, especially the freeways, which were anything but free. They were their own kind of overcrowded prison—thousands and thousands of steel boxes crammed together on concrete with their prisoners staring ahead for hours on end. Then again, I suppose we all live in one kind of prison or another. Mine was my head.

Following the Google map I'd printed earlier in the week, I drove my white Toyota Corolla down the Riverside Freeway and caught the 15 headed north, cursing at the trucks when they barreled down my tailpipe or pushed me to the shoulder. But the hour drive with all of its hazards didn't distract me from a larger reality pressing in on me.

I'd just ground up a finger and rinsed it down the drain. Maybe Danny's finger.

It's difficult to express just how much I loved him. He was my rock, my adviser, my lover in better times. I leaned on him for everything and he seemed to return the favor.

Take my job, or lack thereof. At twenty-seven years old I ought to have had a decent job, and believe me, I'd given it a shot. Not because I needed the money—Danny had given me enough to buy the two-bedroom condo in a quiet corner of an upscale complex and live without working for seven years. I needed a job because we both knew I had to find a way to enter a thriving social context if I didn't want to go nuts.

During one of my weekly visits to Ironwood, Danny suggested I try something that didn't require too much interaction with complaining customers, and ease into the workplace that way.

"Like what?" I asked.

He shrugged across the table and gave me one of his crazy, blue-eyed grins. "Like a night watchman. Put your skills to good use."

I sat up. "Seriously?"

His grin faded. "No, not seriously. It was a joke."

"But I could do that!"

"You couldn't do that. I was just having fun."

"No, I could. The only people I would have to worry about would be the ones looking down my barrel."

Now his face was flat, that determined expression he uses when he wants to cut to the chase. "Don't be ridiculous. You're tiny. The first thug that comes along weighing three hundred pounds would smash you flat."

"You're saying I don't have what it takes?"

"I'm only saying that you'd be putting yourself in the way of danger. Please, Renee, do not consider this. For my sake if not for yours."

See, I liked that Danny tried to care for me even while locked up. And while a part of me loved the idea of going up against a three-hundred-pound thug who might crush me if he tripped in my direction, the thought of using a gun again did bother me some. And I was a bit small to do any real business with a nightstick, if that was all they gave me.

"Then what else could I do at night?" I asked.

"Anything, I suppose. Drive a truck."

"You're serious?"

"No, not really. Just trying to—"

"That's it! I could drive a truck. Right? One of those big 18-wheelers."

"I think that's pretty heavy work, don't you?"

"Are you kidding? It's all lifting gizmos and electric power stuff. It's mostly listening to the radio and steering down a long road, right?"

"Hydraulic lifts."

"What?"

"They're called hydraulic lifts. The lifting gizmos."

"Oh. Right."

"So then try it," he said.

And I had. The instructor thought I was a bit nuts at first, but he quickly learned that my mind wasn't quite as frail as my body. I think it was during those few months trying the whole truck-driver thing that I first entertained the thought that I was too skinny. A lot of the best drivers have at least a few extra pounds of fat and muscle. Frankly, I was a bit jealous.

But here's the thing about being a truck driver: once you get out of school and get to working for a real company (General Electric in my case, which was why I had GE appliances) you realize that you spend a lot of time with men in dirty warehouses. And too many of them don't mind putting their filthy paws on your shoulder, your arm, your thigh, or your butt. Not a bad thing if you're interested in them and their hands are clean, but I wasn't and these weren't.

I also tried selling magazine subscriptions from home, but the continual abuse was inhuman and I found myself fighting the urge to help ungrateful customers see their way to a better life despite repenting for my previous indiscretions.

All the while, my neurosis seemed to get worse, and after two years of periodic trials and failures I finally gave up. Point is, Danny supported my decision. He always did. I had been through a nightmare, he said. I just had to take some time and find myself.

Tears came to my eyes as I drove north, praying that Danny was still alive and had all of his fingers. My emotions ran a ragged edge, from rage to remorse to abject fear. I should never have listened to his nonsense about finding myself another, suitable man. The thought of living without him seemed profane now.

I still remembered every word of that conversation. It was on another one of my regular visits to Ironwood State Prison that Danny stared me in the eye and brought up the unthinkable. I knew he was working up to something critical in his mind because he gave me that long, I'm-sorry-for-what-I'm-about-to-say look and took my hand.

"Now listen to me, Renee. Please, you have to listen very carefully."

Already, I didn't like it. "I am listening, Danny."

"We've been over this before."

"Over what?"

"You know that I'm going to be in here fifty years."

"Paroled in twenty-five," I said. "Twenty-five years."

"I don't know that."

"I do." The fact that he had escaped death row, which at first I was so sure would be his fate, emboldened me. If he could cut such a deal with the DA, what else might be possible? A twenty-five-year parole, of course.

He glanced at the door. "What happens to me isn't really in my control, Renee, you know that. It's a war zone in here. Things happen."

"They can't hurt you, Danny," I said. "Look at you!" He had been a powerful man before his incarceration but had gained thirty pounds since, all of it muscle. "You could take any of those thugs one-handed, show them who you are! Have any of them been through a real war?"

"Prison *is* a real war, but that's not the point."

"You've managed this far," I said. "Right? Just defend yourself."

"It's not that simple. Defending yourself means defending your people, and that means resorting to violence. I can't do that. But really, that's not the point."

"Then what is?"

"Fifty years is too long."

"No, Danny, it's not. No, you have the will of a bull!" Guilt was swamping me. He was in prison and I was free. I clung to his hand as if it were my last lifeline. "You have to do whatever you need to stay alive."

"It's not me I'm worried about, Renee."

"It's me? You want me to confess?"

"No! Please, no!"

"You want me to break you out?"

"Renee. My love. You're missing the point."

"Then what *is* your point?"

Danny stared at me for a moment, then lowered his gaze. He was never one to cry easily, but when he looked back, I saw that tears had filled his eyes. He swallowed hard, took a breath, and made it clear. "The point is that you can't wait for me, Renee."

"Of course I can. And I will."

He lifted my hand and kissed my fingers tenderly. "No, Renee. You can't. You're going to fall apart without someone to hold on to. You know how much I love you, but you have to let go of me and find someone who can—"

I slammed my palm down on the table and bolted to my feet. "I don't want anyone else!"

"Sit down," the guard watching us near the door barked. I gave him a harsh stare and sat.

Danny spoke in a placating tone. "Please, darling. You have to be practical. As much as we both hate it, this is unfair to you."

"I can decide what's unfair to me. Thousands of prison wives do it. What's unfair is that you're in prison and I'm not."

He ignored my last statement entirely. It was a moot issue for him. "I'm not suggesting that you can't decide for yourself, and I have the highest respect for those who stand by their loved ones doing time. I'm only saying that you need to be realistic." His jaw flexed, and he continued, "And you have to start thinking of me as well."

I gawked at him, aghast.

When he took my hand again, his was trembling. Danny's hand never trembles. He has one of the softest hearts I know, but the rest of him is made of steel. "Listen to me, Renee. I can't do this knowing that your life on the outside is difficult because of your loyalty to me. You may argue that you're fine, but I know you, dear. And I know me. You have to find someone to take care of you, if not for your sake, then for mine. Someone who will hold you at night when your fears come, someone to laugh with during the day. I can't be that man."

"You *already* are that man!"

He shook his head gently. "We're not like the rest—you have to begin accepting that. I didn't surrender myself for you to be alone except for an hour each weekend for the rest of your life." A tear slipped from his eye and my heart began to break for him.

We're not like the rest. It was the truth, and I'd long known it. Having decided even before we married to take the fall for my sins, Danny never officially filed our marriage license and

93

other necessary paperwork in Bosnia. In the eyes of the law, we never technically married. He wanted to make it easy for me that way, knowing this time would come. But he couldn't know then that I would be forever married to him in my heart, regardless of the law.

"I'm strong, Danny," I said. But I had started to cry with him.

We tenderly spoke for an hour that day at Ironwood, and when it was time to go I clung to him, sobbing, until the guard pulled us apart. The next time was no easier. But as time passed I began to admit my own loneliness to myself.

It took me another three months to accept his reasoning, and then only with the help of my therapist. Danny was only looking out for me, knowing that I really did need someone on the outside. He could not be persuaded otherwise. His need to belong to me was outweighed by his need for me to have constant companionship. Because I really was interested in honoring his needs above my own, I couldn't dismiss them.

The problem was I still loved Danny and he loved me. Even after finally agreeing to entertain the idea of dating another man, I never worked up the courage or the desire to pursue any other relationship. I would love Danny till the day I died, even if he wasn't my husband.

I left the city behind me and followed the train of trucks into the scrub-covered hills. The day was overcast or smoggy or both; a thick haze hugged the mountains. I couldn't shake the feeling that when I emerged on the other side of the mist I would find myself lost. Thinking the radio might help, I turned it on, then off after a few minutes of talk about things that didn't interest me.

By the time I reached Highway 138 the mist had thickened and I felt downright spooked. The traffic on the two-lane road snaking through the hills was spotty, which was a relief. But the lack of movement on either side made me feel more isolated. And it was quieter. Large limestone outcroppings rose from the ground like ghosts on guard.

A mile and a half later I reached Lone Pine Canyon Road, turned left onto the narrow two-lane road, and headed into no-man's land. It was called the Angeles National Forest, but the forest was mostly shrubs and dirt here. The road turned, then rose and fell gently, following aboveground power lines.

The cutoff for Basal came suddenly, a few miles farther, announced by a single blue sign that read Basal Institute, with an arrow directed across Lone Pine. I swung my car onto a blacktopped driveway and it was then, driving into tall and ominous-looking trees, that I began to doubt my spontaneous decision to come and make something happen on my own.

I really had no idea what I could accomplish. For all I knew, I would never even reach the prison. There would be a gate and guardhouse long before I reached the actual entrance and, without the necessary paperwork, I would be turned away.

The driveway was long, at least half a mile, descending slowly as it snaked around the hills. The trees grew even taller. The mist was thicker. I rolled forward, alone on the road, breathing shallow.

The mist to my left suddenly thinned, offering me my first view of the valley. I blinked at the sight and veered to the left shoulder. Shoved the car into park. Threw the door open and stood with one foot in the car and the other on the graveled shoulder.

Below me in a large clearing half a mile away lay a fenced compound. In the center of that compound rose a beautiful stone building shaped like a cross. I saw it all in a glance and my pulse thickened.

The only similarity between Basal and Ironwood were the tall fences, three of them running in parallel, set back from the institution. Where Ironwood looked like four huge factory buildings, Basal looked more like an oversized mansion. Or an old sanitarium for the mentally ill. Or a massive cathedral. No guard towers that I could see.

The walls rose high and were topped by a green metal roof that sloped upward to meet a glass dome that allowed light to filter into the area below. Windows every ten or fifteen feet peered out from the cells, but they were tinted, the one-way kind used in some office buildings. There were no bars, only leafy vines that crawled up the walls at each corner.

And then I saw what could pass as guard towers, built into the corners of the building with a clear view of the exterior compound.

If so, the guards were out of sight. A green lawn, maybe a hundred yards wide, separated the monolithic structure from the three fences, which alone marked the compound as something other than a uniquely designed resort.

Haze drifted by, thickening to obscure the valley for a few moments before thinning again.

There were no patrol cars driving along the perimeter road, no correctional officers pacing the lawn. A single paved road bordered by a shorter fence stretched between a sally port near the perimeter and what I took to be the front entrance. The sally port was a system consisting of two gates that could not be opened at the same time. Any vehicle coming or leaving would have to pass through the first gate, then wait for it to close behind before being admitted through the second gate—a security measure used at all prisons.

A large fenced parking lot with a pedestrian sally port encompassed thirty or forty cars on the far left side. Otherwise there was no indication that the building was even occupied. Deliveries probably came in from the back, where there would be a third sally port, but I couldn't see over the building.

For a moment I imagined that Danny's world had just been filled with a ray of bright hope. Surely this would be a better place than Ironwood. But then the voice from the phone drifted through my mind and the illusion faded.

Danny was somewhere within those walls, cut off from the reality known by the rest of the world. For all I knew they were conducting experiments on the inmates inside. Even if they weren't, someone was going to kill him.

"Can I help you?"

I spun back and saw that a car with an orange light on its roof had approached without my hearing it. A man dressed in black slacks and a white collared shirt stood at the open passenger door, hand on the frame, looking at me. Inside the car, a driver watched me through the windshield, idly tapping his thumb on the steering wheel. I stared, caught completely off guard.

"Do you have an appointment?"

"Ah…no. I just…" I stepped around the hood of my car. "But maybe you can help me."

He didn't respond. He was a kind-enough

looking fellow with blond hair and a neatly trimmed goatee. The car's door sign identified it as Grounds Control. No weapons that I could see. Not even pepper spray.

"My husband was brought here from Ironwood this morning and I'm having trouble getting a message to him. This is Basal, right?"

"Go through his attorney. Quickest way. It'll still take at least a week."

"A week?"

He was eyeing my body and I glanced down. Only then did it hit me that in my frantic haste to leave the condo, I had quickly pulled on a pair of jeans but forgotten to change my top. Or fix my hair. Not that my hair needed fixing—I normally wore it down, and messy hair was somewhat in style. But my yellow-checkered flannel top screamed pajamas...

"I don't have a week."

"I'm sorry, but this is a restricted area. You need to turn your car around and leave."

"Just like that?"

"Just like that."

"You don't understand. You have an inmate

inside whose life's in danger. I have to talk to the warden. Please, I'm begging you."

"And you know his life's in danger how?"

I hesitated. "I was told."

The guard didn't look impressed. "Ma'am, if even one in a hundred threats made in correctional institutions were carried out, the prisons would be graveyards. Let me put your mind to rest. Your…husband, did you say?"

"My friend."

"Trust me, your friend's in the safest prison in California," he said, "in part because of Basal's strict policies regarding isolation. He's been selected for the program for a reason, and you're going to have to trust in that."

I looked back at my car, scrambling for an angle, but I couldn't find one. Maybe I was overreacting. It wouldn't be the first time. Then again, maybe not.

I faced the man, who clearly had more patience than I did. "I got a phone call from a stranger this morning threatening to kill him."

"Kill who, did you say?"

"I didn't."

The corners of the man's mouth pulled up into a cockeyed smile. "I wouldn't worry about it."

"I got a shoe box."

"A what?"

No, I couldn't go there.

"Someone's threatening to kill him, so like it or not, I am worried."

"Look, Basal has a zero-tolerance policy regarding violence. Without weapons at their disposal, inmates use words. All the time. That's assuming the threat came from Basal, which is highly unlikely."

"Why do you say that?"

"He just got here this morning?"

"Yes."

The guard shook his head. "I doubt he's met any of the prisoners yet, much less had time to make enemies. Besides, all phone calls are monitored. Is your friend a violent man?"

"No." Not anymore, anyway. Although I had no doubt Danny could put both of these guards on their backs without breaking a sweat.

"He make a habit of screaming obscenities at people who walk by?"

"Of course not."

The guard shrugged. "He's perfectly safe here. Wherever that call came from, it wasn't Basal. And whoever made it will have an even harder time getting in here than you. Follow? What prison did you say he was transferred from?"

"Ironwood."

"There you go. Impossible to spend time at Ironwood without making enemies. Now, if you don't mind, you really need to turn your car around and leave. And just so you know, the minute any car hits our blacktop, we know. Go home and take a deep breath. If you still think you need to get a message inside, you best work with an attorney."

"Do you know an inmate named Bruce Randell?"

The guard's eyes flickered and I knew I'd hit a chord.

"Not directly, no. I'm not at liberty to speak about any members. I think it's best for you to leave."

I knew then that I had no hope of getting in to see Danny without someone's help. That's when I decided to start with whoever had first put Bruce Randell behind bars. Know your enemy's enemy, Danny had once taught me. They will likely be your ally.

"Thank you," I said, eager to leave. "What did you say your name was?"

"I didn't." He grinned. "Martin. Please don't return until you have the right paperwork. There's an armed gate around the corner a hundred yards up. No one gets past it unless we want them to. Follow?"

"Follow," I said.

But the only path I was following was the one that led me to Danny, and that path now led me to Bruce Randell, Danny's newest enemy.

6

THE DINING HALL was located in the south wing, just off the hub, a self-serve affair that rewarded those who lined up for chow with a compartmentalized plate not unlike those sold as TV dinners. Today's lunch consisted of one spoonful of fake whipped spuds, three or four small chunks of corned beef, a dozen green beans, an apple, a thick slice cut from a French roll, and something like margarine spread thinner than a snitch's word across the surface. Choice of drink: water, apple juice, lime soda, or lemonade.

The hall contained thirty long tables, three rows of ten. According to Godfrey, the prison had a maximum capacity of 300 but was considered full at 250, allowing the warden the spare cells needed to shuffle members between wings as required. Lunch was served to the commoners in two shifts, although privileged members, currently numbering forty-seven, could eat in the hall if they so desired. At least half took advantage of the better meals delivered to the guest rooms, as the privileged cells were called. Members in the basement meditation wing were fed rolls of highly enriched bread in their cells.

On Danny's first day there were roughly a hundred members in the room, seated at the tables or in line, talking quietly, casting glances only occasionally at the table where Danny sat alone with Godfrey and a very shy Pete Manning.

The boy looked young for his twenty years, hardly more than a pubescent teenager, not because he was small but because his features were fine. Short blond hair covered his head, straight but slightly disheveled. The lashes above his light blue eyes were long, and the fingers holding his plastic spoon as he toyed with his whipped spuds looked like they hadn't seen a day's labor in years. He was pale and his skin was unblemished except for a bruise on his right cheekbone.

The only sign that he was anything but perfectly normal came in the way he carried himself, delicately and on edge, as if he knew of some imminent danger hidden from the rest of them.

A quick count identified seven privileged members eating at the tables, and five employed in the serving line, all easily distinguished by their street clothes in a sea of members dressed in blue pants and tan shirts. Roughly half were white, perhaps a third were black, the rest, Latino. Danny found this odd, considering the overwhelming percentage of minorities imprisoned in California's prison system, one of the great injustices of law enforcement.

A single CO—or facilitator, Godfrey had called them—lounged in a chair near the door, apparently bored stiff. In most prisons, guards were sparsely stationed for efficiency in high-traffic areas. A show of force was only required when trouble erupted. In some larger institutions, inmates might see corrections officers only a few times over the course of several days unless there was trouble nearby.

The custody and security operations at Basal were fairly typical. One captain, Bostich, oversaw three lieutenants, one for each wing: the east privileged wing, the west commons wing, and the basement meditation wing. Under each lieutenant were three sergeants, one for each eight-hour shift, for a total of nine sergeants. The sergeants oversaw the corrections officers, ranging in number from two to seven depending on the shift and the wing. Each of the four towers on the perimeter were manned by an armed officer, who made up the balance of the security detail.

But at Basal they were all simply called facilitators, regardless of position. Danny could account for five of them—two at the commons wing, one in the hub, one in the dining hall, and one rover—as he ate and listened to Godfrey's philosophy.

"You do realize that most get locked up without a violent bone in their body. Two percent for rape. Ten percent for murder. That's it, Danny boy. There's been no increase among violent offenses per capita in this county for decades. There has, on the other hand, been a seven hundred percent increase in the number of nonviolent offenders put in prison since the seventies. You ever wonder why?"

"Since the warden mentioned it," Danny said.

"There aren't more rapists out there to justify the increase. Not more murderers. Not more violent husbands. Instead, there are simply more laws."

The older man continued with a twinkle in his eye.

"The land of the free has only recently undertaken a grand experiment of sorts, incarcerating far more of its citizens than any other society in history has ever attempted, Hitler's incarceration of Jews notwithstanding. Is it working? Is America now safer than it was in the seventies, eighties, or nineties? Nope. Is it safer than Canada, which is far more lenient? Not close. Europe? Again, not even close. You ever think about that?"

"I haven't dwelled on it, no."

"Well you should. Politicians are obsessed with passing new laws that give them power and satisfy smug constituents. Fact is, hundreds of thousands of the inmates inside are no worse than those who live in freedom. Know what their problem is?"

Danny didn't answer.

"They were caught out of sync—wrong place, wrong time. They crossed the road on the wrong day. They said the wrong thing to the wrong person in the wrong country and were accused of hate speech. They placed the wrong chemical in their mouths. You ever do drugs?"

"Can't say that I have."

"Me neither. Still, an interesting case. In the early nineteen hundreds, most of the drugs now prohibited in the United States were legal. Millions consumed elixirs and medicines loaded with cocaine and opium and other drugs on a daily basis. No one considered their consumption immoral any more than the consumption of wine or fast food was immoral. But then the laws changed, making first drugs and then wine illegal. You see?"

Godfrey paused only a moment, then answered himself.

"New time, new law. Same species: human."

He took a bite of egg and went on, speaking around his food.

"Predictably, the consumption of alcohol was

hardly suppressed by the new laws—people who wanted to drink still did and always will—but prisons began filling with those who were caught deviating from the new norm. And then the laws changed again and the country went about happily selling and drinking wine in freedom. You see?"

"I guess I do."

"New time, new law. Same species: human. Humans don't change their behavior to conform to new laws as much as they take pains not to get caught breaking the new laws. Fact is, more than half of all Americans have broken federal laws—mostly tax and drug laws—for which the penalty is prison, but have never been caught. You think we should put half the country behind bars, Danny?"

"Doesn't make sense."

"What will happen when society changes its political mind and makes wine illegal again? Or decides that all unregulated herbs like ginger root should be illegal to possess? Or that anyone caught using trans fats or selling fast food should be imprisoned?"

Godfrey liked to talk.

"And it ain't just alcohol and drugs. Take

murder. Murder is murder, course it is, but not all forms of taking human life are illegal or considered immoral. Infanticide is legal in some societies, partial-birth abortion in others. Abortion in most. But what if the laws change, as they invariably do?"

Godfrey glanced at Peter, who sat beside him, keeping to himself.

"Or take sexual deviance as defined by law. Pete here is in for statutory rape, right? But based on current California law, Jesus himself, the so-called son of God, was raised by a statutory rapist. Isn't that so, Priest?"

It was. Joseph had been at least thirty years older than his fourteen-year-old bride. Joseph would have been sent to prison for statutory rape if he'd lived in the United States of America.

"Different time, different law, same species: human," Godfrey said. "Were Joseph and Mary stupid? No. Were they immoral? No. But change the laws and they would be classified as deviants along with all of their peers. It's cultural, not moral. But a politician makes a new law to get elected and, suddenly, previously acceptable behavior is deviant. So the question is, what to do with all those deviants created by changing laws?"

"Build more prisons," Danny said.

Godfrey smiled. "Now you're thinking. Build more prisons. You'll need them. Not for the scumbags of society, like you and me, but to segregate and punish those caught deviating from the rules. Just like the rules at Basal. Don't break the rules, Danny. There's a price to pay. Isn't there, Peter?"

Peter nodded without looking up. "Yup."

The efficiency and order on display among the members of Basal was nothing short of unnerving. Pape's system seemed to be working surprisingly well. The program was too new to account for any early paroles, but the reports coming out of Basal, which Danny had read in his handbook, would undoubtedly be a source of pride for reformers and a thorn in the side of those who wanted to keep prisons just the way they were.

Many of the rules for the commons were plainly objective. Lights out at 9:00 p.m., no later than 9:02. Follow pathways where marked, in the lunch line, for example. No swearing. No contraband, the list of which filled three single-spaced pages including such items as tobacco, alcohol, drugs, a long list of "weapons," images of half-naked or fully naked men or women, and novels that contained inappropriate language including any swearing, nakedness, sexuality, or excessive violence.

Shirts could not be unbuttoned below the first button. No jewelry of any kind could be worn. New tattoos were prohibited. Nicknames were prohibited. Cleanliness was held next to godliness, and as such each member was required to shower and brush their teeth once per day using only cold water. The list went on and on.

But some of the rules were entirely subjective, placing members at the mercy of the facilitators' judgment.

No raised voices, for any reason at any time, including but not limited to yelling, laughing, cursing, threatening, or questioning. But what constituted a raised voice?

In addition to swearing, no coarse language at any time for any reason. But what constituted coarse language?

No displays of affection, which might be construed or mistaken as an invitation to sexually deviant behavior. Again, how many ways might a simple glance be interpreted?

No threats to members or facilitators. No disrespect to any member unless authorized by the warden for disciplinary reasons. In addition, members were required to demonstrate a progressive attitude and a full willingness to learn nondeviant behavior. Yet again, *threats*, *disrespect*, and *attitude* were all wide open for interpretation.

And perhaps the most disturbing of all: no questioning authority, or the rules, or the doctrines upon which the facility stood, except as a matter of formal petition and due process. In other words, members weren't free to spout off complaints. Instead they were required to file a petition and could voice such questions or complaints to the warden only if permitted. As in a courtroom, free speech in Basal was limited, forfeited as part of the waiver Danny had signed in the warden's office.

This was Basal's cultural norm, and deviation from that norm constituted deviant behavior, and deviant behavior would be punished.

What kind of punishment? Restricted privileges. Isolation. Shunning. Meditation. An eye for an eye. What precisely that meant, Danny didn't yet know.

The other members watched Danny with interest, but as Godfrey had predicted, they didn't speak to him as they passed through the hub, nor during a quick survey of the tiny yard nestled between the east and south wings, nor in line for lunch. Not a word anywhere. Speaking to the priest was prohibited.

Godfrey ran down a short list of members in the dining hall that he thought might interest Danny. Carter Beagle, a convict who'd been locked up for over twenty years, transferred in from San Quentin. He was in for homicide, a gas-station robbery that went wrong when the proprietor's girlfriend came out of the back room with a shotgun. Carter's first shot went off by accident and struck the proprietor in the chest. He had taken half a load of buckshot in his right leg, which was why he limped.

Now he was an old-timer like most at Basal—those who just wanted to do their time in peace, unlike younger inmates who still thought they could prove something on the inside.

There was Max Demarko, a mob guy in for

grand larceny, also an old-timer; Sterling Maxwell, in on weapons charges in the sixties; Pedro Rivera, a teddy bear of a man who had raped a woman twice his age while strung out on crack back in the day. Godfrey knew them all, and most of them shared one thing in common: they were program convicts who'd long ago abandoned any desire to buck the system.

Their silence was part of Danny's indoctrination, but at the heart of that programming was the young man who Pape claimed would determine Danny's fate at Basal.

Peter Manning.

Danny studied the boy while Godfrey murmured that the knuckleheads must have eaten their lunch at the first serving. His mention earned an apprehensive sideways glance from Pete.

During the ten minutes since Godfrey had motioned the boy to the table, Peter had looked Danny in the eye only once, and then for less than a second. He ate quietly, eyes fixed on nothing of note, lost in a world trapped in his mind.

That this boy could have been convicted of statutory rape was hard to imagine, much less believe. And yet here he sat, locked up to keep society safe and to help him see a better, nondeviant way.

Godfrey nodded at Danny, took a drink of lemonade, and cleared his throat. "Pete, why don't you tell Danny your story? Hmm? The one you told me. The truth."

Peter made no sign that he'd heard Godfrey. He remained hunched over his plate with one hand on his lap and the other around his spoon. Perhaps a more direct approach was called for. Confession wasn't new territory for Danny.

"Maybe it would be better if I told you my story, Pete," Danny said. "Sometimes we do things because we're hurt. We wish we could take it back but it's too late. I know, because when I was fifteen I killed some men, and now I wish I hadn't."

Pete glanced up at him, held his gaze for two seconds, then shifted his stare into space as he chewed his food.

"That's not why I'm in prison. At the time I lived in Bosnia with my mother and my two sisters. Men came into our house and raped my mother and both of my sisters. That's why I killed them."

Pete's eyes darted toward Danny. After a moment, he spoke. "Rape is evil," he said.

"Yes. It is. Do you know why?"

"It's a very bad thing."

"Yes, but do understand why it's a very bad thing?"

"It's evil."

Danny now understood what the warden meant when he'd used the word *dense*. Pete was slow. He likely suffered from some mild form of cognitive disability. How he'd found his way to prison was a curiosity. Although California law allowed for a felony conviction in cases of statutory rape in which the victim was under the age of eighteen and three or more years younger than the victimizer, typically only nonconsensual statutory cases resulted in felony convictions.

Most cases of statutory rape involved consensual sex between a boyfriend and girlfriend who'd fallen in love and engaged in sex at the wrong age and on the wrong side of the marriage laws. Pete was twenty, meaning he'd been found guilty of having sex with a girl no older than seventeen, presumably nonconsensual sex. Otherwise he would have received a misdemeanor conviction. Either way, surely the court would have taken his cognitive impairment into consideration.

"How long have you been in Basal, Pete?"

"Four months," Godfrey said when Peter didn't answer.

"He was the last before me to be admitted?"

"Yes."

This, along with the fact that the warden had specifically set Pete aside for Danny to help didn't sit right. Perhaps he was reading too much into a coincidence. Either way, Danny now felt compelled to learn the full details of Pete's crime and conviction.

"Did you rape a girl, Pete?"

No answer.

"It's okay, you can tell me the truth. I used to be a priest, and although I'm no longer a priest, I've always tried my best to help people who've made mistakes. Believe me, I'm no stranger to mistakes myself. Maybe I can help you."

Pete looked up at him again, this time searching his eyes for trust. The boy's defensive mechanisms had started to break like the first crack in the shell of a hard-boiled egg. Danny had seen the look a thousand times.

Pete looked over at Godfrey, who nodded. "Go on, tell him. He's a good man, a deviant like the rest of us, but he knows that deviant behavior doesn't mean wrong behavior. Just like I told you."

If Pete could understand that much, his cognitive impairment couldn't be too great. Danny helped him along.

"Did you have a girlfriend?"

A mist swam in the boy's eyes and Danny knew he'd gotten through.

"What was her name?"

"Missy," Pete said softly, and the mist settled into thin pools at the bottom of his eyes.

"Did you hurt Missy?"

"I will never hurt Missy." He said it with enough conviction to secure Danny's confidence that the boy believed it.

"How old was she?"

"Fifteen. I met her at the park." His eyes brightened. "She likes me. We spend time together. I would never hurt Missy."

"Missy has a soft spot for people in need," Godfrey said. "I don't think she was slow, but don't know for sure."

Danny returned to Pete. "You were twenty and she was fifteen?"

"Missy is seventeen. She's going to be a nurse."

"So you were twenty and Missy was seventeen when they arrested you. Was she your girlfriend?"

A tear slipped from Pete's right eye and he lowered his head again. It occurred to Danny that his breaking down in the cafeteria might not go well with the facilitator at the door or the other members.

"It's okay, Pete," Godfrey said. "Maybe it would be better if I told Danny what you told me. Can I do that?"

The boy hesitated, then nodded.

Godfrey addressed Danny, voice low. "A classic case of forbidden love. Missy comes from an upscale, conservative family—unlike Pete, whose mother is indigent and long ago divorced. No other family he speaks of. No brothers, no sisters. They met at a church event at a park when Pete was eighteen and Missy was fifteen, just two fledging birds who developed a deep bond of friendship. At first Missy's parents had no problem with the boy their young daughter was trying to help out. Who would? Isn't that right, Pete?"

"Missy loved me."

"Exactly. But Missy's parents grew worried about the relationship when their daughter preferred spending time with Pete over other boys in her peer group. High school stuff." Godfrey dismissed the notion with a flip of his hand.

"They tried to discourage their daughter, but Missy spent most of her time with Peter. Not sure it was really a romantic relationship as such, but they became inseparable."

"And yet he was convicted."

"Because Missy's parents, terrified that their only daughter was getting too friendly and wasting her life away, threw a fit. Missy reacted by running away from home to be with Pete, whose mother had just passed away, leaving him the sole beneficiary of their little crumbling house. After a week the parents decided an intervention was the only way to save their daughter. Maybe it was understandable, but they overreacted."

"Did they have any evidence of nonconsensual—"

"They had a case worker who reported a confession by Pete that he'd pushed himself on Missy. Absurd, but there you have it. As a priest, you're probably aware that in California, confidentiality is waived in cases of rape."

"And you think the parents paid off the case-worker."

"What better way to keep a vagrant from your daughter than have him thrown in prison?"

"Missy didn't come forward?"

"She was removed to a camp for troubled teens in Arizona. A letter alleging misbehavior and shame served as her testimony. It took me an hour to learn this much, you understand, and I may be missing some of the details, but that's basically what happened. Am I right, Pete?"

"I would never hurt Missy."

"I know you wouldn't. The rest is plain enough. Missy's parents had Pete arrested, their attorney fed the DA all they needed, Pete had a public defender who caved under the case. The judge sentenced Pete to two years in state prison despite his pleas of innocence. The warden managed to rope the boy, and here we sit."

Godfrey had been right—the boy's story broke Danny's heart. For the most part, law enforcement and the courts got their implementation of the laws right, despite the questionability of some of those laws. But when they got it wrong, they could get it very wrong. Unfortunately, the plight of the innocent in prison was mostly lost on an angry, cynical public.

"If everything you're telling us is right, you didn't do anything wrong," Danny said.

"I didn't do anything wrong."

"I know. Do you remember the name of the judge?"

Pete shook his head.

To Godfrey: "The court didn't take his condition into consideration?"

"You tell me. Worst part is that the convicts consider him a pedophile. I keep telling him to keep his head down and stay to himself, but that can only help so much."

"Someone's bothering him?"

The boy's eyes flickered across the room. No one in particular that Danny could see, but the bruise on his cheek held more significance now.

Even so, Danny would be hard-pressed to lend any assistance other than empathy, consolation, and advice. And really, in any other prison Pete might have already suffered far worse than he had here. Despite the warden's oddities, Basal might just be Pete's best chance of surviving his time, short of living in segregation.

Danny was lost in these thoughts when it occurred to him that the room had quieted. He followed several stares toward the door and saw a white commons member walking toward their table. The man was big, well over six feet, with arms the size of small trees and a neck built like a trunk. The man looked like a Viking who thought with his fists and offered rebuke with his eyes, harsh glares that would shrivel all but the strongest opponent. Behind him and to his right walked a smaller, thin man, his dark hair slicked back with grease, wearing a crooked smile. Both had tattoos that ran down their arms, but no gang markings that Danny could see.

"That's Randell," Godfrey muttered of the larger man, and the moment he said it, Pete's head whipped around. The look of terror on the boy's face could not be mistaken.

Both Godfrey's and the warden's advice to stay clear of Randell flashed through Danny's mind. The warden had asked him to help Pete because he and the boy shared a common enemy. Randell.

But helping the boy would only infuriate that enemy.

The large man spoke to Danny before he stopped at the edge of their table. "Stand up, you FNG."

Randell's challenge drew no attention from the facilitator at the door, who watched them from his chair, tilting it back on two legs. Across from Danny, Pete was trembling. Danny remained calm. The warden had made it clear that he'd be tested.

"You deaf, punk? I said stand up and face me."

Bruce Randell's lips were as pale as his face, two strips of bleached leather on a pocked, lunar face. An albino bulldog. Danny remained seated, unguarded, refusing to allow his anger to rise. He should say something— silence was its own form of disrespect—but considering the man's blatant disregard for the established protocol, what would that be?

"I hear you just fine," Danny finally said. "My instructions from the warden are to avoid you.

I think it's best I stay seated. But I assure you, I'm listening."

A smile crept onto the man's face. "A fancy talker." His eyes dropped to Pete, who was staring down at his plate, still trembling.

"So the two diddlers are already playing together," Randell said. "What do you make of that, Slane?"

The man with slicked-back hair had his eyes on Pete. "I think they both need to know what it feels like."

"An eye for an eye," Randell said. His stare drilled into Danny. "I don't like priests. If you don't stand up I'm going to let my friend loose. And I promise you it'll be bloody."

A surge of adrenaline flooded Danny's veins, but he refused to give in to the sudden impulse to set the man straight. He'd given in to such weaknesses once and paid a heavy price. More important, he'd taken a vow of nonviolence in an effort to follow a truer way.

Proper execution of the people's law was the only way to handle injustice, and Basal had its law. He was legally and morally obligated to follow it even when that law failed. Who was he to judge?

The man called Slane bent down and whispered something into Pete's ear, his eyes fixed on Danny. There was darkness and hatred in those eyes.

Pete spun off the bench, rounded the end of the table, and dropped down on the seat next to Danny, effectively placing his new protector between himself and Slane.

Danny stilled another urge to help Randell see the light. His impulse to defend the weak would never leave him, he knew; neither would his resolve to control that impulse.

Randell glared at him. "Welcome to Basal. You may think the warden's your problem, but you'd be wrong. That would be me." He leaned forward and spoke, close enough for Danny to smell his stale breath. "I'm going to make you hate yourself, Priest. And then I'm going to kill you."

Randell brought a gnarled hand up, gripped Danny's cheeks between his thumb and fingers, and shoved his head back. "Remember that."

"Back off, Randell." The facilitator had finally decided to step in.

Danny couldn't deny the anger he felt. But he'd faced far worse and learned that his refusal to engage, although initially painful, eventually rewarded him with peace. Turning the other cheek made sense only if you did it every time.

Randell lifted his arms in feigned surrender and stepped away.

The facilitator, a thirty-something with a hook nose that looked as if it might have been broken more than once, was on his radio, calling for backup. He pointed Randell and Slane away from the table, then glared at Danny.

"Why is it that all the FNGs cause trouble?"

"Forgive me, Officer, but—"

"Shut up! Did I ask you a question?"

"Actually—"

"Shut up!"

In the space of ten seconds Danny knew he was being introduced to the way justice worked inside of Basal. Fair enough—his life wasn't his own. Marshall Pape owned it.

"When another member asks you for a simple courtesy, you give him that courtesy, you hear? You don't sit there like a wart. Now stand up and step away from the table." The facilitator had produced a pair of handcuffs.

Danny did as instructed.

"Zero tolerance, get used to it. Turn around and place your hands behind your back."

The facilitator cuffed him. Two other COs had arrived and stood to one side in a show of force. They needn't have bothered. Danny had no intention of speaking, much less resisting.

There was no outcry from the other members, despite the obvious injustice of the event. Randell stood to one side, showing no emotion. Godfrey sat still, watching Danny, but he made no move to defend him. It was prohibited and would only invite more trouble. Still, it was strange. At Ironwood, inmates would invite trouble for the sake of solidarity. A few days in the hole was a small price to pay and even more, a sign of strength.

Not in Basal.

The facilitator gave him a nudge toward the door. "Let's go. The rest of you, back to lunch."

Two guards led him through the hub, past the security gate that led to the administration wing, and through another reinforced steel door with the words Meditation Floor stenciled in black above it. Not a word was spoken.

The concrete steps descending into the basement were bare and well worn. Caged incandescent bulbs lit the way down one flight, then a second, before opening into a long, dimly lit hall with cells running down the right side. The sound of whimpering echoed through the corridor.

The meditation floor. Fifty cells, according to Godfrey.

"Did I tell you to stop?"

Danny walked forward, past the cells. The doors were solid steel with small slats at waist level and similar openings near the floor, used to fasten or unfasten a member's wrist and ankle irons as well as to deliver food and water.

The smell of urine and feces hung in the air. No light reached past the cracks in the steel doors. Other than the padding of their feet down the hall, the only sound came from the whimpering in one of the cells. It made Danny wonder how many inmates were being held in segregation.

When they drew abreast the cell of the whimpering man, the facilitator banged his stick against the steel door. "That's another week, Perkins. Shut your foul mouth!"

The whimpering shriveled to a whisper. No due warning, no filing, no due process or hearing. A clear violation of the California penal protocol.

They passed eight additional cells before the guard stopped him. "Hold up."

The facilitator unlocked the cell door and swung the door wide. Inside was a concrete room four feet wide and maybe eight feet deep. A raised slab of cement, three feet wide, formed a bed of sorts next to a sealed steel panel on the floor. A metal sink and toilet combo hugged the corner. That was it. No bedding. Nothing else.

"Take off your shoes, your socks, your pants, and your underwear."

Still cuffed, Danny did as ordered.

"Inside."

He stepped into the concrete box, immediately aware of the temperature drop. Behind him, the cell door clanked shut. A bolt was thrown and the upper slat door squealed open.

"Back up to the slat."

The facilitator uncuffed him through the opening and withdrew the restraint, leaving Danny free to move his arms.

"Take off your shirt and pass it out."

He unbuttoned the shirt, shrugged out of it, and passed it out.

"You can consider due process served. The warden will make his recommendation. If you're lucky you'll be out in a few days."

The slat cover slammed shut, leaving Danny naked in the dark. The accommodations were poor. It was cold. There wasn't a single soft surface in the small room. He stepped to the sink and turned the faucet. No water. It was likely on a timer or controlled manually from the outside, as was the water for the toilet.

It was rumored that some of the cells in the death-row segregation ward at San Quentin were set up similarly, although the inmates were allowed to wear their shorts. Cups had been banned because any vessel could be used to collect urine and feces to throw at an officer who opened the slat. Clothing and sheets could be used to commit suicide by way of strangulation. Mattresses could be torn apart or used to block entry into the cell.

But this wasn't San Quentin. Danny wondered if anyone outside these walls knew the true nature of administrative segregation in the bowels of Basal.

The door at the end of the hall slammed shut, leaving the entire floor in an eerie calm.

Danny found the edge of the raised slab and eased down onto the bed. He lay back on the cold concrete, stared up into the darkness for a full minute, then shut his eyes and sought God, who is love.

Slowly, he let his mind still, seeking out the light between his thoughts and emotions. There, in simply being still, he found solace.

7

WEDNESDAY

KEITH HAMMOND, THE sheriff's deputy who'd taken down Bruce Randell, wasn't eager to be found. I might have just given up and gone to the authorities to find him if not for my own aversion to the law. Danny had done a good job steering me clear, and when my dedication finally paid off two days later, I was relieved to learn that Keith was no longer professionally tied to the law.

He lived in a condo on Acacia Avenue in Huntington Beach, a twenty-five-minute drive from my home in Long Beach without traffic.

The neighborhood, only ten blocks from the ocean, was populated by free-spirited types who would rather head to the beach than to work. The condo was nice enough—white with green bushes along the base of the building and a bright green canopy leading up from the side-walk. Several large palm trees in the back rose over the roof. But it wasn't the neighborhood I cared about, it was the man who lived inside 1245 Acacia Street #3. I was now pinning my hopes on him. All of them.

I sat in my Corolla down and across the street, gently picking at my lower lip as I obsessed over how best to meet him. When to make my move. What to say. How to determine if I could trust him. Whether he would be willing to help. If he still had the mustache from his days in the Los Angeles County sheriff's department, as pictured.

He didn't have a Facebook profile, which was fine, because neither did I. He hadn't made any news for a few years. Good enough—I hadn't either, at least not for three years, and then only as an unidentified subject in a rather nasty slay-ing.

What he did have was a two-year history

working as an attorney, and five years in the sheriff's department before that. Best as I could fit the rather disconnected pieces together, Keith had joined the sheriff's department right out of law school, served for five years, entered private practice, and then dropped off the scene altogether a year or two ago.

The *Los Angeles Times* had at least a dozen stories that included the name Keith Hammond in their archives, five of them about the bust and the high-profile trial of a meth cook and distributor, one Bruce Randell.

Bruce: the viper doing time in Basal who hated priests and was now going to kill Danny. Over my dead body. Likely both.

Keith spoke of his reason for leaving the sheriff's department in an article about Martinez Boutros, the only client from his two years of law practice that I was able to identify. Boutros was a twenty-six-year-old Mexican immigrant who'd been charged with murder in a drug case. He was wrongfully accused, Hammond claimed, and then he was acquitted. And the *Times* came looking to find out why Keith had switched sides from drug buster to busting out druggies.

In a short statement Keith claimed he'd left the sheriff's department to find true justice. When pressed about how the department lacked true justice, he sidestepped the question.

Conclusion: Keith left because of corruption in the system. Maybe not, but honestly, that's what I hoped for. Then he took up practicing the law to defend the innocent. And then...well, then he'd quit on the system altogether.

That's what I pieced together. That and the fact that he'd gone through a bitter divorce eight years earlier, about the time he quit the sheriff. He'd been twenty-seven years old at the time and was now thirty-five, same age as Danny.

I had my attorney, albeit one who no longer practiced law. I had my defender of the weak, righter of wrongs, and, most important, I had someone with a common enemy: Bruce Randell.

But that was only in my mind. In reality, I didn't have him at all. He lived in the condo across the street, and for all I knew he'd moved there to get away from people like me.

The sun was long gone, and I was about to

give up in frustration when a black Ford Ranger approached the condo, turned up the driveway, and pulled into the garage on the first floor. I could hardly mistake the face of the man through the windshield. The man who would help me save Danny had come home.

How he could help, I didn't know. But that wasn't all I didn't know. Short of storming Basal with an Uzi—and believe me, I'd thought about it—I didn't know how to get to Danny. I didn't know who I could trust, who I could get to listen, who I could hire. I needed someone to help me think. To be with me, because alone I was lost.

The instant the garage door closed, I opened my car door, stepped out into the gray dusk, and headed across the street. I climbed the three steps to the condo's landing, pushed the doorbell, and stepped back. Hoping to make a good impression, I'd washed my hair twice, blown it half-dry and combed it out so that it laid naturally. The Miss Me jeans I wore were boot cut, better than the skinny jeans I used to wear. My top was a brown BKE with dolman sleeves. I knew these things because I bought all of my clothes from either the Buckle at the Irvine

Spectrum Center or from the online store, and I stick to what makes me comfortable without looking shabby. Jane had introduced me to the Buckle two years earlier, and I hadn't found the need to switch.

I rarely wore a bra around the apartment, but out was a different matter. I'd chosen one of two padded bras that I owned. There's no way to make B breasts look like double-D breasts, and even if there was, I wasn't interested. Still, I was on a mission and I figured a little help wouldn't hurt.

The door opened and Keith Hammond stood in the condo's entry light. His short hair was blond and tossed but still somehow neat, his face was clean shaven but he still looked rough, his jeans were marked but not torn, his shirt was a blue button-front with short sleeves, but it wasn't buttoned. How he'd gotten so casual so quickly was a bit of a mystery, but my first impression of him was hopeful.

He looked like the kind of man who wasn't confined by the system.

"Sorry, honey, whatever you're selling, I'm not buying," he said.

"You're Keith Hammond?" I replied.

"That would be me."

"Can I come in?"

"Umm, why?"

See, that's what I would have said. He wasn't only outside the system, he was cautious. That was good.

"Because I have some information you might find interesting, that's why. And I'm not selling it."

"And who are you?"

"My name is Renee Gilmore."

"Information, huh? And what makes you think I need any information, Renee Gilmore?"

"Because you and I have the same enemy."

His brow arched. "Is that so? And who might that be?"

"Bruce Randell," I said.

Up to that point Keith had worn the face of a man who is mildly amused. But when I gave him the name, the light went out of his eyes.

"I wouldn't say that Mr. Randell is my enemy," he said. "Our paths crossed once, but that was a long time ago."

"Do you know where he is today?"

"Chino, last I heard."

"He's in Basal."

"Basal?"

"Basal Institute of Corrections."

"The experimental prison."

"The inmates call it Basal."

"And why should that concern me?"

"Because Danny's there too."

"And who's Danny?"

"My husband," I said. "Well, not technically. Sort of."

"Sort of?"

"Can I come in?"

"You do realize I don't practice law any-more."

"I'm not looking for a lawyer."

"How did you hear about me?"

"I tracked you down. Can I come in?"

He studied me for a moment, then stepped aside. "Be my guest. But I can assure you there's nothing I can do for you. Unless you're looking for a drink and dinner. That I think I could manage."

I ignored the compliment and looked around his condo. Stairs to my right descended to what I assumed was the garage and maybe a room or two. The brown carpet was lint free. Beyond the living room, a tiled breakfast bar divided the rest of the living space from a spotless kitchen, although I couldn't see the sink from where I stood—sinks always speak the truth. By all appearances Keith looked to be a clean man who was comfortable enough in his own shell to leave his shirt unbuttoned when answering the door.

But I wasn't here to judge his cleanliness. I wanted his help.

He stepped past me, doing up one button in a respectable show of modesty. "Look, Renee...I know you think there's a connection between us, but I'm afraid you're mistaken." He put a hand on the stair rail and crossed one leg over the other. "You've obviously done your research and know that I helped put Bruce Randell behind bars, but like I said, that was a long time ago. I really don't care what he's doing, as long as he stays where he was put."

"He's trying to kill Danny," I said.

"Your not-really-husband husband."

"That's right. And I can't get into Basal to warn him."

"What makes you think I can? Assuming I wanted to. Prisons are run by wardens who all share at least one goal: preventing violence.

You should be talking to the warden, not to a washed-up cop-turned-attorney who walked away from it all. I dabble in stocks for a living now, did you know that too?"

"That's why I need your help."

"Why? Because I trade stocks?"

"Because you're washed up. Like me."

He glanced at my name-brand jeans. "You don't look washed up to me."

"That's because you don't know me," I said, and then I pushed the point, thinking I had to use what I could for Danny's sake. "Would you like to?"

The light sparked in his eyes, or maybe it was only my imagination. "Boy, you're full of surprises, aren't you? Thank you, but no, I'm not really looking for a romantic relationship with a woman right now."

"Did I say romantic? I just assumed by your history that you are a kind person interested in doing the right thing. Like helping a woman who has nowhere left to turn."

"Then you don't understand my history. I had my chance to help people and I turned my back on it. All of it. I wish I could help you, but I'm not the person you're looking for."

It wasn't going well, but, considering my options, I wasn't about to let him off the hook that easily. He was like me, you see. He just wanted to be left alone to live his life in peace.

I stepped past him, walked into his living room, and sat down on a stuffed tan chair, keeping my eyes on the window. I didn't intend to appear distraught, I just wasn't interested in his dismissal.

He hesitated, then followed me and eased into the couch opposite me without a word. We sat like that for a few moments, silent, an odd stalemate of sorts. And he didn't seem inclined to break it.

So I did.

"I received a call on Monday from a stranger who told me he was going to kill Danny. He was just transferred to Basal and there's no way for me to make contact. That same afternoon a woman named Constance came to my apartment and told me that an inmate named Bruce Randell was a threat to Danny."

"None of this really matters to me—"

"I got a finger in a shoe box," I said.

"A finger?"

"Or something that looked like a finger. It was a warning."

"From who?"

"Who do you think? Randell."

He eyed me. I'd finally gotten his attention.

"Either way, none of this is really my concern," he said.

"How can you say that?" I snapped. "You haven't even heard what I have to say. You may be all cozy, sitting here trading stocks and drinking beer with your poker pals, but there're people out there in the system who'll die if you don't help them. Me included."

"You're assuming I can help. And for the record, there's no way to fix the system. It's broken. Trying to fix it will only break you."

"I'm already broken!"

He peered at me, unmoved, either a broken man himself or someone who didn't care about anyone but himself. I had to hope it was the first.

"Do you still have your law license?" I asked.

"I haven't practiced in over a year."

"But you have it, right?"

"Yes."

"Will you at least hear me out? It's not every day a helpless woman comes knocking on your door asking you for help. Don't be so cold."

Keith leaned back and looked out the window. "That's fair." Eyes back on me. "So tell me."

His insincere attitude toward my distress was infuriating. I almost stood up right then and left. But I didn't have anywhere to go or anyone else to turn to. So I told him what I thought he needed to know. Nothing Danny would have disapproved of, mind you. Nothing about my past, only about Danny's conviction and the events that had led up to my receiving the shoe box.

He listened to all of it, asking only a few questions, like an attorney making inquiries of a client he was considering taking on.

"And so you came here and waited for me," he said after I'd finished.

"Yes."

Keith nodded thoughtfully. "And that's all?"

"Pretty much. Yes."

"I'm really not coldhearted, you know."

"I didn't say you were. I only asked you not to be."

"Any other time in my life and I might be all over this. But for reasons I'm not at liberty to share right now, none of which have anything

to do with your predicament, I just can't represent or assist you. Still, maybe I can give you
some advice."

It was a letdown, but not enough to dash my
hopes. For the first time he was showing real
interest in my predicament, as he called it.

"What kind of advice?" I asked.

"Your coming here, for starters. I don't mean
to alarm you, but the woman was right. People
like Bruce routinely reach beyond the walls of
their cells and destroy people on the outside. I'd
advise against walking up to complete strangers
and telling them the kind of things you've told
me."

"You're underestimating me," I said. "The
only reason I came to you was because I had
nowhere else to turn."

"Just because someone's a warden or a cop
doesn't mean they're not working with people
like Randell. Trust me, I've seen it from the inside."

"Which is precisely why I'm here. You're *not*
on the inside anymore."

"Just be careful. Also, I wouldn't assume that
Randell was the person who called you."

"The timing doesn't line up, right?" I said. "I

know, but it's still technically possible. Who else would call me?"

"Someone on the outside. It could even be un-related to Randell's beef with Danny. You said Danny confessed to killing two people. For all you know there were more. And he probably had run-ins with others he didn't kill. Could be one of them. Was there any press on his arrest?"

"No." His reference to Danny's past sent a chill through my arms. Not only because he'd guessed the truth so quickly, but because his conclusion was one that had haunted me for the past two days. A ghost from our past had found us and wanted us dead.

"You can't assume there were others," I said.

"No, but it's a possibility, and it makes more sense than Randell calling you. Actually, I think you could be as much the target as Danny."

None of this was news to me, but again, hear-ing Keith say it made the threat sound more real. Why else would the caller have contacted me?

Keith's reading of the situation didn't fill me with fear as much as it focused my anger. I had been backed into a corner before, and Danny taught me to come out swinging. Or maybe I'd taught that to myself. Either way, whoever was coming after us wasn't just going to pick us off like little varmints. They were playing the same kind of game Danny himself might have played before he'd taken the high road.

"And your point is?" I asked.

"Be careful."

"I'm the most careful person in the world."

"Good. You said Danny could take care of himself. So let him. Nothing from the outside's going to help him. You could try an attorney, but even if one can get a message inside, warning Danny won't help him as much as you might think. Prisons are a world unto themselves, understood only by those who live in them. Warning someone to watch his back in a prison is like telling a driver out here to watch out for other cars on the road. Unless he's an idiot, Danny knows of the threat already."

"You sure?"

He leaned back and shrugged. "Either way, there's nothing you can do about it. If Randell really wants him dead, one of them will end up dead. That's the kind of man he is."

My gut felt like a sauna for bed bugs. Billions of them.

"So what do you suggest I do? Lock my doors and bar my windows and hope for the best?"

"No. I suggest you start trying to figure out who in either your past or Danny's past might have a reason to come after you. You can't stop Randell. He's in a closed system. Forget him. Find out if someone else made that phone call. Find out who sent that shoe box."

"Then help me do that," I said, knowing that there was far more to the past than I could ever tell Keith.

It didn't matter. He shook his head. "I can't. I'm sorry. I wish I could but I just can't."

"You still have connections in the legal system, right? You know cops. You know the criminal world..."

"I also have a history that takes me out. I wish I could be more help."

He was looking at me kindly enough, and if I wasn't mistaken, his eyes betrayed interest in me as a woman, but he wasn't going to bend. He'd made his point as plainly as he could. I'd probably said way too much.

"You can, you just don't want to," I said, standing up. "Where's your cell phone?"

"My phone?"

"I'm going to give you my number. If you decide to help me out you'll know where to find me. Or you could just call and breathe heavy."

He studied me for a moment and smiled, then dug his phone out of his back pocket. "Give me your phone number."

I did and he keyed it in. But I knew it was wasted time.

"Got it?"

"Got it," he said.

"Can I have yours?"

"I'd rather not."

"Of course not."

But I hardly cared anymore. Someone was coming after me and there wasn't a soul in the world who could stop them, including Keith Hammond. I was on my own.

It was time to go home and dig out the nine-millimeter.

THERE ARE TIMES in life when everything a person thinks he knows is challenged.
Undercurrents suck him under and threaten
to pull him into a bottomless sea. Tsunamis
rise up after an unannounced earthquake and
sweep away every trace of reason in a matter
of seconds. That's why the wise man builds his
house upon a rock.

But what happens if he unwittingly picks the
wrong rock with the best of intentions, only to
discover that the foundation under that house
can crumble?

In Danny's case, the storm that threatened to
test his rock did not roar in like a tsunami in a

matter of seconds. It rose slowly over the course of the three days he spent in meditation, and even then it managed only to erode a small part of his foundation.

Personal suffering he could manage, only because he'd faced so much of it through the war. But the suffering of others…that was another matter.

He didn't know the names or the crimes of those who suffered in segregation with him, only the odor of their excrement. Inmates came and went during his stay, and the routine became plain.

A code of complete silence was strictly enforced on the meditation floor. Any deviance was handled swiftly. A single loaf of heavily enriched and dreadfully tasting bread was delivered once every day. The water to the faucet ran for five minutes three times a day, signaled only by the hissing in the pipes. The toilet flushed only once a day.

Once every two days, each cell was properly hosed down with the occupant inside. The water and refuse drained through a trap door in the floor, opened during the cleansing. For the day following the bath, the entire wing stank of chlorine and whatever other chemicals they'd put in the water—Pape's answer to sanitation concerns, which doubled as a mild form of torture, leaving them shivering in the damp cold. There were undoubtedly showers in the wing to meet all requirements set by the Corrections Standards Authority, but Danny guessed they weren't used except during inspection.

What had the others done to deserve such inhuman treatment? They'd deviated from the rules established by the world in which they lived.

Who made up those rules? A few of them had been established by the warden, the rest of them by the department of corrections. By extension they were all the rules of society.

Why follow the rules? Because the consequence of *not* following them was painful. They should have all known better. It served them right, people would say. If a law says you stop at a stop sign, and you don't stop, you are guilty and should pay a price. You run a stop sign, you pay a certain penalty, even if it's on a deserted road at four in the morning and there isn't another car within ten miles. Why? It's the law.

If the law says you cannot look at a guard a certain way and you look at a guard that certain way, you will pay a penalty. Why? Because it's the law. Looking at a guard wrongly at Basal might be compared to looking at a woman wrongly in some cultures.

Deviant behavior. Do the crime, do the time. Made sense.

After four days of shivering in Basal's dark hole, however, it made less sense. Not because of Danny's own suffering, but because of the suffering around him. Still, to maintain order, every society had to establish rules and follow them.

Even then, it wasn't the plight of those around him that eroded Danny's rock. It was the face of the young man named Peter Manning.

More specifically, the abuse the boy might suffer at the hands of Randell and his viper, Slane.

Even more specifically, Danny's own reaction to that abuse. It was clear that any attempt on his part to intervene would constitute a deviation from the established law in this society called Basal. He would be taking the law into his own hands, so to speak, something he'd done before. But by doing so, he'd finally found it lacking. Man did not have the right to subvert society's laws to enforce his own, even if doing so brought about good.

But therein lay the conundrum eroding his rock. Was it morally right to stand by while another suffered? What of the poor, the diseased, the hungry, the abused, the disadvantaged? Didn't he have a moral obligation to come to their rescue?

If so, wasn't he justified in wanting to prevent Randell from harming Peter? If he was required to break the law to save the boy, he would endure Pape's punishment. At least the boy would be spared his suffering.

And yet this reasoning only delivered him back to the philosophy he'd embraced as a vigilante, saving the abused who were overlooked by the law.

Danny lay on the concrete slab, and he thought of the boy, and he thought about Renee, and he wept because he knew that if it were Renee up there instead of Peter, his wrath would know no bounds. And yet Peter was deserving of as much love as Renee. So, for that matter, was Randell.

But love wasn't administered by a gun. He knew that. In his very bones he knew that. Randell was a monster because he'd been loved by hard steel instead of a warm heart his entire life, and such love was not love at all.

The facilitators came for him on the evening of the fifth day, the captain, Bostich, and a CO Danny hadn't had the pleasure of meeting. They asked him to stand outside his cell and dress before cuffing him, which was itself a humiliating show of superiority. But Danny did as they asked, and they led him from the hall of silent, tormented deviants.

"I'll take it from here," Bostich said, locking the steel door that led down to the meditation floor.

The other guard nodded and stepped away.

"This way."

Bostich led Danny to a sparsely furnished office in the administration wing and closed the door behind them. He motioned toward a gray metal chair next to the desk.

"Sit."

Still cuffed, Danny sat.

Bostich leaned back on the desk, crossed his arms, and returned Danny's stare. The dark-eyed man with bleached hair looked like he'd come out of the womb angry and hadn't yet found a way to punish the world for accepting his birth. Danny felt compelled to glance away. A clock on the wall indicated that it was 8:37 p.m. They'd timed his release to coincide with lockdown. Why? Danny didn't yet know, but he was sure that every detail in Basal was carefully orchestrated for maximum effect.

"Look at me," Bostich said, then continued when Danny faced him. "I'm going to give you the same speech I give every member after their first stint in meditation. If you think that was hard, think again. If you think that was unfair, you should have thought about that before you did whatever you did to get here. The only one who decides what's fair is God, and in Basal, the warden is God. Is that clear enough for you?"

"Yes."

"And if you think opening your mouth about your sacred experience down there'll bring attorneys running to set things straight, well then you just don't understand the nature of your predicament, do you? You talk to any member about your time below and you go back down.

You talk to anyone on the outside about it, ever, and anything can happen to you. The only thing protecting you in here is the warden. Am I clear?"

Danny had no reasonable choice but to answer in the affirmative.

"Good. I won't lie. The warden thinks you're good for this place, that you can somehow be a model citizen headed for early release. Me, I hate you. I don't trust you. I see you and I see a knucklehead, and the only knuckleheads in my prison are the ones I know I can trust. One more stunt like you pulled back in the cafeteria and you'll wish you were never born."

That would make two of us, Danny thought, but he said nothing.

Bostich glared at him. "Now that you know how things work, the warden thinks you should be given a little more freedom. He wants you to keep an eye out. Half the members in this place are snitching on their cellie but no one's a snitch, if you catch my drift."

Meaning no one was labeled as a snitch, because it would break the convict code and subject them to hatred, and yet half the members were giving up details when called upon to do so anyway.

"An efficient way to—"

"Shut up. If you see anything that strikes you as out of place, you have permission to inform the warden, but only directly or through me, you got that?"

"Yes."

The captain stared at him for a full ten seconds without blinking once.

"Fine. You're going back to your cell. You open your mouth even once before lockdown and you're going back down. Stand up."

The hub was deserted except for four privileged members who sat around a table, playing a game of checkers. Most of the inmates would already be in the housing units. Two members were in a discussion with the facilitator on duty in the commons wing when Danny stepped in. Another small group loitered near the top of the staircase. Several dozen stood at their cell doors or on the tier above, leaning on the railing, wasting away their last few minutes before lockdown.

The hall quieted the moment he entered. Heads turned and watched, silenced by his appearance. Danny's last hose-down had been earlier that day. He still smelled of chlorine. His hair was a mess and his hands were scraped from the concrete, but his clothing covered the bruises that had developed on his hips and shoulders from hours of shifting on the hard bed in an attempt to ease his pain. He'd lost a few pounds since arriving; otherwise there would be no other sign that he was worse off for the wear.

"Up."

Danny mounted the steel staircase, aware of the surreal silence interrupted by the sound of his feet thudding up the steps. Even if this was a common occurrence, his unearned reputation as the new deviant priest probably had more to do with this audience than his return from the hole. He was still a curiosity, singled out to be crushed with the help of Randell and his thugs.

As such he was a potential enemy to all. The warden expressly reserved the right to impose restrictions on the entire wing due to one person's deviance. Most of the members were likely far more interested in Danny's compliance than in his help.

A quick glance at the top of the staircase

showed no sign of Randell or Slane. A member with a barbed-wire tattoo on his neck and a crooked grin on his face watched him from his cell door at the top of the staircase.

"Yo, ya priest," he said with a slight southern accent. "Name's Kearney."

"Whoa!" Bostich stopped Danny and looked at the member who'd spoken. "You begging for trouble, boy?"

"No, siree."

"Then keep your trap shut." He lifted his chin down the tier. "In your cells, all of you."

They pulled off the railing and stepped into their cells, some more quickly than others.

Danny headed down the tier, keeping his eyes ahead, but he could see the members in his peripheral vision, making idle use of their last minutes before the ward shut down. At Ironwood a similar hall might be cut with the sounds of a banging locker and loud laughter, punctuated by vehement demands or loud objections.

Danny's thoughts were cut short as they approached his cell. A man stood inside the cell next to his own, fingers wrapped around the bars, peering out at him, wearing a thin grin. It was Slane. Hair greased back like a wedge on his narrow head.

Danny drew abreast of the cell and stopped. Beyond the grinning Slane sat Peter, rocking back and forth on the lower bunk, staring into oblivion. Bostich didn't order Danny forward, didn't shove him toward his own cell, made no effort at all to keep him from seeing what he was meant to see. They had transferred the predator into Peter's cell with clear intentions.

Danny met Slane's daring eyes and for a moment rage flooded his veins. He couldn't seem to pry Peter's plight from his mind. What kind of savage would place such a boy in the arms of a beast like Slane?

He told himself to move on, there was nothing he could do. He willed his feet to move, but his feet weren't responding. There was the predator and there was his victim, and here stood Danny, helpless to stop the one or help the other. And even if there was a way to help, could he?

Would he?

A stick in his back finally pushed him forward and Danny moved on, pulling his mind back from that place of fury that had once swallowed him.

Godfrey lay on the bottom bunk, reading Tolstoy's *War and Peace*, which he immediately set down. The door crashed shut behind Danny.

"Lights out in two."

Bostich nodded at Danny. "Sleep tight, Priest." He retreated down the pier, evidently satisfied that he'd escalated Danny's misery by setting up Peter in the cell next to his.

Godfrey closed his book and laid it on the mattress beside his head. "So you survived your first opportunity to meditate. That's good, everyone does."

"When did they move Slane into Peter's cell?" Danny kept his voice low.

The older man's head swiveled toward the bars. "What do you mean?"

"The man's in the cell next to ours."

"Now?"

"Now."

"Peter's with him?"

Danny shrugged out of his shirt and walked to the sink. "Yes." He turned on the faucet and splashed his face, ran his wet fingers through his grimy hair. There was no mirror.

"Lockup!" the CO shouted. The electronic

locks on the cell doors engaged with a loud clank.

"You see what I mean?" Godfrey muttered. "There's no end to their games. And there's nothing you can do, don't kid yourself. Guaranteed, this is as much about you as Peter. They are begging you to say something. Take my advice, don't."

"Lights out!"

Danny grabbed his towel from his locker and wiped his face. The bulb blinked off, leaving only pale light from the tier to reveal the outlines of the room. A faint whimper sounded from the cell on Danny's right.

He stood still for a moment, unable to move, unwilling to give any more space in his mind to the rage boiling in his gut. For three years he'd methodically steeled himself against the fury directed at the monsters of society, fully aware that he was essentially one himself. His only reasonable course of action now would be to console the boy and provide him with a ray of hope in the morning.

Danny stripped, rolled into his bunk, and prayed for the boy's safety. But he could not pray to be Peter's guardian angel. That task would have to be left to higher powers.

The facilitator on duty walked down the tier, checking each cell door.

"Keep to yourself, Priest," Godfrey muttered.

Why the man thought Danny needed this encouragement was a mystery. Was his indignation so obvious?

For half an hour Danny's senses remained tuned to the hall's noises, listening for the slightest sound from the cell next to his. Surely Slane wouldn't go so far so quickly. Surely there was a limit to what he could do with impunity in Pape's sanctuary. An eye for an eye, Pape had said, but surely he wouldn't demand an eye from someone as innocent as Peter. And yet, in Pape's world, everyone was guilty, whether or not caught and—

A short cry sliced through the dark night. At first Danny couldn't be sure of what he was hearing. But then the cry came again, this time a whimper that stopped his heart.

"Please! Please..."

Danny sat up.

"Think, man. Get a grip," Godfrey whispered.

Although the boy's cries were muffled now, they did not stop. The wing was gripped in perfect silence except for those stifled cries, now accompanied by other sounds of struggle.

Danny sat rigid, overwhelmed by a craving for justice that refused to bow to any calculated reasoning.

No one could help the boy in this moment, Danny. Your only course is to hope that Slane's sending a message, not carrying it out.

A bead of sweat ran past his temple; his body was already covered in a sheen of it. It was the warden's willingness to throw the boy away simply to break Danny that stirred up the worst of his anger.

In this world only the warden had true power. He was using terror to ensure compliance as much as some might think God would use a tornado to wake up a sleepy town.

The boy's stifled cries became louder, and Danny felt his hands begin to tremble. His mind bent to the point of snapping. Peter was that unwitting participant in a grand scheme, lost to the complexities of rules and protocol yet somehow subject to all of it. Peter was in his own hell, suffering punishment while the warden's message hung over them all: everyone is guilty and everyone suffers and only I can save you.

Beneath Danny, Godfrey's breathing was heavy. Surely he'd been confronted by similar injustice many times during his incarceration. He knew to keep his offense to himself, no matter how deep it ran.

Danny, on the other hand, wasn't as practiced, not here, not in Basal. But he could learn. He could suppress his hopeless urge to defend the defenseless. He could refuse to act. Didn't the whole world do the same? Didn't everyone turn a blind eye to the plight of others less fortunate?

A muffled scream reached past the cell wall, and for an endless moment that cry belonged to someone else. It was his mother's.

No, Danny, this isn't your mother...

But Danny's mind wasn't cooperating. He was a boy, hiding in his room in Bosnia. In the next room the Serbs were raping his mother. He was only a boy; he could not stop them. His two sisters were already dead. Now they were going to kill his mother, but he could not stop them, he couldn't scream, he couldn't even breathe.

The sounds of his mother screaming stopped. Their house was suddenly quiet. And Danny hid in the corner, shaking violently. This time he could not allow them to kill her. His foundation began to crumble. He was only vaguely aware that he was sliding off the bunk, desperate to stop them this time.

"Stop it!"

Danny's mind snapped back to his cell. He was on his knees, fists balled like twin hammers.

Silence smothered the echo of his cry.

In the next cell, Slane cackled. His hand must have slipped off the boy's mouth because a shriek cut through air.

"Help me! Help—" But the cry was stifled once again.

The bulbs suddenly popped bright, flooding the commons hall with light.

"Priest!" Bostich's voice rang out from the hall below the tier. The electronic lock on their cell door snapped open. "Step out of your cell!"

It took a moment for Danny to reclaim his poise. The heat on his face began to subside. What had he done? But he knew only too well.

"I won't say it again—step out of your cell!"

"Lord have mercy," Godfrey breathed.

Danny swung his feet off the bed, dropped to the ground, and exited his cell. His had been the only door opened. He stepped up to the railing and saw that Bostich stood by the guard station on the first floor, hands on hips, staring up at him.

"Do we have a problem?"

Danny had been under the warden's thumb for less than a week and the man had already fractured his resolve? He took a deep breath and considered the captain's question, then chose his words carefully.

"I would like to request an audience with the warden, sir."

The captain hesitated. "There's protocol for that, and it doesn't include screaming out in the middle of the night." But Bostich's curiosity pushed him further. "Regarding what?"

"Only clarification."

"You're confused, is that it? No one else seems to be confused. Are all priests as thick-headed as you?"

"I only need clarification about your latest request."

There was another pause as Bostich seemed

to consider his reference to snitching, surely knowing that Danny had nothing on which to snitch other than what was obvious. But it was enough to pique the man's interest.

"You're going back into meditation, you do realize that, don't you?"

"All I'm asking for is a word with the warden as part of due process before you take me down. Nothing more."

"Get back in your cell, keep your mouth shut. I hear of one more word in this ward tonight you're all going on lockdown for three days. That includes you, Slane." He faced the CO to his right. "Shut it down, Tony."

9

THURSDAY

IT'S AMAZING WHAT even the most bland mind can conceive of when properly stimulated. But press the more imaginative among us and there is no limit to the kinds of wild thoughts that fill our heads.

There I stood, at the end of my bed midday Thursday with all of my tools lined up like footwear on a Buckle shoe rack, carefully rehearsing the use of each item. I had gone through the exercise twice already, the night after returning from Keith Hammond's condo, and again that morning, after rising from a fitful sleep.

On the far left lay a Bowie knife with a ten-inch stainless-steel blade, good for hacking down a small sapling in the forest if you were stranded following a single-engine airplane crash and needed to make a platform in the trees so the bears wouldn't get you at night.

Or for cutting off someone's head.

Next to it rested a smaller, more manageable six-inch Boker tactical knife, sharpened on both sides like a dagger, good for drilling holes in the thin walls of a shack in the forest if you wanted to stay out of sight and spy on whatever deer or porcupine might wander by.

Or for stabbing a rapist's forehead.

There was also the folding survival knife, good for more than slashing. The wire, good for many things beside strangling. The small but very powerful Steiner binoculars, good for watching more than ugly neighbors. A set of lock picks, good for entering any locked door but my own. A pair of handcuffs for restraining a bad guy. And a four-inch can of pressurized Mace pepper spray readily available from Amazon. Good for turning even the largest man into a squealing little pig.

I'd selected the tools from a chest containing many, many more. It had sat in my closet, unopened, for three years running. These would all fit neatly in my kit, as Danny had taught me to call it—a small black leather bag that some might confuse for a large purse and others a doctor's medicine bag, although doctors no longer used such things.

Eight tools on the end of my yellow-checkered comforter. And one in my fist: the Browning nine-millimeter gun with a nine-clip round slammed up its handle. Copper hollow points with enough power to stop a much larger person than me in a full rush.

I snatched the gun up to shoulder height and twisted to my right into a firing position. The mirror on the wall said it all. Small package, major punch. Long black hair flowing over my face. Cropped black tank top and yellow-checkered flannel night shorts. Other than being too skinny, I looked like Lara Croft ready to face the world. Well, at least from the waist up. My flannel shorts and white thighs were anything but threatening.

I straightened and examined the gun. Released the clip, checked it quickly, slapped it home, chambered a round—*clank, clank*—and pointed the gun at my fluffy white tiger.

I tilted the barrel up. "Sorry, Tigger."

But I wasn't. Yes, I hated the gun in my hand. I'd never used the wire or the handcuffs or the pepper spray or most of the tools on my bed, not on another human being, at least. They all took me back to terrible days when they'd been necessary.

In the end it had been a gun that saved me. I would be dead if not for a gun, I was sure of it.

I paced out to the living room, checked the door to make sure it was still locked, and went to the refrigerator for a glass of water. The memories of that night four years earlier rushed through my head. I'd been shot up with heroin, a bag of bones after being manipulated and crushed by a man who wanted me only as his toy. He and his buddies had chased me down an alleyway. I was stumbling, falling, desperately tying to get away. It was raining. Hard.

You see, if I'd had a gun then, I might have been able to defend myself. But that would come later. I was saved by a stranger that night. A stranger who turned out to be just as bad as my first captor. Maybe worse. After a year, I finally set the world straight—and I did it with the help of a gun.

So you see, I hadn't touched the nine-millimeter in my hand for three years because I hated it. But I also loved it. How could I not love something that had saved my life?

Danny was a purist, locked up because he always had done and always would do what he thought was right, even if that meant serving the rest of his life in prison. And although I agreed with his vow of nonviolence, the new threat to both of our lives superseded his conviction. At least it superseded mine, maybe because I wasn't as strong as Danny.

If that meant blowing a hole in Bruce Randell's head, so be it. I wasn't going to let him kill either Danny or me.

I had spent hours rehearsing my options and settled on two possible courses of action. One, I could simply hole up in my apartment and wait it out, trusting that Danny was fully capable of taking care of himself. I mean, he'd survived the front lines of the Bosnian War, hadn't he? And he'd done it as an assassin who routinely penetrated enemy lines to take the lives of key players. Danny could handle guns and explosives like most people handled breathing. More important, he could handle his wits even better than he handled guns.

Holing up in my apartment would also keep me off the streets, where I'd be a target for verbal abuse, kidnapping, rape, murder, waterboarding, thievery, blows to the head, and other disturbing possibilities. If anyone tried to break in, they would be greeted by a bullet. I would eventually have to go out, but I could get Jane to buy me a few groceries—my list wasn't terribly complicated or long. If I didn't drive, I wouldn't need gas. I could pay all my bills over the Internet. Anything else I needed I could get from Amazon overnight or by using two-day prime shipping. I could live in my apartment for a few months without going out if I had to. And I would always have my phone to call Basal until they finally let me talk to Danny.

I paced back to my bedroom swimming in thoughts. Holing up in my apartment was one plan, but it didn't deal with the obvious: if Danny and I were being threatened by someone on the outside and they had waited this long, avoiding them for a few months would only delay the inevitable.

A second option would be to go ahead and hire an attorney, then get a message to Danny asking for a list of all of his victims and anyone associated with them who might be in a position to come after us. Armed with that list, I could go on the offensive with Danny's help once he earned his visitor privileges. I could track down each one covertly, working with Danny to identify and neutralize our enemy. Danny's old terms.

My pacing took me back out to the living room. The problem with working with Danny to identify and neutralize our potential enemies was in the identifying part, because he wouldn't want a list out there with all of his victims on it. And in the neutralizing part, because Danny no longer believed in neutralizing. Of course, if he knew my own safety was at risk, he might have a change of heart.

There was always the possibility that the threat was coming solely from inside the prison, after all. Bruce Randell might be the only threat, and Danny might still be unaware. But I doubted it. Randell had to be working with someone on the outside, as Keith had suggested, and that someone was likely one of Danny's enemies.

I glanced at the front door, just a nervous habit of a glance, and I started to turn when the white envelope on the floor caught my attention. My first thought was that mail had been delivered through the slot in the door earlier than it normally came, around four. My second was that someone could fill the entire apartment with a deadly gas through the same slot. It was a hole in my dam.

My heart skipped a beat. I pinched the white envelope by its corner using my left hand and lifted it. It was sealed. No name or address.

Maybe Jane had come by and, not wanting to bother me, dropped off the twenty dollars she'd borrowed from me two weeks earlier. No, she would have at least put my name on it. Or called. Someone else had delivered the envelope in the last few minutes, and only one name popped into my head.

Bruce Randell. Someone working for Bruce Randell.

The gun was in my right hand. Whoever had delivered the envelope might still be making a getaway, hurriedly walking away as I stood frozen.

I dropped the envelope on the counter, disengaged the nine-millimeter's safety, snapped open both dead bolts on the door, and pulled it wide, gun raised to the outside world. Pointed straight ahead at the cars driving by on Bixby Road.

My pulse was thumping and my palms were already sweaty on the warm steel. I stuck my gun out, then my head. They couldn't have gone far.

But the yard was empty. So was the sidewalk. A woman was walking casually for her car in the parking lot, and, as she turned her head my way, I lowered the gun to my side. She would undoubtedly misunderstand my intentions. Or, worse, understand them just fine and call the police.

The woman turned away and I glanced to my right and left, searching for a sign of whoever had delivered the mail. They were gone. And I was neither in the right clothes nor the right frame of mind to go running around the complex with a nine-millimeter in my hands.

I ducked back into the apartment and locked the door.

The envelope was clean. Careful not to disturb any fingerprints on the surface, I slit it open using a butter knife and shook the contents out. A sheet of lined paper from a yellow pad fell onto the counter. On it were words written in red ink. Not just written—scrawled, as if they'd been written left-handed by someone who was right-handed.

I knew, without reading a single word, that the same man who'd breathed heavy in my ear had now followed up his call with a letter.

I slowly opened the folded sheet and read the red words.

Renee Gilmore,

I am watching. Always watching.

I saw you drive up to the prison. I saw you go to that scumbag last night, dressed in your tight skanky jeans. Both you and Hammond will go to hell. The priest did what he thought was right in the sight of man, but he made one mistake. He didn't kill them all. If you go to the cops the priest will die. If you go to an attorney the priest will die. If you go to the warden both you and the priest will die. I will be watching.

I laid the page down on the counter, fingers trembling, and I took the rest of the note in quickly, as if by reading the words I could make them go away.

The writing filled the page, laying out careful instructions for me, and with each line my anxiety rose. The reality of the threat grew exponentially with each paragraph. The note ended plainly.

I'm as serious as the devil in hell.

I stood there in my flannel shorts and black tank top, unable to get enough breath. My fingers gripped both sides of the letter and the gun sat on the counter to my right, and all I could think was, *He's serious. He's as serious as the devil in hell.*

And then I was running for my office, searching for the number I'd written on the bottom of one of the pages I'd printed out, the one with information about Keith Hammond. I didn't have his cell phone, but I'd found his home phone through a reverse directory, which cost me $4.99, charged to my Wells Fargo debit card.

I found it, dropped onto the edge of my chair, and punched the number into the phone by my Mac.

Pick up, please pick—

"Keith."

"I just got a letter from him. He knows about you."

"Renee?"

"Yes, Renee. Could you come over?"

"*Who* sent you a letter?"

"Didn't you hear a thing I said last night? Someone's stalking me and he knows I was at your house last night."

"Slow down. What kind of letter?"

"The kind someone would write when he knows way too much and is threatening to kill you."

"What do you mean kill me?"

"He said that if I don't do what he says he's going to kill us. All of us."

That brought a short pause. "Can you read it to me?"

"You need to read it yourself."

"Is he there now?"

"No, someone pushed the letter through the mail slot in my door. The point is, if whoever is playing this can reach me this easily, he will reach you. I'm dead serious. This isn't funny anymore. You're involved, whether you like it or not."

One more hesitation. When he spoke again I could hear the nervousness in his voice, and it brought me more comfort than I like to admit.

"What's your address?"

10

"I AM WATCHING. Always watching," Keith muttered, reading aloud.

He stood with one hand on the counter, running the other through his short blond hair, studying the scrawled red words on yellow-pad paper. He'd read it twice, hardly giving my apartment a second glance.

I, on the other hand, had read the letter at least a dozen times as I paced, waiting for him to arrive, and then again with him. My nerves were too raw to pay any attention to common courtesy, which would have suggested I change into jeans before he got there. And that I put away my kit or close the door to my bedroom. Maybe offer him a drink.

But the contents of the letter had wiped all social grace from my mind. It was the writer's claim that there was only one way to save the sinner's soul that had me worked up. The demands were all there, in red, unmistakable.

If you want to save the priest you will do exactly as I say without question. Fail once and the priest's sins will be exposed to the Los Angeles Times. *Fail twice and he will die. And if you doubt my ability to snuff out the priest's life, you are a fool. Test me and know that I am he.*

You will put one million dollars on my plate. You will confess to the murder of the person you kill. You will spend the rest of your life in that sanctuary of penance, paying for your sins. Do this and the priest will be set free. Maybe he can save you.

Time to live, Renee: Go to the Rough Riders bar in Long Beach at 10:00 tonight. Alone. I'll know. Find my next message at the public phone in the corner. Do what it says.

I'm as serious as the devil in hell.

Of that, there was no longer any doubt.

"The question is, how?" Keith said. "Randell's on the inside and unless he has frequent phone access or has a cell phone stashed in there, it would be very hard for him to get timely updates from anyone on the outside."

"So it's more than him, obviously."

"Someone with a grudge against the priest. One of his previous victims."

"His name is Danny," I said.

Keith was taking it all in stride. He did, after all, have sheriff's blood in him.

He nodded. "They're using your attachment to him as leverage."

"Leverage for what?"

"Evidently a million dollars."

"How can we be sure this *is* actually Randell? Maybe it's just someone on the outside."

Keith took a deep breath and blew it out slowly. The sleeves on his blue T-shirt were short and exposed the lower half of a tattoo on his left shoulder—a sheriff's badge with something about honor and death. His eyes flitted over to my gun, which still lay on the counter. He'd hardly given the Browning a second glance when I'd first let him in, which made sense. He'd expect someone like me to be packing after receiving the threats I had.

"The money points to Randell," he said. "When you know the whole story."

"What story?"

"But it's about more than just money. They want you to know they know about Danny's past, which validates their threat. The real question is, who got away from the priest and is back to make him pay?"

"What story?" I asked again.

Keith scanned the letter once more. I knew he was holding something back and I needed to know what it was. I also needed him to work with me. Having him beside me provided far more comfort than I was used to, and I can't say it bothered me.

"Okay, look," I said, covering the letter with one hand so that he would look up at me. "Let's get one thing straight. It's not just a coincidence that you're here. If the woman hadn't given me Bruce Randell's name, I wouldn't have tracked you down and you'd be back home right now, watching football and drinking beer. But she did, and I came to you and whoever is stalking me now knows about you. They may know you're in here right now. You're involved, like it or not. So we're in this together. Right?"

"So it seems."

"You're either going to help me or you aren't. Which is it?"

He studied me with his hazel eyes, then nodded. "We're in this together."

I removed my hand from the letter and stepped back. "Good, because I need you."

He glanced over my shoulder and I followed his stare into my bedroom. There were my criminal tools, spread out like a smorgasbord.

"Looks like you can handle yourself just fine," he said.

"Yeah. Well, every woman living alone needs to protect herself." Which explained pretty much all of the tools on the bed except the strangling wire.

"True. Okay, let's start over." Keith walked into the living room where he paced, letter dangling from his right hand.

"For starters, there's no way I'm going down to this bar of his," I said. "Who does he think I am?"

"A person he has in a corner."

"Then he doesn't know me."

"Let's hope not. From the top. My best guess:

The priest...Danny...is transferred to Basal, and in a matter of hours you get a call from someone on the outside who knows Randell. One of them had to know Danny was going to be transferred."

"How? That's protected information."

He waved my assertion off with a simple flip of his wrist. "Forget that. Obviously we're dealing with people who have access. Money buys you anything, honey. As anticipated, the phone call had you scrambling."

"They wanted to scare me."

"Just enough so that you would dig, knowing that you would quickly learn just how impossible it is to reach Danny. Isolation is critical to them. Danny belongs to them now, not to you. They hold that card. And we have to assume they wanted me involved."

"Why would they want you involved?" I answered my own question. "Because he knew you would confirm the threat. Everything that's happened so far—the call, the woman, the shoe box, the letter—it's all to make sure I take them seriously." I let it set for a breath. "Tell me about the money."

"I'm getting to it. The letter mentions

Danny's failure to kill all of his victims. Any ideas?"

"He was convicted on two counts of murder. Jonathan Bourque and Darby Gordon. Both scumbags in their own rights. But he was a priest who didn't mind using a gun. I'm sure that he scared the heck out of more than a few in his time. Injustice drives him around the bend."

"You don't know any of them?"

"No. He was very private." Mostly true. I knew about the pedophile he'd killed and a few others, but they were all dead.

"Well, now one of them is back and with a vengeance."

"And what about the money?"

"Are you always so persistent?"

"Only when my life's on the chopping block."

"Okay, the money. We were able to close down on Randell because of information leaked to us by an anonymous source who claimed to be Randell's partner. I always knew the informant was high up, but I didn't understand his motivation to betray Randell until later. This guy—who's still unknown, by the way—kept a large sum of money that should have gone to Randell. I would guess that Randell thinks he can now get to the money using you."

"Why me? Why not just have one of his contacts on the outside go get it?"

"I'm getting to that. He can't trust them. His operation turned on him and fed him to the wolves. But this man who hates Danny—Randell can trust a man like that. You give him a means to the money in exchange for Danny. In the end they both get what they want."

"Randell gets his money back—"

"And his pride."

"And his pride. And this brute on the outside makes Danny and me pay."

"That's right. I would guess that whoever Randell's working with doesn't just want you dead. He wants you to suffer. Thus the game."

"Which isn't going to happen. We're going to stop them first."

"Maybe. But it'll be risky. We can't go to the authorities without running the risk Randell will know we've done it. There's also the fact that the wheels of justice turn very slowly, as they say. There's a gulf between the law we know and the prison system. Two different worlds. If Randell wants Danny dead, the warden will have a tough time stopping someone from putting a shank between his ribs."

I glared at him.

He shrugged. "I'm sorry, but we have to be realistic."

"Danny's tougher than that. Last night you said wardens are good at suppressing violence."

"They are. But if someone like Randell has nothing to lose—he doesn't care if time is added to his sentence—there's not much the warden can do for long. And that's assuming the warden isn't in on it. Point is, going to the law or the warden will probably make things only worse for Danny. And certainly for you."

None of this was particularly new, just a little clearer. I had always feared for Danny's life on the inside. His strategy for staying alive in the prison system was to stay out of trouble, period. Show strength but never use it. He'd managed three years at Ironwood without making enemies. That had all changed the moment he stepped into Basal.

"Okay, so where does that leave me?" I asked, picking up the gun. I needed a reminder that I wasn't powerless in the face of these thugs.

"Don't tell me you expect me to play this game of his."

"I don't know. We have to think about that."

"Then think about this. I say we cut this game off at the head." I said it waving the gun at the ceiling in frustration. "We don't know who's messing with us on the outside, but we know about Randell. So we take out one side of the partnership. Without Randell, the guy on the outside can't threaten Danny or manipulate me by doing it."

Keith's brow arched over his right eye. "Break in?" He seemed to consider it for a moment. "No way."

"Why not?"

"We don't have access, for one. Even if we did, it's a crime."

I stepped up, snatched the letter from his hands and held it up. "What do you think *he's* demanding from me? Community service?"

"No. But he's not demanding we walk into a prison and take the life of a prisoner."

"Right. Instead he'll demand I kill some innocent bystander on Long Beach Boulevard."

"We don't know that yet. But breaking into Basal to kill Randell is out of the question."

"Then use one of your contacts to do it."

He shook his head. "I don't have those kinds of contacts."

We stared at each other, silent for few seconds.

"You're actually suggesting I do what he wants?" I finally said. "Go to this bar tonight?"

"Not necessarily. I'm just talking this out." He gently plucked the letter out of my hand and lowered it to his side. "I'm only suggesting we consider all of your options."

"*Our* options," I said.

"Okay, our options."

"And if the warden's crooked?"

"Then it's game over. The warden is judge and jury on the inside." He paced, one hand in his hair. "Look, I don't trust legal channels any more than you do, but given our alternatives, maybe it is your best option. I might be able to reach out to some people and find a way to the warden. Maybe—"

"And risk Danny's life? Or mine? You already made that case!" I had the distinct impression he was having second thoughts. "I can't do that. You have your reasons for quitting the law, I have mine. They know too much about Danny's past. And mine."

"And what's in your past?"

There it was.

"Let's just say I stood by Danny."

He nodded slowly. "Fine. Short of any legal route, the only play we have is to gain both you and Danny some time. And the only way to do that is to go through some of the motions."

Short of trying to kill that snake Randell, which I think I preferred, Keith was right. I took a step to the couch, sat down, and dropped the gun on the cushion beside me. "Do you mind sitting? You're making me anxious."

"Sure." He sat down in the chair opposite me, letter in hand. "We have to figure out who this guy on the outside is. He's probably the one pulling the strings. We need time."

"So we play his game." I said it plainly but my stomach was turning.

He looked at me with tender eyes for a few moments. It was in that look that I first saw his compassion for me. I hardly knew Keith, but he'd come from a hard world—his résumé made that clear enough. Up until this point he'd been all business.

"Read it again," I said.

He lowered his eyes and read, "You will put

one million dollars on my plate. You will confess to the murder of the person you kill. You will spend the rest of your life in that sanctuary of penance, paying for your sins. Do this and the priest will be set free. Maybe he can save you."

"He wants me to trade places with Danny," I said. "But there's no way anyone could set Danny free."

"Unless..." I could see the wheels spinning behind his eyes as he stared at the drawn curtains. "I know you say you don't know, but is it possible Danny could have gone after someone in power back then? A judge, for example?"

It hit me. Danny's first victim, the pedophile, was the adult son of a judge. Which judge, I had no idea. But a judge.

"It's possible. But I wouldn't have a clue who."

Keith watched me. "The right judge could suspend Danny's sentence. If a judge is involved and we can turn that judge...But it's more likely whoever wrote this note's leading you on."

It was my first real thread of hope, and I grabbed it like a falling monkey snatching a vine. From that moment I knew, without the slightest reservation, that I would play this sicko's game.

I snatched the gun, pushed myself up, and paced. "Okay. So I play along. I go to this Rough Riders bar at ten tonight. What then?"

"Then we don't know what. But I don't want you to get the wrong idea. Even if we take the claim at face value and assume the writer of this letter can free Danny, which is highly unlikely, it would require that you do everything he demands. That's not going to happen."

"We don't know what's going to happen. Like you said, the only way to buy us time and flush this sicko out is to play his game."

"Flushing him out won't be easy..."

"So what are you suggesting? That we play or that we don't?"

"I'm suggesting we play. But don't get your hopes up. This could all go very wrong."

"It's already very wrong. I have nowhere to go from here but up."

He nodded. "Sicko, huh?"

"Sicko."

Keith tapped his thighs and stood, as if that was that. "Okay. We play Sicko's game."

"So you'll work with me?"

He offered a grim smile that he probably intended to appear forced, but I saw more than simple willingness in his expression.

"I don't see that I have a choice," he said.

I stepped up and stuck out my hand. "Thank you."

He took my hand, and I saw that softness in his eyes again. It was remarkable how eerily similar this all was to meeting Danny. Coming out of a place of such loneliness and desperation, I could have hugged him.

And then I did. A short, spontaneous hug. "Thank you for helping me."

"You're welcome."

I pulled away. "Now what?"

"Now you show me your toys." He jerked his head over his left shoulder. "In the bedroom."

"My toys?"

His cheeks reddened and he gave me a crooked little smile. "Your weapons."

Oh.

"You think I'll need them?"

"Honey, you're going to need everything you have."

11

THE FAINT SOUND of Peter's crying in the next cell finally stilled, and the night passed without further incident. But Danny lay awake for several hours, rehearsing his own misstep, gathering resolve to recover himself, layering his mind with reason once again.

His mind soon filled with an image of Renee, and with it a terrible longing to hold her again. To be held by her. To hear her whisper in his ear. *It'll be okay, Danny, you're a good man. It's not your fault I turned out the way I am. You saved me, Danny, and I love you.*

But he'd also shown her a brutal way, and for that he wept also.

The sound of a loud buzzer brought the prison to life at 6:00 a.m. sharp. The night's events felt a world removed.

Slane had vanished from Peter's cell by the time Danny stepped over to check on the boy, who was still under his sheet, sleeping. He slipped in and shook the boy by his shoulder.

"Wake up."

Peter gasped and jerked back, terrified. Then he saw that it was Danny and twisted his head around to find Slane. Seeing that they were alone, he began to settle.

"Are you okay?"

A tear slipped down the boy's cheek. Danny checked the sheets for any sign of blood and was grateful to find none. It was entirely possible that Slane had only intended to terrify the boy. Infuriate Danny.

He'd succeeded on both counts. But that was now past.

"Are you hurt?"

Peter curled into a ball. "No." He began to cry.

"All right, but you need to be checked anyway."

Godfrey stepped through the door. "Is he okay?"

"He appears to be. I think Slane only meant to scare him."

Godfrey muttered something about a system gone off the deep end.

"You need to get up, Peter. You need to be strong and show them that they can never destroy your heart."

Godfrey said something else under his breath. Peter refused to speak. It occurred to Danny that the boy might need some privacy to deal with his shame.

He squeezed Peter's hand and faced Godfrey. "It's okay, I have this."

Godfrey eyed him, then the boy, then nodded and left, mumbling, "An eye for an eye will kill us all."

"Why don't you get up and see if you're okay, Peter. I'll be right next door, okay? Slane's gone now. It's safe, I promise."

"I don't want to go back down," Peter whimpered.

"Down where? To breakfast?"

He shook his head.

"To the segregation ward? Meditation?"

His answer came in a cracked whisper. "To the other place."

"What place?"

But the boy only huddled up in his sheets and Danny didn't want to disturb him further.

"You're not going to be punished, Peter." He patted the boy's hand. "I'm going to talk to the warden and I'll make sure that you aren't punished. Don't worry, you're safe now. Okay?"

Peter finally nodded.

He left the boy alone, knowing that his words were hollow, a false promise of hope when there was no hope in this bloody sanctuary for a boy like Peter. Danny would make his case—he'd rehearsed it when reason had returned to him—but in the end they were all victims of the warden's whims. And the warden seemed to think his version of hell was the way to fix the world.

By 7:03, according to the large white clock on the wall, the second wave of diners had filled the cafeteria including Godfrey, Danny, and Peter, who had emerged from his cage to follow Danny like a shadow, hovering close, bumping into his heels twice on the way to the dining hall.

With the exception of Godfrey, Peter, Randell, and Slane, Danny hadn't spoken a word to any of the other members yet, in part because of the gag order the warden had placed on them all, and in part because he'd spent most of his time in disciplinary segregation. But apparently the order had been lifted. The prisoner with the barbed-wire tattoo around his neck, Kearney, had spoken to him on the tier last night.

Danny sat in the cafeteria and scanned the members dressed in blue and tan. Who were they? What had brought them here? What were their stories?

Answer: they were humans, and deviance had brought them to Basal, and each of their stories was as fascinating or heartbreaking as anyone else's.

As in any society, the humanity of those incarcerated rose above the culture of incarceration. What made one truly human, perhaps more than genetic code, was the human experience. As much as dignity, respect, and honor, a person's story gave him a human identity.

Other than Godfrey and Peter, Danny knew little about other members' unique identities. Basal members seemed more amenable to toeing the warden's line rather than trying to draw their own.

He sat with Godfrey and Peter at a corner table in the cafeteria slouched over a plate of powdered eggs, two pieces of soggy toast, a lump of ground meat that approximated sausage, and a glass of orange juice. As he ate, Danny finally began to put flesh to the warden's sanctuary.

The first to join them was the man with the barbed-wire neck tattoo, Kearney, a bright-eyed fellow in his upper twenties who seemed less interested in speaking than smiling. In fact, he said nothing at first, and Danny was content to let him eat in peace.

Kearney was soon joined by two others who sat quietly for about a minute before breaking the silence.

"You have a name, Priest?" the short pudgy one with gray hair and a round face said.

"Danny."

"Just Danny?"

"Just Danny."

The man nodded. "Okay then, Danny. Name's John Wilkins."

"Tracy Banner," the man next to him said. Banner was older as well, maybe in his early fifties, but much taller, with dark hair and a thick scar on his right cheek. Probably a lifer like his friend.

"Yo, dat took some balls, doin' what you done last night," Kearney said. "You lost it, huh?" His accent wasn't as much southern as hackneyed, part everything with some street thrown in.

Danny took a sip from his cup.

"You a real priest?"

"No."

"You *were*?" the scarred Banner asked.

"I was."

"I said yo last night," Kearney said.

"You did. Appreciate it."

"I went down for manslaughter. Got bump't in the taillight at a stop by a Toyoter truck. Buddy 'n' I went on a joy ride 'n' chased it down. Never had even no ticket up till then."

"Nineteen," Godfrey said.

Kearney glanced at him. "Nine years 'go. Truck went clean off the road and hit a tree. Passenger was preg and lost 'er baby. Made me sick. Never did no drugs, no tickets, no nothin' and then—bam—I'm in the big house. My bad. None else."

But manslaughter wouldn't bring a life sentence, and Kearney wasn't a fish. "Why are you still here?"

"Got shanked by a southerner in Lancaster back when it was the way, you hear me? Said no baby-killer deserved to breathe. Next time I was goin' down, so when he come at me 'gin I lost it. Got twenty for killin' him."

"Tough." He wasn't a lifer, but Danny understood why he'd made it into Basal. Kearney wasn't a killer at heart.

He took a bite of eggs and nodded at the oldest of the three, Wilkins. "I'm guessing you're a lifer?"

"Like most in here. Murder. A lifetime ago when I was young and stupid."

"Same," Tracy said. "Shot a man I caught with my wife."

They ate in silence for a minute. Danny's mind turned to his request to meet with the warden. He still had no idea if, how, or when it would happen. Even less if he could do Peter any good.

"Godfrey says you help't someone see the light," Kearney said. "That your ticket?"

"One way to look at it. The foolish idealism of an imperfect man."

"Word to the wise, Priest," the round-faced Wilkins said quietly. "You might think you can shed a little of your light in here, but don't kid yourself. God knows half of us would like nothing better, but the only light in here is the warden's light, you hear?"

Danny gave him a nod.

"You seem like a standup guy," said Banner. "Most of us are old cons who know how to do smooth time. Basal's not the place to do hard time, trust me. He'll put your balls in a vise and make you wish you were dead. I don't care what kind of wiseacre stories other cons'll tell you about this prison or that segregation unit. Nothing comes close to Pape's hell. Drink the Kool-Aid, keep your mouth shut, and smile along with the rest of us, you hear?"

"Believe me, I'm not looking for trouble."

"What he's saying," Wilkins said, "is that neither's anyone else, knuckleheads included. You haven't seen what the warden's capable of, and you don't want to. Upset him and everyone pays. Consider the knuckleheads on his payroll 'n' part of the program. Enforcers. Helps him keep his hands clean, but they only do what he allows them to do, if you catch my drift."

"Like I said, no trouble."

"Not to say what you did last night wasn't a trip," Kearney cut in. "A priest, huh?"

Danny shrugged. "It won't happen again."

"You think we didn't want to flush that sick jocker's head down the sewer where it belongs?" Wilkins said. He cast a sideways look at Peter, who sat hunched over, keeping his eyes elsewhere.

He lowered his voice. "Makes me want to puke, but you gotta remember where we are. This is hell. We don't need anyone turning up the flames. Godfrey should have told you that."

"I did," Godfrey said. And then after a pause, "But everyone has their limits."

"And everyone can just stretch their limits."

"Easy," Kearney said. "Some lowlife tried to hurt his daughter."

Godfrey's eyes shifted and held on Danny for a moment. "And that lowlife no longer walks the earth," he finally said.

"Neither do you," Wilkins said. "You walk in Basal."

The room suddenly grew quiet. Next to

Danny, Peter stiffened. One look at the boy's pale face betrayed his terror. The surest cause would be Slane or Randell.

But when Danny followed Peter's stare to the cafeteria's entrance he saw that he was wrong. It was neither Slane nor Randell. It was the warden. Marshall Pape was gracing them with his presence.

The immaculately dressed custodian walked into the silent cafeteria, slowly scanning the long tables. His black suit was pressed and his white shirt was starched. He looked in no way evil or monstrous, only immaculate and sure of his place. A good marshal come to keep the peace in a town of misfits. There was no gun faster than his, no word so firm, no foot so sure.

His patent-leather shoes clacked on the concrete as he walked into the room. The captain, the first-watch lieutenant, and three correctional officers spread out along the walls adjacent their superior.

Pape nodded. "Gentlemen." When his bright blue eyes reached Danny, he stopped and held his gaze. Somewhere, someone cleared his throat. For a long moment it was the only sound.

Danny understood immediately.

"I hear that there was an incident in the west wing last evening," the man said. "A request was made for a conference with me." He smiled and spread his hands. "Well, I'm a simple enough man. Here I am. So tell me, what would the priest like for me to clarify? Surely, if such an educated man of the cloth is confused, the entire flock must be courting similar confusion. Why not shed the light on the whole bunch at once?"

Danny kept his eyes on Pape, aware that the man had placed him in an impossible situation. What was said for all to hear wouldn't bring any good unless it was accepted by both sides. The members were Danny's potential enemies as much as the warden was. Perhaps more so.

The warden lowered his hands. "I'll tell you what. Why don't we play fair? Ask me any question you like. Voice any concern or doubt you have. I give you my full blessing. If I am unable to satisfactorily answer your concern, then I will acknowledge my oversight and grant either you or anyone of your choosing quarters in the privileged wing."

Danny could hear Peter's heavy breathing beside him.

"But if your concern proves to be misguided, then I will send Peter deep. After all, I believe it was the boy who started the ruckus last night. Fair enough?"

Deep? Someplace other than meditation. Peter's comment earlier, that he didn't want to go down there, returned to Danny.

He had no ambition to confront the warden in public. But he also knew that it would prove valuable for Peter to see someone standing up for him, regardless of the consequences.

"What do you say, Danny?" Pape asked, wearing a good-natured smile. "Be a good sport. Stand up and be heard. Please, I insist."

Danny pushed himself back from the table, calmly stood, and faced the man. Only now, standing, did he see Randell at a table across the room with Slane and several other knuckle-heads. Smirking.

"Speak up, Danny. Tell me what's so confusing to you."

He turned his eyes back to the warden and spoke with stoic resolve and calculation.

"It's my understanding of deviant behavior that's unclear," Danny said.

"Oh? How so?"

He couldn't implicate Slane directly without snitching and thereby violating the strict convict code. Rat on one, you'll rat on us all, it was said.

"I wonder if morality is as important as deviance in Basal. By that I mean—"

"I know what you mean, Danny. I'm not a fool."

In another place, another time, he would have recoiled at such condescension. Now he only took the man's dismissal in stride.

The warden continued. "You're wondering if I accept immoral behavior in my sanctuary as a means of punishing deviance. And the answer is, you're missing the point entirely. But that's understandable, you're only a fish here."

"Then perhaps you could explain your point to this fish."

Easy, Danny. Don't push the man.

The warden lowered his chin. "I intend to. The point is, I have no control over the morality of the members in our institution. The point is, morality cannot be legislated. It occurs primarily in the mind. Anger, jealousy, envy…all matters of the mind. As the good book says, every soul walking the earth is guilty. They are all evil. Surely you know that, Priest. Morality rests with the judgment of a higher authority."

He clasped his hands in front of him and continued:

"Deviance, on the other hand, can be measured by man. That's why we have the law. To monitor and control behavior, not morality. Does that clear things up for you?"

"And should a member of society be punished if he deviates from that law to protest or prevent a grave injustice?"

"Didn't you hear me, Danny? No? Then I'll repeat myself. It is for a higher authority to decide what injustice to punish, and at Basal I am he. If a man doesn't want his eye plucked out, he shouldn't pluck out someone else's eye. If your boy didn't want to be hurt, he shouldn't have hurt whoever he hurt to land himself in this hellhole."

"He hurt no one. He is innocent."

"Again, please pay close attention so that I don't have to keep repeating myself. *No one* is innocent. *Everyone* is guilty. Injustice is in the heart of *every* man. Truth be told, the whole world belongs in here, where justice is true. It's quite simple, really: you do wrong and you pay the price. The members of this institution should consider themselves fortunate enough to be given the privilege of learning this here, before they face much worse, wouldn't you agree?"

No. But already Danny saw the futility of this exercise. No good could come of it. His only hope now was to make his position clearer for the members, irrespective of the warden.

"I've found that grace and love, which come from the highest authority, are better teachers than punishment," Danny said. "But I'm sure you know that all too well. I suppose it's why you have the privileged wing. I only wonder what grace can be shown to the guilty who live among the commons."

The warden stared at him for a moment, then faced the rest, smiling. "You see, this is why I brought a priest here. His fancy words, his big heart—you would think you're in *his* sanctuary. Such comfort for the masses. But he's as guilty as the rest. A murderer like so many of you. And as for grace..."

He faced Danny, mouth flat now. "Grace is a sham. It's only another word for obedience. As the good book says, if you only believe and accept you will be saved. What they don't tell you is that belief and following are the hardest work. There is no free ride. Even your faith teaches that you must do something to be saved. And that belief is pronounced dead if not accompanied by good works. So you see, grace is no grace at all. All that matters is reward for obedience and punishment for deviance. And that, dear murderer, is what my sanctuary is all about."

A slight but crooked grin twisted the warden's face. "You do believe in punishment, don't you, Danny?"

"I'm trying to understand it. The God I love *is* love. How punishment works within the context of that love is a mystery known only to him. My part is to love, not judge or punish. Morality *is* love. As such I try to be a moral being, finding love and grace in my heart."

"Oh? And here I thought you believed that the end result of your actions is what determined your morality. Isn't that how you justified your numerous vigilante murders as a priest? Killing evil men to free the oppressed under their thumb? Ring any bells?"

Danny's heart stalled. *Numerous...*

He was certain in that moment that the warden knew far more about his own unconfessed crimes than he had any business knowing. There was more to the man's decision to bring him to Basal than Danny had first known.

And if Pape knew more about his guilt, he might also know about Renee's. Concern swelled in his mind. He could not allow anything or anyone to compromise Renee.

"I was wrong."

"Yes, you were," the warden said. "And frankly, you're still that same man, willing to unleash your wrath. Which is why you are here. I intend to show you that much."

"By unleashing your own wrath on a boy like Peter? On the rest of us? We are both men trying to understand love and serve God."

"That's where you're wrong, Danny. In here, *I* am God. And you must be taught obedience, which begins with the understanding that you're still rotten to the core. My punishment will help you see that."

"By extending punishment, rather than grace?"

"Punishment wasn't my idea, it was your God's. I am only subjecting you to your own

God's way of correction." He cocked his head, brandishing a daring grin. "You think my punishment for not following the prescribed way is harsh? I'm an angel, Danny. Far too softhearted, really. As the holy book says, 'He that curseth his father or his mother shall surely be put to death.' Do you see me stoning twelve-year-old girls? I'm not so harsh as your Jesus, who, according to Christian doctrine, was the same God who made that law."

Pape's eyes flitted to the other tables. "And if there's one law that all of you should be eternally grateful I don't borrow from the priest's God, it's that anyone who shows contempt for a judge should be put to death. So you see, relatively speaking, I'm a merciful man filled with grace."

Danny held his tongue. Here then was the core of the dilemma that had haunted him for too many years. The great mystery that only elaborate theological arguments could attempt to unravel, finally acquiescing to blind belief.

"You've failed to make your case, Danny. The fact is, I think God was on to something. Punishment works. Everyone is guilty. And, clearly, as I've shown, his so-called free gift of grace isn't free at all. You now live in the big house where I am your God. How you do your time depends on how well you follow the rules. And those rules include not crying out in the middle of the night as Peter did. He did the crime and now he will do the time, it's simply the law. He should have known better."

Pape looked at the captain. "Take the boy down."

Bostich nodded at the facilitators, and two of them began to cross the room. Peter shifted behind Danny and grabbed his pant leg.

"Excuse me, sir, but I have one final request."

The warden held up his hand and stopped the guards.

"Oh?"

"If not for my need to learn your ways, you wouldn't have put Slane with the boy last night, and he wouldn't have been in a position to cry out. I was the one who objected. Send me down instead of the boy. I'm the one who stands to gain more from learning your ways."

The room could not have been more still. But by the look in the warden's eyes, Danny wondered if Pape had anticipated this, wanted this.

He was a master chess player, one step ahead at every turn.

"The boy paid his price last night," Danny said. "I haven't."

"The boy wasn't hurt."

"Not his body, but you've crushed his spirit."

The warden nodded. "The next time it'll be more than his spirit. But since you insist..." The warden nodded at Bostich. "Take the priest deep."

12

I SPENT TWO more hours with Keith before he ducked out to run some errands. I'd shown him my kit, and, unless I'd completely misread him, he was impressed. Not with what I had, but with my knowledge of knives and guns. Naturally, I felt obligated to show him how each should be used. Sure, I didn't look as natural as Danny or Keith, but, to use Keith's words, I would get the job done.

He asked why I thought I needed all of it. The gun, he understood. The knives, sure, although the Bowie was a behemoth in my hands. The pepper spray, even the handcuffs—who doesn't have a pair of handcuffs, right?

But the wire was a different matter. I told him it had come as part of a detective kit I'd ordered online. Truth be told, I don't know why I thought I needed a wire. It's not like I had any plans to run up behind a robber and strangle him until he dropped what was in his hands.

When I told Keith this, he smiled and shook his head. "No, but you'd be surprised how effective it can be in a tight spot. I'd say you take the folding knife, and the wire, nothing else."

"The wire?"

"You can't pack a gun, they'll just take it from you. If they search you, they may find the knife, but the wire, they'll never find. Not unless they strip search you."

"Hide it where?"

"Around your hips. Under your jeans. If everything else fails and you still have use of your arms, you get to it and you get it around their neck from behind. Then you hang on for your life."

Made sense. The knife went in my right pocket—I had to give them at least something to find.

The plan was simple: I would play the naïve damsel in distress, willing to do anything to save her man behind bars. Keith would approach from a side street and park his Ford Ranger in an alley one block away. If things went wrong, I would push the small reset button on a black wristwatch he'd given me. A page would be sent to his iPhone, which was tracking mine through its GPS. If things went terribly wrong, I had the wire and the knife.

I had a pair of short black leather Harley boots with inch-thick soles that I'd bought two years earlier, thinking they looked cute. After wearing them for a week whenever I went out, I decided they were too heavy and I hadn't worn them since. I also had a black leather Harley vest I'd bought with the boots. Over a cropped red tank top I looked quite the biker chick. A skinny one with a white belly.

The Rough Riders bar was located on the Pacific Coast Highway in Long Beach. It was a fairly typical bar from what I could tell by its website, trying hard to appear inviting to nonbikers without alienating bikers.

I parked my Toyota in the small parking lot on the north side of Rough Riders at 9:55 and called Keith.

"I'm here."

"Good. You're sure you're up for this?"

"Does it matter? My palms are slimy, what does that tell you?"

"It's not too late to—"

"Of course it is. We both know I don't have a choice."

He said nothing.

"I can handle myself, right? I've been in worse situations, believe me. Just be ready to bail me out."

"I'm right here, Renee. Anything happens, you page me."

"What if they take my watch?"

"We don't even know there will be a they. You just go straight to the phones and find whatever he's left for you. Then get out. I'll meet you at Brady's Diner as planned. That's all that's going to happen."

"What if they want me to do something crazy?"

"We've been over this. Anything illegal and you get to the bathroom and get me on the phone."

"What if they're listening to my phone right now?"

"Renee…"

"I know, too many what-ifs."

"We *don't* know. But this guy used a letter, not an e-mail, to deliver his demands. He doesn't strike me as a tech-head."

"That doesn't mean anything."

"I know. But it's a comforting thought. Just get in and get out. If I haven't heard from you in fifteen minutes, I'm coming in."

My questions were only my way of coping. We'd gone over all the details a dozen times already.

"Okay, I'm going."

"Renee..."

"Yeah?"

"Just don't do anything stupid."

"You think I'm stupid?"

"No. I think you're probably smarter than me. But the kind of people who would be connected to Randell are scum. Resist the temptation to set them straight. They also tend to have hair triggers."

"Okay. I gotta go now."

"Be careful."

"You're repeating yourself," I said, then disconnected.

It was 9:59 when I stepped up to the door

with the large red and blue neon sign that said Rough Riders. Seven bikes were parked out front, at least a few of them Harleys. The sidewalk was empty except for an older man with a cane who hobbled away with his back to me.

Okay, Renee…okay, just any biker chick in on a Thursday night, looking for her old man.

I pushed the door open to the sound of Guns N' Roses playing "Sweet Child of Mine" and stepped into the dimly lit establishment. The bar was to my left. Two bartenders served six or seven meaty guys and one woman seated on bar stools. A dozen tables with oak chairs sat on a well-worn wooden floor that ran up to a small dance floor. A railing separated the main bar from a brown-carpeted lounge that had two pool tables and a couple couches. The walls were lined with beer lights and biker paraphernalia.

All of this I saw at a glance.

That and the fact that the floor needed to be scrubbed and swept, that the poor lighting failed to hide stains on the walls from one too many thrown beer bottles, that a bad shampoo had failed to remove all the spill spots on the carpet. I was walking into bacteria heaven.

Two things I didn't immediately see: One was the public phone. It was probably by the bathrooms around the bar. The second was the people, because I hadn't come to meet the people, only get to the phone as quickly and quietly as possible.

But then my eyes took in the patrons and I found myself returning stares. Not one or two, but a dozen of the thirty or forty people in the bar, looking at the skinny white biker chick with the black leather vest who'd just entered their sacred realm. Ripe for the pickings.

From what I could see the room was seventy percent men, thirty percent women, half of them bikers, half wanting to be. Many of them had beards and even more had tattoos on their arms. They were mostly dressed the way you would expect biker chicks and dudes to dress, in jeans, T-shirts, and jackets or vests. A thin fellow with a silver chain looping from his pocket was slow-dancing with a girl who had a big bottom, but he was looking over her shoulder at me, not at her.

I avoided all their stares and walked along the bar, feeling their eyes on me. I headed to the left, where I saw the two prehistoric pay phones on the wall between the men's and women's bath-rooms. It was even darker in the hall than in the bar.

So far so good.

I didn't know what I was looking for, and my heart was beating like a jackhammer. There was no package on the ledge under the phones, no folders or envelopes on top of either, nothing but two phones long ago stripped of their phone books.

Relieved that the hallway was clear, I stepped up and frantically searched the first phone, ducking around it to get a better view of what might be under, above, or behind it. Nothing but years of crud. I grabbed the phone and tugged, half expecting it to tear free, but it didn't budge.

So I hopped over to the second phone and bobbed around again. This time I saw the small folded note tucked underneath the metal box, and my heart missed a beat.

"Can I help you?"

One of the bartenders, drying a glass, had stuck his head into the hall—a tall guy with curly hair and long sideburns. He weighed at least three of me.

"No thanks."

"You need change for the phone?"

"No. I was just going to the bathroom."

"Well that's a phone, honey, not a door opener. Bathroom's to your left."

"Not a door opener, huh?" Keith's warning not to help people see the errors of their ways whispered warning in my mind. I took the three steps to the bathroom door and turned back. He was still looking.

"I collect old phones," I said, offering him a dumb smile. "Someday they'll be worth a mint."

"Huh. Never thought about it that way."

I ducked into the bathroom and closed the door behind me. Took a few calming breaths. Okay, I had to look more natural, not like some junkie searching for loose change and making strange comments about collecting phones. But at least I'd found the note.

"Wow, those boots are adorable."

I jerked my head to the side. There was an open toilet stall facing me, and on the pot sat a woman. She was peeing. Her eyes were adoring my boots in a way that made me wonder if she wanted to confess a fetish.

"I always liked those kind of boots," she said. "You get them at the Harley shop?"

The place smelled like fake pine-tree spray and urine, and it occurred to me that with every sharp inhalation I was breathing in thousands, maybe millions, of bathroom bugs.

"I got them online," I said. "Same with the vest."

She said something about her birthday, but I was already halfway out the door, relieved to see that the bartender was gone. Using my thumb and finger, I pinch-plucked the note out from under the phone and unfolded it. The sheet was one of those tiny pages ripped out of a spiral-bound notebook. It was too dark to read the words, but I immediately recognized the handwriting.

Sicko.

I edged down the hall into better light and read the four words written in red ink.

Dance with the bear.

I turned the note over. Nothing. That was it.

Dance with the bear.

* * *

My mind raced, considering a retreat to the bathroom to think through the meaning of the instructions. But there was a woman who adored my boots peeing in there. Dance with the bear—what was the bear? Wasn't that Russia? Dance with a Russian bear? I imagined myself doing a Russian folk dance, but no, that couldn't be what Sicko wanted. He wanted me to steal a million dollars.

Was *bear* another term for prison? A judge? A powerful woman with a beard? Or was it a who? If so, the note would have said just bear. *Dance with Bear* with a capital B. Not *Dance with* the *bear* with a small B.

I had the note. I should go back out to the street and call Keith, who at least would have an opinion on what Sicko could possibly mean. If he wanted me to rob a bank, why didn't he just say that? But then I knew, didn't I? Sicko was more interested in unraveling Danny and me than in getting the million dollars. That was Randell's interest, not Sicko's.

I shoved the note into my left jeans pocket and made a beeline for the main room. Head down, eager to get out and breathe some fresh air, I passed by the patrons seated at the bar. But halfway to the door I glanced up. In that single glimpse, I saw the four men gathered around the table closest to the dance floor. They all had tattoos and beards. Three of them wore vests with patches. Two of them were staring at me.

One of them wore a black T-shirt with the words Don't Screw with the Bear written above an image of a roaring bear head.

The man's eyes held mine and he winked.

I made it to the street in five seconds flat and had Keith on the phone in another five.

"You good?"

"No, not really. He says 'dance with the bear.'"

Keith paused. "The note said 'dance with a bear'?"

My hands were shaking. "There's a man in there with a T-shirt that says Don't Screw with the Bear."

"And the note just reads 'dance with the bear'?"

"The man winked at me."

"He winked?"

"Sicko wants me to dance with the fat,

bearded man in the T-shirt. The bear-man is working with him."

"Hold on, we don't know that. You sure there was nothing else on the note?"

I turned and looked back at the red and blue neon Rough Riders sign. "He wants me to dance with the bear. It's the man with the shirt."

"Maybe, but we have to be certain."

"He winked at me, Keith! What else do you need?"

I could hear Keith's silence and it only reinforced my conviction.

"If I don't—"

"It's a test," Keith interrupted.

I headed back, walking on feet that seemed to move on their own now. The letter in my apartment claimed I would find my next test at the phone in the Rough Riders. I had found that test. It was to dance with the bear. The man in the T-shirt was that bear. If I was wrong, I would find out soon enough, but if the man *was* the bear and I didn't dance with him, Sicko would make Danny pay.

"I have to find out," I said.

"You're going to dance with him?"

"I have to. Right?"

A beat.

"Just don't get yourself in any trouble, Renee. Don't do anything rash. Stay calm."

"I have to go."

"Call me as soon as you get out. Please, just be careful."

"I'm a very careful person, Keith. You'll get to know that about me." I hung up the phone, shoved it into my pocket, and turned into the Rough Riders bar.

For the second time in ten minutes the skinny white girl with the black leather vest and the heavy but adorable Harley boots stepped into the realm of bikers and wannabe bikers. But this time she did not stop at the entrance and take note of how dirty the place was.

This time she walked straight toward the table with the four men closest to the dance floor and looked directly into the eyes of the man wearing the Don't Screw with the Bear T-shirt.

I was halfway to the table, determined to deal with the bearded man, when another man stepped away from the bar and looked down at me with smiling brown eyes.

"How 'bout I buy you a drink?"

I almost pushed past him but then thought better of it. He looked like a regular here, sidled up to the bar as he'd been, and it occurred to me that he might be able to help me.

"A drink?"

"Sure. Just a friendly drink. You look like you could use one, darling."

"Well, I guess that depends."

"It does, does it? Depends on what? 'Cause I'd hate to see a pretty girl like you lost in a bar like this. Are you all right?"

"Of course I am. Do you know Bear?"

He cocked his head. "Bear? Can't say that I do."

"That man behind you in the bear T-shirt. You don't know him?"

He threw a glance over his shoulder, saw that the man in the bear T-shirt was staring at us, and offered a curt nod. "Yup. That's Bill." He turned back to me. "Why, you know him?"

"Should I?"

A knowing smile slowly formed on his face. "Well that depends if you like three hundred pounds of man smothering you."

"You ever see him wear that shirt before?"

He looked again and shook his head. "Nope.

Can't say that I have. You want him? Because I think he could be persuaded."

"That depends."

Without waiting for me to lead the conversation any further, the man turned and called out, "Hey, Bill, I think the pretty girl here likes you."

The cacophony of background voices faded, leaving the sounds of AC/DC blaring alone.

"Well, heck, send her over," Bear roared. "Come on over here, sugar."

That was one way to approach Sicko's test. I was now fully committed, and I let my impetuous nature lead me on. With only a moment's hesitation, I stepped past the man who'd offered to buy me a drink and walked up to the table where Bear and his three friends sat, wearing impish grins. They needed baths, all of them. And, hairy as they were, they should have at least had the decency to trim the hair poking out of their ears.

"Are you Bear?" I asked.

The man scooted his chair back and patted a thigh as thick as an oak trunk. "Come to papa, sugar."

Now, I could have told him where to shove

his sugar, but I refused to let my disgust distract me from what I'd come to do.

"Actually, I'd rather dance," I said.

That earned a chuckle from the man to his right, a thin fellow who looked half Bear's age. "That's right, Bear. She wants to dance for us. Honey, you can dance for me anytime you like."

"Shut up, Steve. Don't you listen to him, sugar." He paused, eyeing me with round, bloodshot eyes, then spoke in a lower voice. "How much you charging?"

Heat washed over my face and it took all of my focus not to kick him in his shin and leave. But that didn't stop me from helping him understand that I wasn't a prostitute and that I hadn't offered him a lap dance.

"On the floor, you buffoon." What if he wasn't the right man? "A friend told me I should dance with a man called Bear. Either you're that man, in which case I would like to dance with you, or you're not, and I can leave you to your beer."

His smile softened, but he didn't immediately acknowledge that he was in fact the bear. My patience was all but gone. I'd gotten the note

and followed what I thought were the instructions. Either there was a bear in the bar or there
wasn't. I looked up and saw the whole room
was now watching our exchange.

"Is anyone else here called the bear?"

They all just stared at me, some grinning,
either pleased with my show of chutzpah or
embarrassed for me.

"No? No one?"

Not a soul spoke up.

I turned back to the hairy man. "That leaves
you. Now either you want to dance with me or
you don't. Your call."

He nodded, tongue poking against the inside
of his cheek. "Sure, sugar—"

"Can you please not call me that?"

Beside him, Steve stifled a laugh.

"You wanna dance, then let's dance." Bear
started to push himself up, and seeing his lum-
bering form rise, I felt a sudden urgency to
know without a doubt that this thug really was
working with Sicko.

"You sure you're the bear?"

"I am for you, sweet cakes."

"Don't call me that either," I said.

He loomed over me, belly out like the nose of

a submarine, and gave me half a bow. "If it'll get me a dance." To one of the men behind the bar, "Give us something romantic, Harry. Foreigner or something."

"You sure you're Bear?" I asked again, needing to be sure.

"Don't worry, sugar, you've found your man."

The music stopped midsong and then started with the intro to "I Want to Know What Love Is." Satisfied, he pulled his oversized jeans up by the belt and walked out onto the dance floor. Spreading his legs, he waved his arms like a belly dancer and began gyrating his hips.

Hoots and whistles filled the bar. "Swing those hips, Big Bear. That's right, show her what you got, Bill."

I stood like a fence post, suddenly terrified by what I had gotten myself into. But this was exactly what Sicko wanted. He was testing me, leading me down a path to see if I would break. Dancing with Bear was the least of my concerns.

I walked out to Bear and stood three feet from him as he moved to the music. My jack-knife was in my pocket. I could have it out in two seconds if he started slobbering in my ear. The wire was under my jeans, but I couldn't see jumping on his back and strangling him out here on the dance floor. But I was over-thinking the situation. He only wanted to dance.

"Come on, sugar, dance with the Bear. Show me what you got."

I was tempted to slap him, but I didn't. Instead, I began to shift my weight to the beat of the music as the chorus swelled.

"That's it, baby. Ooo, yeah. Show me what you got."

"Shut up," I said, loud enough for only him to hear over the music.

He moved closer and reached for my hand. "Move that skinny little butt like you want it, baby."

That was it. I stopped. "Okay. I've danced with you, now what?"

"You call that a dance? I don't think so. You show me what you have or you don't get what I have."

"So you do have something for me?"

"Maybe. But you're going to have to dance with me, sugar. And I do mean dance."

"Is *sugar* the only word you know for 'woman'?"

He winked. "Melts in your mouth and in your hands."

I couldn't help thinking it would be pretty easy to poke him in one of those big eyeballs of his. But that wasn't what Sicko had in mind, so I reluctantly let him take my hand and went through a few motions with his bulbous belly pressed against me.

Slow now. "That's it. That's the way you dance with the papa bear." He pulled me closer and whispered into my ear. "I have what you want but not out here. Follow me after the song."

He pulled back, lifted both hands above his head, and swayed to the music. More whistles and catcalls. I could barely hear the music over the surge of encouragement. But I now knew I'd found the right man, and I played my part, offering a forced smile for the benefit of the on-lookers.

The song began to wind down and Bear took my hand. "Come with me, darling." He led me toward the hall and the bar began to settle behind us, punctuated with a holler from Steve: "Bill's gonna get himself some."

I assumed Bear was simply leading me into the hall so that he could give me whatever he'd been paid to give me. But I was wrong.

He waddled down the hall and entered the women's bathroom. Left with no clear option, I followed him in. The woman who'd occupied the stall earlier was gone. I was alone with the hairy and now sweaty bear, and with the smells of a badly cleaned bathroom.

"I got what you want, sugar," Bear said, eyeing me as if I were a piece of candy. "But it's not going to be that easy."

He was making no attempt to hide his interest and my thoughts flashed to the knife in my pocket. Then to the wire around my waist. But if I pulled either out now, he would only pull out whatever hidden weapon he had, and I would either leave empty-handed or not at all.

He drew one hand through his beard. "How about a little kiss. Hmm?"

"How about you give me what you were paid to give me. I danced with you, didn't I?"

"Oh, yeah you sure did. But that wasn't the deal."

"Well that was *my* deal, so please, just give me whatever you have for me and no one gets hurt."

Bear chuckled. "Is that what you think you're going to do to me? Hmm? You gonna hurt me?"

He shouldn't have said that. He couldn't have known it, but he'd put me in a whole new frame of mind, no longer as concerned with what weapon he might have hidden in his pocket.

But he'd also opened a door for me, hadn't he? Bear was a pervert, and there's more than one way to deal with a pervert. Summoning my full reserve of control, I forced my mind off the knife in my pocket and offered him a thin yet seductive smile.

"Is that what you want?" My stomach turned. I placed a hand on his chest, then gave him a gentle shove.

"And how do I know you have what I'm looking for?" I asked in the same tone. I closed the space, leaving only six inches between us. "How do I know you're not just an imposter trying to step in on another man's fun?"

"Because I have it," he said.

"Have what?"

"The note."

"Show me."

He hesitated. Then reached for his jeans without removing his eyes from mine. Wearing a coy smile, he slowly pulled the leading edge of a folded note out of his pocket. "See? It's right here."

I smiled and slowly slipped my hand up his thigh toward the note while I leaned in and gazed into his eyes. Every nerve in my body was on fire, but not in the way he hoped.

"Good," I purred. And then I closed my fingers around the note and brought my knee up into his groin with enough force to break a watermelon in half.

He gasped and I let my rage get the better of me. I slapped him across his face. Hard.

"Shame on you!"

Bear roared in pain, more from my knee than from my slap, I guessed, but I didn't hang around for clarity. With the note firmly in my left hand, I flew to the door, ducked out, took one deep breath, and headed back out to the bar.

I have no idea what the patrons thought I'd accomplished in such a short time alone with Bear, but a few of them whistled and called out their congratulations. I simply smiled courteously and walked past them all without a backward glance.

The moment the door swung closed behind me, I was running for my car. I can't lie, I felt a strange euphoria—the kind you might feel after narrowly escaping a rushing rhino. What was more, I'd maybe helped Bear gain a new appreciation for women, especially those who were a third his size. For a moment there, I came close to whooping and pumping a fist above my head. I had the note. I was alive. Danny was safe.

Victory.

But a few other words quickly pushed the thought of victory from my mind.

I'm serious as the devil in hell.

I turned into the parking lot and pulled up, breathing hard. This was just the beginning, wasn't it? And Danny...My heart broke thinking about him. Danny had no clue. If he knew, he would carve Sicko up into small chunks and throw his body parts into the ocean.

In that moment, standing alone ten yards from my Toyota, I wanted Danny to do just that. I wanted it with all of my heart.

13

DEEP MEDITATION.

Prisons were not simply constructed at the whim of one man, but subject to committees' reviews for approval, always under the scrutiny and guidelines established by the Corrections Standards Authority.

In the Basal case, Warden Marshall Pape had been involved prior to the prison's construction, but he answered to a director in the Division of Adult Institutions. Who in turn answered to the chief deputy secretary of Adult Operations, who answered to the man at the top: the secretary of the California Department of Corrections and Rehabilitation, appointed by the governor of California to his cabinet.

The entire system was closely watched by the Office of the Inspector General, the equivalent of an internal-affairs watchdog. Scrutiny, more scrutiny, and even more scrutiny.

The question that first presented itself to Danny when he was led into the bowels of the prison was how the section Bostich called deep meditation could have possibly been constructed under so much scrutiny.

The answer was plain: it couldn't have. The room had initially served some other purpose, only to be modified after the prison was opened. And it was likely done so with the knowledge of the director in the Division of Adult Institutions, perhaps also with the agreement of someone in the inspector general's office. Surely nothing short of such cooperation would have allowed the warden to create, much less operate, deep meditation with impunity.

The man might be a tyrant, but he wasn't stupid. Rigorous control of the staff, the inmates, and the flow of information in and out of the prison was critical.

The captain and a CO named Mitchell Young had placed a spit hood over Danny's head— typically used to keep prisoners from spitting on corrections officers, as the name implied—then cuffed his wrists, chained his ankles, tied both into a strap around his waist, and led him from the administrative holding room to a flight of stairs. Where the flight of stairs was, he didn't know, because they walked some distance before descending.

It was steep, like the stairwell that led to the meditation wing where he'd spent his first few days. It led to a second door, which creaked on its hinges and opened to a much cooler room.

They took two right-angle turns, then stopped. Bostich demanded he stand still, then proceeded to open an entrance that required a full minute and included scraping and pounding not associated with the simple opening and closing of locked gates or doors.

"Hold still."

It took only a moment for them to cut through his clothing, strip him bare, and remove his shoes.

They led Danny through the entrance into an even colder space before suggesting he watch his step because they were going down. The leg irons allowed him just enough movement to negotiate the concrete steps. Only when they passed through yet one more door, which they closed behind them, did Bostich remove Danny's hood.

A single caged bulb shed very dim light on the room. The bare concrete space was perhaps fifteen feet to a side and may have once been used for storage or as a cistern. A single wooden table that held a small crate sat against the wall to his right. He could see no doors, but the back wall was nearly obscured by darkness.

"What's a matter, you were expecting worse?"

Danny blinked, allowing his eyes to adjust to the darkness.

"I asked you a question."

"I didn't have any expectation," Danny said.

The red-faced man wore a sneer. "You will. We reserve deep meditation for the worst of the worst, and you're about to learn why. There's two ways to do this. We can either knock you out, or you can go willingly. Either way, you're going. Clear?"

Going to where, Danny had no idea.

"Yes."

But then the restraints on the back wall emerged from the shadows and he did know. They were going to strap him up on the wall.

The captain saw his stare and smiled. "They never see it when they first come in. It's a pain getting you up there when you're out cold, but it's your choice."

"I'll go willingly," Danny said.

"We'll see. One wrong move and you get a Taser in the neck, you hear? I'm gonna take off your restraints, but Mitchell's quick on the trigger. Keep that in mind. No sudden moves."

Danny nodded. He had no intention of showing any aggression. It would only prove pointless.

"Walk to the wall and turn around."

Danny shuffled forward, eyeing eight eyehooks set in slats that could be adjusted to fit varying body sizes. He turned around a couple feet from the stained concrete wall. The CO named Mitchell, a rail-thin man with a long face that held too-big eyes, stood with his legs spread and Taser ready, as if he was facing off with a bear.

"Don't move," he snapped.

Bostich approached, holding a single strap in his left hand. He reached behind Danny, tied the restraint at his waist off to an inset eyehook, and cinched him tight against the wall. He released the irons on Danny's wrists and ankles before stepping back.

"Sit tight."

The man retreated to the crate on the table and withdrew a fistful of cables with leather cuffs. In less than two minutes each of Danny's wrists, knees and ankles were snugged firmly in padded, three-inch leather restraints. Each of these six cuffs were then hooked into cables that latched into the sliding eyehooks on the wall.

Working now in silence but for their heavy breathing, Bostich and Mitchell pulled first his arms, then his feet, then his knees wide into a spread eagle on the wall. They returned to the arm cables one at a time and stretched him wider. They repeated the same exercise on his legs, pulling them up off the ground and away from each other.

Danny said nothing. All of his attention was on pressure in his joints and tendons. He was a strong man, but Bostich seemed determined to mitigate any advantage Danny might have.

As of yet, he felt no pain, but he knew that would soon change.

When they were done, the facilitators stepped back and studied their handiwork.

"Good enough?" Mitchell said.

Bostich smiled. "Oh, yeah. Two things you should know," he said to Danny. "One, you're in here for forty-eight hours. Don't you worry, we'll check on you and give you water. You're going to need it. Two, this is just for fun. Every second you're on that wall, you remember one thing: it can get worse. Much worse."

Danny just stared at the man.

Evidently satisfied, they turned their backs on him, turned off the light, exited the room, and shut the door. The *thud* reminded Danny of a heavy crypt being sealed, and hanging on the wall in the pitch darkness, he couldn't escape the subject of his own mortality.

Already his arms and legs, with which he supported most of his weight, began to tire.

The only thing he could see was inky darkness. The only thing he could hear was his own breathing. The only things he could feel were the stretching of his muscles and his naked skin, which had already started to shiver as a means of generating body heat to ward off the cold.

But these weren't the most unnerving to him. The fact that he was even *in* such a predicament reserved that place in his mind.

And the fact that such a place even existed in a free country that despised abuse. The fact that word of this room would bring a thousand human-rights advocates and their fully armed attorneys running. The fact that no human being deserved this kind of treatment, much less a simpleminded boy like Peter.

And yet here Danny was, strapped to a wall in Basal's bowels. If the warden inflicted such punishment on the members, it was only because he could. How, Danny wasn't entirely sure, but his adversary was far more organized than even Danny had imagined.

No one of Pape's intelligence would dare open the doors to this place without taking every precaution to mitigate fallout that might threaten either him or his precious sanctuary. Any objection from any member subjected to such treatment would likely bear terrible consequences or death, the threat of which would follow them into their old age.

Corrections and rehabilitation at its finest, a shining example for the rest of the world. California's prison system was being fixed by someone who thought himself far wiser than the politicians who ran society, all to one end: the salvation of that society.

Punishment and reward, as it had been demonstrated throughout history. Basal: heaven and hell in one building.

The first half hour was quite tolerable. The next was less, forcing him to use more of the muscles in his arms and shoulders to take the weight off his burning calves and quads. During the second hour, his strength began to fail. His weight shifted from his muscles to his tendons and joints, which increased his pain.

And then Danny began to lose his sense of time, because every minute seemed to stretch far beyond its capacity. It was cold but he was sweating. His muscles were toned and strong, but he was trembling like a frail reed. His intelligence and stoic reasoning had served him through the worst of human experiences, but now they began to fade.

Danny shut down his pain to the best of his ability and hung on the wall, naked, stripped of all thoughts but the worst of all.

What were they doing to Renee?

14

BRADEY'S DINER WAS a hole in the
wall three blocks from the biker bar, nearly
empty when Keith and I got there at ten fifteen
that night. We sat in an isolated corner booth
with two cups of coffee, having assured a waitress in an orange dress that we wanted nothing
else. Nothing at all.

"You kneed him in the groin?" Keith asked.
"You couldn't have just grabbed the note and
run?"

"And risk him coming after me?"

"Not likely in a place like that. Besides, you
did what was asked. The man's job was done.
He'd have no reason to come after you."

"He was a pervert."

Keith couldn't quite suppress his grin. "You really can handle yourself, can't you?"

I shrugged. "I suppose, if I have to."

"Just keep in mind that we aren't in this to teach perverts a lesson. We do what we need to do and nothing more that might draw attention to ourselves. That includes physically assaulting a pervert. We have more immediate concerns, right?"

"Right."

"Although I can't say I blame you. Let me see it."

I checked the restaurant, saw that the waitress was clear across the joint gabbing with a cook, and pulled out the bear's note. It was on lined yellow paper, same as the first note, folded over eight times.

Keith opened it carefully and smoothed it out on the blue Formica table. We sat side by side, staring at Sicko's third message:

Good girl.

Nausea swept through my gut. The idea of being anybody's good girl jerked me back to the days when I had stooped far too low to please others and suffered abuse at their hands. For a moment I lingered on those two words, terrified that I was being drawn back into a similar place.

It had started with Cyrus Kauffman, who pulled me into the world of drugs and tried to kill me when I refused to prostitute myself to make good on a debt. Danny had saved me from that, but what if Sicko was about to resurrect my old self?

We all have memories of darker days pushed back into the corners of our minds, but mine were sucked up to the surface with those two words. *Good girl.*

Keith slid his hand over the note. "You okay?"

I nodded.

He put his hand on mine. "Look, sometimes things look bad, but we get through them. The truth is, you're a free person. You could probably fold up shop and go on the run now...never look back. It would probably be your safest course of action. Frankly, half of me thinks that's just what you should do."

"Then you don't know me."

"Actually, I'm getting to know you better. That's what I'm saying. You could do it, but you won't because you love a man that society has all but thrown away."

A knot gathered in my throat. I nodded.

"So you're doing this for love. Me, I'm sitting here for far less noble reasons. Self-preservation. The fact is, my own past is catching up to me."

"By making an enemy in Randell." I looked across the diner again. We were alone now except for one old couple on the far side.

He nodded. "But I did the right thing. I put him behind bars for the right reason, and now it's coming back on me. You try to do the right thing and sometimes you pay a price."

"You could walk away."

Keith lifted his hand from mine. "I've been telling myself that all afternoon, but the truth is, I can't any more than you can. If Randell's working with someone who can do this to you, they can do it me. *Are* doing it to me. This goes deeper than either of us can guess. They could probably find a way to reach out and crush me anytime they wanted. We're in this together, period. Okay?"

He was trying to ease my mind, and after my little episode with Bear, I needed him to.

"Okay. You should know that what Danny did, he did with a noble heart. He hurt some people, but only those who deserved it. No different from what you did."

"Maybe."

"No, not maybe. He confessed and now he's paying a price. But to be honest, I love him even more for it."

"Then remember that. You're doing this for him. The truth is, no one else can help him now."

I dipped my head, pinched the edge of the yellow paper, and slid it out from under Keith's hand. Sicko's note stared up at me.

Good girl.

There's an old warehouse at the end of Sherman Road, Morongo Valley. You will be there Saturday night at eight o'clock. I'm watching. If you go to the police, I will know. If you go to the prison, I will know. If you deviate in even one detail, I will know.

Do what you're told, Renee. The priest is suffering but he's alive. Don't make me kill him. Set him free.

There was no salutation, no name. Only the blatant assurance that whoever had written the note had all of the strings in his fingers and was eager to pull the ones that would end Danny's life.

Keith turned the note over, then flipped it back. "That's it."

"Saturday? We're supposed to just sit around for two days?"

"Keep it down."

"I danced with that pervert for this? Why didn't he just say this in his first note?"

"Because that's the way it works. He playing with our minds, knowing that you would react exactly the way you are. So don't."

"We can't just do nothing! Something's not right."

"Nothing's right! That's the whole point."

"We've got to find out what's happening to Danny. I can't just sit on my hands for two days."

"Slow down. That's exactly what he'll expect."

"What?"

"You doing something crazy. Going to the cops. Finding an attorney. Trying to contact the warden—anything and everything he's said not to. If we do that this guy's going to carry through."

"So, what? We're just his puppets now?"

"No." Seeing the waitress headed their way, Keith folded the note and slipped it into his pocket. "Hold on."

The smiling server with stringy mud-blonde hair held out the pot. "Need a freshen-up?" She smiled wide, bearing front teeth that should have been put in braces when she was younger.

"No, thank you," Keith said.

She faced me. "How about you?"

"Nope." I sounded snappy, I know, but I was at the end of myself. It struck me as her face fell at my retort that Keith was right. This was exactly what Sicko wanted. But could I help it? I didn't think so.

In fact, if it were only me I'd probably run into the bathroom, lock the stall, and have a good cry.

"No, thank you," I said, as she walked away. She flashed a faint smile over her shoulder.

"Sorry."

"No, it's fine. I'm not suggesting we do nothing."

"Then what?"

"We have two days to think. To research. To try to figure something out. Then we go do what he says. Other than that, we go dark."

"Dark."

"He's watching. We don't react the way he expects us to. In fact, we do the opposite. We don't break his protocol, but we don't panic."

I understood immediately. "Play his game."

"Play his game. Try to shake him."

"Make him second-guess us."

"That's right. We go about our lives as if nothing's happened. We get a beer, we shop, we go to work…do you work?"

"No. And my routine is pretty simple."

"Fine. We assume he's listening to our phone calls, so we don't talk on the phone. Only outside, in a park, on the beach, out of earshot. But we don't act concerned or panicked."

"Seems like a pretty weak play."

"It's a start. It'll at least make him wonder. More importantly, it gives us some control—and trust me, honey, we need some."

I took a sip of coffee, black, the only way I can force the stuff down. One cup and I'd be up all night, but I doubted I'd do much sleeping anyway. The next forty-eight hours were going to be screaming torture—Sicko's whole point. Still, the thought of doing nothing without knowing what was going on with Danny was going to double me in half. I'd have to visit my therapist.

"Okay."

"Trust me, it will drive him nuts. Take consolation in that."

"Nuts," I said, nodding. "We'll drive him nuts."

"Bananas."

"Bananas."

But all I wanted to do at that point was find Sicko and shove a gun down his throat.

15

SATURDAY

TWO DAYS COULD be a lifetime: this is what Danny already knew but learned once more as he hung from the wall in the bowels of Basal. The human body was an incredibly durable vessel: this is what he had learned too many times in Bosnia and never wanted to learn again.

When the body was subjected to an overload of pain, it tended to spare the mind prolonged duress by shutting down. Unconscious, it does not shiver uncontrollably or feel pain or scream. Danny was comforted only by the thought that he'd likely spent at least half of his time in that oblivious state before his body rebooted in darkness and flared with agony.

Conscious, he also had to live with his thoughts and his emotions, which flogged him just as relentlessly. Strapped to the wall, he was acutely aware that his thoughts and emotions, though only temporal things, could affect as much pain in him as harm to the body could. Through the years he had willed himself to live in simple consciousness, stripped of the thoughts and emotions that dragged him into suffering. The brief periods of time in which he succeeded filled him with peace and clarity.

He'd often wondered if such a place of clarity was the closest thing to heaven to be found on earth. Finding it this time proved more difficult than before because of his incessant fear for Renee's safety and his empathy for Peter's circumstance.

Some advocated surrender as the path to peace, but Danny had always known that his mind was too strong to surrender to anything. Instead he controlled it with raw determination and willpower, a process that sometimes worked better than others.

He'd once been taken captive by the Serbian Christians in Bosnia and, because he was suspected of numerous infiltrations into their strongholds, was questioned over a two-week period before he managed to escape. Their interrogation methods had become increasingly forceful. It was the first time he'd been forced to endure tremendous amounts of carefully directed pain.

Marshall Pape's version of hell did not match that torture, but the pain of deep meditation was severe enough that a boy like Peter would likely never survive a second encounter.

And wasn't that the purpose of the warden's sanctuary? To scare the wayward straight by subjecting them to the threat of extreme punishment?

Doing his best to ignore the pain in his nerves, his thoughts, and the torment inflicted by his emotion, Danny sought the stillness beyond, peering into the darkness, searching for awareness of God's love and beauty in his own spirit. It wasn't easy to find.

Bostich did not come with water as promised. No one did. No one came at all. The promise of water was only a hope deferred to make the heart sick, one little twist of the knife to increase his suffering. Without any food or water, his body might have shut down completely had they not come for him after forty-eight hours.

When Bostich and Mitchell did come, they came with a hose, which they used to wash him down while he still hung on the wall. He sucked in as much of the water as he could.

They finally released him from his restraints, a process that heaped pain upon pain, then stood back as he collapsed in a heap.

"Get yourself together. We'll be back."

Bostich left a neat pile of folded clothes on the table and left Danny to recover, this time with the light on. It took him an hour to get to his feet, work out enough of the aches in his joints to dress, and compose himself.

"I'd like to see the warden," he said when they returned.

"Well, you're in luck, 'cause he wants to see you too."

Several minutes later, Danny sat in the same chair he'd first used outside the warden's office, waiting for an audience. The clock on the wall read 7:26. Saturday evening, if he guessed correctly. He'd been at Basal for a mere six days that overshadowed his entire three years at Ironwood.

And yet he wasn't disheartened. His resolve had not been compromised. He was only glad that he and not Peter had endured deep meditation.

As for his own reward, he expected to be presented with an opportunity to determine what the warden might or might not know about Renee. If his suspicions were confirmed, Danny would set his mind on discovering a way to warn her. Confined as he was by both prison and his resolution never to resort to violence, his options would be limited, but there were always options.

There had to be; Renee was all that mattered to him now. Renee and, to a lesser extent, Peter, the boy who was as innocent as she herself once had been—Renee and Peter and those trampled underfoot by society's failures.

And yet his determination to defend the weak had proven pointless once before. No man had the right to exercise ultimate judgment over another man, certainly not the way Danny had.

He could not save Peter by killing Pape.

Nor could he sit by while Peter suffered.

Two compulsions in conflict. The disparity threatened to fracture his mind. Something was askew in his worldview.

The warden's door swung open and Pape's familiar form emerged, smiling. "There you are. All cleaned up and ready to join a more reasonable world, I trust."

Danny got to his feet slowly. The pain in his joints had already begun to fade, but he knew it would return with a vengeance after a night's sleep.

"Need some help?"

"No thank you. I'll manage."

The notion that he was more pathetic than noble whispered through his mind. What kind of weakness would prompt a man to say "No, thank you" to a man like Pape in a moment like this?

"Please come in."

Danny entered the office and sat. The warden picked up a black pen and tapped it on a form before him. For a few long moments he watched Danny, expressionless.

"You're a strong man, I'll give you that. Unfortunately, it only means I have to work harder to get through to you. It's only my job, you must realize that."

Danny was here for Renee's sake, not his own, so he kept his mouth shut.

"I'm sure you feel that my methods are extreme. That's understandable. But as I pointed out in the dining hall, they are no more extreme than other methods condoned by your God."

After another moment of silence the warden continued.

"Although I admire your mental strength, I need you to respond so that I can determine your progress. Is that fair?"

The man seemed more gentle somehow. Amenable even.

"I'll do my best."

"Good. Then you *do* understand that harsher methods than mine were at one time condoned, even embraced, by good people."

"I can see how you draw that conclusion, yes."

"But you disagree with them..."

"It's not my place to judge your treatment of me. I accept that I'm your prisoner."

"I'm not referring to my treatment of you. I was thinking more of the others."

"Meaning whom?"

"Meaning Peter, for example."

"We both know that Peter's innocent."

"Must we really go through this again? Innocent of what? Rape? And is rape more or less deviant than other expressions of deviant behavior? Everyone is guilty of some infraction of the law, Danny. Everyone breaks the law. It's my job to correct those deviants, once and for all. Murderers, for example."

The warden studied him with knowing eyes.

"You know about murder, don't you?" He tapped his pen on the surface of the desk. "Why did you kill them, Danny?"

"Kill who?"

"Please, I know you killed more than the two men you confessed to as a part of your plea bargain. The question is, why? There's no clear motivation cited."

"I was foolish enough to think I could change the world."

"By what? Setting a few of the wayward straight?"

"As I said—"

"Then we're the same, aren't we? You see people in need and you rush to their defense. I

273

see society in need and I rush to its defense. In a way I admire you for attempting to do outside the law what society has failed to do within that law. Isn't that why you killed?"

"A few years ago, I would have agreed."

"But not now?"

"No."

The man watched him for a long moment, then stood and approached the family portraits on the wall, hands behind his back.

"Maybe it would help if you understood my own motivation." He nodded at the picture of himself with his wife, his daughter, and his son. The daughter was perhaps fifteen, a younger reflection of her mother apart from her hair, which was straighter than the wife's fluffy curls. Both had bright blue eyes, the same sharp nose, rosy cheeks, and small mouths. Both were beautiful and wore red dresses.

The son looked more like his mother than the warden as well. He wore a crew cut and was perhaps two years younger than his sister.

Pape pointed to his daughter. "This is Emily. She was fourteen when this picture was taken. Nate, my son, was eleven. Everyone says they both look like my wife, Betty. Wouldn't you agree?"

"Very similar, yes."

The warden glowed with pride. Nothing about his pleasure seemed remotely disingenuous. Reconciling Marshall Pape the warden with Marshall Pape the loving father might prove difficult for many, but Danny had seen a thousand hardened soldiers in Bosnia who fought out of love of their families, he being chief among them.

Marshall Pape was first of all a human being, in the same way that the inmates under his thumb were. Really, none of them was a monster. They were all just trying to make sense of their world in this subculture called prison.

"They're now six years older," Pape said. "Emily's studying medicine at UCLA, Nate's the starting quarterback on his high school football team, quite a player at only seventeen." He faced Danny, still smiling. "Perhaps one day you'll father a child, Danny. I can assure you, there's nothing more rewarding than watching a child grow through the years. Nothing."

There was a heaviness in the warden's voice that forecasted the frown that slowly overtook his face. He looked at the photograph again.

"But who am I kidding? Those are only my

dreams. Unfortunately, I'll never see Nate or Emily grow up. In truth, this is the last picture taken of them before they were killed. Ten days after we sat for this photograph, actually."

Danny recoiled at the revelation.

Marshall Pape faced him. "They were both at a convenience store in Santa Monica when a paroled felon named Jake Williams came in with only drugs and money on his mind. The store owner had a gun, and in the ensuing face-off, Nate was killed by the felon. Emily was accidently hit in the head by a bullet from the storekeeper's handgun. They both died at the scene."

The warden had suddenly and dramatically become a victim along with his children. Danny could not ignore his empathy for the man.

"I'm sorry. I can't imagine how you must have felt."

"The store owner received a two-year sentence for involuntary manslaughter. The felon was killed. My wife suffered a mental breakdown and left me a year later. She still blames my son's and daughter's deaths on me. Do you know why?"

"Because you are a warden, responsible for keeping people like Jake behind bars."

Pape forced a smile. "Very good. It's a stretch, don't you think? But she had a point, Danny." He held up two fingers. "Jake Williams had *two* previous convictions for robbery. He did his time in one of those monster factories only to be paroled, unchanged at his core. So you see, the system failed my son, and weak gun laws failed my daughter." His eyes were glassy, misted with tears. "Now both are dead."

"I am so sorry, sir. I'm truly terribly sorry."

"I lost my children, I lost my wife. I also lost my sister, Celine, who was murdered before all of this," Pape continued. "I knew then that God was sending me a message, and I took an oath. Never again would I oversee deviants without helping them accept their failure in the very core of their being. Never again would a single soul under my supervision rejoin society without first being completely changed from the inside out. Three years later, I became the first warden of Basal."

This was Marshall Pape's religion, to help deviants become new men, transformed by the renewing of their minds, a noble pursuit to say the least. He was just going about it wrong.

"I can understand your ambition," Danny said.

"Yes, I suppose you could. Is that why you killed? To help men see the light?"

"Yes." And then he said something he was sure the warden couldn't know. "My mother and my two sisters were raped and killed in Bosnia."

The warden's eyes held on him, wide. "Then you do understand."

"God's love and grace are the path to healing. Not condemnation or punishment."

"Then your world is full of naïve idealism," Pape said. "Grace is only a word that masks a new kind of law. Like I told you before, true grace doesn't even exist. He who offers it still demands adherence to some kind of behavior. A new law. There is no free ride. And breaking the law always comes at a cost. There must remain the very real threat of punishment and torture. I'm surprised you don't seem to understand that, being a priest."

Danny remained silent. The warden's argument, however uniquely put, represented the conundrum that faced all religions and institutions that sought to modify behavior for greater good. From Pape's perspective, Basal made perfect sense.

"In the end the quality of life is always about some kind of law. You would think I'd be agreeable to a man gunning down the murderer of my son and daughter before he had the chance to kill them, wouldn't you?" the warden said.

They were on dangerous ground; Pape was describing Danny.

"But you would be wrong," Pape continued. "That would be illegal. The law is in place as it stands for good reason, tested by centuries of trial and error. I lost my family because both a well-meaning man and a felon deviated from the law. The law, my friend. No one must break the law. Ever. Everything I do at Basal is geared toward this one end. You may not like my ways, but I do it for the millions of Nates and Emilys who only want to go to the convenience store for an ice-cream sandwich. I am their protector."

He returned to his chair, eased himself down, and sighed. "But you, Danny, you would break the law to save an innocent boy like my son, wouldn't you?"

Danny hesitated, careful not to take the warden's bait.

"No? You wouldn't kill a man to save an innocent boy? How about someone like Peter?"

"No."

"So you would not cut off a man's penis to stop him from abusing an innocent boy, is that it? Danny?"

The air went still. There was no mistaking Pape's reference to the pedophile that Danny had first killed—Roman Thompson, son of Judge Franklin Thompson. How could the warden know? Who else had known? Renee. And a handful of victims he'd shared the detail with as a means of motivation.

Renee would never share the knowledge, that much he knew. Which left those victims he'd shared the episode with, all of whom he was sure were dead.

Or were they?

"So you see how closely our worlds are entwined?" the warden said. "I know more about you than you might have guessed. I have powerful friends who can change lives with the stroke of a pen. But you're wondering how I know about Roman Thompson, the pedophile you killed. Am I right?"

At least the pedophile's death in no way implicated Renee. He'd killed the man years before she'd come into his life.

"I'm not sure I know what you're talking about," Danny said.

"Then let me refresh your memory." The warden sat forward and rested his elbows on the desk. "The man you killed had a father. A judge named Franklin Thompson. Surely you know that much. What you can't possibly know is that the Honorable Franklin Thompson knows more than you think he knows. He has no physical evidence, of course, you were too good for that, but he isn't without his means."

"So that's what this is all about? Forcing a confession out of me?"

"No." Pape leaned back in his chair, comfortably smug. "No, I doubt I could ever manage that. My objective is to help you see who you really are, so that you can truly repent and be whole. And to that end, I will now confess that there's more to Peter's story. How do you think a young man like Peter ended up in Basal?"

The facts lined up in Danny's mind like crows on a high wire. A ghost had come out of his past to haunt him. The father of his first victim had found a way to send an innocent boy accused of rape to Basal, not to teach Peter a lesson but to destroy Danny.

They intended to push Danny to his end.

"So, now you think you know. An eye for an eye. How far will you go to protect Peter? Hmm? Me, I think you would kill again. That your vow of nonviolence is only an empty promise to appease your guilt. I intend to find out if you still have self-righteousness in you. And I promise to push until you do. Randell isn't my wolf, Danny. You are."

Danny let the judgment sink in, aware even as he sat across from the warden that he now faced a world of impossible choices. Already the heat of familiar rage was spreading up through his chest and face.

"How about Renee?" the warden said. "How far would you go to save your precious wife?"

Danny's mind went dark, then brightened with panic. But he didn't dare reveal his terror at those words. He couldn't allow any focus to linger on Renee.

"She's not my wife," he said, bringing all of his resolve to mind.

"No. No, she isn't. You'd better prove that you've changed, Danny. You'd better come clean and tell me everything and show me that you're a fully rehabilitated man no longer willing to deviate from the law. Each of my children is unique, each with his own rehabilitation plan. But you're special. You're a man of the cloth; you should have known better."

"Then deal with me on my own. Don't subject Peter to punishment to teach me. Let me prove myself to you on my own terms."

The warden drew his hand across his mouth to dry his lips. The man was still reeling from his own tragedy.

"Well, my friend, as it turns out, I'm one step ahead of you. I always will be, remember that. In this case, I've already had Peter transferred to the privileged wing as a sign of good faith. The boy's suffered enough for the time being. As the good book says, 'There's a time for peace and there's a time for war.' But know that I'm watching you. If you slip—if you allow your ugly, violent nature to emerge without my express direction or permission—then it's war. Fair enough?"

Danny hesitated, then nodded. "Thank you."

"You see, I am a reasonable man. I only want to know that you've truly changed, Danny. Punishment will haunt those who do not confess their sins and embrace a new life at my mercy. Are we clear?" He stuck out his hand. "Friends?"

Danny had little choice but to take the man's hand. "Again, thank you for showing the boy some kindness."

"Grace, my friend. As the good book says, 'It is through grace that you are saved.' No need to boast, but I feel good about myself in moments like this. Don't you?"

Danny felt a measure of relief that Peter had earned himself some peace. But he felt no connection whatsoever with the warden's form of grace. And the warden's earlier claim that grace was no grace at all floated like a harbinger in the back of Danny's mind.

"Yes," he said. "I suppose I do."

"Good. One last thing and I'll let you go. Like I said, I have friends, many more outside these walls than inside. Breathe a word about deep meditation to a soul, now or ever, and I will have you hunted down and killed. Am I clear?"

"Yes."

"Good." He pressed the intercom. "Send Mitchell in. The prisoner's ready."

The gaunt facilitator with big eyes came in, restraints in hand.

"No need for chains." Pape waved them off. "We have an understanding."

"Yes, sir."

"Take him to the hard yard as we discussed. I'm sure the man would appreciate some exercise before lockdown."

16

KEITH'S SUGGESTION that we go about our business as if nothing in the world was wrong was fine. I got it, I really did. If we were being watched—and we were—the reports that found their way back to Sicko would needle him, which was in and of itself a small advantage. He was obviously as interested in manipulating me as he was in achieving whatever end he hoped for.

He needed to feel his power over me, Keith said. It was why he insisted I play his game. Not rewarding him with the satisfaction of seeing me cower was our only hope of pushing him off his own game. That was probably why he was making us stew for forty-eight hours, he said. Either that or he needed the time to set up whatever awaited us.

It all made perfect sense, it really did.

It also felt impossible.

We had nearly forty-eight hours before we could go to the warehouse to learn what twisted fate awaited us, and we spent only five of them together, at Heartwell Park off of Carson Street, rehearsing every possibility and angle a dozen times, but doing it like two free-spirited hippies burning up time. Long but only a block wide, the park offered an open line of sight from either Carson or Parkcrest, and we expected to be seen lounging on benches, strolling with hands in pockets, or carelessly kicking chunks of bark along the grass, arms folded.

Under the facade, my heart refused to slow down, and my skin felt sticky. Yet with each passing hour the realization that any other course of action would only bring tragic consequences became more certain. Still, we rehearsed them all, more for Keith's sake than mine, because I already knew what was going to happen.

We were going to play Sicko's game. The fact was, *someone* certainly knew I had killed two men. And they knew Danny had killed more than two. And if they knew, they could talk. I had to get to that person, end of story. It was the only way to protect both of us.

But Keith didn't know that. He'd suggested we play the game, but like a good lawman, his mind was always looking for the angles, the alternatives, the way out with the least amount of risk.

"For the sake of argument," he said, "we could still involve one of my old contacts at the sheriff's department and get him to make inquiries into Basal, just enough to put the prison on notice."

"We'd have to assume Sicko would find out," I said, my tingling hands stuffed in my jeans.

"There are ways—"

"Like what? Meet in the dead of night in a park like this one? We don't know who we can trust or who's watching. The first call into the prison would alert them that someone's leaked something. If someone on the inside is in on this, they'll carry out their threat."

Keith glanced around nonchalantly, scanning

for a driver or pedestrian watching us. He was always looking, always observant. "There's got to be someone who can find out what's happening in there without tipping them off."

"Yesterday you said no. Now you think there is? How?"

"Probably not without tipping them off, no. Not in the time we have."

"And you don't think the warden's involved," I said.

"It would be a stretch."

"This whole thing's a stretch. You made the calls, right? Like you said, Pape keeps the place quieter than a corpse in Siberia. Why? Maybe this is all his doing?"

"Possible, but not likely. Going around the law isn't as easy as it may seem."

Unless you're Danny, I thought.

"Either way, I'm not willing to take that chance," I said. "This is Danny's life we're talking about here."

"Fine. But if the warden's involved, and I doubt he is, then we're screwed."

"This is news?"

"No. But I mean really screwed."

"Like I said, this is news?"

He nodded and tapped a small stone to the side with his foot. The fact of the matter was, Keith couldn't have the same motivation I had to protect and save Danny. He could only help me. God knew I needed his help, but at what cost to him?

"Maybe I should do this alone," I said, crossing my arms. "Really—"

"It's too late for that," he interrupted. "People smart enough to use Randell are smart enough to tie up loose ends. I know way too much now to let go."

I hadn't really thought of it that way, and I felt a pang of guilt for demanding he help me. In my urgency, I'd sucked him into a place of terrible danger for my own gain. I was using him.

I pulled up, struck by the thought. He turned and looked at me with those hazel eyes. But there wasn't any fear in them, only resolve. He was a good man, a very good man. I couldn't help wondering what it would have been like to meet a man like Keith before Danny came into my life.

Now there was only Danny. Forever.

"I'm sorry," I said.

"Don't be. I was meant to be here."

"No, I came to you."

"Only because I put Randell behind bars and you were smart enough to find me. Frankly, whoever is behind this may have wanted you to find me."

"Seriously?"

"Why not? I could verify the validity of Randell's threat. It was probably at Randell's request—you're not the only one who has enemies. This is what he gets out of it."

"What if I hadn't come to you?"

Keith shrugged. "He'd probably have found another way to get me involved. Doesn't matter now, we're here. Let's walk."

We moved on, and my mind returned to Danny. A question that had ridden my mind through the previous night served me again.

What would Danny do?

"We could go through a judge," I said. "Take them at gunpoint and force them to shut the prison down."

"You know one who could do that?"

"Don't you?"

He considered the question. "Nope."

"Not even if we told them the whole thing? Showed them the notes?"

"Without corroborating evidence, what would stop a judge from thinking *you* wrote those notes as a way to get to Danny?"

"And that corroborating evidence would have to come from inside the prison," I said. I knew all of this, but for both of our sakes I had to get it out one more time, if only to line things up again, like checking a lock on a door three times just to be sure.

"Basal's a self-contained city with its own rules," he said.

"Same with the inspector general's office?"

"OIG would be our safest best, but it would still take way too much time and require an investigation that would probably be leaked to whoever's monitoring communications."

What would Danny do?

"Then we go straight to the warden," I said. "Not at the prison, but at his house. In the middle of the night."

Keith glanced at me. "We could. You want to take the risk Sicko won't find out? The note said no warden."

It also said I would have to kill someone. The wind was blowing my hair in my face and I was too distracted to care. "You think Sicko's just going to let us walk when this is over?"

"Nope."

That was quick.

"But you think we can find a way out before it gets to that point," I said.

"He's gotta keep pulling a lot of strings to make this happen, so yeah. There's a good chance he'll slip up sooner or later."

"Sooner, I hope."

"So do I. Like you said, until then we're screwed."

I nodded and swallowed. "Don't worry. I'm good at playing games."

But I was lying, wasn't I? A gun I could handle. Bedbugs I could starve to death. But games drove me crazy, and I was already too crazy.

The hours crawled by, and the millions of people around us went about their business, oblivious to the stakes we faced. I spent the three hours prior to our journey to Morongo Valley pacing my home, repacking my kit, then checking and rechecking my nine-millimeter with an unsteady hand. Then I cleaned the gun and checked it yet again, because three years had passed since I'd used it, and in my shaken state, I wasn't sure I'd done everything right—even though I knew I had, if that makes any sense.

It was five minutes before eight when I turned off my headlights and rolled the Toyota to a stop on Sherman Road, where we'd been directed by the note. I had suggested taking Keith's truck because the route was a gravel road way out in the middle of nowhere, but he'd dismissed the idea out of hand. Whoever was watching would want to see me driving my car.

Glowing haze from the city to the west hid the moon, and there were only a few stars visible above us even though it was dark. The old warehouse one hundred yards ahead rose into the night sky like a massive ancient tomb.

The car's engine barely purred; the air-conditioning vents whispered. I sat with both my hands on the steering wheel, staring at the darkened building, mind filled with ghosts and dead bodies.

"You sure you're up for this?" he asked.

"I can see why he picked this place. There's not a soul within ten miles but us."

"And whoever's watching."

I glanced out the side window. Scattered scrub pine hunched on the otherwise barren ground.

"I don't like this."

"I don't either," he said. "Just don't panic."

We sat in silence for a beat. Keith's plan had all seemed so simple—we'd both go in together, armed. The note hadn't said anything about me coming alone this time, just without authorities. Sicko needed us alive, Keith insisted. There wouldn't be a threatening confrontation here, probably only more nonsense, but I knew he was saying some of that for my benefit.

Nonsense wasn't in Sicko's vocabulary. He liked to communicate with bloodied body parts in shoe boxes and perverted bears in biker bars. Looking at the dark warehouse, a terrible fear gripped my mind. Despite Keith's warning, cries of panic told me to throw the car into reverse and roar away under full power before it was too late.

But the panic lasted only a few seconds before anger shut it down. If we were going in, we were going without hesitation.

I snapped on the headlights, shifted my foot

off the brake, and floored the accelerator. The tires spun on the gravel, found some traction, and hurled us forward.

"Whoa..."

"Hold on."

The rings of my headlights expanded on the warehouse's old gray sides.

Keith gripped the dashboard. "What are you doing?"

There was a door, dead center and closed. There was a knob on it. My eyes centered on that knob, as if it was the only thing that stood between me and Danny. As if this was Danny's prison and I was here to bust him out.

"Slow down—"

I released the gas pedal and braked hard. The car slid for twenty yards and came to a lurching halt a dozen paces from the door. Dust roiled around us, drifting through the shafts of light from the headlamps.

"Okay. That's one way to do it," Keith said. "Keep the lights on." He pulled out his handgun, chambered a round, and eased his door open.

I'd lost my cool, collected self there for a moment, I knew, but that was okay. The note had instructed us to come, and we'd come. And now here we were.

What would Danny do?

He wouldn't have come in like a bat out of hell. He probably would have scoped the place out first, found all the exits, all the windows, surveyed the surrounding landscape. Heck, he probably would have counted the number of shingles on the roof. There was a reason why he never got caught until he turned himself in, and it was in part because he didn't come roaring up to his enemies in a Toyota spewing dust and gravel for the whole world to see.

I shoved the stick into park, grabbed my gun, and was out of my door before Keith had two feet on the ground. Staring at that warehouse, it had all became very plain to me. Keith was right—Sicko needed me. I was the key to their money. I was their leverage. I was their subject of torment. Without me, there was no game.

I was also Danny's only hope.

So without waiting, I walked through the illuminated dust, straight for the door, both hands snugged on the butt of my gun. Keith cut in front of me, one hand raised to hold me back, eyes on that knob.

He put his hand on it, glanced back, and gave me a nod. "Easy...Follow me." He twisted the silver knob and pushed the door open.

Darkness.

Keith slipped a small black flashlight from the pocket of his jeans, snapped it on, and shone it through the gap as I peered around him.

Empty space. Concrete floor.

Shoulder against the door frame, Keith poked his head in quickly, then pulled it back.

"What do you see?" I whispered.

He gave me a sharp look that pretty much said *shut up*, waited a count of three, then spun in and pulled up, wrists crossed so that both his handgun and the flashlight were pointed forward.

"Anything?"

He still wasn't moving, so I stepped up beside him and saw the dim interior with a single glance. The warehouse looked like any empty warehouse, except for what appeared to be clothes heaped in the far left corner. Dirty floor, cobwebs on the sloping wood ceiling, three windows on each side all covered up by brown paper. Nothing else that I could see.

My eyes skipped back to the heap of clothes.

Only it wasn't a heap of clothes. A dark-haired head protruded from the top. Two arms to the sides. And two legs.

Keith ran forward, light twisting wildly in the dark. The image jerked around my field of vision as I ran, but I began to piece together what I saw.

What I had mistaken for clothing in the flashlight's farthest reaches appeared to be the slumped form of a young man or woman with short dark hair, chin resting on a blue Bruins sweater—asleep, unconscious, or dead. A gray blanket was heaped over the person's torso, and from it protruded two legs in jeans, doubled back to one side so that only the knees showed.

Each arm was chained to the wooden framing on either side.

Keith dropped to one knee beside what I now saw was a teenage boy, maybe sixteen or seventeen.

I felt sick. "Is he alive?"

Keith pressed his hand on the boy's neck to check for a pulse, but it was as far he got. The boy's head jerked up, eyes wide.

"No!"

"No, no, no, it's okay…" Keith removed the

light from the boy's eyes. "We're here to help you. It's okay." To me. "Get his hands free!"

"No!" The boy's frantic cry echoed in the vacant warehouse. "No, you can't!" His frantic eyes darted from Keith to me and then to his right hand. "He cut off my finger."

I saw the bloodied hand. Three fingers. The index digit was missing, cut off at the base. An image of the shoe box filled my mind and I swallowed against the nausea rising from my gut.

The boy stared up at me with the wildest, bluest eyes I had ever seen. Tears trailed through dust on his face.

"He...he cut off my finger."

I lowered myself to both knees next to him and rested my hand on his shoulder. "I'm so sorry. We're here to help you. What's your name?"

But the boy was too overwhelmed to answer. It occurred to me that nearly a week had passed since I received the shoe box. If the finger sent to me belonged to this boy...

"He was moved here," Keith said. "There's no blood on the floor. The wound was cauterized. Did they hurt you anywhere else?"

The boy began to cry. He shook his head.

"Do you have a name?" I asked again. I had to know. I had to know because in my mind's eye, this was Danny. And he was me. At the very least, the boy was here *because* of me.

"Jeremy," the boy said.

My hand on his shoulder was shaking.

"Why can't we take the restraints off, Jeremy?" Keith asked.

"He...he said the letter first. You..." The boy was so distraught that his words came out jumbled. "It's under here; you have to read it first."

Keith glanced at me, then pulled the blanket off the boy. His jeans were stained where he'd wet himself. In his lap lay yellow paper folded down to a two-inch square.

There was no food or water around that I could see. Keith picked up the note, shoved the flashlight under his chin, and quickly unfolded the paper.

I took a calming breath and gently rubbed the boy's shoulder. "Okay, listen to me, Jeremy. I need you to tell me how long you've been here."

"I don't know." And then, "A long time." His face was wet with tears, flowing freely now.

"When did they take you? Do you remember what day it was?"

He stared up at me again, eyes pleading. "Sunday."

"From where?"

"Pasadena," he said.

"You live in Pasadena?"

But he only lowered his head and began to cry silently. Something in my mind began to break. Not because Pasadena meant anything to me, but because Jeremy was an innocent boy who lived in Pasadena and was abducted on Sunday so that Sicko could use his finger to make sure I got the message. Jeremy would suffer the rest of his life on my account.

I felt faint. He needed water, and I had water in the car, but for a few moments I couldn't move. And then I was up and running for the door. Slipping on the gravel outside, dust flying. Lunging into the car for the water.

When I burst back into the warehouse, Keith was standing with both arms at his sides like a zombie, staring down at Jeremy, Sicko's note in one hand, flashlight in the other, pointed at the ground. The sound of the car's engine faded behind me, replaced by the pounding of my feet on the concrete.

"What is it?"

Keith didn't respond.

"Why can't we get him out of those things?" I demanded. "The poor kid's been in here for a week!"

"You should read this," Keith said. His voice didn't sound right.

The boy's chin was on his chest again, passed out again. Poor boy...I dropped to my knee and tilted his chin up. "Wake up, Jeremy." His eyes slowly opened as I pressed the water bottle to his mouth. He drank thirstily, gulping like a bird. Water spilled down his chin, soaking his shirt. When he finally shifted his mouth from the bottle, he was already fading.

I set the bottle down. "We'll get you out of here, I promise. You're going home, Jeremy, okay? You'll be home soon, I promise."

Keith took my elbow and led me to the side. "Just read it."

So I did, taking the flashlight from Keith to illuminate the note myself.

Good girl.

If you would have been one minute late, the boy would already be dead.

At midnight Monday night you will go to an address I will give you. You will force a full confession from the owner of the house and learn where he put the money. If he refuses, you will kill him and wait for my next instructions. If he confesses, you will have forty-eight hours to retrieve the money. Once you have the money, you will return and kill the man and wait for my instructions.

Either way, you will kill the man. If he's alive in four days, both Danny and that scumbag you're with are dead. He crossed the wrong man.

Be a good girl and do what you're told.

P.S. Cut off another one of the boy's fingers. Remind him that if he tells anyone about what happened to him, we will kill his mother.

My hands began to tremble.

17

DANNY WAS ESCORTED from the warden's office clean, dressed in the blue slacks and tan shirt of the general population, bearing no mark or sign that he'd just spent two days in hell. The hub was half full of convicts playing checkers, watching television, wasting time an hour before lockdown.

Hustles were going down, bets were being made, arguments unfolding, scores settled, gossip passed, all with the warden's approval. And only with it. Evidently, if a member proved his loyalty, he was allowed certain lenience. It would take some time to understand what limits could be pushed without reprisal. Danny had no intention of exploring those boundaries.

Mitchell led him past the cafeteria, past a door that led to the infirmary, to a short hall that opened to a gymnasium.

"Stay out of trouble," the CO said, giving Danny a gentle shove through the double doors. He turned on his heels and left him standing alone.

The room was roughly half the size of a typical gym, all concrete. Gray walls, cement floor, open to the night sky above except for a wire mesh. Bright lights hung from metal beams overhead.

Some members were engaged in a game of pickup basketball around a netless hoop that jutted from the far wall. Pull-up bars were fastened to the adjacent walls, most in use by other members going through typical prison yard exercise routines.

The hard yard. No lines on the floor to mark courts, no nets for tennis or volleyball, no bins full of balls or stacks of weights. Just one hoop, the pull-up bars, and eighteen or twenty inmates. Among them: Randell, Slane, and two other knuckleheads he'd seen with them in the dining hall.

He was briefly tempted to turn around and walk out, but the warden had specifically sent him to the hard yard, clearly for a reason.

"You okay?"

Danny turned and saw that Godfrey and Peter had entered behind him, the old man wearing concern, Peter oblivious to anything but his own delight.

"The warden put me in the privileged wing." Peter beamed. "You like my jeans?"

Indeed, he was dressed in a pair of jeans at least three sizes too large. He'd neatly tucked a bright red T-shirt, also oversized, into the waistband.

"You're looking pretty snappy there, Peter. Where'd you get them?"

"From the warden. He gave me my own room in the privileged wing. It's a big room and it has a pillow."

"It does, does it? Well, I'm sure you deserve at least three pillows."

The boy laughed, snorting once in his exuberance. "I can eat anytime I want, and they have chocolate milk. The warden is being nice to me."

"Good."

"He said that if I'm good, he won't hurt you, Danny."

Danny exchanged a quick glance with Godfrey, who forced a grin. The older man rubbed Peter's shoulder. "The Pete's living large, my friend. He's finally made it. Isn't that right, Peter?"

"Yup. And I'm going to be good. I promise."

"Did the doctor check you?" Danny asked.

"He said I wasn't raped. I was just scared, that's all. Did…did the warden hurt you?"

"Not too much, no."

"We'll be good, and everything will be good. I promise, Danny. You can come live with me if you want."

The exchange could hardly have been more surreal, standing in the hard yard, talking about being good so the warden wouldn't hurt them. Such was Peter's simple understanding of Basal. It broke Danny's heart.

"I would like that."

The boy's eyes looked past Danny and went wide. Danny turned around to see Randell, Slane, and the two other cronies headed their way.

"We'd better go," Godfrey said.

Slane's hair was slicked back, his lips twisted.

"I need to stay. Peter…" When Danny turned back, the boy was gone.

Godfrey stepped up next to him. "You don't need to do this, Priest."

"Stop calling me that. And you're wrong. I do."

"I've seen him put a man in the hospital with one hit. You should leave."

Randell was halfway to them, basketball under one arm, face drawn and red, whether from the heat or from anger, Danny didn't know. Likely both.

"No one's fighting. The warden set this up."

"Like I said, you should leave," Godfrey said.

There were three ways to handle Randell. The first and most obvious was to leave, as Godfrey suggested, but doing so would only postpone the inevitable confrontation, one which Danny was sure the warden intended.

The second was to stand up to the man. Even in Danny's condition he was confident he could hurt Randell enough to plant permanent doubts in his thick head. But that choice would place Peter in terrible danger.

It would also land Danny back in deep meditation.

The third option was the only course that made any sense to him.

"Go get the others," he said to Godfrey.

"Say what?"

"The other members. As many as you can, get them in here. Be quiet about it."

Godfrey hesitated only a moment, then spun and hurried out.

Danny walked forward, arms limp at his sides. He wouldn't hurt Randell, but he could make the man second-guess himself. There were no guards that he could see. The other members had turned their collective focus on Randell marching across the concrete floor.

Such an obvious schoolyard confrontation would never have gone down at a prison like Ironwood, where inmates and gangbangers tended to be more calculating, waiting for the right moment to slip a shank out of their sock and shove it into a victim's side before the guards could stop them.

But this was Basal, where each member was hardly more than a piece on the warden's chessboard. Randell was approaching Danny only as

intended by Marshall Pape, who was undoubtedly watching via one of the security cameras at
this very moment.

Danny stopped when they were ten feet
apart. "Good evening, Bruce."

The man shoved the basketball at him and
Danny caught it easily, then dropped it behind
him.

"I realize we got off on the wrong foot."

"Shut up, you FNG."

Danny was tempted to smile but didn't, out of
respect. Instead he attempted respectful reason.

"You do realize how ridiculous that sounds,
my friend. Why don't you just talk to me the
way you would in any other prison? I've been
called many things, never an FNG. But you
can't use common language in here because the
warden finds it offensive. And we don't want to
upset the warden, do we? We're not free men,
you and I. We follow someone else's rules to
avoid terrible punishment."

The patter of feet announced the arrival of
other members through the door behind
Danny.

"And so we should. As I recall, one of those
rules is that we respect each other. To that end,

I've given my word to the warden not to disrespect you in any way. All I want is to do my
time in peace."

Randell stood like a thick tree. His didn't
glare or crouch with fists clenched, he only
watched Danny, expressionless. Suddenly composed. And in that unexpected calm, Danny
saw Randell for what he really was, stripped of
a role given to him by the warden.

A more dangerous man than he'd estimated.

Twenty or thirty members had made their
way into the hard yard and fanned out now,
all watching, wary and focused. There was no
taunting, no agreement or disagreement. Vocal
support or outrage would undoubtedly be
noted and punished. They all seemed to know
that what happened here was meant to happen.
It was all part of the warden's program.

Danny spread his hands. "Really, Bruce, you
and I are on the same side. I respect you, you
respect me, we both respect the warden, no one
gets hurt, we all go home early. Those are the
rules."

"You're missing something," Randell said.

"What's that?"

"You're a priest."

With that the man calmly walked up to Danny, balled his hand into a fist, and slugged him in the gut with enough force to shove him off his heels and back a foot.

The blow didn't take his wind—he'd anticipated it—but his time on the wall had weakened him, and pain flared through his abdominal muscles.

"I'm not going to fight you, Bruce," Danny said. "I only mean to show and earn respect. You should know that I'm not a priest."

Randell blinked, perhaps caught off guard by Danny's unflinching resolve. He stepped up and struck Danny on his chin, a bone-crunching blow that snapped Danny's head around and dropped him to one knee.

Danny's world spun, darkened for a moment, then slowly came back into view. The concrete was there, only two feet from his head, and he wanted to lie down. But that would only compromise his standing before them all.

The confrontation would have to end as he'd expected it must.

Danny slowly pushed himself to his feet. Blood trailed down his chin and dripped on smooth concrete.

"I don't think you understand," he said. His jaw ached and he wondered if it was broken. "I'm not your enemy. We're all in this together."

Randell's calm broke then. His face darkened and his lips pulled back in a snarl. He came at Danny like a prizefighter, thundering his rage. And Danny let him come, knowing he would have to bear only a little more pain before it was over.

The man's next blow glanced off his ear, inflicting a sharp pain like a knife to the side of his head. But it didn't knock him down, so Randell threw his left fist in a wicked uppercut that landed squarely on the bottom of Danny's chin.

He staggered back and felt his legs start to go.

"This is insane," someone muttered.

It was the last thing Danny heard before Randell knocked him down with an elbow to the right side of his face. A boot smashed into his ribs. Another struck his neck.

Danny lay still, bleeding on the floor, only dimly aware of his surroundings now. If Randell killed him, then he would die and the warden would have no further reason to punish Peter, he managed to think.

And maybe then Renee would be safe.

"Break it up!" Mitchell, the skinny guard who'd wanted to Taser him in the basement, was yelling above the ringing in his head. "Get out, all of you!"

Hot breath whispered into his good ear. "The next time I'm going to break every bone in your face, Priest."

18

WE STOOD NEXT to the car's hood, two ghosts in the halo cast by the bright headlights. Keith paced, one hand rubbing his cheek, the other holding the note. Neither of us was quick to speak. The boy had passed out, at peace for the moment. We had to think, and the only thing I could think with any amount of clarity was that I had to find a way to end this. How, I didn't know, but I couldn't follow the letter's draconian demands. My life was caving in on itself.

"We can't cut off one of his fingers," I said.

"I know."

"They'll hurt Danny if we don't."

"I know."

"We can't go and kill this other person."

"I know."

I stood still, desperate to do something, gripped by a dreadful certainty that there was nothing I *could* do.

"Who would *do* something like this?"

"That's the problem, isn't it? Who?" He faced me, jaw fixed. "And why?"

"What do you mean, why? Because someone you put in prison wants the money."

Keith stared at me and I knew he wasn't satisfied.

"And because someone's after Danny," I added.

"I know that. But there's more to it, isn't there?"

If he only knew. There was much more, like the fact that Danny had taken the fall for me. Like the fact that Danny wasn't the only one with enemies. But I wasn't free to tell Keith that.

"Like you said," I said. "Randell's working with someone who wants to hurt Danny using me."

"And now that person's demanding we cut off an innocent boy's finger," he said.

"We're can't do that."

"And that we kill Randell's partner to get to his money."

"We're not doing that either."

"I know we aren't. But we need to know more about the man doing all of this on the outside, and that means I need to know anything you know."

"I told you, I don't know Danny's enemies." And that was the truth. "A judge, maybe, but even if it is a judge, I don't have a clue who."

"Think! There has to be something Danny said. Some mention of someone. Please, Renee, you have to think!"

"I told you, the pedo—" I stopped short, realizing I'd said too much.

"The pedophile? What pedophile?"

I hesitated. "I don't know. Just something he said. Danny has a thing against pedophiles, but who doesn't?"

"Okay, that's a start. He killed a pedophile?"

"I told you, I don't know any specifics. You'd have to ask him."

"Well, that's not possible, is it?"

I said what at the time seemed the most obvious thing in the world to me. "So we break him out."

Keith blinked once. "Crazy. Not a chance. Which pedophile?"

"I don't *know*, assuming he even killed one."

Keith lifted one hand shoulder-high in a sign of surrender and turned away. "All right…all right, fine. I accept that. But you do understand what kind of predicament this places us in."

"The same one we've been in since the beginning."

He glanced sideways at me, face strung with worry. For the first time, he'd been directly threatened by Sicko, and he didn't like that.

"All right…" He was nodding again, pacing. "All right, let's just take a deep breath and think this through. The way I see it, we have two days to figure out who's behind this. We could start with judges. Maybe a judge connected to a pedophile. We could also run through all of Randell's known associates on the outside, but I've already picked through them a dozen times."

He stared out into the darkness and continued, talking to himself as much as to me. "If we come up with nothing, on Monday we could still go to the address we're given. Use that as a starting point. Whoever Randell wants us to kill has to know more than where this pile of money is. With any luck, we catch a break with him. One way or another we have to start flushing out names and contacts that might lead us to Sicko."

I walked from one headlight to the other, then back, eyes on my black boots, which were now coated with a film of dust. Somewhere in the back of my mind I was telling myself I had to polish them the second I got them off. And wash my socks. And my feet. Take a shower. Maybe two.

"Maybe we're approaching it all wrong," Keith said.

"How so?"

He stared off into the darkness, then shook his head and shrugged his shoulders. "Obviously Randell is only part of the equation, but he's a piece we actually know about."

"Okay. And?"

"And Danny's in the equation too. He has information we need."

I nodded slowly. "And?"

"And they're both inside the prison."

He was rethinking breaking in. Now that he was directly threatened, his horizons were broadening.

"I thought you said breaking in would be impossible. You could figure out how to get us in?"

"I said crazy. Illegal." He dismissed the idea again with a wave of his hand. "It's pointless. Even if I could get us in, we'd never make it back out."

"And what do you call this?" I shoved a finger toward the warehouse. "If we could get to Randell, their leverage would fall apart. You're right, everything we need's inside Basal. Randell's in there. Danny's in there."

"I don't know what I was thinking. It's a federal crime. Like I said, plain crazy."

"So we do what? Cut off the boy's finger? Not a chance. I'm sure that fits somewhere in the crazy-federal-crimes thing as well."

"We take him home to his family," Keith said.

"Sicko will know."

"That's a chance we have to take."

"And then what? Kill this guy Randell wants us to kill?"

"No." Keith paused, staring at me. "Not unless we have to."

His willingness to consider it surprised me. But then it didn't, not really. It depended on who the guy was, what he'd done, what he would do. For all we knew he was a John Gacy with a dozen bodies in his basement.

Again, what would Danny do?

Danny wouldn't kill anyone, period. Not anymore.

"If we have to kill anyone, I vote for Randell," I said. "He's the man on the inside. Without him Sicko's leverage goes away, and we can bring in the cops."

"Randell isn't controlling this."

"Then we force a confession from him."

Keith let out a long breath and began to pace again. "No... We do the only thing we can do: we play along. We buy time. We keep fishing, we keep looking, but short of any new developments, we go to the man's house and we play Sicko's game."

"Fine." My throat felt frozen.

Keith glanced up at me. "You're sure?"

You're sure?

Those two words sliced through my mind.

Sure? Sure about what? I wasn't sure about anything anymore except that I had to do whatever was necessary to save Danny, but even that was getting foggy.

My mind flashed back to a memory of Danny holding my hand, telling me that he'd decided to turn himself in and take the fall for me. His life of violence was over; he'd made a terrible mistake and now he had to pay his debt to society. Me too, I'd said, but he'd flatly refused.

Now I'd been sucked back into that place of desperation and violence. And I hated it.

"Like you said, what alternative do we have? We go to the cops, we're screwed; we go to the warden, we're screwed; we go to the media, we're screwed; we go to the prison, we're screwed. All that's left is playing along."

Keith saw the despair in my eyes. "Renee..."

I turned toward the warehouse door and took two steps, then stopped, smothered by a sense of hopelessness. A knot clogged my throat.

"Renee..." He'd walked up behind me. "I'm sorry, I know how much you care for Danny."

Images of Danny spun through my mind. Whips and chains and knives and blood. His enemies would hurt him now, I was sure of that. What if they cut off Danny's arm? Or his foot? What if they cut out his tongue?

Sometimes my mind seemed incapable of turning itself off. Keith put his arm around my shoulder. I know he was trying to comfort me, but I almost resented him for it because really, it should have been Danny standing next to me, not Keith.

He was a good man, the broken cop, but I wanted my broken priest.

What would Danny do?

He would lay down his life if he had to, and that was what scared me most.

I couldn't break down. Jeremy was waiting. So I swallowed the pain in my throat, took a deep breath, breathed a prayer, and put my hope in Danny, which was the best I could do in that moment.

"Danny's a strong man," I finally said. "He might not be as easy to hurt as Randell thinks he is."

And then I walked into the warehouse to save the boy.

19

MONDAY

THE INFIRMARY AT the Basal Institute of Corrections and Rehabilitation was large, considering the size of the prison. Nothing less than a top-notch facility that met the highest standards for professional medical care, in or out of prison. Danny wasn't a stranger to hospitals. He'd spent time healing in several during the Bosnian War and even more time visiting patients as a priest. The level of sophistication at Basal surprised him. Certainly it was a far cry from the more clinical atmosphere at Iron-wood.

He'd awakened in the ward eight hours after taking his beating in the hard yard, his head splitting with pain, still groggy from whatever medications they'd injected into his system, but otherwise sound. His lip was cut and swollen, and his ear had required several stitches, but none of his wounds prohibited his return to the commons.

The warden's orders, however, did. It was for his own safety, the nurse had informed him. Basal's policy was to segregate injured members long enough for the warden to stabilize the situation.

The infirmary was laid out like an emergency room, with six spaces separated by drawn blue curtains, each of which contained a hospital bed, an IV stand, and a sealed rolling cart that housed various instruments, none of which were pertinent in Danny's case. Twelve recovery rooms housed longer-term patients on both sides of the hall outside the primary care facility.

In most prisons, patients who needed critical care were transported to hospitals and then returned upon recovery, but with the high quality of care available at Basal, only members with more serious medical conditions were transferred. It was yet one more way the warden limited his members' contact with the outside world.

Danny learned that a doctor had inspected him and sewn up his ear, but otherwise the only human contact Danny had was with a male nurse, Garton Kilburn, a large fellow with unflinching eyes, few words, and no evident emotions.

"Looks like you'll be fine," the man said after a cursory inspection of Danny's wounds on the first day. He wore blue scrubs over a white shirt and carried a stethoscope around his neck.

The nurse checked the leather restraints that tethered Danny by the wrists and ankles to the bed's steel rails, standard operating procedure following a fight.

Danny lifted his right arm as far as the bindings would allow, no more than six inches. "I think it would be best if I moved around a bit, don't you think? My joints could use some loosening up."

The man offered him a curt nod and left him without a word, his version of *whatever*. Danny was their property and would be allowed to move around when they determined him either fit or deserving.

In Danny's case, that was two days later, in the evening, long after his joints had all but frozen in place following his time on the wall and his subsequent beating. During those two days, he'd spoken only to Garton Kilburn and only on three occasions. None of the conversations had proven more inspiring than the first. The man's function was evidently limited to delivering trays of food three times each day, freeing Danny of all but one restraint so that he could use a commode rolled in twice each day, and changing the bandage on his ear twice before removing it altogether.

Considering the nature of deep meditation, the medical staff likely attended to inmates whose bruising would raise the most eyebrows. They, as much as the correctional officers who knew about deep meditation, would have earned the warden's trust. Connecting with their patients in a personal way that might test that trust was obviously not part of the program.

Odd, how being property of the state changed a person's outlook on freedom and identity, Danny thought. Three years earlier, accepting this kind of treatment would have been inconceivable. The war in Bosnia had filled him with a profound need to protect the abused, and that need had extended to protecting his own life. But he'd walked into the hard yard and let Randell hit him without raising a finger to protect himself. Not once but three or four times, with enough power to kill most men.

Why? To what end?

Was he less of a man now than when he'd taken up a gun at age fifteen and avenged his family's deaths?

Was he weak in the face of Peter's suffering?

He'd taken a vow of nonviolence and he intended to stand by it. Judge not lest you be judged; turn the other cheek; love your enemy; rather than rebel against the authorities who stripped you of your dignity and slaughtered thousands, bow to them and pay them their tax. These were the precepts that had finally drilled their way into his heart.

But he could not shake the questions that begged him to reconsider.

Was it even possible to follow that way when

boys like Peter stood in your path, begging for help?

But, no. No, he couldn't go down that path again. It was precisely that kind of questioning that had led him to violence in defense of the helpless.

A correctional officer came for him on the second night after dinner. Danny's muscles still ached, his joints were stiff, a dull ache still hung in his head like an iron weight. Once again he was led through the hub. Once again he climbed the stairs to the second tier in the commons wing. Once again he was ushered into his cell.

There was a change in the others this time, he thought. The member in the hub watched him with more than just mild curiosity. They wore uncertain faces, either confused by or genuinely interested in him, perhaps a little of both. The prisoners along the tier moved back from the railing without being told to.

This didn't mean they'd found more respect for him. In all likelihood word of his beating solidified his reputation as a weak prisoner. He was prey for the predators, the kind of man who could not stand up and defend himself or his brother. A punk. It didn't matter. He wasn't in prison to win approval, only to do his time.

Peter was in the cell with Godfrey, waiting for Danny. This was surprising, considering the danger that he might find in the commons now as a resident of the privileged wing. Clearly, the boy saw him as his savior.

"Danny!" the boy blurted, bolting off the lower bunk. Peter bumped his head on the frame, but the blow didn't discourage him from stumbling forward and throwing his arms around Danny.

"Hello, Peter."

"You're back!"

"I am."

Danny patted the boy on the back, shifting to maintain his balance. Peter's tight hug aggravated the pain in Danny's ribs, and he was thankful when the boy released him of his own accord.

Godfrey grinned, one hand on the bunk, the other in his pocket. "Anybody who can take a beating like that and walk out of the grave three days later is a priest in my book," Godfrey said.

"It's been two days."

"Either way."

"Simon says you're a strong man and that I should thank God I have a strong man on my side," Pete said.

Danny offered the boy a slight smile, but he wanted none of the conversation, not now.

Pete stared at his stitched ear. "Why did you let him beat you up, Danny?"

Once again, Danny was confounded by the irony of innocence held captive in such a brutal environment. The boy was guilty of deviating and was paying his price without really understanding either the rules or the price.

"You crazy, man." Kearney had walked up behind Danny and leaned on the door, bright eyes twinkling. "And you still walkin'."

"Not crazy, no. I just don't like fighting."

"Don't worry, Danny," Peter said, beaming. "It's not like that in the privileged wing. It's nice."

Danny grinned at the boy and rubbed his head. "Well, I'm glad for you. They're treating you well then?"

"I have chocolate milk in my room. And last night I had a steak. That thick." He pinched an inch of air with his thumb and forefinger. "It was juicy."

"Steak," Godfrey said. "Now there's something I would be willing to spend a day in the hole for."

"You can come!" Peter exclaimed, eyes darting between them. "You can both come. If you're good, you can have all the steak you want. And I have a new friend. His name is Jack."

"Seriously, why'd you do it, Priest?" Kearney asked.

Danny walked to the sink and turned the water on. "Like I said, I don't like to fight."

"Ya, but to git yur butt whooped like that... They sayin' we got a half-baked priest here."

He splashed water on his face. There was nothing more that needed saying. Maybe he *was* half-baked. Silence filled the cell behind him. He glanced over his shoulder and saw that they were watching him.

"They take you deep?" Godfrey asked, voice softer now.

Danny grabbed a towel from the top of his locker and shook it open. The warden had made it clear that no discussion about deep meditation was allowed. For all Danny knew, his mention of the experience would find its way back to Pape and all four of them, including Peter, would pay a price.

He shoved his head into the towel and dried his face. "I'm fine. Just a bit tired. What time is it?"

No one responded.

Danny pulled the towel from his face and turned toward the door. Kearney, standing there only a moment ago, was gone. In his place stood Warden Marshall Pape, watching Danny, one hand in his pocket fiddling with keys or coins, the other limp at the bottom of his black suit jacket.

"It's almost eight, Danny," the warden said. "Time for Peter to leave us."

Peter stood still, transfixed by the sight of his greatest oppressor.

The warden stood aside and indicated the walkway with an open palm. "It's okay, boy. Run along."

Peter hurried past him, turned down the tier, and was gone.

Pape stepped into the cell. "I hear you took quite a beating," he said in a gentle voice.

"I'll be fine."

"Of that I have no doubt. You've proven to be quite a stubborn man, I've got to hand it to you."

The soothing tone of his voice would have come across as disingenuous before their most recent discussion, but now Danny knew the truth about this man. Marshall Pape was just like the rest of them: a wounded man who was doing what he knew to cope with difficult circumstances.

At his core, the warden *was* a gentle man. His motives were as pure as any father who'd suffered the loss of his family. He, like so many well-meaning religious types, truly thought he was doing the right thing.

"You know, at times I worry that some people are too strong," Pape said. "They refuse to own up to their own inadequacies. It bothers me. But I have to believe that good can come from even the most vile situations. And I think that maybe you'll show us all a more perfect way, Danny. I don't think I've ever seen anyone face punishment with so much courage. It's inspiring."

Danny nodded. "I suppose every man has his limits. I can only pray I never find mine."

"Well said. I'm sure you're still sore. The nurse informs me that he neglected to give you any medication before you left the infirmary." The warden pulled his hand out of his pocket and held out two white capsules. "Normally, we don't allow narcotics in the wings, but I think the situation warrants it. Maybe this will help you sleep."

Danny looked at the capsules. "I'm fine, really..."

"I insist. It's the least I can do."

Alarm bells were ringing in Danny's head, warning him that taking the medication, whatever it might be, would end badly. But he also was sure that not taking them would be considered insubordination.

So he stepped forward and took the pills from Pape's hand.

The warden gave a little flip of his wrist toward Godfrey. "Give him some water, Simon."

Godfrey picked up a water bottle and handed it to Danny, who hesitated only a moment, then threw the pills into his mouth and swallowed them down with the water.

"Good. That's good. Sweet dreams, Danny. You're going to need them."

He left Danny standing, clueless to his intentions. But that wasn't entirely true, was it? The warden had already made his intentions perfectly clear. He was well-meaning, but he was also hopelessly deceived.

He was going to help Danny see the light.

He was going to crush him.

20

THE MAN THAT Sicko wanted us to kill lived at 1227 Sunrise Street in Beverly Hills—that was all we learned from the distorted male voice that called my home phone at ten o'clock Monday night. Two days of dread hadn't brought Keith or me any closer to a better understanding of the note he'd left with the boy Jeremy, the words of which were permanently inscribed in my fractured brain.

> *...you will kill the man. If he's alive in four days, both Danny and that scumbag you're with are dead. He crossed the wrong man.*
> *P.S. Cut off another one of the boy's fingers.*

Remind him that if he tells anyone about what happened to him, we will kill his mother.

We knew we were being watched, but we hadn't cut off another one of the boy's fingers. On this point we felt compelled to call Sicko's bluff. We freed Jeremy from the warehouse, helped him into the backseat of my car, and drove him to Santa Monica.

He'd leaned against the door, silent and numb for most of the ride, and all I could do was rest my hand on his knee and promise him that he was safe now. We would find who did this and make him pay, I said. We were this devil's victims too. I was so very, very sorry.

None of what I said did anything to settle my mind, because the fact was, Jeremy had lost more than his finger. He'd lost a part of his innocence through abuse, just like I had before Danny had saved me.

As we drove, Keith was the one who finally brought up the threat in the note.

"I know this has all been a nightmare, Jeremy, but I need to know if there's anything else you can tell us about this man."

The boy sat mute, staring absently at his

hand, which we'd wrapped in a clean white rag from my trunk.

"Anything at all?" Keith pressed. "Besides the fact that he wore a ski mask and gloves? What kind of car he drove, maybe?"

"He put a bag over my head," Jeremy said. "I couldn't see."

I felt nauseated. His abductors had evidently chosen him at random, an easy target riding his skateboard in an alleyway near his house in Pasadena. A club to the head, a bag, and that was all he could remember. When he woke, his finger was missing. He'd spent the next several days in a dark room, mostly sleeping under the influence of the drugs they'd given him to keep him quiet.

We drove on for a bit before Keith continued, glancing up at the rearview mirror. "He made a threat in the note he left us. Did he say anything to you about that?"

The boy looked out the window. "He said I couldn't tell anyone or he would kill my mother."

Keith glanced at me in the mirror. "That's going to be hard, Jeremy. I know how difficult this is, but I think he means it. Your family and the police will want to know everything about how you were taken, exactly what happened, about us…everything. But he cut off your finger, which means he's serious about what he says. Does that make sense?"

"Yes."

"You'll have to tell them something, I understand that. You don't have any information that could lead them to whoever did this, so it's probably okay to tell them what you know, that you were taken and you don't know why. But if you say anything about the note, or about us, I think whoever did this might carry out his threats."

It was true. Sicko knew that if the boy led the police to us, we could lead them to Randell. We were the link that could incriminate him.

"Tell the police that whoever took you brought you back and dropped you off a block from home. Don't tell them about the warehouse or about us. I know that may not sound right to you, but I can't think of a better way to go. Trust me, we'll get to the bottom of this, and when it's safe everything will come out. Until then, you can't say anything about us. Fair enough?"

"Yes."

My heart was already broken, but I saw my-self in Jeremy's shoes, and it was everything I could do to remain calm. I gave him a long hug and helped him out of the car a block from his house in a low-rent district on the east side of Pasadena. We followed him at dis-tance until he entered a duplex, safe.

But really, he wasn't safe. Neither was Danny.

Only two days had passed between the time we drove away from Jeremy's house and the time we drove up to the large white house on Sunrise Street, but those two days felt like a week to me.

"This is it?" I asked, pulling the car to a stop twenty feet back from a stucco mailbox marked with the brass numbers 1227.

"That's it." Keith shoved the Google map into the car's door pocket. "Kill the lights."

I did.

"Turn the engine off."

I looked at him, then up the driveway at the house, which was lit by an array of exterior lamps affixed to the stucco walls. Two white pillars bordered a tall arched ironwork door. Using Google's satellite view, we'd zoomed in on the house, complete with red adobe tiles on a dozen roof lines. It was clear then that our target was wealthy. But we still didn't know who owned the property or who we were supposed to kill, only that he lived here.

My palms on the wheel were clammy with sweat. "I think we should leave it running," I said. "We might need to get out quick."

"Saving the three seconds it takes to start the car isn't worth the risk."

"Risk of what? It's Beverly Hills."

"These are public streets. A cop comes by and wonders why the car's running? No, turn it off."

So I did. "What time is it?"

"Eleven fifty-one. We have nine minutes."

"So I just go up and knock on the door, right?"

Keith reached back and grabbed my black kit. "Just like we agreed. You go to the front door, I hold back until the door's open. Assuming you're still good with that."

Was I?

The plan was mine, dredged up from my better days with Danny. He would have insisted on a thorough surveillance, but the timing

Sicko had given us didn't allow for that. The home owner probably wouldn't see any threat in a skinny girl like me dressed in *Miss Me* jeans and a bright blue blouse. Once he had the door open, Keith, who was dressed in black, would step in from the side with his gun and force the man back in the house.

Looking at the house, I was having second thoughts. We didn't even know if the owner had a wife in there, or daughters, or guards, or dogs.

"What if he's the wrong man?"

Keith pulled out his gun and chambered a round. "Whoever's pulling our strings is too meticulous in his planning for that. The man they want is in that house, guaranteed."

"And then what?" I asked.

"And then you leave it up to me."

"I don't like it."

"I don't either, but trust me, it's the best way. Go in fast and hard and control the situation before he has a chance to react."

Something about the look of that fortress struck me as odd. Maybe it was my frazzled nerves, maybe my suspicious nature, maybe my fear of bedbugs and rats—I don't know.

There was too much we didn't know about our target. Too many things that could go wrong. I knew that as a cop Keith had been through his share of similar situations, but nothing had gone right for us so far. And we'd failed to follow the instructions on the last note. It was suddenly all happening too fast.

What would Danny do? I'd asked that question a hundred times in the last two days, but staring at the house, a part of me saw our present situation differently. My instinct to start out with deception was good, but the part about barging in with guns drawn wasn't sitting right. We didn't know enough!

Danny would already be on the perimeter circling the house. He would be patient. He would find a weakness first and then exploit it, right?

"You ready?" Keith asked.

"Read the note again," I said.

He turned his head. "We've been over this."

"I have OCD."

He stared at me, then pulled the note out of his pocket, fished a penlight out of my kit, and read the note under its light.

"'At midnight Monday night you will go to an address I will give you. You will force a full confession from the owner of the house and learn where he put the money. If he refuses, you will kill him and wait for my next instructions. If he confesses, you will have forty-eight hours to retrieve the money. Once you have the money, you will return and kill the man and wait for my instructions. Either way, you will kill the man. If he's alive in four days, both Danny and that scumbag you're with are dead.'"

He lowered the note.

"You know what I'm thinking?" I said, eyes still on the house. "This isn't about the money. Whoever lives in that house has all the money Randell could want. He doesn't need us to get it; he could find another way."

"We've been over that too. Randell doesn't know who he can trust on the outside anymore. His partners turned against him."

"It's not about the money," I said. "He's obsessed with us killing whoever's in that house. That's all that matters to him. But why us?"

"And we've been over that too. Revenge."

"Against who?"

Keith looked up at the house. "Me. You. Danny."

I nodded and looked at the side of his face. "Okay. But what about whoever's in the house? What if he's more than just a drug dealer? If it's not really about the money, why does Sicko want him dead?"

"We don't know." His voice took on a frustrated bite. "We don't know squat—you don't think I know that?"

"That's what I'm saying...we don't know."

"We know Sicko's enraged about something Danny did. Revenge. You kill this man, you take the blame, you go to prison. It's his way of messing with Danny."

"I'm not going to kill him," I said.

"You sure about that?"

I didn't answer. It still didn't make complete sense to me. There was something else we didn't understand in play. Maybe that was what made me rethink the whole barging-in thing. Whoever was in the house might be our only real shot at getting to Sicko.

"Like you said, we need to know more," I said.

"We don't have *time* to know more!"

I glanced at my phone. Three minutes till midnight. My heart was racing. Danny's first

rule had always been to know your target, and
the best way to do that now was on the inside of
that house. Not with guns blazing.

"I'm going in first," I said. I grabbed the kit
off his lap. Pulled out my knife. Stuffed it and
the Mace into my pockets. "Give me five minutes."

"You can't go in there alone and unarmed."

"I'm not going in with a gun. We need to
know who this guy is before we do anything.
The second he sees a gun, he sees us as a threat.
I need to know who he is before that."

"Then let me go in first."

"No, he'll see you as a threat. Me, he sees as a
lost girl looking for some help."

"That's your plan now? Go in looking for directions?"

I took a deep breath and opened my door. My
desperation gave way to a kind of fatal hopelessness.

What would Danny do? He would do whatever was necessary to save me. I had to save
Danny, and the only way was to know his enemy.

"I'm going in, Keith. I have to. Wait for me
outside and be ready."

"Ready for what? A smoke signal?"

"I don't know." I put my foot on the street and stepped outside. "I'll think of something."

"Renee—"

"Give me ten minutes."

"Ten? Or five?"

"Ten. Wait for me."

"Renee—"

I shut the door on his voice and hurried toward the house. I'd done this before. I could do it again. I had to. For Danny's sake, I had to.

21

THE PILLS THE warden gave Danny were a sedative, a powerful narcotic that began to pull at his mind within ten minutes. Not a numbing drug, but a sleeping agent, which made sense if Danny understood the warden's intentions as well-meaning. He'd been through a nightmare. It would be good for him to sleep it off so that he could face whatever came the next day.

But Danny could not understand any such benevolence on Marshall Pape's part. Or could he? Yes, actually he could. From Pape's point of view, everything he was doing was well-meaning. There was simply a disparity between his and Danny's understanding of *well*. In Pape's world, it would do Danny *well* to conform to the punishment he'd earned. Breaking Danny would do the world *well*. Any suffering was *well* deserved, as was the suffering of every member in this sanctuary.

These were the thoughts that mumbled through Danny's mind as he sat on the upper bunk, looking at Godfrey, who watched him with the gentle eyes of a man who knew more than he was willing to say.

"He wants you out cold. I can see it in your eyes," Godfrey said, reaching for one of his books on the locker. "I don't know what you've done, Priest, but I've never seen the warden so fixated on breaking a man, not in the first week." Godfrey faced him. "So tell me, what did you really do?"

The older man's image grew fuzzy for a moment, then came back into clear focus. "I told you. I killed some people."

"No, that's not it. There's something else. I don't know what, but you did indeed truly cross the wrong man. The question is, why does the warden want you out cold now? I've seen a lot of things in my time, but I've never seen him help an inmate sleep."

Danny had been transferred to the prison eight days earlier, and in the space of that week he had spent two days in the hole, two days in deep meditation, and two days in the infirmary, leaving him only one day in general population—this all without so much as lifting a finger or raising his voice to harm a soul.

But that was precisely the problem, wasn't it? Like a loving father, the warden meant to flush out all of Danny's deepest, darkest, most violent impulses and lay them bare in the light of his own justice, so that Danny might be transformed into the kind of man who never again deviated from society's rules.

And tonight that loving father had given him two pills to put him to sleep.

"He wants to break me," Danny said.

"Break you from what?"

"I used to kill my enemies." The drug was flooding his veins now, pulling his mind lower into darkness.

"He wants to break you from killing your enemies?"

Danny felt his head shaking, slowly—*no*. He put his hand on the edge of the mattress to steady himself.

"I took a vow to love my enemies," he said. His tongue felt thick. "I don't think he likes that."

Godfrey held his eyes steady. When he spoke his voice was knowing. "So he wants you to expose you. The bastard wants to justify his punishment of you by making you do it again. He wants to turn you back into a monster in his monster factory."

It wasn't a new thought for Danny, but hearing it so clearly, he felt a stab of panic penetrate his foggy mind.

"But darkness can't drive out darkness, only light can do that," Godfrey said. "Hate can't drive out hate, only love can do that. Martin Luther King said that."

"Yes," Danny remembered saying.

And then he remembered nothing. Not what, if anything, Godfrey said next. Not lying down, not falling asleep.

He wasn't even aware that he was on his bunk, dead to Basal, drifting through a peaceful world in which he had no enemies. Time drifted by, bringing with it vague images and whispers that were gone the moment they appeared. From the fog emerged a vision.

Peter was there, smiling, holding out a plate
with chocolate cake on it. Where, Danny
didn't know—just there, right in front of him.
Beaming.

"Do you want some, Danny? If you're good
you can come to my room and we can eat some
cake."

"I would like that, Peter. I would like that
very much."

"I will never hurt a girl again, Danny."

It was a strange proclamation, but not so
strange in the fabric of a dream.

"Did you hurt her?" Danny asked.

"The warden said I did." Tears flooded the
boy's eyes. "I don't want to go back into the
room."

Danny felt a lump rise in his throat. He
reached out and laid his hand on the side of
Peter's head. Drew his thumb over the boy's
temple. "Don't worry, I'm not going to let that
happen."

The smile returned to Peter's face. He held
up the chocolate cake. "It's okay, Danny, we can
eat cake now. I'm good now."

Another voice spoke. "Danny?" The female
voice was etched into his mind for all time.

He turned and saw that Renee was standing there, in his dream, looking at him with her clear eyes. Immediately that ancient warmth of hope and affection flooded his chest, swelling through his throat and face.

In his mind he was running for her, throwing his arms around her and swinging her through the air as she laughed.

Why haven't you done that, Danny? Why haven't you called her and wept on her shoulder and told her how deep the ache in your heart runs?

Then he saw her face and his heart froze. There were tears on her cheeks.

"Danny," she said. "I can't find you, Danny."

"I'm here, darling! Right here!"

She stared at him and swallowed deeply. "Are you doing well?"

Yes! he wanted to say. But he couldn't form the word.

"And are they treating you well?"

Yes, my darling. Yes! But he couldn't speak. Because in truth he wasn't well. In truth he was falling. In truth he was melting down.

Standing there in his dream, facing the woman he loved more than his own life, he realized that he was afraid. That he was terrified.

That he was only a shell of a man, powerless to save Renee.

Overcome by sorrow and unable to find solace through meditation because of the drugs, Danny began to cry.

22

I WALKED UP the three steps that led to the mansion's glass and ironwork door, fingers tingling, and without allowing even a pause, I rang the illuminated doorbell button that was set in a brass intercom.

I assured myself that I was safe. Apart from the knife and Mace in my pockets, I wasn't packing threatening weapons and I had no intention of leaping on anyone with fists flying. I was only a lost soul who desperately needed to use a phone because the one in my back pocket was dead. My presence was totally innocent. Nothing strange, nothing crazy, nothing but me being neurotic, and there was no crime against that.

I rang the bell again, and this time I saw light come to life past the glass. Clean, sparkling glass. This was it. I stepped back, heart pounding, but otherwise calm and collected—not counting my fingers, which were trembling. I shoved my Mace deeper in my right pocket so it wouldn't stick out.

"Can I help you?" The low male voice spoke over the intercom, startling me.

"Yes, um ... I'm sorry, but I was wondering if you could help me. I need help."

A pause. "It's midnight. What help?"

"I need to make a call. I'm sorry, I know this is strange, but my phone's battery died and I think I might be in trouble. I have to make a call. I couldn't find a gas station or anything ..."

"It's midnight," he said again.

"You don't understand, my husband is in terrible trouble. I have to make a call. Please, I'm a respectable girl who needs a helping hand. Just one minute, I promise."

The intercom was silent.

I was about to push the button again when a figure distorted by the angular glass stepped into the dim light inside, unlocked the deadbolt, and pulled the door open a foot. A tall man with a goatee stared at me through round spectacles. He was maybe fifty or older, dressed in casual black slacks and a turtleneck, and he didn't look anything like a drug dealer.

"The phone?" he asked.

"Yes. Please."

"Wait here a moment." He started to close the door.

"I also need to use the bathroom," I said quickly. His right eyebrow arched. "Unless you'd rather I pee in your bushes. Look, I've been out here for an hour and I'm sorry, but I really have to pee."

He hesitated, then opened the door. "Please hurry. The phone's in the kitchen."

"Thank you."

I stepped in, and just like that I was in the house of the man Sicko wanted Keith and me to kill. Looking around, I didn't see anything remotely threatening, much less piles of guns or cocaine. The house was mostly dark, but in the shadows sat expensive furnishings made of leather: brass lamps with animal hides for shades, large oil paintings on the walls. It was the kind of decor you'd expect to see in a colonial mansion in Beverly Hills, I supposed.

To my right, a twisting staircase rose to a catwalk. Living room dead ahead. Kitchen to my left. An office or a library next to the kitchen. A clean house. I liked that. But my fingers were still trembling.

I stuck out my hand. "My name's Renee Gilmore."

He studied my eyes without taking my hand and I immediately withdrew it, thinking he would notice how clammy it was.

"I thought you needed to make a phone call."

"I do. And pee."

"Then use it." He indicated the archway leading into what I could see was the kitchen. "The bathroom's down the hall to the left." He nodded at a hallway next to the kitchen entry.

"Thank you."

Worst case, I could slip into the bathroom and call Keith. The man didn't seem to know my name, and we wouldn't be meeting armed drug lords. The man we were to kill seemed entirely respectable, not the person I'd imagined trying to force a confession out of over the last two days.

Was he alone?

I headed for the kitchen. "Sorry for bothering you, I'll be out in a second."

"Make it quick," he snapped.

I stopped and turned back, determined to take him off guard. "Look, I've had a hard night. You're nice and comfortable in your mansion here, but there's a world of hurt out there. Please, some kindness would be nice. I just need to use your phone and pee. We should be thankful we have running water and phones to share, not hoard them. In some places they pee on the ground and communicate with drums."

Disarming was good, Danny had always said. Maybe I was crossing the line between disarming and alarming. I softened my voice and changed the subject.

"You have a family?"

"Yes."

"And you're afraid I'll wake them?"

"No, I'm here alone."

"Do I look like a thug who's going to rob you?"

"I don't know, are you?"

"Of course not."

"Then why are you carrying a knife and Mace?"

I blinked at him, surprised he'd laid me bare so easily.

"My security system scans for more than movement, dear. There's more to this house than meets the eyes."

He'd used something like one of those airport scanners on me? Keith wouldn't have made it in. It also explained why it had taken him so long to answer the door. He was checking my naked self out on some monitor. Was that even legal?

"A knife and Mace are common sense for a girl like me."

"In this neighborhood?"

"I'm not *from* this neighborhood. And if you don't mind me asking, what kind of person has an airport scanner hooked up outside their house?"

"A man with many enemies."

"You don't look like the kind who hurts people. Why would you have many enemies?"

"Because I'm a judge, dear. The kind who puts very bad people behind bars."

A judge? My pulse quickened. For a brief

moment all I could think was that I was looking directly into the eyes of Sicko himself. But
that made no sense. Was this the judge who
could be furious with Danny for killing his son,
the pedophile?

No, that couldn't be. Nobody but Danny and
I even knew about that judge, so how could he
be connected to Randell? More likely this was
the judge who'd sentenced Randell, in which
case Keith would recognize him.

Or maybe it was just a coincidence.

"A judge, huh? Wow, that would make you
pretty powerful. You ever hear of Basal?"

His face seemed to turn into stone for a moment. Or maybe I was just imagining it.

"You're right, we're not in the jungle," he
said. "We have phones, so please, use mine and
then leave."

"Now you're trying to get rid of me?"

"You can understand why I find all of this
a bit unusual. You come into my house with
Mace and a knife under the pretext of using my
phone but you seem more interested in the fact
that we have flushing toilets in America. And
prisons. I think it's best that you just use the
phone and leave. It is, after all, my home."

"So you do know about Basal. Because that's where my husband lives."

He stared at me. "Then I doubt you'll be getting through at this hour. What's this all about?"

"Does the name Danny Hansen mean anything to you?"

This time I knew I wasn't imagining anything. His face did turn to stone.

"I think you should leave." He frowned. "Now."

"I haven't made my phone call."

"I don't care. I would like you to leave now."

My mind spun.

"I need to pee." And I dashed into the bathroom before he could object.

I'd backed myself into a corner. But that didn't matter anymore. The man Sicko wanted us to kill was a judge familiar with the name Danny Hansen.

I was a tight bundle of nerves as I closed the door of the small half bath. Normally I would have lingered on thoughts about the cleanliness of that room—the sink, the toilet, the mirror, the toilet, the floor, the toilet—but all I could think as I flipped on the switch and stared at the image of skinny me in the mirror was that I was in the house of a judge who knew something about Danny. I had to know what and why and how, and I wouldn't leave until I did.

What was his connection to Danny?

What involvement did he have with Randell?

What were his ties to Sicko?

Why did Sicko want us to kill him?

Why had he gone stiff when I mentioned Danny's name?

How could he help me save Danny?

I grabbed my phone from my back pocket and pressed the favorites button with a shaking thumb. I thought to turn on the water in case the judge was listening. I had to get Keith in before the judge forced me out. Getting back inside the house would be difficult if not impossible.

I pressed Keith's name and lifted the phone to my ear. *Pick up! Pick up, pick up, pick up!*

He did, on the second ring. "Renee? What's happening?"

It occurred to me that my voice might carry beyond the door. The running water wasn't loud enough to cover it. If the judge heard me he'd know I wasn't talking to myself. That my phone wasn't dead. And any judge with security scanners would also have a gun.

Fear came over me then, as I looked at the brass water faucet, then at the closed door. Then the faucet again.

"Renee? Are you there?"

I shoved the toilet's flush lever down. The toilet roared and I quickly whispered into the phone.

"Now! Hurry!"

"Renee? Are you there?"

He couldn't hear me over the flushing toilet!

The sound of the door squeaking behind me sent panic through my bones and I started to turn, but in that moment of raw alarm I remembered that I had the phone to my ear. So I dropped it.

It plopped into the toilet and rattled around the whirlpool of flushing water.

I spun around as the door swung wide.

The judge stood in the opening, goatee jutting from his sharp chin, staring at me, arms down at his sides. There was a gun in his right hand.

But he didn't lift his gun or threaten me with

a scowl or scream at me. He was too resolute for that. He spoke in a calm voice that I could take as nothing less than a direct order.

"Leave this house," he said.

I couldn't. I had to stall him.

"My phone fell out of my pocket," I said. "It's in the toilet."

"Leave it!"

"It's my phone. I can't just leave it." *Hurry, Keith!* He would be running, maybe coming up to the door already. I had to let him know the judge was armed.

"Why are you holding a gun?" I said, loud enough for my voice to ring in the small bathroom. "You invite a girl into your house to use the bathroom and then you pull a gun on her? Are you going to rape me?"

The judge lifted his arm and pointed his gun at me. "Get out of my house. Now!"

I lifted both hands shoulder high. "Okay. Okay, calm down. Just let me get my phone…" I began to reach for the toilet bowl.

"Leave it."

Something snapped in my mind with those words. When he said *leave it*, all I heard was *leave Danny*, and that was sickening. I wasn't going to leave without this man's information or one of his bullets in my head.

"I'm not leaving my phone!" I snapped.

"I said leave it! Get out!" A vein stuck out on his temple where his sideburns were graying.

"You're going to murder me because of a phone?" We stared each other down. "Just let me get my phone and I promise I'll leave. I'll find some other house without a maniac and call my husband there."

"You weren't going to call your husband! He's in prison!"

"He's not the one I was going to call. I don't know if I'm coming or going here because your gun is pointed at my head. I'm getting my phone." I lowered my hands. "Shoot me in the back if you want. Judge kills skinny girl who dropped her phone in his toilet. That'll go over big."

"Lower the weapon!" Keith's voice rang through the hallway, and the judge twisted his head to his right.

Keith stepped into view and held his gun to the man's head. "Put it down. Now."

The judge slowly lowered his arm. "What's the meaning of this?"

"The meaning of this," I said, stepping forward and jerking his gun from his hand, "is that we're smarter than you. And if you don't get smarter really quickly, we're all going to die."

23

THE SOUNDS OF shuffling feet and grunting nudged Danny from his dream. But that couldn't be true; he was still in a drugged fog. It had to be the slap on his face. But that couldn't be true either. Renee wouldn't slap him. Neither would the boy. Neither would Godfrey.

The ghosts were groaning in the night. Renee was nowhere now. Vanished. Had someone slapped him?

His eyes slowly opened, and for a moment he stared at the ceiling three feet above him, the surface a dingy gray in the dim light. The sound of his own breathing reminded him that he was still alive. One of Randell's blows had bruised his ribs.

Why so quiet, Danny?

Cool air drifted over his body. He'd fallen asleep in his blue slacks, shirtless.

Danny closed his eyes and began to drift again. The fog settled and he turned his mind back to the vision of Renee. She was all that mattered now. Through his sacrifice, she had life. Because of him, she was free. If he lost her now, there would be no more reason to live.

Why so still, Danny?

It was a good question, spoken from the fog of his mind. So he opened his heavy eyes and thought about it.

Why so quiet? Prisoners had no privacy. The snores and coughs and grunts of other inmates were never-ending in the dead of night. But now the commons wing was perfectly silent.

He blinked. *Why?*

Danny listened, heart now throbbing with thickened blood. Not a sound beyond his own breathing. Maybe his ears weren't working properly because of the drug the warden had given him. Maybe he'd slept through the night and the others were gone to the yard.

Maybe something was wrong.

He pushed himself up onto one elbow and tried to clear his head. It was still night. The clock through the bars on the hall's far side read ten past midnight. But the wing was lit beyond his cell, not dark as it normally would be after lockdown.

His head felt like a steel ball as he turned it and glanced around the room. Gray. Undisturbed.

"Simon?"

The name chased emptiness around the room. Propped up on his elbow, Danny gripped the thin mattress with both hands and leaned over the edge.

The still form in the lower bunk took shape in the darkness. Its eyes were not closed. It was not sleeping. It was not clothed. It was not breathing. It was not Godfrey.

It was not alive.

Danny reacted without thinking, hurling himself off the top bunk. If not for the drugs, he would have landed on his feet. Instead he hit the concrete floor with his hip and left shoulder. Pain spiked his bones and jerked him to full awareness. He rolled to his left, slammed into the lockers with a loud clatter, and sprang to a crouch, eyes locked on the bed.

Peter stared at him, eyes wide, mouth parted like a dead fish. He was facedown, with his cheek flat on the mattress and his knees pulled up under his torso, as if bowing in prayer. His left hand dangled over the bed. Pale, delicate fingers pointed at the floor.

They'd cut him in a dozen places. They'd beat him to a pulp. They'd violated him and placed him here to beg forgiveness in supplication.

Danny staggered back, mind revolting.

"Godfrey?" He jerked his head around. No sign of the old man.

Danny pushed himself to his feet, shaking. Dear God, what had they done? Dear God, what had they done? Dear God…

And then Danny knew what they had done, because the words scrawled in blood on the wall behind Peter's body made it plain.

WELCOME TO HELL, PRIEST
I LIKE GIRLS TOO
GOD

This was Randell and Slane's doing, but he'd known that the moment he'd seen the naked body.

His second thought was of Renee.

In Danny's mind, the boy and Renee were suddenly one. They were the same, and it was because of him that they were bloodied and butchered.

For a long, unending breath that failed to fuel his lungs, Danny stood unmoving, unable to reason properly. The boy's white flesh looked ashen, stained by black blood and angry gashes. His eyes stared at him, pleading.

In the bowels of this sanctuary, Marshall Pape's truth was a lie. His justice was revolting. An eye for an eye.

Nausea swept through Danny's body. He stared back at Peter and let that familiar friend, rage, seep back into his bones. It swelled, then stormed, then shook his body.

He was suddenly moving toward the door. His steps carried him with only one thought.

Justice.

He reached his cell door and twisted the latch. Open. But of course it was open. This had all been planned. He stepped out onto the tier, turned, and quickly walked past vacant cells. There was no guard at the night station. There were no prisoners in their beds. The wing was empty except for Danny and the boy he'd failed to save.

The warden had moved them all out so they couldn't see what happened next. Whatever that was, it could not be good, because there *was* no good in the warden's sanctuary.

Images of the boy blinked through his mind. Peter and the girl who loved him, walking hand in hand through the park, smiling, delighted by birds. His bright eyes and eager voice: "Do you like chocolate, Danny?"

His fingernails dug into his palms, deeper with each breath.

"Oranges or grapefruit, Danny?" Dear Renee… "Grapefruit!" she would say before he could respond. "It's better for you. I'll put some sugar on it!"

He hated grapefruit but he would never tell her.

He hated prison. He hated the warden. He hated Slane. He hated himself. He hated the whole world because in the end it all came down to this.

To a deviant on his knees, bloodied and bruised because he'd been a naughty boy.

Danny spun around the rail at the stairs and took them down, one at a time, feet bare. They were waiting, he knew that. He was doing what they wanted him to do, he knew that as well. The monster would make him a monster, he knew that more than anything else.

So then, they would have their monster. None of them knew what he was capable of. None had stood by his side when he vindicated his mother's death. None had faced him on the streets where his way of justice would drop them to their knees, begging for mercy.

The steel door that closed off the commons wing when it was locked down was open. Why wouldn't it be? A way had to be left for the bull to be drawn to his slaughter. The rest of the prisoners had been moved to a safer place, where they could not witness what was to be done.

What the warden didn't know was that the slaughtered could also slaughter. That there was a time for peace and there was a time for war and there was a time to rip their heads from their skinny necks.

The thoughts pummeled Danny as he entered the hub. In a single glance he saw that it was empty except for a lone CO, who stood at the door to the administration wing. The facilitator had his arms crossed, watching him without emotion.

But in that moment he saw one other thing: this third-shift guard was also a man.

Not a facilitator or an officer or a machine or a monster, but a man. Dressed in a black uniform. In that moment it was the only thing that distinguished him from those in blue and tan. They all had families. They all had their favorite TV shows. They all had their enemies and their loved ones.

This realization was the first to fracture his rage, but the effect vanished when he turned his head and saw that the door to the gymnasium was cracked open. Behind that door waited the warden. If not him, then his henchmen. If not them, then Randell and Slane.

There was now only one path ahead of Danny, and it ended with Randell. The man would never again hurt another soul. The warden wanted Danny to kill Randell or Slane or both. In retrospect, the message had been clear from the outset. And now Danny would comply. He would put both men in their own personal, eternal grave.

His feet padded on the concrete floor, the sole sound in the great room. He reached the door to the hard yard, took hold of the lever, and pulled it wide. Two more steps, through the threshold, and he stopped.

The lights were on, blazing bright. Over a hundred prisoners lined the walls, all eyes on him, watching in dead silence. An armed guard stood in each corner, rifles in hand. The center of the room was cleared of all but stained concrete.

Danny stood still, mind spinning, scanning the faces, most of whom he knew only by sight. He didn't know them and they knew him only as the stubborn priest. Now they would learn more about him. Much more.

Some were dressed, some wore only shorts, as if they'd been awakened and herded here quickly. He saw Godfrey halfway down the right side, frail between two larger members. Danny quickly picked out Kearney, then Tracy Banner and John Wilkins. He didn't immediately see Randell or Slane.

No other prison could possibly produce such a moment. No other warden would allow, much less facilitate, a similar confrontation. No other inmate population would stand in wait, silent. There would be calls and taunts; the room would be full of bitterness and objection.

A whistle sounded from the far corner, and Randell stepped out from behind the line of members to Danny's left.

"You looking for me?" Randell walked toward him wearing a twisted grin. "You don't like what you saw?"

Danny moved forward, taking even, confident strides. The simple fact of the matter was that he could destroy the larger man. The world had seen too much evil from this devil.

"You want to fight me, is that it, Priest?"

Slane stepped out from the opposite corner. "How about me, boy?" His hands were bloody.

Danny stopped halfway across the hard yard, mind flashing back to that singular moment so many years ago in Bosnia when he hid behind a stove in his house and shot three killers. His life had come full circle. The victim was Peter now, but his mind was drawing no distinctions.

"You killed the boy," Danny said, staring at Slane's body, his bloody hands and arms.

"Oh, I did much more than that," the man said.

Danny dipped his head. "Then come here and do it to me," he said.

24

WE STRAPPED THE judge's arms and legs to a wood chair in his office with the duct tape from my kit. Keith pulled the shades and turned on the lamp that sat on a large cherry-wood desk. Hunter green wallpaper with black pinstripes covered the wall and ran behind paintings and bookcases. The office, which apparently doubled as a law library, was trimmed with a rich mahogany wainscot and crown molding.

Sicko's plans for us were clear. We were supposed to find out where the judge had his money and then kill him. Period. For twenty minutes, Keith paced in front of him, demanding answers to questions about drug money and Randell, with all the success of a man trying to wrestle answers from a brick wall.

In regard to minor details, Keith had more success. We learned his name: Judge Franklin Thompson. We learned that he presided over the Second District Court of Appeals; that before being elected to the court, he'd practiced law for fifteen years in the Bay Area; that he was divorced and had one son living in Boston; that he'd graduated from Yale Law School; that he'd smoked pot in college; that he had a boat in Marina del Rey, and that he was a narcissistic man who feasted on his own importance.

We also learned that he was loaded with money.

But I no longer cared about the money. I wasn't even sure Sicko's game had anything to do with money. What I did know was that the judge was my only outside link to Danny. I stood by the desk with my arms crossed and let the two of them hammer through their one-way interrogation, biting my tongue, eager to get on to Danny.

"How many times do I have to tell you? Even if I did know about Bruce Randell's conviction or incarceration, I'm bound by confidentiality," the judge was saying. Thompson's blotchy red face was sweaty, and his graying hair had fallen down over his forehead. "You must believe me, I don't know. I did not preside over the case and I have no clue about any drug money. Or any other money connected to this man. This is absurd."

Keith squatted down in front of the man and rested the barrel of his gun on the judge's lap. "And how many times do I have to tell you that we don't have a choice here? Someone thinks you have their money. You either tell us where it is, or all three of us are dead. All of us. I *know* it's absurd. I also know that I don't want to die. So either you tell us where the money is, or it's over. It that really too difficult to understand?"

"I don't *have* your one million dollars!" the man snarled.

Keith's hand flashed out and slapped the judge's cheek. "Wake up! Where's the money? Why do they want you dead?"

The room fell silent. Blood edged the corner of Thompson's mouth.

"I don't think you understand," the man said bitterly. "I am in no way connected to any drug money, so I have no idea why the people behind this would want me dead. Even if I agreed to give you a million dollars I couldn't get to it until the banks opened and it would take some time. You can't just muscle your way into a judge's home and demand a million dollars."

"This isn't our plan. It's someone else's, and they aren't giving us options."

"Who?" Thompson demanded.

"You tell me."

"I don't know!"

"Think!" Keith snapped. "Forget the money for a minute and think about who would tell us to come to this house and put a gun to your head. You have that security system in place for a reason. Who would want you dead, for any reason?"

Thompson blinked. "I have more enemies than I can count."

"But there has to be someone…A case that stands out. A sentence that kept you awake at night. Anything above and beyond."

The man hesitated, then shook his head slowly. "We do our best."

"Well tonight your best is going to get you killed."

"And you'd spend the rest of your life in prison. As you said, I have security. It includes surveillance. Both of you are already on tape, off site. If anything happens to me, the law's going to see that footage."

That caught us both off guard. Keith glared at Thompson. "The law's the least of our concerns. None of us will survive long enough."

I lowered my arms. "Keith, can I talk to you a minute?"

He faced me, flushed with frustration, then gave a shallow nod. We stepped outside the office and around the corner. The house was still dark except for the light from the office, and more spilling down the stairs from a wall lamp.

"He's lying," Keith said.

"Probably, but if he's got the money we'll have to tear the house apart to find it or wait until the banks open tomorrow, like he said. I don't think this has anything to do with Randell's drug money. I don't like it."

"None of this makes sense." Keith waved his gun absently. "None of it! Why would he send us here to kill a judge?"

"That doesn't matter now."

"He's got us on tape."

"We're being played, Keith. You said it yourself, this is about Danny. A judge who has it out for Danny."

He looked up at me. "You think *this* guy's Sicko?"

I glanced at the door and kept my voice low. "No. But I mentioned Danny's name before you came in, and he recognized it."

"You're sure?"

"I know a man's face. I want to find out what he knows about Basal and Danny."

"We're screwed now, I hope you realize that. He's got us on *tape*."

"We've been screwed for a week," I said. "Forget about the money. We have to find out what he knows about Danny." I stared into his eyes, determined. "I don't care what it takes."

"We need leverage, something to hold over his head."

"All right, we need leverage, but this is about Danny. And I want to do it my way now."

"Fine. Your way."

"I want to talk to him alone."

He wasn't expecting that. "Alone? Why?"

"Because I think I can talk to him as a woman."

"I don't see what—"

"Sometimes a woman can do things to a man that a man can't. Just give me ten minutes with him. Alone. With the door closed."

He stared at me, unsure.

I reached my hand out. "Give me the gun."

"You can't use the gun."

"I need leverage. What do you think I'm going to use, my body? Give me the gun."

"You can't kill the man."

"I'm not going to kill him! We have nothing to lose. Gun."

He hesitated, then handed it over. "I don't like this."

"You don't have to. Just watch the front door."

I entered the office and closed the door behind me. Locked it. I'd made a vow to never divulge any of Danny's crimes, which meant Keith couldn't know what I knew about Danny's first victim.

The judge couldn't either. Unless he already knew.

Thompson had managed to move his chair a few inches closer to the side of the desk. I had no idea what he hoped to accomplish. His hands were taped to the chair's rear legs. It wasn't like he was going to reach some hidden weapon.

I yanked a tapestry off the wall and wrestled it under the front legs of his chair to keep the carpet clean. Then I grabbed a second wooden chair from its grouping around a small chess table in the corner, plopped it down in front of the judge, and sat facing him with my hands around the gun on my lap. For a few seconds I just stared at him, torn between grabbing his hair and knocking it against the desk until he told me what he knew, or taking a more crafty approach as I knew Danny would.

"Now you listen to me, judge. I'm not a violent person, you have to know that. I'm not like the murderers and rapists you send away for life. What I am is a woman. I need you to understand what that means. Do you know how it feels to be a woman?"

He looked at me with blank eyes.

"No, you don't. Then let me help you out. Most women give birth to babies. It's in their blood to protect those children at any cost. They can't help it. It's in their DNA. You can't convince them otherwise, because it's actually a part of themselves they're protecting. They'll give up their lives to save their children if they have to. Even you...If you had a son, you'd do anything to save him. Wouldn't you?"

It took him a moment, but he finally dipped his head. *Yes.*

"Maybe even if that son had done something wrong," I said, thinking about that pedophile.

The man's eyes held steady.

"Take that impulse you feel, and double it," I said. "I don't have a son, but I still have that crazy-mother DNA, and I have someone as precious to me as any child. I'll do anything to save him. If that kills me or puts me in prison for the rest of my life, so be it. Nothing's going to stop me. Which means you have a very serious problem in front of you. You have a desperate woman who will do anything, and I mean *anything*, to find out what you know about the man she would give her life for."

His breathing was even. No denials, no confessions. Not yet.

"I lived in a nice house like this once," I said, glancing over his shoulder at the curtains. "It had very thick walls. Like yours. And at least double-pane glass. I don't think the neighbors will hear a gunshot, do you?"

"Using a gun won't save anyone." His voice was firm.

"It's not just anyone, it's my husband," I said. "His name is Danny Hansen. You don't fear me because you look in my eyes and you know I'm not a killer." I lowered my eyes to the gun and turned it over in my hands. "But there're other things I can do with this gun."

I stared at his knees, then at his crotch. I didn't know if Thompson was the father of the pedophile Danny had killed, but in my mind's eye he became that man. Danny had cut off his son's penis because he'd abused and killed a boy after being released from prison early, thanks to some fancy footwork by his father, the judge.

My eyes lingered on his zipper, then I drew them up his chest. To his face.

"I think you know why I'm here, Mr. Thompson. I don't expect a confession. Frankly, I don't care what you've done in your past. It doesn't matter what you did to upset whoever sent us here. I really don't care what you do tomorrow or the day after that. But tonight...tonight you're going to tell me what you know, do you understand?"

"I've told you what I know. Nothing."

"But you see, that's a lie. Nothing you say can change the fact that you've been fingered by someone who has a very elaborate plan that isn't sloppy or misinformed. There's nothing arbitrary about us being sent here. Nothing you say can change that. I may be small, but do I really look that stupid?"

Nothing.

"This is just between you and me now. To be honest, I'm not sure my friend has what it takes to blow off your penis. But you and I know about things like that, don't we?"

"I don't know what you're talking about."

"You don't know about a certain son of yours who was convicted for pedophilia?"

I dropped the bomb and watched, and the twitch in the corner of his right eye closed the loop for me.

"That's what I thought," I said. "The good news for you is, I don't care about that. Everybody's paid a price. What's done is done. Your secret's safe with me. All I need to know now is how you're connected to Basal."

"I don't know what you're talking about." He took two shallow breaths. "I told you, I don't..."

I didn't hear the rest of it, because my true nature flexed its full will and darkened my mind. I stood up, took one step forward, bent over, put the barrel against his right brown loafer, and pulled the trigger.

The shot crashed through the room and Judge Thompson jerked upright, roaring with pain and outrage.

Keith tried to open the door, found it locked, and banged on it.

"Renee! What are you doing? Open the door!"

"You shot me, you little whore!" Thompson snarled.

"It's okay," I snapped at Keith. "I just shot off his toe."

"Open this door!" he shouted.

But I had no intention of opening the door.

"I'm not done," I said. "I still have eight bullets."

25

"THEN COME HERE and do it to me." Danny's challenge hung in the hard yard, blasphemous and demanding a response.

Someone cleared his throat; otherwise there was no sound in the heart of that sanctuary. Randell stood fifteen paces away, left of center; Slane, fifteen paces right of center. The room was already turning in Danny's mind, transformed into a three-dimensional model examined by a student of the fight. The distance to the walls, the positioning of the members, the sections of the concrete floor that were smooth or rough, the lights, the switches, the clothing his opponents wore, all of it. Like a gladiator

armed only with his fists. Adrenaline had suffi-
ciently cleared his mind.

"Who do you think you are?" Randell asked.
There was a note of sincerity in his voice. "You
think you're gonna change anything?"

"Yeah, you think you're gonna change anything?"

"Shut up, Slane," Randell snapped at his
punk. The man's face flattened.

The big man jabbed his chin at Danny. "You
think a priest like you has anything on us
scum?"

"I'm not the priest who abused you," Danny
said. Randell stiffened. "I'm the priest who
found a boy abused by your punk. I'm the one
who defends boys like you."

Randell's face flushed red. "Shut up."

"They don't know you were raped by a priest
when you were a boy?"

"I said shut up!"

Randell was moving already, marching forward with his thick hands balled into fists.

"Not so fast, Bruce." The warden's voice rang
out from behind Danny.

Randell wasn't stopping.

"Back!" The order was that of a master commanding his dogs. This time Randell pulled up, eight paces away.

Pape's hard-soled patent-leather shoes clacked and grated on the concrete as he strolled out into the middle of the yard, one hand in his pocket. Danny let him come into view without removing his eyes from Slane or Randell.

"You think this is an unfair fight?" the warden asked Randell. "That you two can take him down? Then you don't know that our priest has made a life out of chewing up and spitting out people like you. When you were a little brat running around the neighborhood stealing old lady's purses, Danny here was in the business of killing men twice his size. More men than you can count."

He faced Danny, lips curved with a hint of a smile that reflected in his eyes. He was nothing less than delighted.

"It is unfair," he said. "Isn't it, Priest?"

Danny watched him. The words he'd spoken earlier were still cycling around his head like stray buzzards.

Do it to me.

"But it wasn't just these two who hurt little

Peter, Danny," the warden said. "No, there were three more." He scanned the members who stood along the walls. "Weren't there? Sure there were. Mason, Ratcliff, Stone. Step out."

Three men broke from the ring of onlookers and approached the center of the yard. Danny recognized two of them, both heavily tattooed white knuckleheads who in any other prison might be scrutinized for gang affiliation. But none of their tattoos was familiar to Danny. Prison ink.

The third was a skinny man with a bald head and a viper's sneer. Of them all, he was likely the most dangerous.

They moved into a circle around Danny. So then, it was now five on one.

"You kin take 'em, Danny," Kearney said from the side.

"You'd like to join them, Brandon?" the warden asked.

"No, sir."

"Then shut up. I will allow the priest to defend his honor and fight those who have so recklessly and gratuitously hurt Peter. The boy was abused, and however much that might disturb me, he was guilty of the same, so justice is served. As the book says, an eye for an eye. But death is a different matter. Just because God slays the wicked doesn't mean you may. Our aim is to rehabilitate, not kill, and one of these five men killed Peter. So now it only follows that the priest kills one of them."

He was speaking to the whole room, but his eyes stayed on Danny. No one seemed to be aware that Pape was contradicting himself, speaking of rehabilitation and retribution in the same sentence.

"If he can."

Danny stood at the epicenter of the grand stage, surrounded by opponents he could not fear, did not fear. Not because they couldn't kill him—a single mistake and they would, and might even if he made no errors. He could not and did not fear them because he'd been trained not to. Respect, yes. Fear, no.

But Danny feared himself.

If he extracted justice now he would be lost, pulled back into an ideology that had once ruined him.

Do it to me, he'd said to Slane. But if Danny struck back... To what end? More dead bodies for his graveyard?

An image of Peter bowed in prayer pleaded with him. Danny's eyes rested on Slane, the one who'd surely enjoyed Peter's abuse the most. And there he saw a man. A hellion, a beast, but one with pretty blue eyes.

"What do you say, Danny?" the warden said. "Will you rise up to your calling?"

And there was Randell as well, belligerent, once abused by a priest. Now he would be killed by one?

Danny felt the muscles in his shoulders begin to ease. He let his fingers relax. There was Brandon Kearney, face stark with hope, eager to see Danny extract revenge. There stood tall Tracy Banner, with a scar on his cheek, watching with some wonder. Down the row, John Wilkins's lost expression begged for answers.

Here stood the whole world. They all wanted to see justice. They all wanted him to spill blood. How much was enough?

"In my sanctuary, I am God, boy," the warden bit off. Danny looked at him and saw that his face had gone flat. He knew.

"Vengeance is mine. When I say march, you march. When I say kill, you will kill. Or, my friend…I swear I will send you to that hole down there that they call hell. And this time your wailing will be heard for miles."

"No."

Pape's eyes briefly narrowed. "No?"

"I was wrong. You're right, I could hurt these men." He glanced at Randell, who looked confused. "I could snap Randell's neck before he landed one blow." Slane. "I could break Slane over my knees like he deserves. That might be fair. But fairness has failed the world."

The hard yard sat in perfect quiet.

"Why did you come?" The warden's voice was tight.

"I came to kill Randell."

"Then you will kill him."

"I was wrong."

"And so you'll let them kill you?"

Danny took a deep breath, knowing already what he would do, what he must do. This wasn't just about him, it was about Renee. He could not die.

"No."

Marshall Pape looked at Randell, then the other four. "Kill him!" he said.

26

"SEVEN BULLETS LEFT," I said, staring at the bloodied tapestry under the judge's chair. He was being stubborn and I'd felt compelled to put a second bullet through his other foot, into the subfloor beneath the thick green carpet. They were hard jackets and passed through cleanly without making too much of a mess.

But none of that lessened the judge's pain.

Keith gave up trying to break the door down after the second shot, when I'd taken a moment to explain what I was doing.

I sat in the chair, unable to steady my trembling hands. "The nice thing about losing toes is that you can cover them up with good shoes.

With good therapy no one but you will even know someone shot them off. But I hear it's hard to walk if you lose too many, especially the big toes."

He was sweating and his face was flushed. Tears of pain leaked down his cheeks.

"You're done," he growled through clenched teeth.

"Not really. Because if I still can't get you to talk, I'm going for the biggest toe." I gave his crotch a significant glance. "I really don't want to do that, but I hope you understand now that I can't control myself. This is something I have to do."

"You can't get away with this."

"But you did, didn't you? You put your son back on the street, and he went back and killed that poor boy. You don't have to confess that. I just want to know how you're connected to Basal. That's all. Think about it. I'm not going to incriminate you. I'd go to prison if what I've done here ever came out. I'd have to spill all the beans and there'd be a full investigation into both of us. We're in the same boat, so we have to keep this all private—me and my crazy DNA and you with your secret. Just tell me and we'll leave. I'm not going to kill you, even though that's what we were sent to do. I'm not a violent person."

He was looking at me as if I was a complete nut, and that was fine by me. The crazier he thought I was, the better.

I kept telling myself it was okay. That I had to do this, that I'd already gone too far to turn back, that this man *did* hold the key to Danny's life, that in some ways Danny was in prison *because* this man had pushed Danny beyond the brink when he'd cut his son loose. But I didn't really know if any of that was true, and I was feeling nauseated.

The judge sat in his chair, chest rising and falling as he tried to control his agony.

"So I have to use another bullet?" I asked.

"This is absurd." The last word was a snarl.

"Is that a yes or a no?"

He only glared at me. So I stood up, leaned over, and pressed the gun to the tip of his right shoe. I was just starting to squeeze the trigger when he spit in my hair. Dirty germy spit.

My crazed DNA reasserted itself. I jerked the gun up and shoved it into his crotch.

"You shouldn't have done that," I said. "I

know what your son did. You think Danny killed him and now you're after Danny. Tell me what you know about Basal or I'm going to pull this trigger."

He swore.

"You don't think I'll do it? Like son, like father."

His jowls were trembling, and for a moment I felt sorry for the man. What if I was wrong about him?

"You have three seconds. Two. One..."

"Okay," he blurted. "I'll tell you!"

"Tell me!"

27

"KILL HIM!" THE warden's order echoed through the hard yard.

The first to come wasn't Randell. The big man had heard something that made him hesitate. The first was one of the heavily tattooed men behind Danny, and he came like a bull, rushing at full speed as if this were a street fight and he could simply overwhelm Danny by force.

Without turning, Danny waited, using the sound of the man's feet slapping on the concrete to judge his distance. The other tattooed member joined the rush, to the right and slightly behind the first man.

By not turning, Danny offered his attacker the false perception that victory was imminent, that if he only moved faster and reached Danny before he could turn, he would be able to break his back from behind. This belief drew the man into a final headlong rush.

Slane was now on the move as well. That made three coming in, no contact.

Danny spun to his right when the tattooed man was only one step away. Hooked his arm behind the man's back, and shoved hard. The off-balance attacker flew forward and collided head-on with Slane.

A bone snapped. They both crashed to the ground with Slane beneath, screaming in pain.

But now the other tattooed man arrived, swinging his fist at Danny's head like a club. Danny shifted and blocked the blow down and away with his forearm. In any other circumstance he would have caught the arm and wrenched it back for either a break or a dislocation.

As it was, he helped the man find the ground with a kick at his ankles and quick shove at his back. Arm deflected and twisting, the man landed on his shoulder with a grunt.

Slane was moaning. He'd been struck with a

head to his arm, now broken. The first attacker was back on his feet, facing him like an ape. But Danny had disrupted their circle and he now backed away from the three standing men, hands lifted in partial surrender.

"I don't want to fight, but I'll defend myself. Please, this isn't necessary."

"Fight!" the warden roared.

All but Slane found their feet and came together, screaming bloody murder. Four grown men unfamiliar with tactics any more strategic than brawling with fists or backstabbing with shanks. Without a dark corner from which to spring, without an element of surprise, with only their fists and muscles, they were at a hopeless disadvantage.

They came fast, sure that four abreast could overwhelm one man. But all four had two legs, and all eight of those legs were propelling them forward.

Danny feinted back one step into a half crouch, but instead of retreating he surged toward them and threw himself down, perpendicular to their path.

He hit the ground at their feet and crashed through them.

The two on the ends had time to jump, but still he caught one of them by the foot. The two in the center—Randell and one of the tattooed men—took the full weight of Danny's body on their ankles. Their forward momentum carried their bodies where their feet could not go.

Another bone snapped. Three of the men sprawled headlong onto the concrete. Two rolled and came up, panting. The tattooed man lay on the floor near Slane, twisting with the pain of a broken ankle.

Danny had missed the skinny one entirely, and now the man twisted back to take a vicious kick at Danny's head.

There was no way to avoid the contact. Danny arched his back and took a glancing blow on his temple.

The man left his legs exposed, and Danny could have struck the side of his knee, perhaps disabling him with one kick. But doing so stood a good chance of putting the man out of commission for more than a single fight.

Instead, he rolled away and came up in time to deflect a second blow aimed at his head. This time he took the man's feet out from under him.

The skinny, bald man landed on an un-padded seat. Hard.

Danny backpedaled on light feet, hands up. "You don't need to do this. You must understand, I won't fight, but I must defend myself. Please…"

"You call that not fighting?" Slane blurted from the ground.

"You're alive, aren't you?"

The warden wore a mild grin, whether truly impressed or shocked and attempting to cover it, Danny didn't know.

"You've made your point," Danny said.

"Have I?" The warden held up his hand toward Randell, who was circling in, eyes crazed. "No, I don't think I have. The point is, we accept only deviants in this place. Bring your broken and wounded and I will make them whole, isn't that the way it works? I will rehabilitate you. But you, Danny, don't want to accept that you're broken. You're as evil as the rest of them, but you really do think you're better. How can I help you if you don't first show me just how broken you are?"

"I *am* broken!" Danny shouted.

"Then kill him!" The warden jabbed his finger at Slane. "Kill the man who broke my rules and killed young Peter. An eye for an eye. Take his life!"

"I can't!"

Pape stopped. Stared at Danny for a moment.

"Captain?"

Bostich took one step away from the wall. "Yes, sir!"

"Kill Slane."

A beat of silence.

"Shoot him, sir?"

"He broke a fundamental rule and killed a man, did he not?"

"Yes, sir."

"Then do the same to him."

"Yes, sir."

Bostich lifted his rifle, aimed at Slane, who was just beginning to grasp what was happening, and shot him through the head before the first cry of protest could be heard. The loud crash of gunfire echoed through the room.

Slane dropped flat, hole in head.

"Now," the warden said, addressing Danny. "Kill Randell."

28

"TELL ME, OR I swear I'm pulling this trigger," I snapped.

The judge was trembling from head to bloody feet, furious that I'd maneuvered him into baring his deepest secret. But he still wasn't telling me.

"I swear…"

"I received a call from Basal this morning," he breathed.

"That's not enough. We'll start over. Three, two,…"

"The warden called me an hour ago." He was breathing hard. "He said there'd been an accidental death. A rape that went too far."

A rape?

"You know the warden? Why would he call you? Who was raped?"

"I was instrumental in transferring a young man convicted of statutory rape to his prison. The boy was evidently raped."

"What about Danny?"

He held his silence and I knew that this was the information that had him resisting all along. He could have told me about the boy earlier, but it was something about Danny that he wanted to keep from me.

"What was the name of your son?"

The muscles along his jawline bulged.

I pressed the gun in tighter. "Tell me!"

"Roman," he said.

"He was a pedophile?"

"Yes. Now move the gun."

So I really had been right. I stood back and lowered the gun to my side, still trying to connect the dots. Franklin Thompson had made the one confession he never imagined making, but I needed more. Danny had killed the judge's son, and for that maybe I was sorry. But that was the past.

"What does the boy's rape have to do with Danny?"

"The warden said there could be some trouble, and he wanted legal advice. If any of this comes out, you know I'll deny it."

"Tell me what I need to know and it won't. Trouble with who? With Danny?"

The man's eyes shifted. "He told me that the inmate behind the rape wants to kill Danny. And that he's inclined to allow it. That's all I know."

"What do you mean kill Danny?" Waves of heat washed over my face. "Who's going to kill Danny?"

"That's all I know! I sent the boy there because the warden said he needed him to break Danny. I didn't know he would be killed. Danny murdered my son!"

"If you could prove that you'd have gone through legal channels." But my mind was on Basal. Randell was going to kill Danny, and the warden was in on it. "You have to help me stop it," I said.

"I can't."

"What do you mean, you can't? You set this up—you have to!"

"I didn't set it up. I only got him the boy."

"Call the warden and tell him I know everything."

"I can't. And you don't."

"Why can't you?"

"The warden knows too much. He would turn on me. My life would be over."

"I don't care if your life would be over! You set Danny up, you get him out!"

Keith banged on the door. "Renee?"

"Hold on!"

Blind with rage, I walked back up to the judge and put the gun against his teeth. "Now you listen to me, Judge. I really have lost it. You hear me? I'm a neurotic, manic mess. I don't care anymore if I live or die. You're going to call that warden and you're going to get Danny out of there, or I swear I'm going to blow off another body part!"

"You don't understand. The warden would start cleaning up his mess the moment I called him! They'd all be dead—Danny, the boy, Randell—all of them. There'd be no witnesses. And then he'd come after me."

My mind was in a dark fog, and all I could see was Danny, the gentle giant who'd taken a vow of nonviolence, turning the other cheek as the warden beat him to a bloody, dead mess.

But somewhere in that fog I knew that the

judge was right. The machine that had growled to life couldn't be stopped with a phone call. Or by the law, not quickly enough.

Danny had awakened a leviathan, and now he was in its jaws. He was in that monster factory, doing his time. Time that was grinding to a halt.

29

DANNY TOOK A step back at the order. *Kill Randell.*

Slane's body lay facedown in a pool of his own blood. The man with the broken ankle was dragging himself away from the body. Randell's face twisted into a pitted ball of rage.

Danny took another step back.

"Kill him, or I'll kill you and she'll be all alone out there, twisting in the wind."

Renee…

Panic lapped at Danny's mind. He could not kill Randell. He could, yes he could, but in doing so he would become only another monster, and a monster could not love Renee.

Randell took the matter out of Danny's hands, no doubt certain that if he didn't kill Danny, Bostich would shoot him too.

He roared and rushed.

Danny's first instinct was to take the man down. Doing so would have been a simple matter. But Randell was built like an oak and wouldn't fall for a simple disabling maneuver again. Danny would have to use force. A lot of it.

His mind scrabbled, grasping for a way out of the warden's impossible game. All he could think of was a fist to the man's throat.

But no, he would crush Randell's windpipe.

His opponent came in like a bull, fists up like hammers, and Danny skipped backward on the balls of his feet.

"Don't do it, Bruce," he breathed. "It's no good!"

"Fight!" the warden shouted. "Kill him!"

"Kill him, Danny!" Kearney shouted. Other prisoners joined in, their mutters and jeers encouraged by the warden's own order. Randell was the enemy to most of them. They all wanted to see his blood on the ground.

They, too, wanted justice.

"Kill him, Danny!" Pape shouted over the din. "Rip his head off!"

This was their coliseum and Danny was their gladiator.

But he would not kill Randell. There was only one way.

Danny ducked out of Randell's reach and stopped ten feet from the warden, eyes on the raging bull.

He held out one hand. "Hold on!"

Randell came on, but he slowed.

"Just hold on!" Danny snapped.

The man was panting, blinking the sweat from his eyes. Desperate to survive.

Danny lowered his guard. He started for the larger man, arms at his sides.

"Let's at least make this fair," he said.

Now only four paces from Randell.

"I can't in good conscience simply kill you. You first. Hit me."

Two paces.

"Hit me with everything you have, you dumb oaf!"

Randell closed the last step, drew his fist back and threw his full weight into a full swing at Danny's head.

He let the blow come, knowing that he was flirting with death. But he saw no other way.

The man's fist landed on his temple, snapping Danny's head to the side and back.

The darkness came quickly, and his contact with the concrete shut off the world. Danny lay on his back, at their mercy.

30

I FACED THE judge and all I could think was that I had to save Danny. Danny had saved me and now I had to save him. The judge was complicit in a plan to destroy him, and I alone knew the full truth.

As I saw it, there was only one way to save him.

I hurried to the door, turned the handle, and jerked it open. Keith spun from where he was pacing in the shadows. I gave the door a shove and let it slam behind me.

"We have to break into Basal."

He stared at me. "What happened?"

"I'm done with this game. I'm going in there and I'm going to kill Randell."

"You think that'll stop Sicko? What happened in there?"

"He's going to kill Danny, that's what happened."

"The judge told you that?"

"The warden's in on it. They're in that institution, free to do whatever they want, and right now what they want is to break Danny. I'm going after him."

"Hold on, slow down." Keith walked to the office door, cracked it wide enough to glance inside and, satisfied that the judge was as he was supposed to be, notwithstanding bloody feet, he shut it and faced me.

"From the top. Before any more crazy talk about breaking into Basal, I need to know what just happened in there. What did he say?"

"I shot off two of his toes."

"I saw."

"He told me that he came to some kind of agreement with the warden to send a boy to Basal so the warden could break Danny. But it's all gone wrong and now Randell's going to kill Danny."

Keith dropped his eyes to the floor. "He knows we didn't follow his instructions. The boy at the warehouse—we didn't cut off his finger. He's following through."

"Either way, we have to get in," I said. "And the judge can't know. All it would take is one call from the judge to warn the warden." I couldn't say anything about the judge's son—Danny's first victim. "We have to go, Keith. It's our only play."

"Slow down…"

"They brought Danny to Basal to break him, but I know Danny. He doesn't break easily. They'll kill him instead."

He hesitated, then nodded. "You're forgetting about Sicko. Unless you think the judge is Sicko…"

No, that didn't make sense, did it? "Sicko wants the judge dead," I said.

"So who's pulling the strings? The warden?"

"Maybe."

He paced, running his hands through his hair. "Why would the warden have a grudge against Danny? I can understand trying to break him on the inside, but why go through all this trouble with us?"

"Because he knows how much Danny loves me. And if Danny knows what's happening to me he'd…" *Lose it,* I thought, but a knot in my throat cut off my voice.

"I don't know. The warden wouldn't risk all this craziness to break a man." He glanced back at the door. "That leaves the judge. But that doesn't makes sense either. Why would he want us to kill him? And why would he make us jump through all of these hoops?"

In a perfect world, we'd have the answers we needed before we did anything crazy, like break into Basal. But we didn't have time to unravel the mess. I had to get to Danny. That was all I cared about now.

"It doesn't matter. We have to get in there before it's too late."

"It always matters."

"We get inside the prison and stop Randell—that's what matters. The answers are there. All of them, there, not here."

He didn't object as quickly this time.

"Assuming we could get in and stop Randell, the warden would just find another way to break Danny," he said.

"Then we stop the warden. We blow the whole thing sky-high!"

"How?"

"I don't know how," I snapped. I took a deep breath and tried to gather myself. "You tell me how. Prisons are built to keep people in, not keep them out. Don't tell me there's no way. We either get in there and stop this or, like you told the judge, we're all finished. All of us."

He lifted a hand to quiet me. "Okay, calm down." He absently scratched at his neck. "But Sicko's still pulling strings. He can't find out we've abandoned the judge. Which means..." His voice trailed off.

"What?"

He flipped me a glance. "His instructions gave us forty-eight hours to get the money. We'd have to do it within the next two days."

I'd won him over, which could be either good or bad, but in that moment all I could think about was Danny, and Danny was in trouble *now*, not in two days.

"We can't wait that long."

"You can't just drive up there and walk in. We'd have to get the right identification, make the arrangements, and plan it down to the minute. And then there's the getting-out part."

"So you know how we can get in?"

He averted his eyes. "Maybe. I've been think-ing…I made a few calls."

"And you didn't tell me?"

"You would have insisted. We didn't know enough to go off half-cocked. We still don't."

"I do." I walked over to my kit open on the floor and shoved the gun into the bag. "Every-thing leads back to Basal. Everything." I snapped the kit shut and snatched it off the floor. "We're wasting our time here."

"What about the judge?"

"We tell him he has two days to gather one million dollars. We'll be back in forty-eight hours."

"And what if he goes to the police? Or warns the warden?"

"He won't," I said. "I know too much about him now. If he can't keep quiet, what I know about him goes to the press."

31

HE DIDN'T KNOW how long he'd been out, only that he wasn't dead. And that he'd been brought back to consciousness by water thrown on his face.

"Wake up, you idiot. Payback time." The captain's voice.

Danny opened his eyes. The concrete ceiling of the terrible room where he'd spent two days slowly came into focus. He was in deep meditation. The place of torment.

But he was alive, which could only mean that the warden had stopped Randell from killing him as he lay unconscious in the hard yard. This was what Danny had hoped for. Death wasn't Pape's objective. His world revolved around compliance and punishment.

But what of Randell?

Danny turned his throbbing head and saw that he wasn't on the ground. Or on the wall. He lay on his back, arms and legs strapped to the wooden table, dressed only in loose shorts.

Bostich stood over him wearing a slash for a grin. Sweat beaded his forehead and darkened the armpits of his uniform.

"Wakie, wakie."

A doctor from the infirmary stood in the corner, dressed in a white smock. There was a black medical bag at his feet. The man was tall and gaunt, with high cheekbones and a balding blond head. He watched Danny, emotionless, hands clasped in front of his waist.

The door opened, and the warden stepped into the room like a sloth, slow and deliberate. He closed the door behind him and straightened his black suit jacket.

Danny saw then that they'd strapped down his shins and thighs as well as his ankles. The low-wattage incandescent bulb on the ceiling flickered once, then remained lit, casting its glow about the room.

Marshall Pape slid one hand into his pocket as he always did, and stepped into the middle of the room. There wasn't a hint of kindness on his face.

"You disappoint me, Danny. You saw what they did to that poor boy. Slane was the kind of person other prisons keep paroling back into society to prey on the weak. The kind who took my family. I'm trying to fix that, and I'd hoped to get a little help from a priest. I was wrong."

But Danny's mind was more on the straps holding his legs. Why? A tinge of fear leaked through his bones.

The warden nodded at the doctor, who bent for his black bag.

"Did your father ever send you into quiet time when you were a child, Danny?"

He cleared his throat. "Yes."

"Think of the hole as a kind of quiet time. But if you keep breaking the rules, things get worse. The next time, your father might take away privileges. Then swat your hand. Then maybe give you a good whipping."

No, but Danny said nothing.

"You may think of this as your good whipping. I hope it's your last."

He stepped aside as the doctor placed his black bag on the table. From it he withdrew a white cloth, which he placed next to Danny, then latex gloves, and something that looked like a silver electric toothbrush without the brush. A small jar of disinfectant and several cotton swabs were next.

The warden continued in a calm voice. "Don't worry, he's very clean. It's important that you don't develop an infection."

The doctor removed a small white case, which he opened. From it, he selected a very thin six-inch needle that went into the end of the device. Or was it a small drill bit, like those used by dentists?

Sweat began to seep out of Danny's pores.

The doctor connected a small air tube to the silver wand and set it down on the white cloth. Taking the disinfectant, he wiped a four-inch section of Danny's shin.

No one spoke now. Bostich stood with his arms crossed, wearing a smirk. The warden watched, hand in pocket, frowning. The doctor calmly went about his business.

"The advantage of this particular form of punishment is that it will leave only a very small mark," Pape said. "The needle will reach into your bone and grind at certain nerves. There will be no permanent damage, but you can expect the pain to be quite intense. It doesn't compare to eternal fire, but you'll get the general idea."

The doctor felt along Danny's shin bone with his thumb until he found what he was looking for. Keeping the thumb in place, he reached into the black bag and turned on a power source. A small air pump.

He lifted the drill and Danny closed his eyes. The device whined once, then twice as the doctor tested it.

"We've only taken one other member this far," Pape continued. "Slane was terribly stubborn when he came to us, and now he's dead. Such a shame, but some people just can't be rehabilitated in their time. As for Peter's suffering, it was short. Yours will last two days. We'll talk then."

He stepped away. The door squealed open, then closed behind him.

Bostich pressed a thick strip of rubber against Danny's mouth. "Bite on this. You don't want to chew off your tongue."

He accepted the piece, bit into it, and marshaled all of his focus to one end: shutting down his mind. The brain controlled pain. The nerve endings might be stimulated, but unless their message was properly interpreted by the mind, the pain would be lost. There was no way to avoid the warden's punishment, but he could endure it by minimizing that pain.

This Danny knew, but he had never felt a thin, whining drill grind into his bones before. The device screeched to life.

"Try not to move," the doctor said. "We have a long way to go and I don't want to tear up your bone marrow."

It was with that word *marrow* that Danny's resolve began to fade.

The tip of the drill touched his skin and a sharp sting shot up his leg. But not so much that he flinched. Then it struck his chin and the sensation swelled, a biting, excruciating pain that brought with it spreading heat as his flesh rebelled.

This too, Danny could manage for some time. He bit down on the rubber with more force and pushed his thoughts into submission, searching for the solace that he'd learned to find beyond them.

But then the drill broke past the surface of the bone and struck a tangle of nerves that shattered any notion he could endure such torment. The pain was not localized; it slammed into his whole body at once, like a thundering wave crashing onto the shore.

Nothing could have prepared him for such intense agony. His body began to tremble from head to foot. His head snapped back, and he clamped down on the rubber, desperate for relief.

"Hold still," the doctor said. "It gets worse with time. Just try to relax."

Danny's jaw snapped wide and he began to scream.

32

I WAS A bundle of raw nerves. Keith drove the rented black Ford sedan down Highway 138 toward Lone Pine Canyon Road toward Basal. He had pulled the entire plan together in fewer than forty hours and, despite the fact that it fell into place so seamlessly, I was certain we'd forgotten something.

We had identification. Getting in would all come down to our Office of the Inspector General ID badges.

Never mind that. Even if we hadn't forgotten anything and getting into the prison proved to be as simple as we thought it could be, we were entering the lions' den. The warden was in there. Randell was in there.

We were dressed like congressmen visiting our constituents, Keith in a dark blue suit and me in blue slacks and a white blouse.

I'd watched a documentary once about the cult leader Jim Jones, who set up a compound for his followers in Guyana called Jonestown. A congressman who had gone in to investigate rumors of abuse lost his life along with more than nine hundred temple followers.

I couldn't shake the feeling that Basal was our Jonestown and I was that congressman.

We'd left Judge Thompson in his estate, assured of his silence and compliance. Knowing that he was complicit at some level, we told him what we wanted him to hear: someone wanted him dead, and unless he got our hands on one million dollars within forty-eight hours, we would have to at least fake his death. We would be back. There would be no contact until then, because we believed that someone was watching.

As to why Sicko wanted the judge dead, the reasoning had become obvious to us: Thompson was a loose end who knew too much to be left alive. If we killed him, we would be implicated in his murder and go to prison, which was one of Sicko's stated objectives from the beginning. It was the perfect setup.

As to why Sicko had led me to the dancing bear, then to the warehouse with the maimed boy before leading us to the judge, the answer seemed obvious in retrospect: he was manipulating me, pushing me further and further, hoping I would snap and kill a man with my own hands.

But now we'd turned the tables on him. He didn't know it yet, but he was now playing *our* game, and in that game I needed the judge alive. In fact, he was invaluable. Assuming both Danny and I survived the next twenty-four hours.

"You're sure these IDs will work?" I asked.

Keith didn't bother answering. He drove the sedan in silence, as he had for most of the drive north. Neither of us had slept more than a few hours since Sunday night.

He'd dyed his hair black and wore a mustache and goatee. He looked nothing like the Keith I knew. I'd found a short blonde wig and wore rectangular, wireframe glasses. True, I was still my skinny self, but Keith seemed certain that the warden wouldn't detect us. Although he had probably seen pictures of us, he hadn't met either of us in person, a key factor in recognition. Our alterations were simple but they would be effective, and I had to trust him on that.

"How long?" I asked.

"Five minutes."

Honestly, most of my nervousness revolved around the thought of seeing Danny again. Would I? What condition was he in? Was he even alive? I stared at the road ahead and tried to imagine seeing him again. Would he recognize me with a wig on? What would I say?

I'd written a letter that laid it all out—everything that had happened, everything we planned. Although the judge didn't know it yet, with his help I was going to get Danny transferred out of Basal. But first we had to keep him alive. We had to stop Randell. We had to deal with the warden. That couldn't be done from the outside because there was too much risk of the warden being tipped off, which would send him sky-high. He'd blow up the whole prison with Danny in it. He'd become the new Jim Jones, and Basal would become his Jonestown.

The letter was folded neatly in my underwear—nothing was as important as getting it to Danny.

Keith gave me a quick glance, then returned his gaze to the road.

"What are you thinking?" I asked.

He waited a while before answering. "I was thinking that I've been over this a hundred times, and I'm still having a hard time believing the system would leave such a gap in their security. They must have retina scans, fingerprints—*something* to identify OIG deputies besides a simple ID."

I gave him our pat answer. "Who wants to break into prison, right?"

"Yeah, but you'd think they'd have more protocols in place. What if someone wanted to break in to kill a high-value target? I know we're not talking witnesses here, we're talking convicted inmates. One gets knocked off and no one really cares much. Still…"

"But you trust your source," I said, knowing the answer.

He nodded absently. "Sources. Three of them."

Our break-in would be made possible because of the separation of power between the California Department of Corrections and Rehabilitation and the governor's Office of the Inspector General, the investigative watchdog that had reporting authority over the way the CDCR ran the prisons. In essence, the OIG could investigate any complaints of abuse in the department of corrections. Misappropriation of funds, theft—any form of misconduct in the prison system was the OIG's to flush out.

OIG deputies routinely showed up unannounced to audit, inspect, or investigate complaints. According to California law, any prison official's refusal to cooperate constituted a misdemeanor. The OIG was seen by some as the governor's Gestapo arm, the adversary, the ones who made the difficult task of controlling prison populations even harder.

But that adversarial relationship gave OIG deputies healthy respect, and we intended on tapping it. We needed only an hour inside, plenty of time to do what we needed to do and get out before any collateral damage was discovered.

There were problems, challenges that would

have been impossibilities without Keith's connections, like getting fake ID badges made quickly. And any investigation into a prison like Basal would immediately put the warden on high alert. He would watch us like a hawk.

After numerous phone calls and hours of digging, the plan that Keith landed on seemed flawless.

We would show up unannounced as two deputies dispatched from the main office in Sacramento. The warden would be familiar with regional deputies. Our papers identified us as deputies Myles Somerset and Julia Wishart. We were investigating a current well-known problem in the system: spiked milk supplied by the Prison Industry Authority. We would take random blood and urine samples from inmates, and milk samples from the kitchen. It would take only an hour and we'd be out of their hair.

The warden wouldn't call the Sacramento office to verify our task, because doing so would cast suspicion on his motives for inserting himself into the investigation. You don't call headquarters and demand to know why the Gestapo are checking out your prison unless you're covering something up. He might be able to make inquiries through back channels, but it would take time. Hopefully enough for us to get in and out.

Once we were processed and inside, we had the authority to ask the staff to help us or stay clear. We would find Randell and Danny, do what we needed to do, and leave.

Simple.

But we both knew nothing was ever that simple.

Keith took the turn onto the winding canyon road, and the silence seemed to deepen, despite the fact that neither of us was talking. The radio was off, the windows were up, the air was turned down. My gut felt inside out.

"Remember," he said softly. "It's all in the way we play it. It's in the eyes and the voice. Who are you?"

"Julia Wishart. OIG. You don't need to worry, I can handle myself."

"I know you can. So does the judge now."

"Maybe I should shoot off Randell's toes."

"Maybe not." We both grinned, but our attempt at humor fell flat.

"We stick to our agreement," Keith said. "We go in, confront Randell, tell him if he touches

Danny he'll spend the rest of his life in a far worse place, learn what we can about Sicko from him, warn Danny, then get out. If everything falls apart, we call the authorities using the number on speed dial. I'd rather be at the mercy of law enforcement than of the warden. If neither of us can make a call and we can't get out..." He blew out some air. "Let's just hope it doesn't come down to that."

"You're sure they won't search us?"

"They could by law but they won't. I've checked. Once they process us we can come and go as we please. Just remember that and wear it on your face, not just on your badge."

"Like I said, I can handle myself."

I wasn't exactly new to this. I knew I could flip a switch if I had to. You do what you have to do when the world is at stake, and Danny was my world.

We passed the bluff where I'd stood and looked down at Basal just over a week earlier. Keith guided the car around a curve, and the prison's first checkpoint came into view. A brick guardhouse with a gate. Two officers stood inside behind the large glass window.

"Here we go," Keith said. "Let me do the talking."

He slowed the car and came to a stop next to the reinforced glass. I immediately recognized one of the men in the guardhouse. It was the blond man I'd talked to on my first visit.

My first thought was that it was over. He'd recognize me. He knew I wasn't with the OIG.

But I wasn't the same woman he'd met, was I? I was Julia Wishart, OIG.

Keith beamed at the man. "Afternoon, gentlemen." He casually stuck out his ID. "Myles Somerset, OIG. We need access to the facility for an inspection, if that's not a problem."

The man stared at Keith, then at his ID, then looked at me. For a moment I wasn't sure how to take his stare. He'd been confident, casual, completely in command when I'd met him before. Now he seemed off guard, and I wasn't sure if it was because he sensed something wrong or because a visit from the inspector general naturally set most prison staff on edge.

"OIG," he said. "What's the nature of your visit?"

"Well now, that would take all the fun out of it, wouldn't it?"

The officer stared at him. We all knew that OIG had no obligation to explain itself. Keith let the question stand for a second, then grinned.

"We're doing routine inspections tied to an investigation of the Prison Industry Authority. You can understand my reluctance to give any opportunity to suppress evidence. It's a supply-side issue. We'll be in and out in an hour."

The guard's eyes met mine again. "Identification?"

I reached across Keith and handed him my ID. "Afternoon, Officer. Deputy Julia Wishart." I could think of nothing else to say, so I just said, "Shouldn't take long."

The man took my badge and dipped his head. "Just one second."

He retreated into the booth, spoke to the other staff member, then lifted a phone off the wall and made a call.

"He's checking," I whispered.

Keith didn't respond. He didn't even look at me, which was message enough. *Shut up.*

The guard spoke into the phone, tapped quickly at a keyboard, then hung up the receiver. Our names would come up on a list of registered OIG deputies because our counter-parts actually existed, far away in Sacramento, probably pushing paper. Keith had done his homework. An elderly man with round spec-tacles somewhere in Culver City knew he'd forged two OIG IDs for the fair price of five thousand dollars, but any admission on his part would land him in prison. We were covered.

Again, I only half-believed it.

The guard leaned back out of the booth and handed Keith the IDs. "Long way from Sacra-mento."

"Tell me about it," Keith said. "They're run-ning this one out of the main office."

He nodded. "Head on down to the first sally port. They're expecting you. A staff member will accompany you from there."

"Thank you, sir." Keith gave him half a salute, put the car back in gear, and headed past the lifted gate.

We drove for a hundred yards before either of us spoke. "Never underestimate the value of a good forgery," Keith said.

"Just like that."

"Not quite."

But it was just like that.

I knew it was too easy. I should have known then that something was terribly wrong. I kept telling myself that it would work, that everything was going to be all right, that the demons screaming inside of me were just a part of my neurosis. I kept thinking that although getting in was the easiest part, God was on our side, because we'd come to set the world straight and sometimes the good side does win.

But then suddenly it wasn't just like that, because we came around a corner and the massive structure called Basal loomed before us.

I sat next to Keith, numbed by our audacity in the face of that fortress. It had all seemed so doable on paper, but driving up to the prison I was suddenly certain that I wouldn't come out alive. If I did, it would be in Danny's shackles because he would no longer need them. He'd be dead.

Then again, maybe it really was just like that, because we were breaking in, not breaking out, and getting into prison was very easy in the United States of America. You can check in anytime you like, but you can never leave.

The first gate at the perimeter fence rolled open as we approached. I sat still and tried to keep my mind on Danny as we rolled into the sally port.

"This is it," I heard Keith say.

"Just like that," I returned.

"Not quite," he repeated.

But it was. A deputy welcomed us, asked us to leave the rental car where it was, and then led us, briefcases in hand, along the fences to steps leading up to the arching front entrance. The massive bolts on the iron doors were drawn back. Some would say that Basal looked stately compared to other prisons, but all I saw was a glorified dungeon. I tried to imagine Danny locked away inside such a beautiful building, but I couldn't and my mind returned to flip-flopping between *just like that* and *impossible*.

Something was wrong.

No, nothing's wrong, Renee. My palms were sweating, but everything was going exactly as we'd planned it.

We were breaking into Basal to save Danny.

We were ushered into a reception area that reminded me of a waiting room at a doctor's office. I stood by the window, looking calm and collected with both hands clasping my briefcase as Keith gave our badges and paperwork to the staff member on duty.

I was thinking that I should do something besides stand there like a coat rack, but Keith was in charge of getting us in.

The CO who'd ushered us in stood by the door patiently, watching me. I gave him a shallow smile and a nod, then averted my eyes. Did he suspect anything at all? Evidently he didn't, because he just stood there for the five minutes it took the clerk to process us and call for our escort.

A staff member dressed in a white shirt and blue tie walked into the room and smiled.

"Welcome to Basal, deputies." He reached out his hand. "Michael Banning, assistant to the warden, at your service. I understand you'd like to inspect our milk."

Keith took his hand. "Just a random inspection, no cause for alarm. We'd like to get started if that's all right with you. We have another appointment today."

"Of course." He offered me his hand and I didn't want to take it, but I did. "I'm guessing you're Julia."

"Deputy is fine," I said.

He grinned wide. "Well then, Deputy it is. The warden is on his way down. Can I get either of you anything? Coffee, a soda?"

"This isn't a social call, Mr. Banning," Keith said. "The warden will be notified of our findings when our investigation is complete. Now if you wouldn't mind, we'd like to get started."

"Of course. But I'm sure the warden would feel he'd insulted you if he didn't greet you himself. It'll just be a minute."

I don't know what came over me at that moment—maybe my fear of meeting the warden, maybe my aversion to waiting one more minute for anything when it came to Danny. But I looked into his eyes and spoke with simple authority.

"Do you know how much evidence can be burned in a minute, Banning?"

Banning. Not Mr. Banning, or Michael, just Banning.

He flashed another grin. "Of course. It'll just be a moment."

Before I could make another pass at setting him straight, the door crashed open and a tall man wearing round glasses and a black suit walked in.

"Who do we have the pleasure of assisting to-day?" he boomed.

This was Marshall Pape, warden of the Basal Institute, I was sure of it. Danny's greatest enemy.

My demons vanished, fleeing the sudden rage that boiled in my gut. I wanted to walk up to him and slap him in the face and demand he take me to Danny immediately, but that would have only made our break-in a disaster.

I stepped forward and spoke before Keith could. "OIG, Deputies Somerset and Wishart. Thank you for having us, Warden. Nice place you have here. As my partner was just explaining to your assistant, we have another appointment, so if you could help us keep this as simple as possible, we'd be grateful." I considered stopping there but kept going. "Nothing to worry about—we just need to take some random samples of milk and question some of the inmates about spiking. I'm sure you've heard of the recent issues with the Prison Industry Authority. Point us in the right direction so we can get out of your hair."

Keith watched me, masking his surprise at my monologue, I'm sure. The warden looked down at me with a kind face, if a bit long in the nose. I wasn't sure if his smile was forced or if he truly found me amusing.

"Right to the point. I like that." He slid one hand into his pocket. "It *is* a nice place, isn't it? We take a lot of pride in what we do here. You have my full cooperation. No one is more eager to root out any irregularity or misconduct, I can assure you." His eyes turned to Keith. "You're not from this region. I know most of the deputies."

"We're out of the main office. Thank you for your help, Warden. We'd like to get started."

"Of course. Michael will take you to our conference room and call up any staff or members you wish to interview. Samples of the milk can be taken from the kitchen."

"The conference room won't work," I said. "We'd like to question the inmates in their cells. It's less formal and more direct. We'll need a roster."

His grin faltered. "Of course. You didn't bring your own records?"

"Policy requires we use the most recent, which would be yours," Keith said.

"Yes, of course."

A moment of silence hung over the room.

"Well then, Michael will be glad to take you wherever you wish to go. My prison is yours."

"Thank you," I said. "But we won't be needing an escort." I looked at the assistant. "Get us a roster and show us around. We'll take it from there."

Another beat of silence.

The warden dipped his head. "Michael? You heard the deputy." He started to turn, then faced me again. "Please be careful, Ms. Wishart. We have a number of men here who would love to get to know you more personally."

He smiled at both of us, and then walked back out the door.

"So then"—Michael Banning clasped his hands together—"follow me."

Just like that.

But it was never just like that.

33

DANNY HAD ENDURED punish-
ment and he'd suffered pain, but he'd never
been taken to the edge of himself as he had over
the last thirty-six hours. There was no escaping
that cell, no refuge from the excruciating pain,
no reprieve from the warden's place of punishment. If he'd been weaker, he might have
passed out, but he could not, and he now regret-
ted his strength.

His body seemed to react without his will
engaged. He'd never screamed as he had on
that table. His muscles had never locked up
so fiercely or shaken so violently without soon
submitting to his control. But there in deep

meditation his physical torment was beyond him entirely, and his body could only revolt in the most strenuous terms.

All of his attempts to muscle his mind into a calm, meditative state failed to attain the peace he sought for more than a few minutes. There in the darkness behind closed eyes, he searched for and found light, but it was fleeting, stamped out by raging pain.

He refused to surrender to the pain. Neither could he surrender his mind. But all of his attempts to step beyond it failed him far more than they aided him. Unending misery was his only friend in that place of torment.

If they hadn't cinched the leg straps so tightly, he might have shaken loose from the restraints. The only reason the bit didn't break off in his bone was because it was flexible, like a very thin cable.

The doctor had taken many breaks, one that lasted nearly six hours, presumably to sleep. But as Danny quickly learned, the breaks only intensified the experience. After thirty minutes of grinding he found that his body began to shut down his nerves of its own accord. The doctor would withdraw the needle from his shin, calmly lay the device on the table, and sit for a smoke or leave the room for ten minutes before resuming his task with the calculation of a brain surgeon.

Initially, Danny had found the break welcome, but the first time the bit returned to the tiny hole in his shin and made contact with his inflamed nerves, he understood their intentions. The pain was even more intense than before and only seemed to increase each time the doctor repeated the cycle. His anticipation of that pain was its own kind of torture.

Bostich had left them after the first hour and checked in on several occasions, each time muttering words that Danny could hardly hear much less digest in his condition.

The ordeal jerked his mind back to the pain he'd inflicted on his victims before taking his vow of nonviolence. He'd never tortured anyone—he didn't have a sadistic bone in his body—but he had used painful force. It was true that each of those he'd confronted were guilty of heinous crimes, but while lying on the table in convulsing agony he wished no pain on the guilty, because he knew his own guilt. Weren't all guilty?

He lost track of time. His life descended into cycles of suffering marked by the doctor's insertion of the bit into one of several holes he'd made in Danny's shin. There was no end; there was only more. At some point he began to forget that it would end. Minutes felt like hours, and hours like an eternity.

Danny was strapped to the table, alone in the room, a shell of himself when the door opened once again. He didn't open his eyes or demonstrate his fear. He'd salvaged that much control over his body.

At any moment a gloved hand would touch his leg. The wire would be carefully slipped into one of the holes. The machine's whir would scream to life and his body would begin to shudder.

At any moment.

But that moment did not come. Instead, a new voice. He didn't hear the words, only the sound of the voice. It took him only a few seconds to connect the voice to the warden, and with that connection came the memory that the warden had said he'd come back when the ordeal was over.

The words gained meaning.

"…that I don't enjoy this any more than you do. But it was necessary."

The punishment was finished. The pain was done. Danny's chest rose and fell as his mind wrapped itself around the warden's voice.

Danny opened his eyes and stared up at the ceiling.

"The doctor said you were brave. I want you to know that I appreciate that."

The warden had come. Danny's mind stalled for a moment, then restarted, surging with question. It was done? No, it was only a ploy. And yet he'd said he would come at the end.

"It's finished." The warden walked up to the table.

From the deepest parts of Danny's soul rose an emotion that he could never have anticipated. It started out as relief but then suddenly became more. Much more.

Gratitude. Appreciation. Wonder. Awe. He closed his eyes and let the emotions spread through his body, flooding him with a warmth and gratefulness that made the pain he'd felt a distant memory.

"I'm sorry, Danny. I truly am. You have to believe that I wish this on no one."

Danny connected his intense relief to that voice. The warden had put an end to his suffering, and for that Danny felt deeply indebted. For that he owed the man his life. For that he loved the man.

He slowly released his grip on the rubber bit between his teeth. The blurred image of the warden's face looked down at him. There was concern in his eyes.

"It is finished, Danny. No more. But you didn't obey me, you understand that, don't you? I don't like this any more than a loving father enjoys punishing his son."

The warden turned his head and looked at the wall, which held the restraints they'd strapped Danny into the last time he had visited deep meditation.

"I lost my children, but the truth is I've gained so many more," he said in an introspective tone. "They're all like sons to me. Even Slane. But Slane refused to accept my help. The terrible task of guiding them to the light falls on my shoulders now. It's the only way I can honor my own son and daughter."

The warden faced him, frowning.

"Say something, Danny. You're a priest, you

should understand these things. Tell me that what I'm doing is right."

He wanted to say something, but his mind was awash with conflict. In the warden's words, he was hearing his own thoughts of not so long ago. He'd never motivated others with the threat of sadistic punishment, but he'd killed them just the same.

"Just say something, for heaven's sake. It's not easy doing this sort of thing."

Danny started to speak, but his voice cracked and he had to clear his throat.

"No," he said. "It's not easy."

"So you approve then."

The overwhelming emotion he'd felt only a minute earlier was gone. Now he felt mostly relief for himself and simple empathy for the warden. He did owe the man his life, because the man had spared his life, but he couldn't find it in himself to voice support.

"You see? You still don't get it, do you? But you will soon. I have great confidence in you, Danny. A profound respect."

The warden let the words settle, then walked to the end of the table and began to release the leather straps that held Danny's legs. When he spoke again, his voice had taken on the firmer, more assured tone that Danny had grown accustomed to.

"The ugly business of corrections is worthless unless we conform to what is right, my friend. All of this is lost unless you can truly expose that lingering core of depravity in your soul. Once we force it out into the light, we can go about correcting it. I hope you can appreciate that more now." He looked up at Danny. "Your legs will ache for a few days, but you'd be surprised at how quickly the puncture wounds will heal."

The doctor wiped the blood from his leg like a tattoo artist cleaning the skin as he worked. A transparent salve covered five tiny red pinpricks on his shin.

"I'll give you a few hours to gather yourself before they take you back up." He unfastened the straps on his left leg. "It'll help if you get the blood flowing through your legs again. You'll have some bruising on your heels, your tail bone, and the back of your head, but otherwise you're no worse off for the wear."

He undid the last strap and brushed his palms against each other. "Almost good as new. Bend your legs for me."

Danny slowly turned his ankles, then drew his stiff legs up, one at a time. A dull pain throbbed in his shin, but on balance he was surprised he didn't feel more.

"See?"

"Thank you." The words sounded empty.

"It's the least I can do." Pape slipped his hand into his pocket and came around the table, staying clear of Danny's legs. "You seem like a good man on the outside, but you're here because you've broken the law. You strayed from a more righteous way. Until I am confident you can be truly rehabilitated, I can't consider you for the privileged wing or for early release."

"I'm not asking for either."

"No, you're not asking, are you? The question you should be asking is are you still a killer?"

"I didn't kill Randell."

"True, but that was hardly a sufficient test. And by refusing to obey you earned yourself some correction. You have to learn to follow my rules, Danny. No one else's, only mine. Do that and perhaps you'll win my confidence. It's really that simple."

"Even if it means killing."

"If I command it, yes. Trust me."

"I've taken a vow of nonviolence."

"Sounds nice and cozy, but if I ask you to go to war, you must. Will you drop the bomb for me, Danny? There's always a time for killing, and in my sanctuary I decide when that time is. Doesn't God kill? As the good books say, 'Vengeance is mine, says the Lord.' And in here"—he spread his hands—"I am he."

"I'm not sure you know who God is."

"Don't be absurd. God is God. They're all the same."

"All of this so that I'll kill again."

"No. All of this so that you never will unless I demand it. I need to lay you bare to see who you really are." The warden lowered his arms. "I'll leave you to consider that. Hopefully the worst is behind us."

Pape headed for the door but turned back when he'd opened it.

"Oh, and a bit of news you might find interesting. Renee has decided to join us. She brought along a new friend."

Danny blinked. "Renee?"

"Yes, Renee. She's been put through the ringer and finally led here, where she can be of some use to all of us. Maybe she can fill Peter's shoes. Maybe you'll get a conjugal visit out of it. Remember to move your legs around. Good for the circulation."

Danny didn't hear the door shut. He heard nothing but the roar of blood rushing through his head. He didn't actually see the warden leave. His vision had gone blank.

One thought alone consumed his mind. Renee was here. Renee was in Basal.

His bride was in hell.

Danny's body began to shake.

34

JUST LIKE THAT.

Keith and I had broken into Basal and were being given a quick tour by Michael Banning, the warden's assistant, and no one was stopping us. All was at ease.

The inmates were hanging out in small groups over card games, or wasting time alone, when we entered the common area, but we managed to attract most of their attention. I did, that is. All of the guards I'd seen were men; I was a woman. A cute blonde with teacher glasses. It made me wonder if the warden knew something in particular when he'd suggested that there were men here who'd like to get to know me better.

"The yard's through that door," Banning was saying, motioning across the large common area. "Think of the layout as like a compass cross and you won't get lost. Administration behind us, that's north; infirmary, cafeteria, recreation, et cetera, directly opposite, south; commons, the largest wing, to our right, west. And the privileged wing, east."

"Privileged?" Keith said. He'd left his coat and his briefcase with the receptionist. Everything we needed was on me, under my loose slacks.

"Essentially an honors program for qualified members who earn certain privileges. Best accommodations in the state."

"I see. And segregation?"

"Below the administration wing. If you need access, just let me know."

"We will," I said.

"Of course. You'd like to go there first?"

"Yes," I said.

Keith glanced at me. "Give us half an hour to conduct a few interviews among the general population first."

"Of course."

Something was wrong, I knew it in my bones.

Sicko was still out there, and we didn't know who he was.

Danny was in here and we didn't know where.

His name wasn't on the roster given to us by the warden's assistant, and in my mind that meant he must be in the hole. I had to get to Danny. I had to see him. I had to speak to him and give him the letter, but we couldn't ask for him by name because that might raise suspicions.

We also had to get to Randell, and his name was on the register, cell 134 in the commons wing.

"Right," I said.

Banning glanced between us, then motioned at the south wing. "Our milk stock's behind the cafeteria. You sure you won't need me to accompany you? It would make—"

"That's generous of you, but it's better for us to maintain the integrity of our inquiries," Keith said. He lifted the stapled roster already opened to the third page and marked off a few names. "If you could please inform these inmates that we'd like to speak to them in their cells, we would appreciate it."

He handed the clipboard to Banning, who quickly scanned the list. "Watkins, Collins, Randell. I can assure you of their full cooperation."

"No assurances needed. Just have them report to their cells as soon as possible. We'll take it from here."

"Of course." He handed the roster back, lifted his radio, and passed the instructions on to a CO, who came back over the air and informed Banning that members Collins and Randell were in the wing and would be in their cells. Watkins was either in the hard yard or the privileged wing. They would track him down immediately.

"The staff all knows you're here," Banning said, and handed the radio to Keith. "The prison is yours. If you need anything, anything at all, just call on that channel. We'll have a special response team standing by, but I wouldn't worry—you'll find our members to be cooperative in every way. We're very proud of our program."

"I'm sure you are."

Banning didn't seem eager to let us go, despite all of his assurances. He finally nodded. "Well then. I guess I'm done here."

Keith nodded once, dismissing the man as anyone accustomed to authority might. I was a basket case under my short blonde wig and stony mask, but Keith's training as a sheriff kept our cover smooth.

The warden's assistant turned and left us on our own.

"Where's Danny?" I whispered, keeping my eyes forward.

"We'll get to him. First things first."

"Then Randell first," I said. We'd planned on getting a few samples of milk first and then interviewing a couple of random inmates to put up a good show before zeroing in on Randell and Danny. But Danny's name wasn't on the register, and that changed everything for me.

"Agreed," he said.

"I don't like it."

"Just stay focused. We'll find him. Let's go."

I walked next to Keith as we headed through the huge domed atrium, struck by just how different Basal was compared to what I'd seen of Ironwood. New and clean, for one thing. Ordered and quiet. My experience visiting Danny was always filled with prying eyes, chattering wives, and families in a crowded visiting room. Kids crawling on the dirty floor, crying.

Basal looked more like a casual resort. The inmates were called members and dressed in neat dark blue slacks and tan shirts. The guards all wore black, cleaned and pressed. If they had weapons they were hidden.

I took it all in, but my mind was buzzing with images of Danny. I was scanning for him, searching every face and coming up only with winks, smiles, and scattered comments as we passed.

"Welcome to Basal, honey. Any time, baby." None of it was loud or obnoxious, just isolated men reacting to a woman. I expected nothing less. If anything, their natural behavior took some of the edge off my anxiety.

I glanced over my shoulder and saw that Banning was talking idly to a CO by the door to the administration wing. Danny was below them in the bowels of the prison, I was sure of it. I wanted to grab Banning by the collar and demand he immediately take me to the member named Danny Hansen who wasn't on their roster.

I wanted to throw myself into Danny's arms

and tell him that I had come to save him. That I'd found a way to get him out of here. I'd found the judge whose son Danny had killed. The man would help us, because I'd heard his confession and would tell the world of his own crimes if he didn't help us.

The commons wing was a long hall with two tiers of cells on one side and a guard station on the other. The station was unmanned. Was that normal?

I didn't have time to worry. We were suddenly there, not only inside Basal, but twenty yards from a cell on the ground floor with the numbers 134 stenciled in black above the barred door.

Two members leaning on the upper tier railing watched us idly as I followed Keith toward Bruce Randell's cell.

"Nice," one of the men muttered.

The whole thing was utterly surreal. The towering gray walls, the barred cages for convicted criminals like Danny, the raw power of incarceration in the great state of California reinforced by billions of dollars and millions of tons of concrete.

And there we were in the middle of it all, audacious enough to think we could walk in and out with impunity. Just like that.

I slowed and trailed Keith as we approached the door to Randell's cell, unsure how I felt about seeing Danny's enemy.

We had to make Randell our friend, because it wasn't enough to put him on notice that we were going to bust his chops wide open if he touched one hair on Danny's body. We also had to convince him to take our side. We might have gotten the keys to the prison, but we needed the keys to the warden and to Danny.

Keith spoke before I could see who was inside the cell.

"Bruce Randell?"

No answer.

I stepped up and saw a large man with a pitted face and light hair staring over a book from the lower bunk, unimpressed.

Keith showed the man his badge. "We're with the inspector general's office and we'd like to ask you a few questions."

Randell sat up, immediately more amenable than he'd initially appeared. Naturally. Among other things, OIG stood alongside prisoners by investigating their grievances. He stood and dropped the book onto the bed.

His eyes glanced down my body, then met my own. I had expected to feel rage and was surprised when I didn't. I only wanted him to help me save Danny now.

"Can we come in?" Keith asked.

"What's this about?"

"Just a few questions about the milk supply. We've had complaints about spiking."

Randell nodded once and stepped back.

I followed Keith into the cell, leaving the door open behind me. There was little privacy, but the cells on either side were unoccupied and no other members were close enough to hear us if we kept our voices down.

"Have a seat." Keith motioned to the bed.

"I'd rather stand."

"Sure. I don't see why not."

"I'd rather you sit," I said, stepping to the side for a better view. "If that's not too much to ask."

Randell gave me a long look, then took a step back, leaned back against the edge of the sink, and crossed his arms.

"Good enough," Keith said. He slipped a pen

out of his pocket, peeled back the first page on his clipboard, and scanned the page.

Our first concern had been whether Randell might recognize Keith, the deputy sheriff who'd put him behind bars, but clearly he didn't. The dye and facial hair threw him off.

"Bruce Randell. Number?"

Bruce rattled it off.

"You've been here how long?"

"Here or in prison?"

"In prison."

"Eight years."

"What were you convicted of, Bruce?"

"Distribution."

"So you know substances, I take it."

"You could say that. I used to, anyways."

Keith lifted his eyes and stared at the man. "How about in Basal? Any that you know of?"

"Nope."

"Really? Because that's not what we've been told. What do you know about the milk here in Basal?"

Randell just looked at him and it struck me that maybe he actually did know something about spiked milk in Basal.

I knew that Keith wanted to play it out and

go through the questioning as we'd agreed to, but that was before I knew Danny was missing. There was an open door at my back and beyond it a prison with a warden who might be breathing down our backs.

I couldn't think of any reason to wait, so I stepped in front of Keith, hoping his body made a good enough shield behind me, and cut to the chase.

"Do you know a woman named Constance?"

He shook his head. "Don't think so. Nope."

His eyes were blank, not a hint of recognition. I'd expected to open the door with that question, but his reaction took me off guard.

"You know nothing about a finger in a shoe box?"

It took him a moment to digest the question before a smirk crossed his face. "You're joking, right?"

"Nope."

Behind me, Keith cleared his throat. This wasn't the plan, I knew that, but it was now.

"What about a million dollars?" I pressed. "Does that ring a bell?"

"Sure, I'll take a million dollars. You gonna get me out of here so I can spend it?"

Not even a hint that he knew about Sicko's game. But he was connected, and I had to know how.

"So you're saying you don't know a thing about any threats to anyone involving body parts or missing drug money."

"I honestly don't have a clue what you're talking about, lady."

"And what about a priest? Know any priests?"

His eyes flinched and I knew two things. One, Randell really didn't know anything about Constance or drug money. That had to be Sicko's doing, which confirmed our assumption that Randell wasn't Sicko.

Two, Randell not only *did* know Danny, but there was history between them.

"Danny Hansen," I pushed. "You know, the priest who was transferred to Basal ten days ago. What can you tell us about Danny?"

"Nothing."

He was lying.

"I think what Julia's trying to ask—"

"Not now, Keith," I said. "We don't have time. You see, my partner and I sometimes play good cop, bad cop—him good, me bad—but we're in a rush, so I'm gonna get straight to the point. This whole prison is about to blow sky-high, Mr. Randell. We're going to give you about three minutes to decide if you want to go up with it. Fair enough?"

He stared at me as if I'd lost my mind. Keith was probably thinking the same thing. I'd mistakenly used his real name.

"Why are you messing with Danny?" I asked.

"I don't know what you're talking about."

"Seriously?" I was incredulous. "You're actually going to drag this out? We know about the threats to Danny's life. We know what's going on in Basal—we just need to decide who goes down with the warden."

"You're lying," he said. "This some kind of test?"

"A test by who? The warden? Because I'll tell you this, I don't care what the warden's told you, it's over. If we don't find Danny alive and well, it's all going to lead back to you, and you're going to end up on a bus to death row."

For a moment Randell looked like he might capitulate, but then his jaw slowly firmed. Whatever hold the warden had over him, it was strong. My ploy wasn't going to work.

So I bent over, hiked up my right pant leg, and pulled out the Beretta I'd strapped to my calf.

Keith touched my shoulder. "Renee…"

I stepped forward and shoved the gun below Randell's belt. He jerked back, grasped the basin with both hands, and stared down at the gun. I knew I couldn't shoot in here—the gun was only meant to be used for leverage if we needed it—but it was loaded and my finger was already tightening.

"Now you listen to me, you pig. I know you were abused by a priest when you were a boy, but the priest you're messing with now is going to get you killed. The state knows everything. We're here because we have reason to believe there's a direct threat to Danny's life as we speak. You're either going to tell me where he is or I'm going to shoot off your toe."

"I don't *know* where he is."

His face was flushed red. I had his attention.

"Renee…"

"Not now, Keith." To Randell: "Is Danny alive?"

His eyes were frantic, looking at me, then at Keith over my head.

"Tell me!" I gave the gun a shove.

"I didn't kill him…I swear he was alive last time I saw him."

"When? *When* did you see him alive?"

He wavered, grasping for the meaning of a woman with an OIG badge shoving a gun at him in his prison cell. I didn't want him to think it through; I wanted him to react without thought.

"You protect the warden and you go down with him. When?"

"Two nights ago."

"Where?"

"In the hard yard."

"What did you do to him?"

"He made me. I'm only doing what I have to do to stay alive in this place. They killed Slane right in front of me!"

"Where's the priest?"

"I don't know!"

We'd been urgent, not loud, but Randell's last denial rang through the hall.

"Shut up," I snapped. "Where would he be?"

"In the hole."

"Segregation?"

"No. The other hole."

"Which hole?"

His eyes were filled with fear.

"Where is it?"

"I don't know!"

"How could you not know? You've never been there?"

He was breathing hard now. I'd reached a part of his mind he didn't want reached.

"They blindfold us. It's below ad seg."

I blinked. The information quickly settled into my gut. Blindfolds? The warden was a brute who was playing games with his inmates. Randell was a pawn who knew nothing. Constance had been a pawn. Messengers and thugs.

"We have what we need, Renee." Keith gently pulled me back by my shoulder. We'd both used our real names, but it didn't matter now.

Keith stepped up to Randell and squeezed his face with a strong hand.

"Now, I'm only going to say this once, so you listen carefully, you hear?"

We had come into Sicko's house. It had to be the warden. We were already naked here. We had to get to Danny and get out!

"One word of this to anyone, and I'm going to

477

make sure you end up on San Quentin's death row for the rest of your life. Not a fun place. Keep your mouth shut and we'll get you out early. And forget about the warden's threats, he's finished."

"You don't understand—"

"No, you don't." Keith released the man's face and slapped him. "It's over! You either go up or you go down. End of story."

"Keith, we have to go!" I said.

He glared at Randell, then turned around, face flushed. "Put that thing away," he said, flipping his hand at my gun.

Danny was being held somewhere off the prison's blueprints, in a hole that made a man as strong as Randell cringe. Keith and I knew we had to find Danny now, but only I knew how. I was going to put a gun to Michael Banning's head and force him to take us to Danny.

I shoved the gun under the strap at my calf, pulled my pant leg down over it, and hurried to catch Keith, who had just cleared the cell's door and pulled up to wait for me.

So I'd thought, but I was wrong.

The sight that greeted me when I stepped out of Bruce Randell's cell stopped me beside Keith.

Not ten feet away stood a thick man with a blond crew cut flanked by two commanding officers in black.

Both of them had rifles hooked in the crooks of their elbows—a major breach of security protocol in any California prison, I knew. Firearms were only permitted in gun rails, towers, and control booths, out of reach of any prisoner, bar none.

The man with the crew cut looked amused. "I hear you guys need an escort," he said.

Keith started forward. "That won't be necessary. We were just finishing up."

The man held up a hand. "I'm afraid the warden insists."

I told myself to run. It had all gone wrong. Instead I pulled out my phone.

"No calls. Put the phone down. Now."

"This isn't your business."

"Well now, that's funny, because the warden told me it was. He instructed me to come find you and escort you. He said go find Renee Gilmore and Keith Hammond and bring them to me. Drop the phone."

I glanced at Keith, who nodded. I dropped the phone on the concrete.

My heart was pounding. The warden knew our names, which meant he knew everything.

The CO flashed a grin. "Captain Bostich, here to serve. Now if you'd please follow me."

This was all a mistake! Basal was official property of the state of California, an institution protected by checks and balances meant to ensure the humane treatment of all prisoners. I was only here because someone—the warden—was going to break through all of those layers of protection to destroy Danny.

In the end none of these thoughts got my feet moving or wiped the smirk off the captain's face.

"Let's go, honey. He has plans for you."

35

THE EMOTIONS THAT raged through Danny as he lay on the table in deep meditation brought not a shred of reason with them. If not for years of training in the bloodied fields of battle he would have reacted to the warden's words as any man might. He would have thrown himself against the restraints on his arms and screamed in a futile attempt to free himself.

But when he learned that the warden had been manipulating Renee all along and had led her to Basal to break him by abusing her, he reacted as only a man with so much training might.

He did nothing.

Rash movement would get them both killed. Nothing prudent could be done without thought. The only problem was, his mind wasn't immediately capable of clear thought. It was fractured by a week of horror and two days of torture, and now it was frozen by a kind of rage and bitterness he didn't know existed.

He didn't thrash pointlessly against his restraints. He lay shaking with rage, trying to grasp at some kind of meaning.

Like demonic drones, the warden's words whispered through his mind. *She's been put through the ringer,* they said, and Danny tried to think of what Pape meant when he said *ringer*. And then he tried not to because the thoughts were too ugly.

She was *led here*, the words said, and Danny tried to think of how that could be. Led how? Under what threat? What terror had drawn her?

Maybe she can fill Peter's shoes, he'd said.

The rage that came with those words shut his mind down again.

He tried to move, he really did, but he wasn't thinking right.

Maybe she can fill Peter's shoes, the warden had said.

For the first time in two days, Danny's mind was merciful to him and shut down completely. His world faded to black and his shaking stopped.

36

MY MELTDOWN BEGAN with that phone call ten days earlier, but sitting in the corner of that dark holding cell at the back of the administration wing, I faded away to nothing.

There was nothing left. I had propped myself up with a blazing sense of purpose and hope for ten days, and just like that it had all been crushed in one final blow. It was done. Finished. I tried to think of a way out, but as Keith had first said, breaking into prison was one thing; breaking out was another. And this wasn't just any prison, it was Basal.

I didn't even question *how* it could be done, I

knew that it couldn't, not now. Not in time to save Danny, not in time to save ourselves.

The cell the captain had taken us to was a ten-by-ten concrete room with a thick metal door, nothing else except for the fluorescent light on the ceiling, which was off.

They'd marched us through back halls at gunpoint and ushered us into the cell without saying another word. With each step I tried to tell myself that something would happen to fix this. The real authorities would come busting in to free us. Keith would throw himself at the guards and give me a chance to escape. Danny would run through the door and save us.

But it was totally hopeless, and I knew that.

Keith tried to reason with the captain, promising to bring the whole prison down under a storm of controversy that would put them all behind their own bars. He was an attorney and knew the law. He had contacts in law enforcement on the outside. He knew congressmen and senators.

His threats fell on deaf ears, and with an ashen-faced glance at me, Keith gave up.

He sat on the floor beside me, slumped

against the wall. Neither of us spoke for a few minutes. My mind was lost.

"You realize what this means," he said. It was a statement, not a question, and I knew the answer.

"The warden can't let us leave this place," I said.

"We know too much."

"He's going to kill us."

"No one even knows we're here," he said. "The records have us as Julia Wishart and Myles Somerset. None of the inmates or guards have any idea what we really look like. There's not a single bit of evidence that Keith Hammond and Renee Gilmore ever came to Basal."

I hadn't thought about that.

"They're torturing the inmates here. The only way that happens without an OIG investigation is through a high level of planning and control. Brainwashing, even. The warden was one step ahead of us all the way. He already knows how this is going to end."

I sat like a lump in that corner, feeling ill. Too sick to cry anymore. A hundred thoughts crammed into my mind. What if I'd gone to the police at the beginning? What if I'd hired the biggest law firm on Wilshire? What if I'd refused to let Danny turn himself in to the authorities three years ago? But none of the questions had any answers.

"I'm scared."

He didn't respond. There was nothing to say.

"So what now?"

"Now we hope we can convince the warden to let us go."

"But he won't."

"Maybe I can call his bluff, say I have a file that will be released to the press if we're not home in twenty-four hours. Something…"

"Maybe," I said. But then neither of us said anything because we both knew the warden was too smart for any of that.

Realization slowly settled in my mind.

"All along Sicko's plan was to get me to break into his sick, twisted prison to save Danny."

It suddenly made more sense than anything else. The escalating threats, the constant pressure, the progression of the game—all of it led me here, into his own house to crush Danny.

"That's why he led us to the judge," I said, eyes straining in the darkness. "He needed us to think we were outwitting him."

"Maybe. But why?"

"Revenge."

Keith sat for a moment.

"There's something you're not telling me, Renee. Something about who would go to all this trouble to set things straight with Danny. If we knew who..."

"I told you, I don't know. The only victims I know about are dead."

"Because that's the key to this whole thing. Who? If we knew, we might be able to use the information as leverage."

"I think it's the warden. But I don't know what he's got against Danny."

The door suddenly rattled, then swung open. Backlit by the hall stood the tall form of the warden, Marshall Pape, in his crisp suit, hand on the doorknob.

He reached over and flipped a switch. The overhead light stuttered to life.

The warden stepped inside, slid his hand into his pocket, and smiled down at us. Keith started to get up, but the warden stopped him.

"Please, remain seated. We don't have much time."

Keith eased back to his seat.

"I thought it would only be fair to explain why I'm going to allow what's about to happen," the warden said. "The common man might cringe, but he can't understand this world any more than the politicians who pass the laws do. They send us deviants and then pass more laws that make correcting their ways impossible. Basal's all about learning to do it right."

I stared up at him, filled with hatred. I hated the smug curve of his lips as he spoke, the round spectacles balanced on his nose, his manicured fingernails, his perfectly pressed suit. His self-righteousness made me sick.

This was a stoning and he was going to cast the first stone.

"There's a reason for the law, my friends. Breaking it comes with consequence. But before you're punished you have the right to know what you've done wrong."

"You make me sick," I said.

"And you, me."

He clasped his hands behind his back.

"Danny's guilty for many crimes that he hasn't confessed yet. His deal with the DA was a sham. He has so much to learn from me. Now you too have broken the law in my house, and

I don't take that lightly. As punishment, I'm going to use you to break him. I hope you'll understand the justice of that."

If his words were meant to unnerve me, they didn't. I felt only rage. Marshall Pape's twisted philosophy of punishment defied reason. I stared at him, too furious to speak.

"You should have known better, you really should have. But now it's too late. The sad part is that you still don't really have a clue. It's going to get very ugly, but in that you will see that I'm not your devil, Renee. By the way, I think Sicko's an adorable name. It's so...you."

He looked at Keith. "As for you, Mr. Hammond, you'll get your turn soon enough. They'll be down for both of you soon."

The warden turned around, flipped off the light, and left us in darkness again.

Keith muttered and cursed under his breath, then fell silent.

The trembling in my bones began then, when I had nothing to do but stare into the darkness as the warden's words rang in my head. I tried not to think about what he meant by *very ugly*, but endless images burrowed into my mind.

I had to be strong, I knew that, but my

strength was all gone. Tears began to fall down my cheeks. It was all so wrong! I hardly could remember what had happened to get me into that cell at Basal.

"I'm so sorry, Renee." Keith rested his hand on my knees.

My tears swelled. I couldn't speak past the knot in my throat.

"Listen to me, this isn't over. There's still Danny. He may still find a way."

I began to sob quietly in the darkness. I knew Keith was only saying that for my benefit, but he couldn't have said anything more appropriate to me in that moment. He was right, Danny was our only hope now.

Danny always saved me.

37

WHEN DANNY'S MIND awoke it did so slowly, like a slug crawling from a hole in the ground.

Though the restraints no longer held him down, he was still on the table where the doctor had worked over him for two days. The light-bulb still glowed on the ceiling above him. His chest still rose and fell in a steady rhythm.

A dense fog hung over his mind, but he was alive. The torture was finished, he remembered that much. There was something else. He couldn't put his mind on it.

He tried to lift his head, but pain flared in his neck and he abandoned the attempt. The warden had told him to move his legs. It was strange that this memory came to him even before the memory that the warden had come at all, but he'd felt pain in his neck and that pain had somehow triggered…

Danny blinked. The warden had come. He'd said something important.

Ignoring the pain in his neck this time, Danny lifted his head off the table and stared down at his feet. Red pinpricks dotted his shin. The leather straps that had held his legs dangled over the sides of the table. But the warden had said something, and as Danny lay with his head cocked up, the words came to him in one lump sum.

Renee has decided to join us.

He'd passed out.

This time Danny moved without calculation. He threw the full weight of his left leg over his right and rolled against the two restraints that bound his arms to the table by his sides. There was no reason in the movement, only a raw reaction. Instinct stripped bare of the training that might hold it in check.

The sudden shift in weight tipped the table as if it had been shoved by an angry rhino. The whole thing twisted wildly under him, wrenching his bound arms as he crashed toward the floor.

But he got his feet down first. Both of them.

He stood half bent with the wooden table strapped to his arms behind him, balanced on one of its legs. Pain sliced through his strained shoulders.

He grunted. But now his thinking was more precise, and his next movement was fully intended for a single purpose: to be freed from the monstrosity on his back.

Roaring as much from pain as rage, he hefted the table onto his back, spun around with all of his strength, and slammed the table into the concrete wall.

Wood cracked, but he wasn't free. So he did it again, grunting loudly as the table crashed into the wall a second time. And a third.

But the table didn't break apart. Instead, the strap that held his left arm snapped on the fourth try.

Ten seconds later, Danny stood in the middle of the room next to the inverted broken table, now missing three of its legs.

He was still locked in the cell, but setting

himself free of the table wasn't pointless. They would be coming for him, he was sure of that. The warden's intentions were plain. He was going to use Renee as he'd used young Peter— as a means of breaking Danny. Pape would keep her alive until then.

They wouldn't know that he'd broken free or that he now had the table legs and splinters of wood to use as weapons. Bostich would have to open the door to the cell, and when he did, Danny would kill him in any one of several ways that quickly came to mind.

Why?

In a moment of clarity he knew that he'd vacated his resolve to eschew violence, regardless of the impulse that called for it. No matter what the situation.

He stood up straight, taken by the deep conflict in front of him. And then another question struck him. Why had the warden left him in a cell with his legs free and a table to break? Why had he told Danny about Renee? The man was as shrewd as any Danny had known.

He glanced down at the leather belt still buckled around his right forearm. It had broken an inch from the buckle, but the rough edge of the tear didn't run the full width of the leather. It had been cut with a knife two thirds of the way through.

The same with the strap on his left arm. The warden had assumed he'd try to free himself once he'd learned that Renee was in the prison. Why? Because he wanted Danny to break out of the deep meditation cell.

Why? Because he intended to lead Danny into a trap.

But that same trap could have been just as easily set by leading Danny with misinformation. Knowing about Danny's unshakable love for Renee, the warden might have only *claimed* to have Renee. How would Danny know the difference?

Renee might very well be safe at home, oblivious to the warden's twisted games. Danny allowed the thought to wash him with hope.

But the moment of reprieve was short-lived because it struck him just as quickly that he could be wrong. The warden might actually have Renee up in the prison as he'd claimed. And with that mushrooming thought, his instinct to save her at any cost reasserted itself like a hurricane slamming into an island.

He stared at the door. The lock was on the outside. There was no getting past it. If the warden intended to draw him into a trap, he would have left the door unlocked.

Danny moved forward on numb legs, eyes on the handle. If the door was open he would go, even knowing that he was being led. He could not remain here while she might be suffering.

He stepped up to the door, put his hand on the latch, and twisted. The latch moved freely and the door pulled open.

His pulse surged. It could only mean that the warden did have Renee. He'd made a way for Danny to find her, knowing that he did not have the strength to allow her to suffer. Knowing that Danny would follow his heart and try to save her.

The light behind him cast a glow down a corridor that ended in twenty feet before turning to the right. From there he knew he would climb one set of stairs to the segregation wing. And another to the administrative wing.

Why?

Why had the warden gone to this trouble? Why hadn't he just come for Danny and led him to Renee?

But then Danny knew. Pape wanted him to come of his own will, even knowing it was a trap. He wanted to lead him as he'd led Renee. The act of going to save someone invested a person in the rescue and intensified the pain of any failure.

The crushing of hope, however thin that hope, was more miserable than having no hope at all.

Even knowing that his disposition now was to overthrow his vows, knowing he was throwing himself on the mercy of his own emotions, Danny retreated, picked up two large splinters of wood, each roughly a hand's span, and slipped them under the waistband of his shorts. One of the table legs had split off at an angle so that it formed a sharp wedge at one end. He grabbed it and strode for the door.

So, then, it came down to this. There was no more room for ideology or thinking. It was Renee up there now, not him. He would crush them all to save his bride.

And if they hurt Renee, he would hurt them.

Danny stepped out of the cell and headed down the corridor.

38

I KEPT TELLING myself the same thing as two guards handcuffed Keith and me and led us through the prison: this was all a misunderstanding. It was a mistake. This was the United States of America. This was California. There were laws, as the warden himself so aptly pointed out, and those laws prohibited the abuse of its citizens, both in and out of prison. As soon as the warden understood that we really hadn't hurt anyone, his thinking would change. As soon as he reflected on how absurd his intentions were, he would come to his mind and return us to a conference room, where we could sit down like civilized people and discuss each of our mistakes—no foul, no harm.

But I knew that I was wrong. This really was my Jonestown, and there really was a new Jim Jones in town, living out his own twisted vision of good and evil right under America's nose.

The world had been shocked by the deaths of the nine hundred people who'd died at Jonestown, because no one believed the rumors of abuse leading up to the massacre. It wasn't possible. It was too much. It was preposterous. Maybe it could happen in the dark ages or in Nazi Germany, but not today. Not in California. Not in the United States of America.

But there I was, like a lamb being led to my own slaughter, and the worst thing about it all was that Keith was right. No one even knew that we were at Basal, not as Renee Gilmore and Keith Hammond. The pieces had fallen almost perfectly into a puzzle of Marshall Pape's design. But I'd given up trying to figure out exactly how and just faced the fact that they had.

The prison was a ghost town. They'd cleared it before we were led through the domed hub. The inmates were probably locked down in their own cells, a common enough occurrence in most prisons. It was usually a form of restriction following an incident that required investigation, or a preventive measure against exacerbation of the incident.

Today, Keith and I were that incident. Danny was that incident. The warden had cleared the prison so that he could deal with us as he wished.

The captain jabbed his chin at the far side of the room. "This way."

Keith hesitated. "Where is everyone?"

The captain gave him a little shove without bothering to answer.

Keith's tie was gone and his white shirt, sleeves rolled up, was smudged along the arms and back where he'd leaned against the wall. He still wore his leather shoes and dark blue slacks.

There were no other guards on duty that I could see. The doors out to the main yard were closed, as were the doors to the housing wings.

Danny, where are you?

We were herded toward the section of Basal that held the infirmary and the cafeteria, but we passed them both and turned into a small hall.

It ended at a door under a sign that said Recreation Room.

The captain reached for the door and offered me a twisted grin. "Welcome to the hard yard." He pulled the door open and stepped aside with the handle still in his hand.

From my vantage, I could see only a gray concrete room—no people. But my mind's eye saw images of black-and-white pictures from old documentaries. Gas chambers from Auschwitz. Slaughterhouses and abandoned basements.

I glanced up at Keith, who was staring in, face masked in stone. His words from the holding cell returned to me. *This isn't over.*

I'd been consumed with Danny and myself, but looking at his stark hazel eyes, I saw a man who'd been pulled into a nightmare because I convinced him to help a damaged woman save the man she loved. Keith was connected through Randell, yes, but as it turned out, Randell had much less to do with the threat against Danny than either of us had thought. Like me, Keith had done what he thought was right. Conscience had only brought him here, to a place called the hard yard, inside of the prison called Basal, which meant core. Hard core.

The captain wagged his head through the open doorway. "Let's go."

It was my Jonestown, but it was also the place where I might see Danny, and so it was with a conflicted mind that I stepped inside their hard yard.

The room was concrete on all sides except the ceiling, which was made of a mesh wire supported by several metal beams. The towering concrete walls sent a chill down my back.

It was as if I had just stepped into my own graveyard. This was my tomb. My crypt, my slaughterhouse, the place where I would finally rest at the end of my life's search for peace.

My eyes flitted over the rest of the room. A sea of faces stared at me, but none of them belonged to Danny. My heart crumbled.

Marshall Pape stood to my left, hands tucked into his blazer pockets, watching me without expression. Ten inmates were seated along the wall, legs cocked up or extended on the floor in front of them. Some were dressed in the common blue-and-tan uniforms of the general population. Some wore street clothes.

Besides the captain and the guard who'd brought us, there were four other COs in the room, one in each corner, all armed with illicit rifles.

Bruce Randell stared at me from the center of the line. I was going to die.

That was how I was thinking of it, but in the most trying times I had a way of letting all of my neurotic tendencies sink into the floor and becoming stronger. I was going to die here—Keith knew that, I knew that, Danny would soon know that—but maybe I was going to take Pape with me.

A low wolf whistle from one of the inmates broke the silence.

"Quiet," the warden said. "This isn't a whorehouse." He returned his stare to me, face still flat.

The captain removed my handcuffs and shoved me from behind. I stumbled forward to the center of the room and was joined by Keith.

For long seconds no one spoke. I scanned the faces of the inmates, trying to guess their intentions or, worse, the warden's intentions for them. *Look at me,* my eyes told them. *I'm only a skinny woman who needs your sympathy. The real ogre's over there. He's the one who we should all fear.*

Some were in their twenties, but most were in their thirties or forties, covered in prison tattoos. Just men, like Danny, who'd been sucked into Marshall Pape's monster factory.

But they didn't look like monsters. One had whistled, yes, and two or three eyed me with interest, but their eyes weren't dripping with lust. In fact, most of them looked at me with uncertainty, even sympathy.

An older man sat at the far end, legs crossed underneath him, and on his face I saw a sad regret I might have expected from my own father, if he were still alive and there.

I was desperate, I know, but I really did feel a surprising sense of kinship with my fellow prisoners at that moment. We were all under the same heel.

I knew they were going to hurt me, but as I stared into the prisoners' eyes I saw Danny. These were the kind of men he'd lived with for the past three years. These were the members of his world now. These were the ones he'd chosen to love. Even Randell, who on closer inspection looked uncertain, not vengeful.

"What we have here, my friends," the warden said, withdrawing his hands from the pockets, "is a perfect lesson in what's so wrong with the world. You see a man and a woman in front of you. They came to our institution under false pretenses, pretending to be two people they were not. But isn't that the way it is with everyone who comes to this place? Isn't that the way it is with the whole world? No one wants to confess their true nature or the evil thoughts in their minds. Everyone's guilty. Pretenders, all of them."

He allowed himself a subtle if insincere smile. "It's my job to peel back the layers, strip you all down to your naked selves, and reveal the pathetic truth of your nature so that it can be rehabilitated. All things must become new, and sometimes that's an ugly process."

The warden wagged his head toward the inmates seated against the wall. "The men you see aren't here by accident. They cannot and will not run to your law, because they're under mine now. They know the cost of breaking my law is far too high to endure for very long, much less forever."

Basal was his religion. The inmates were his flock. It made me sick.

"The question I put to you two today is, who are you underneath it all?" He looked between Keith and me. "Please show them who you really are. Both of you."

I'd forgotten about my blonde wig, and it took me a moment to understand what he was asking. But then Keith reached up and started peeling off the goatee and mustache he'd glued to his face. I pulled off my wig. I'd left the glasses in the holding room. They were pointless anyway.

"You see? They aren't Julia and Myles, after all. They broke into my prison with the intention of killing Randell, because they believed Randell intended to kill the priest."

He walked up to me, and I suppressed a sudden urge to spit in his face, because for a moment he ceased being human in my eyes.

The warden began to pull the pins out of my hair, letting it fall around my shoulders.

"So pretty on the outside," he said. "But inside no different from Slane." He continued pulling down my hair. "You've abused me," he said matter-of-factly. "You've breached my walls and violated my sanctuary. And that is no less of an offense than the torturing or taking of another human being. So now I have no choice but to return the favor. An eye for an eye, as we all know."

"You can't do this," Keith bit off under his breath.

"Oh, but you're wrong. I can. This is Basal, and in Basal, I preside."

It hit me that this might have nothing to do with Danny. The warden was going to let them hurt me and Danny would be nowhere near to stop them. Maybe he was already dead. My breathing thickened.

"Now that the preliminaries are out of the way, let's get on with the messy business, shall we?"

"How can you stand here and—" It was as far as Keith got before the warden slapped him.

Keith glared, face flushed. I had never seen such a look of hatred from Keith, and seeing him stand up to the devil both scared me and gave me a surge of confidence.

The warden turned to me. "Take off your pants."

"No—" Keith's objection earned another slap, this time backhanded, hard enough to startle me.

"Bare yourself!" the warden thundered. "Show us who you really are!"

Danny had worked his way through the underground passages and found his way to the administrative segregation wing. No guards. No attempt to stop him. They knew; they had to know. Why else would they have left the cell open and let him pass?

It was all planned. Danny wasn't about to execute some clever, eleventh-hour rescue that would sweep Renee from danger without significant collateral damage.

But he could not stop, because he also knew that he had to go to her.

There were other possibilities. He could make an attempt to gain a hostage. He could hole himself up in the warden's office and threaten to expose the prison. He could find a more suitable weapon, a knife or a gun. He could try to get to a phone and an outside line and call the authorities.

But the warden was no fool. All his bases would be covered. There was only one way to save Renee. There was only one thing that the warden wanted more than Renee, and that was him.

Danny was the key to her survival. Only Danny.

He paused at the bottom of the concrete stairs that led up from ad seg, breathing hard. A single bulb lit the stairwell and exposed the sealed steel door that led into the administration wing. From there he would head down the hall to the guarded door into the main prison.

They wouldn't stop him, he already knew that. They had all been instructed to let him pass, let him find Renee, let him try to save her. Let him see her die.

His greatest advantage was their underestimation of his skill. They'd seen him take blows and suffer punishment, but they hadn't seen him fight.

His right leg felt like it was filled with hot lead, and his head pounded with swelling pain, but none of it compared to the rage tearing at his heart. Again, a quiet voice deep within objected to the sudden change in him.

An image of Renee silenced that voice.

There were more ways to kill a person than to save one. A thousand times in the yards and halls of Ironwood, he'd been close enough to kill another inmate, but he'd never given the matter a passing thought. He'd put those days behind him forever.

But now he would put his vow behind him as well. How many would have to die in order for him to save Renee?

A new thought occurred to him as he took his last few calming breaths before ascending into the warden's trap. If there was a guard stationed near the door, they might see his weapons and react out of fear, even if they'd been instructed to let him pass. They might force a confrontation early. That risk was too great.

He tossed the chair leg into the corner, where it clattered and rolled to a stop, then he pulled out the two pieces of splintered wood from his waistband and dropped them to the ground.

Barefoot and naked now except for his shorts. It was him, it was Renee, and it was the warden. At least one of them would die, and Danny only cared that it wasn't Renee.

He put his right foot on the first step and began to climb.

I stood in front of the warden, dressed only in my white, short-sleeved blouse and my underwear. Standing there half-naked in my bare feet, staring at Keith because I couldn't bear to look at the warden, my last strands of hope began to disintegrate.

It was what Pape wanted.

I looked over my shoulder at the door, begging to see something that would give me hope, but the door was closed.

When I turned back, my tears were already snaking down my cheeks. I could feel my naked legs trembling beneath me. I wanted to be strong for Danny, but I couldn't seem to find any more strength in me.

"All of it," the warden said. "I prefer that you are yourself, naked in my eyes."

Keith stepped out, positioning himself between the warden and me. "You've made your point."

"Oh? And here I thought rehabilitating Danny was my point."

"By holding torture over his head?"

"Sometimes the threat of torture is the only way to get the wayward to confess their depravity. Danny is still pretending to be good."

"You can't force this on people. It's monstrous!"

Marshall Pape arched an eyebrow. "Well then...perhaps she would like to save herself. Would that ease your mind?" He paced to his right. "How about it, Renee, would you like to save yourself?"

I only half-heard their exchange. My mind was cringing in my nakedness. I didn't know what he meant by saving myself.

"All you would need to do is demonstrate your willingness to follow me. Make just a simple gesture of your love for me. Hmmm? Do that and I'll save you from all this."

My mind wasn't working properly. He'd extended an olive branch to me, that was all I really heard. But he'd also used the word *love* and that confused me, so I didn't respond.

"I'll tell you what," he said. "I can see you're terrified, so let's make this real easy. Don't bare yourself. Just give me a simple gesture to confess your allegiance to me. Choose me, and I'll set you free. Be my Judas; give me a kiss."

The room was perfectly quiet. I could feel all of their eyes on me, some sad, some hardened by too many years in the warden's sanctuary. All I had to do was kiss him and he would spare me?

It all struck me as a carefully rehearsed drama in which I, the unsuspecting victim, had been led onto the stage.

Nausea was flooding my belly and rising up through my chest. I had to be strong, I knew that. I had to save myself so that I could save Danny.

But I couldn't move my feet. I couldn't speak past the lump in my throat.

"No? Not even a simple single expression to be saved?"

"You're a monster," Keith growled.

"*I'm* the monster?" The warden's words rang through the hard yard. He turned to the members. "Is that how you see me?"

None of the prisoners spoke. How could they? They'd all either come to believe him or were too fearful of their own fate to question his ways. His power over them was absolute.

"You see, Mr. Hammond, I'm not the monster here. She is. *You* are. You're two puppets dangling on the end of a rope while the fires burn at your feet."

The warden slowly walked up to me again, hand in his pocket now, grin screwed on his face.

"What would you do to save yourself, my dear? You won't remove your clothes and stand naked before me. You won't even acknowledge me with a kiss. I'll tell you what...why don't you kiss Keith here? Show me that you care about someone besides yourself and maybe I'll reconsider."

He was playing with us. Manipulating. Leading us down his twisted path, determining just what we would say or do to save ourselves.

"Just kiss him, and I'll reconsider. It's a sign of friendship, dear, not betrayal. Prostitutes don't kiss, you know."

The thought of doing anything the warden suggested felt like a betrayal of myself. But I was desperate to stay alive. For Danny.

"You can't even do that, can you?" the warden said.

"What exactly will you reconsider?" Keith demanded.

"Everything. Isn't that what you want? She can become yours. Isn't that what you've always wanted? And now the choice is hers."

For a few seconds neither of them spoke, and it was just enough time for me to get hold of myself and make a decision.

I stepped over to Keith, lifted my hand to his neck, pulled his face down toward me, and kissed him. His lips were warm and he was breathing hard.

Something inside of me broke, and I couldn't let go. He put his arms around me and pulled my head into his shoulder.

"Sh, sh…It's okay, honey," he whispered. "It's going to be okay, I promise."

I clung to him as if he were my last hope in that insane world.

Keith hushed me again. "It's okay."

"Don't let them hurt me," I whispered into his shirt. "Please."

"They won't."

Behind me, the door into the hard yard crashed open. Keith lifted his head and stared. I twisted in his arms and saw what he saw.

A man stood at the door, naked except for a pair of black shorts. His dark hair was swept back, wet with sweat. My heart bolted in my chest.

It was Danny. Staring at us with fiery eyes.

I was already halfway across the room, running for him. I was already throwing myself into his arms and curling up in his chest and vowing my undying love. I was doing all of that already, but only in my mind. I hadn't moved. I was still in Keith's arms, which were tightening around me.

Then I saw that Danny's eyes weren't directed at *us*, but on the man who held me. On Keith.

And from Danny's eyes spilled all the rage of hell itself.

39

DANNY KNEW THAT he was being led to her. He knew there were no guards to stop him because he wasn't meant to be stopped. He knew the only door that remained unlocked led to the hard yard, because Renee was in there. And he knew that when he found her, he would not like what he found.

But he did not know that he would find her in the arms of a beast.

He saw the whole room in the space of a breath. Four guards stood in the corners, armed with rifles. Bostich was near the center of the room overlooking a dozen inmates seated along the wall. The warden stood close to a man who held Renee.

The man was Keith Hammond.

Danny had first met the man when Keith was a rising star in the sheriff's department who liked to take out his frustrations on his wife, Celine Hammond. Celine had come to confession at Danny's parish for a year, each time crying her shame. Her husband beat and abused her weekly.

Danny approached Keith after failing to convince Celine to go to the police. He took the deputy to a warehouse, bound him to a chair, and spoke to him plainly about his choice to inflict suffering on his wife. Keith had shown all the humility of a belligerent bulldog, but Danny was persuasive and the man had finally capitulated, realizing he would lose his life if he did not.

Unfortunately, Keith abused his wife again, and Danny would have ended his life then if not for Celine. Emboldened rather than deflated by his boast that he would beat her in spite of the death threat, she'd gone to the sheriff's department and exposed their rising star.

The department offered Hammond a deal. If he stepped down and granted his wife a divorce, his secrets would remain safe with his employers. He agreed to their deal, however embittered, and Celine moved out of state six months later. Danny put the issue behind him.

Now Keith Hammond was back, evidently here to take Renee because Danny had taken Celine from him.

Keith stared at him over Renee's head and a smile pulled at his lips. The hatred in his eyes could only be that of the devil.

"Take your hands off of her."

Keith's smile broadened. "It's been a long time, my friend."

Renee gasped and tried to spin free, but the man had a fistful of her hair. He jerked her back and backhanded her face.

"Stay!"

She twisted around, eyes flashing with terror. "Danny?"

Three of the guards lifted their rifles and trained the sights on him. It suddenly all made sense. Hammond was working with the warden. If they'd gone to such lengths, the end, too, was already orchestrated. Keith would hurt Renee, and the warden would push Danny to kill, testing him to his breaking point in an attempt to prove he hadn't truly changed.

Renee's face was white. "Danny?"

Keith's hand flashed again, striking her face with enough force to knock her down. He let Renee drop.

Danny stood breathless, immobilized by indecision. They wanted him to rush forward in an attempt to save her. He couldn't play into their hands so recklessly. He had to choose the moment carefully despite the terrible rage washing through his mind. He had to act with precision. How and to what end he was no longer sure, but there had to be a way. There had always been a way.

And if not?

Keith grabbed Renee's hair and yanked her head off the floor.

"She has a new name for me, Danny. She calls me Sicko. Unless you care to stop me, I'm going to hurt her. Bad, my friend. Real bad."

Danny's heart began to stutter.

Sicko. Keith was Sicko...

I was on the floor, held by my hair. My jaw ached and my lips were bleeding from the blow, but it was all made moot by the sickening violation I felt.

Every conversation between Keith and me pounded through my head. Revenge, Keith had kept insisting. One of Danny's victims was obsessed with revenge, but I'd never suspected the victim to be Keith. Now it all came to me.

Constance had told me about Randell because they knew I'd go in search of the man who brought him down. Constance was working for Keith. The phone calls had come from Keith. The boy had been taken and mutilated by Keith or someone who was working with him. The two-day waits now made perfect sense. He'd needed the time.

Keith knew about Judge Thompson because Danny, sometimes telling that story to unnerve his victims, had shared it with him. Keith had somehow tracked Danny down, found him at Ironwood, and worked with the warden to get him transferred to Basal, where he could destroy us both.

Keith, not the warden, was the mastermind behind it all. Keith was Sicko.

Everything he'd done during the last ten days was to earn my trust and push me to the brink with nowhere to turn but to him. He wanted me in the prison, in his arms. I'd been manipulated, yes, but that didn't temper my revulsion. I'd kissed him.

I lay limp on the floor, but something in me changed when I understood what Keith was trying to do. I couldn't understand all of his reasoning or the depths of his fury, but I could understand that he was getting what he wanted.

He was crushing Danny. Right there, right then.

Two more guards stood in the doorway, both wearing sidearms. Danny had stopped ten feet in front of them, frozen, and I felt my heart breaking for him. I didn't know what the warden had subjected him to, but I knew those eyes staring at me all too well, and I was appalled by the desperation in them. No man had ever suffered so much for all the right reasons.

And now his suffering was for me. I couldn't let that happen.

With a ferocious grunt, I hurled myself away from Keith, twisting with all of my strength. His grip on my hair was firm and my head jerked back for a moment before it tore free, leaving Keith with strands spilling from his fingers. Then I was stumbling forward and running for Danny.

I went like an angel, rushing across the room to save Danny. I wasn't thinking about anything other than comforting him. I didn't feel any danger or anger or bitterness. I only saw my broken Danny, who needed to know how beautiful he was.

My intent wasn't to crash into him. I really meant to be gentle and touch him with a soft hand, but I couldn't seem to slow myself because the closer I got, the more anguish I saw in his eyes. The more I saw that he really was breaking apart, and I couldn't bear the sight.

With a loud sob I plowed into him and threw my arms around his neck. His arms wrapped around my body and held me as tightly as I clung to him. I could feel his heart pounding in his chest, smell his skin, taste his sweat on my lips.

Danny was like a boy in my arms, unsure and crushed, and it ripped my heart in two.

"No, Danny...it's okay, Danny. You've done well."

His whole body, all 240 pounds of bone and muscle, began to tremble.

Terrified, I pulled my head back and gently took his jaw in my right hand. "No, listen to me." His eyes were closed and his face was twisted with remorse. "No, no, Danny, listen to me. You did well. You saved me. You came for me."

He was trying to stop, trying to be strong, but he couldn't. Tears began to seep from his eyes. I'd never seen him so undone. What had they done to my Danny?

Or was it because he knew that there was no way out for either of us now? That he'd failed?

"I'm so proud of you. You haven't failed me. You've done good."

My words sounded hopelessly pathetic in the face of his pain, but I couldn't bear to see him this way. I wanted to claw the warden's eyes out!

I kissed his face and eyes and I tried to wipe his tears. "You've done everything for me, Danny, I know that. I love you. You've done well. You've done so, so well."

He couldn't speak, but he didn't need to. I had never felt so much like a woman as I did then, holding Danny in my arms. He could have given me no greater gift than his tears, because it was Danny, you see, and now Danny had even given up his strength for me. Only a very great and mysterious love could reduce him to this. And in truth, it was no reduction at all.

The man in my arms was Danny at his greatest.

He loved me. I knew it then more than I had ever known it. Danny loved me and I loved him, and I didn't care if I lived or died anymore. As long as I was his and he was mine.

But my heart was breaking because Danny's whole life came down to knowing if he'd done well. If he'd done the right thing. If his life, his work, everything he'd done to save and protect, had been done well.

Only I knew the full truth—that every hour he'd spent in the dark, shivering from cold, he'd spent for me. Every blow he'd suffered he'd suffered to save me. Every cry of agony, every moment of torment, every turn of the screws—all for me, because he loved me.

And still he was surely wondering if he'd done well. I could feel it in his quivering skin and I wanted to scream my love for him. I wanted to take his place in that moment and weep my regret for putting him through such suffering on my behalf.

But all I could do was hold him and offer those simple words with tears streaming down my face. "You've done well. I'm so proud of you, Danny. Nothing matters now, you've done it all so well, it doesn't matter what happens now. I'm so, so proud of you."

My words didn't calm him. They pushed him deeper into that place of unyielding emotion, and I knew that I'd touched something beyond his own understanding, a core of his being that was beyond his unflinching control.

For long seconds the hard yard remained silent around us. They were giving us time to endure our own kind of suffering, but they could not know just how much healing was flowing between us.

And then, as suddenly as his tears had begun, he pulled them back with a deep breath and swept me to one side, slightly behind him.

I saw the reason: Keith was walking toward us, mouth twisted in a wicked grin that made him look like he was wearing a Halloween mask.

"So sweet, isn't it?" The man stopped, eyes on Danny. "To be in the arms of the woman you love."

Danny watched the man approach then stop close enough to speak without putting himself in danger of being overheard by the inmates.

527

Danny could have reached Keith and broken his neck before any of them could stop him, but in doing so he would leave Renee exposed long enough for one of them to end her life.

You've done well, Danny. Terrible emotion he hardly understood surged through his chest again, and he forced it back down.

Godfrey was there, and Randell, and a few others Danny recognized. Godfrey had tears on his cheeks. The rest looked on, stoic.

"She loves you, Danny." Keith spoke in a gentle tone. "Trust me, I've been with her for ten days. She loves you as much as my wife loved me. But my wife's dead, isn't she?"

He knew then that Keith had killed Celine. He had followed her out of state and murdered her.

"You took everything from me," Keith said. "My wife, my career, my life. All of it."

"How did you find me?" Danny asked.

"It wasn't easy." Keith kept his voice low. "Your mistake was telling me too much in your little game of manipulation. I figured out you were a priest—your little story about the pedophile helped. A year ago I heard about a priest who'd cut a quiet deal with the

DA. Having connections in the department does have its advantages, even for the scumbags they force out. So I checked it out and I found you. How could I ever forget that face?"

"My face was covered."

"Not the whole time. I saw your reflection in the window, when you pulled your ski mask off as you were leaving. I'm a cop, remember? I notice things."

Danny was asking the questions not for himself as much as for Renee. He had to buy her time. He had to reset the stage somehow. He'd once played a game with this man and won; now he was caught in Keith's game, playing by new rules. The only way out was to reinvent those rules.

"Why didn't you just have me killed at Ironwood?"

"I didn't want you dead. I wanted more. And when I told my brother-in-law how a man of the cloth had betrayed his vows, destroyed me, and murdered my wife, he had a better idea. And I liked it."

The warden was Keith Hammond's brother-in-law. He probably never knew that Keith had abused his wife. Worse, he believed that Danny was responsible for his sister's death.

"That's right," Keith said. "My wife, Celine, the one you so lovingly took from me, is Marshall's sister. She's dead because of you. When I was in a better position, I helped Marshall out from time to time. Got him a job in the prison system. Now, as you know so well, he's a warden. A bit religious for my tastes, but hey, it works for him."

The warden stood across the room with his hand predictably in his pocket, watching them with smug assurance. Pape had mentioned the murder of his sister when he told Danny his tragic story, but at the time Danny had no reason to connect the name to his own life.

"The part of his thinking that resonates with mine is that what comes around goes around," Keith said. "You took my wife and now I'm going to take yours. You took away my playmate, now I'm going to replace her with yours. An eye for an eye. How does it feel?"

"I didn't kill Celine. You did." Danny looked over at Pape. "Surely you know that much."

"He knows that you would say anything to save yourself," Keith said. "Don't be absurd."

Danny saw no value in pursuing the truth of the matter. Keith had obviously anticipated the charge.

"You saw Renee in my arms, Danny boy. I like it best when they come willingly without knowing what awaits them." Keith spread his hands in an open invitation. "Of course, you can always try to stop it. Prove the warden's theory that you really haven't changed and need more correction. He'd love nothing more. He's become a bit obsessed with you, a man of the cloth who should know better. I think you remind him of himself."

Danny looked at Renee, who was watching him. He'd forgotten how beautiful she was, how strong and yet so innocent; how smart and yet so naïve.

She wasn't smiling but her eyes were bright, full of courage. Her sweet voice still whispered in his ears. *You've done well, Danny.* But he hadn't. Not if he allowed them to torture and kill her. Not if he died, because his death would undoubtedly precede hers. They would never allow her to live now.

He scanned the room again. There was only one unpredictable element in the hard yard: the members. The anxiety that had pushed him up out of deep meditation had vanished, replaced now by a stoic resolve to let his training guide his path. He could not allow any more emotion. Renee's life might depend on his ability to exercise acute control over his mind and body.

Danny showed his hands in a sign of surrender and slowly stepped away from both Renee and Keith toward the others. No one stopped him.

He eyed the line of members. Godfrey. Randell. All of them staring.

"You're all fine with this?" he asked them.

"Of course not," Pape said. "Do you think a good father likes to beat his child? My children feel as much regret and sorrow as I do."

"I didn't ask you. I asked them." Danny moved closer, toward the center of the room, eyes on the other members. "She's an innocent woman. The warden's going to torture her in an effort to break me. That doesn't bother any of you?"

"No one's innocent," the warden said.

"And that includes you. But here you stand, judging us all."

"It's my role in this sanctuary."

"And it's mine to speak the truth." Danny

looked at his cellmate and spoke before the warden could. "How about you, Godfrey? You're just going to stand by and let this happen? Or you, Randell? You saw what he did to Slane...you think you'll escape the same fate? He can't let any of you leave this place now. You know too much. The warden will destroy all of you to protect his precious sanctuary. You're just going to blindly follow him?"

"So that's it, then." The warden stepped out. "You come in here vowing to turn your cheek, and now you ask them to resist. You see what I mean, Danny? You really are a charlatan. You're finally showing your true heart, as I knew you would if pressed. And the party has hardly started."

The words seared Danny's mind. Like a fire, they spread through his bones, scorching his heart with that one awful truth: In the end, he really was just as he once was. When all else failed, he would resort to violence and death to save the one he loved. He would do wrong to correct what was wrong, though he'd vowed never to do it again.

And wasn't that exactly what the warden was

doing, defending society from deviants by using violence to fight that violence, rather than love as Danny had vowed to love?

His world suddenly made no sense to him. He was standing before the whole room, making a plea for sanity, but in the end it was his own sanity that was at risk.

Danny wanted to continue his plea—the power of argument had always served him well—but his reasoning faded and he couldn't bring up the right thoughts or words.

He looked down the line of inmates and saw that they were lost. He'd spent ten days inside and hardly knew them—the warden had seen to that. But they all had one thing in common: they were governed by their humanity, and yet they feared the warden's consequences too much to question the true nature of that humanity. Even Godfrey, who knew better but could not escape the warden's hold on his mind.

"You see what I mean, Danny?" The warden came closer, speaking gently now, like a father making his final point to win his son's heart. "She's right, you've done well. You just haven't done well enough. So today I'm going to let you prove yourself. Your reward will be great, I promise you."

Renee could not guess how profoundly Danny had failed her. He stood tall and strong here on the floor, heroic, having endured more pain and suffering than all of them, but inside, his collapse was certain.

He couldn't save her, he knew that now. Not this time. The simplicity of that realization fell into his mind as if the sky itself had shattered. The walls came thundering down and smothered him.

"Now you see, Danny…"

He couldn't save her because he simply could not become that man who had taken so many lives.

The warden was saying something, but Danny couldn't hear it. Something was happening behind him, but he couldn't seem to move.

You've done well, Danny.

He had done well. And now Renee would pay for all that he had done so well.

He had to be strong for her. He could not fail her in this way. He would look at her and she would see how great his love for her was.

535

She knew that he would gladly give his life for her. She would understand his heart. She would take strength from his eyes.

But he could not compromise his vow of non-violence to save her. Doing so would only undo all that he had come to stand for. There could not be violence in the name of love, no matter what the circumstance.

And yet...

"Danny?" Renee's thin voice cut the silence.

Terror sliced through his heart. *She needs you, Danny. You must be strong for her.*

"Are you going to just stand there like a pathetic statue?" the warden demanded.

Struggling to remain composed, legs as heavy as lead, Danny turned around.

Renee stood in the middle of the room fifteen feet away, staring at the door. She swiveled her head and looked at him, frantic eyes brimming with tears of desperation.

He saw her standing there, begging for his help, and he was powerless to give it. Then he saw the reason for her fresh tears. Two guards were setting a table down in the middle of the hard yard. This was for Renee.

You've done well, Danny. You've done so, so well.

The same doctor who'd administered his punishment had entered the room, carrying the same black case he had in the deep meditation room. He was going to subject Renee to the same torture Danny had suffered.

Danny found that he could not breathe. He could not think. His mind was crumbling.

40

I DON'T THINK God himself could have stopped what happened next. Danny certainly couldn't, and so I forgave him even then, before it all ended.

I'd clung to his naked chest while he trembled, you see, so I knew that he was in anguish. I'd smelled the fear on his skin and tasted the agony in his sweat. So when he stood still with his back to me, facing the other members, I knew he'd come to the end of himself.

I knew that he couldn't save me. I knew that he was telling himself that he hadn't done well enough, and I was going to rush over to him and take hold of him again and try to convince him that it was all a lie.

But then it all happened too fast. The warden was speaking and they were bringing in a folding table and setting it down in the middle of the room between Danny and me. A doctor walked in with a black case, which he set down on a bench next to the table.

He pulled out what looked like a dentist's drills, and I knew then that he was going to do something terrible to me. Wild imaginations screamed through my mind, and in them I saw him grinding down my teeth while they held my jaw open. I saw a bit whining into my skull and into my brain. I saw a saw cutting into my spine as agonizing pain sliced through my nerves.

And I knew that if I could imagine those things, the warden's punishment would be worse. I began to panic. When I spun back to Danny he had turned around. He was watching me with dread in his eyes, like two pools of night.

"You're going to watch this, Priest." Keith was glaring at Danny. "You're going to feel the pain I felt when you stole my wife from me, and you're going to wish you were dead. And then, if you're lucky, you will be."

Danny saw it all and knew that he was now faced with a moment that would forever alter his carefully constructed understanding of the world. Pushed by rage, he'd become a celebrated soldier, killing the enemy with ruthless precision until the war ended and there was no enemy to kill. To honor his mother, he'd become a priest, and then, confronted by gross injustice, he'd rescued the oppressed by once again killing, this time monsters who preyed on the weak. In both cases, he'd considered himself the arm of God in a holy war, only to learn that he'd become a monster like those he killed. An eye for an eye, a life for a life, a system of justice he could overturn only with love, by turning the other cheek and dying to save, not killing to save.

But now consideration, logic, and reason yielded nothing but a terrible mystery of contradictions for which there seemed to be no answer. If God loved Keith, was Danny not also meant to love Keith? Wasn't Pape just another confused man twisted by the violence of others? Was it Danny's to judge?

The doctor was going to drill into Renee's shin and tickle the nerves deep inside her bones. Danny could not bear the thought.

And yet the only way to stop that pain was to destroy the guards who held the weapons, leaving their children in a nearby town fatherless and bitter.

There was only one option left for him, borne in that moment of intense suffering for which his mind had no answer, much less escape. He'd never surrendered his mind. He'd controlled it with uncanny vigor and suppressed it in search of peace, but he'd never surrendered it entirely, as was the practice of the mystics. This, they said, took the greatest power of all.

"Strap her down," the warden said.

Danny's mind began to shut down.

He slowly sank to his knees, steeled his thoughts as best he could, and gave in to raw emotion. The pain of surrender was far greater than the pain he'd suffered in the bowels of Basal. He did not cry out, did not weep, did not tremble. He only submitted his mind and accepted the anguish that squeezed his heart.

But even as he did, he knew that his heart could not contain the pain.

* * *

I watched Danny sink to his knees, and I knew that it was over. His eyes were blank and dark, and a terrible sorrow etched deep lines in his face. The sight of it was so horrible that my mind seemed to blink out. I forgot where I was.

"Strap her down," the warden said.

I was there. I was with Danny, and I was thinking that I had to comfort him.

Danny's legs suddenly gave way and he dropped, eyes now shut.

Everything in the room seemed to stall. They were all watching him. I could hear his heavy breathing as he sucked air through his nostrils. I watched a slight quiver take to his hands. Tears flooded my eyes—not for me, but for him.

For the man who had given his whole life for me.

We all watched in stunned silence—the members, the guards, the warden, Keith, all of us—staring at the priest on his knees, mouth shut, breathing hard.

"Get up!" Keith snarled.

But Danny did not get up.

"You can give it but you can't take it? Get up!"

Danny was in a different place, and his sorrow left no room for modesty. His muscles were strung like cords; his fists were white.

Keith cursed and started for me, and only then did my mind return to my own horror. He was going to strap me down on the table. They were going to torture me in front of Danny.

Keith's hand grabbed my arm and I cried out. It was only a single outburst of terror, but that simple tone silenced Danny's heavy breathing.

The emotions ravaging Danny could not find words for expression. They were felt, not described except by approximation. Like a ravenous beast with ferocious fangs, they tore into his heart. His mind told him that he was breaking down. That, confronted by the torment of the one he loved as much as God loved her, he'd finally snapped.

He had been her savior and yet now he would not save her, and the truth pushed his pain deeper into what could only be insanity.

A cry sliced into his consciousness. Renee's.
God help them all...

He felt the last tether of emotion snap and he watched it drift away, like a balloon with a cut string. Immediately, a simple awareness awakened in Danny's being. Finally, he'd stepped past his thoughts and emotions and found himself simply and profoundly alive.

But there was more. Awareness, not thought, occupied him. Awareness of light and love and a profound peace. The anger and sorrow and fear were behind him, chased into hiding by the very fabric of something new in his consciousness.

Pure, unadulterated surrender to what was. To God.

His eyes snapped wide and he saw Renee, and in that moment he was aware of what he must do, not through a process of thought or reason, but through simple consciousness, rooted in the very fabric of creative power and being.

He would not punish. He would save.

I jerked my head up and saw he'd become a different man. A switch had been thrown deep in his mind, and the Danny I once knew had come back to life.

His head was lowered and a look of stoic confidence left his face plain. He moved suddenly, without uttering a single sound, hurling himself forward.

The strangest thoughts overcame me then, seeing him in that state, an impossible mixture of horror and pride, a brew of anguish and exhilaration. He was throwing himself away to save me, you see? His love for me surpassed even his most sacred vow never to harm another man again.

He was now beyond reason, reacting only out of desperate love. There were seven armed officers in the room and Danny had only his hands, but if there were a hundred he would have done the same.

Twenty feet separated my priest and me, and he rushed in like a lion, head low, eyes fixed on his prey.

Danny was halfway to the table before the first shot rang out. I saw the impact of the bullet as it struck his thigh, but it only knocked him sideways for one step and he was still rushing, undeterred, mindless of his own wound.

Then Danny was in the air, hurling himself over the table with his head forward like a battering ram. His left hand snagged the edge of the table as he flew, and in that single motion he did two things: he tipped the table up to give me a semblance of cover, and he crashed into Keith. I saw and heard it all as I fell backward with the table on top of me.

I saw Keith take a desperate step in retreat.

I saw the crown of Danny's head slam into his face, saw Keith's head snap back.

I heard the bridge of Keith's nose crack as Danny's full weight slammed it up into his brain.

Keith was dead before he hit the ground, and Danny was sailing over his falling body.

I don't know if Danny planned every move or if it came to him reflexively, but by the time he landed, he was in a roll and halfway to the guards in the near corner.

The closest CO already had his rifle up and was firing. If he'd been a hunter accustomed to taking down charging rhinos, his shot might have hit Danny, but it missed the rushing target.

"Fire!" the warden was screaming at the other guards. "Kill him!"

But it was all happening too fast, and the guards must have realized they would be shooting directly at the other guards.

Danny struck the correctional officer's chest with the palm of his right hand and sent him crashing back toward the two at the door, jerking away the man's rifle as he flew.

The captain had pulled out his sidearm and finally managed to get a shot off toward the corner. It clipped Danny's shoulder and smacked into the forehead of the guard behind him.

Danny came up with the rifle already in full swing. The first of the two remaining guards by the door threw up his arm and tried to duck under the weapon but failed to avoid the blow. The rifle clipped the top of his head before striking the second guard squarely on his temple.

I lay on my back, head twisted, watching it all from the ground, thinking it was all impossible. There were too many men with guns aimed at Danny! He'd killed Keith and disabled three of the seven armed men, but Bostich and three others still had their sights on him, and surely one would find its mark!

And then one did.

A shot crashed from my left and Danny lurched forward as a slug slammed into his back. Bostich had taken a second shot.

Even when things happen so fast, or maybe especially when they do, certain images and thoughts are remarkably clear. When I saw that second bullet hit Danny I knew that he was going to die defending me.

I shoved the table away and screamed. "Danny!" I was still on my back, and the table was off of me, but it blocked my view of him. Frantic, I rolled to my side and clambered up to my knees. "Danny!"

He was in a pile of three bodies, and he'd already pulled one of them over his own. Two bullets smashed into that body before Danny rolled away and came up on one knee with the rifle at his shoulder. His jaw was fixed and his dark eyes showed no sign that he was even aware of the wounds he'd taken.

It's crazy, I know, but such a surge of respect and pride flooded me that for a moment I couldn't cry out, though my mind was shrieking.

Danny's first shot took Bostich in the forehead and slammed him backward onto his seat. His second chased the first, like a rolling thunderclap, toward the guard in the far corner past Bostich. The bullet struck that man's shoulder and spun him around. The man's rifle crashed to the floor.

Danny shifted his aim and held the weapon on the warden.

"Drop them!" he shouted.

His order rang through the hard yard. There were two more guards in two opposite corners, one to Danny's right and one to his left. He kept his eyes on Marshall Pape's ashen face, keeping the other two in his peripheral vision.

For a count of three, no one moved. They had all just watched Danny take down five men in under fifteen seconds, and they were probably rethinking their allegiances. The doctor stood back, hands half-raised.

I was on my knees, staring at my Danny, who knelt, bleeding from the wounds in his side, back, and his thigh, and I waited for the end.

"Lay your weapons down." Danny's voice was even now. Almost regretful.

The two guards gave the warden the courtesy of looking at him, but with Danny's rifle on the man, they needed no further encouragement. First one, then the other lowered the barrels of their rifles.

Danny stood. "On the ground."

Their rifles clattered to the concrete.

A surreal quiet settled over the room. Randell rose to his feet, eyes wide and on Danny. Slowly, the others rose with him.

The warden's face began to settle. A smile crept over his mouth as he stared down the length of the rifle still in Danny's hands.

"You see, Danny," he said. "I knew you could do it. She's right, you've done well. Now put the gun down and let's clean up this mess."

The man had the audacity to think it was over, as if this little lesson simply had proved his point that Danny had broken the law. And maybe he did, but this wasn't over.

If I'd had a gun, I think I might have shot the warden myself.

"Mark, Rodrick…please leave your weapons on the floor," the warden said.

I glanced over and saw that one of the guards Danny had hit was within reach of his handgun. He didn't look interested in reaching for it.

"You see, it's all over, Danny," the warden said.

"I don't think so."

"This is my sanctuary. I decide when it's over.

We'll never get along until you fully realize that."

"It's over for me," Danny said. "But I think it's just beginning for you."

The warden smiled. "You're forgetting something, my friend. I hold the keys. Keep that tone and you'll earn yourself another trip below."

Danny spoke as if he hadn't heard the man. "You've broken too many laws and ruined too many lives now. We'll let the courts decide what happens to me, but I already know what they will decide about you."

"Don't be a child, Danny. No one will ever even know any of this took place. It happens all the time. And now you've demonstrated that you're no different from me. You've just killed to save your precious lamb."

"I killed only in self-defense."

"You have no rights to defend yourself here. Put the gun down and God may forgive you this time."

Bruce Randell stepped away from the wall, walked up to the warden from behind, and brought both fists down on the man's head with enough force to crack a log.

Marshall Pape grunted once and dropped like a rock. He lay on the floor, legs bent oddly under his torso, breathing but unconscious. Randell stared down at the man, fists shaking.

"You're gonna get us killed," someone muttered. It struck me then that none of the others had moved. Whatever grip the warden had on them was so strong that even now, with their tormentor on the ground, they couldn't see their way free to deal with him.

All but Bruce Randell, who lifted his foot and was about to bring it down on the warden's head when Danny cut him short.

"Leave him," he said.

Randell stared at him, foot cocked.

"He's suffered enough."

Randell hesitated a second, then lowered his foot. The other inmates stared, still stunned by what they'd witnessed.

Danny nodded and faced the guards, who were clearly in shock. "Everything will come to light and California's going to erupt. I'll take whatever punishment the courts decide is fair for what I've done, but you must know that you will as well. I doubt they will be very kind. Tell me if I'm wrong."

None of them spoke. With Bostich gone and the warden out, they were like lost sheep, not unlike the prisoners. I felt a stab of pity for them.

"You can side with the warden and go down with him, or you can stand up for justice. Either way, Renee must be set free. Now. Do you understand? I'm going to escort her out of here, and then you can take me into custody."

He was going to send me away? The thought terrified me.

"No, Danny!" I pushed myself to my feet.

Danny faced me and our eyes met. He was bleeding, his life was in danger, he had to get to a hospital as quickly as possible—but I was thinking something else as I walked toward him.

"You're leaving with me," I said.

"Renee…" Tears misted his eyes again, the good kind, pressed out by the gentle hand of Danny's loving God.

I stepped up to him and lifted a finger to his lips. "Sh…I've spoken to a judge," I whispered. "He'll set you free."

I didn't know it to be a fact, but I was sure that Judge Thompson could be persuaded.

Danny looked unsure.

I had to be careful what I said in the hearing of others. "The one who knows your case. He'll set you free. Trust me, I have a way. You didn't do what they put you in here for. You're wrongly imprisoned." That was true. I had killed the two men he'd confessed to killing. "I can't live without you, Danny. Not anymore. You have to be free to take care of me until we grow old. I'm not leaving without you."

His eyes searched mine, and for a moment I was sure he would protest. But now his need to love me was greater than his desire to follow a more idealistic path.

Danny didn't believe in violence, but to save me he would kill a hundred men. I saw it in his eyes, a terrible love that quieted any other reason or logic, however well-informed.

I stood to my tiptoes, brought my lips to his cheek and kissed him lightly. "You did well, my love," I whispered. "You did very well. Now take me away from this hell."

Danny faced the guards, hesitated one moment, then nodded once.

"We're leaving now," he said. "We're going to set things straight. Do you understand?"

The correctional officers glanced at each

other, then nodded. I think they wanted us to leave. I think they wanted us to tell the world about what had happened because, out from under the warden's thumb, they wanted to set things straight as well.

"No one will stop us," Danny said again, taking my arm. "No one."

And no one did.

EPILOGUE

TWO MONTHS LATER

IT'S AMAZING HOW much power the courts hold to define deviant behavior on the winds of social change and law. Jesus didn't condemn slavery, but that was two thousand years ago.

I'm glad to say our judge used the law as he saw fit—in this case, to our benefit. Under my threat to expose his connection to his son's crimes, Judge Thompson directed me to an investigator, one Raymond Kingerman, who filed a petition to reopen Danny's case. As it turned out, Danny's confession became his strongest ally, because, armed with that confession, the district attorney hadn't conducted a full review of the physical evidence. Danny withdrew his confession because it was in fact untrue. I, not he, had killed the two victims in question, though we neglected to inform them of this detail. Apart from that confession, there was nothing that linked Danny to the murders.

Judge Thompson reviewed the case and overturned the conviction based on lack of physical evidence.

In a separate ruling, he also found that the deaths of Keith Hammond and Captain Bostich were a matter of self-defense under California law.

With a few strokes of the pen, Danny became a free man, seven weeks less one day after I broke into prison to save him. For four of those weeks I waited in limbo, afraid that I would go to prison for breaking in. In the end I was absolved, primarily due to the extenuating circumstances and the department's desire to keep the matter quiet.

Basal was no more. The California Department of Corrections and Rehabilitation transferred all of its inmates to other facilities and shut down the prison pending a full review.

Warden Marshall Pape was awaiting trial and would likely spend many years, if not the rest of his life, behind bars.

That left Danny and me free to embrace life together, two lovers bound together by the kind of profound affection and loyalty that can only really be forged by a lifetime of harsh reality. We were free, yes, but in our own ways we were each in our own kind of prison—I still caged by my obsessive-compulsive mind, and Danny by a history that will probably haunt him to his grave.

On the eve of his release, we walked hand in hand down Santa Monica State Beach, carrying our flip-flops as dusk settled over California's coastline. We hadn't talked about what had gone through Danny's mind in the last moment before he snapped and saved me. I thought the topic was too personal to broach before we knew exactly where fate would land us. But now we were free, and I was doing backflips inside.

Danny had saved me. I had saved Danny. Nothing could separate us now.

Nothing.

I looked at the bare sand smoothed by receding waves. It was like a clean slate, a fresh start. "Freedom is a beautiful thing," I said.

He frowned and stared at the shoreline. "It is. And yet so few really are free. Nearly all people live in prisons of their own making, regardless of their faith, creed, sex, or race."

"That's my Danny."

"Pape called Basil his sanctuary. In truth we all exist in our own sanctuaries—but I don't mean cathedrals or prisons. I'm talking about our hearts and minds, which imprison us in anxiety, fear, insecurity, anger, and other forms of misery. The walls and bars that keep most in a constant state of suffering are thoughts and emotions, not concrete and steel. It's a disease. Insanity. Most are afflicted by it, regardless of which side of the law they find themselves on or where they lay their heads at night. To be free of this, Renee, is to be free indeed."

"Still, I'd rather sleep in my own bed at night," I said.

He grinned. "And so would I. So would I."

"Danny?"

"Hmm?"

"Can I ask you a question about that day?"

He hesitated, but his voice was strong when he answered. "Of course."

I'd rehearsed the phrasing of the thoughts that plagued me for weeks.

"You were once a priest who used violence to protect the innocent."

"That is true."

"And you then took a vow of nonviolence, because violence isn't consistent with your understanding of love."

"That is also true."

"You endured terrible pain in the prison, standing by that principle."

"Yes."

I nodded. "So are you still committed to nonviolence?"

He spoke without a moment's pause. "Of course."

I looked up at him as we walked, and he turned his face to smile at me.

"But you snapped in the prison. You saved me. What was your reason?"

Danny looked ahead, smile fading.

"I had no reason," he said. "I surrendered all

of it in a moment of clarity. I didn't snap; I became fully aware for the first time."

Danny is a man who lives by reason. His logic is impeccable. Knowledge and certainty guide every aspect of his life. And yet he had surrendered his reason? I had to know more.

"Then why did you kill Keith, and those other men? What did you see?"

"That I had to save you. That's all. I could argue that Keith had already given up his right to life and stepped into death when he took you...that I was only finishing what he'd committed himself to, but that's not what went through my mind. Or through my emotions, for that matter. I simply did what I knew I must for your sake."

Keith gave up his right to life. I'd heard the argument before.

"Then your love for me was stronger than your logic," I said. "Because your own logic rejects violence in any case."

"True. Love has its own logic that sometimes defies the mind. I didn't act out of my mind or my emotions, but from a deeper place of light and perfect peace. Perhaps for the first time in my life I truly found God. I have no other way to understand what happened to me in that moment."

"But you still don't believe in violence."

"I would never hurt another human being. It's inconsistent with my understanding of love."

"And if someone came to kill me?"

"I would stop him," Danny said. "By any means necessary."

"Why?"

"Because I love you."

I can't say I was disappointed. In fact, I found his conviction exhilarating, all reason aside. My heart was pounding as we walked through the soft sand.

"So you would never hurt another man, for any reason."

"That's right."

"But if a man came to kill me…"

"I would stop him." He gave me a gentle look, wearing a whimsical smile. "And, my love, if you loved yourself as much as I love you, you might find yourself free of the prisons that hold you. In the meantime, I will love us both."

"Spoken like a good priest."

"Spoken by one whose mind has been broken. Thank God."

We were both silent for a few seconds. What would Danny do? He would lay down even his sound reasoning for me. And I for him. It was everything I could do not to throw myself into his arms and cling to him.

"It's a paradox," I said.

"It's a mystery I doubt I'll ever be able to explain. But we can smile at that mystery rather than try to understand what is by definition unknowable."

"It defies the mind."

"It's not a matter of the mind or the emotions. The truth is, the only key that will unlock the prisons we all live in is love. Unconditional love, like God's. And even that is a mystery."

I loved him for his mysteries. They'd saved my life and brought me back into his arms.

"Danny?"

"Yes?"

"Will you always take care of me?"

"I live to take care of you."

"Will you allow me to love you forever?"

"It will be my greatest honor."

Everything in me was like warm water. I was

drowning in a sea of beautiful, unreasonable love. My mind was telling me I should be saying something appropriate. That I should kiss him and tell him how proud I was of him. I should make sure he knew that I would die for him as quickly as he would for me.

Instead I spoke the only words that made it to my mouth.

"I adore you, Danny," I said.

"I adore you," he said.

And that was all we said for a while.

ACKNOWLEDGMENTS

Although *The Sanctuary* is a work of fiction, many of the details concerning the state of the US prison system and the laws that lead so many citizens into its care are well established. I owe a tremendous debt of gratitude to dozens of documentaries and books which held my rapt attention for many months. Among all of the professionals I spoke to in preparing this story, I want to single out one who worked with me through the entire process, from beginning to end. Eric Messick's 29 years of experience at all levels within the California prison system, primarily as a corrections officer at the San Quentin State Prison, has given him a wealth of firsthand, inside knowledge which he generously shared for the benefit of this book. Thank you, Eric.

Acknowledgments

Millions of Americans now find themselves behind bars made of iron, but in truth we all find ourselves imprisoned by difficult circumstances or challenges, sometimes beyond our control, and all too often of our own making. I want to thank the power of story for the mirror it places in front of each of us. For you who have eyes to see, please...go ahead and see.

ABOUT THE AUTHOR

TED DEKKER is a *New York Times* bestselling author of more than twenty novels. He is known for stories that combine adrenaline-laced plots with incredible confrontations between unforgettable characters. He lives in Austin, Texas, with his wife and children.